COBRA 405

Damien Lewis is a former war reporter and one of the nation's 'twenty favourite authors' (World Book Day). He is a prolific writer, penning over a dozen books and topping bestseller lists worldwide. Many of his books are being made into movies or TV series, and he scripts his own work as films (time permitting!). His military books include the No. 1 bestseller *Zero Six Bravo*, and his man-and-dog at war true stories include the phenomenally successful *War Dog* (*The Dog Who Could Fly* in the USA), both of which are being developed as films. His war victim memoirs – *Slave, Tears of the Desert* – have won a string of awards, and were top international bestsellers. He also writes thrillers, and his first, *Cobra 405*, is being made into a movie by LA-based Safadi Entertainment. The first computer game with his name attached is 'Damien Lewis's Zulu Response' – www.zuluresponse.com – based around the true story of Rorke's Drift, in the Anglo-Zulu War.

Praise for Damien Lewis

'A true story of British courage and daring'
Sunday Times

'Riveting' Richard & Judy

'Grotesque, glorious and utterly gripping'
Bolton Evening News

'A rollercoaster journey into the very heart of darkness'
The Gerry Ryan Show

'The most dramatic story of a secret wartime mission ever'
News of the World

'Tom Clancy without the boring bits' *BloggerNewsNetwork*

'Exciting and revelatory' Duncan Falconer

'A remarkable read' Max Arthur

'As g___ ___ ___ _thrill___

'A rock___ ___ ___ ___ ___r
its best. ___

30

D0262760

Damien Lewis
COBRA 405

arrow books

1 3 5 7 9 10 8 6 4 2

Arrow Books
20 Vauxhall Bridge Road
London SW1V 2SA

Arrow Books is part of the Penguin Random House group of companies
whose addresses can be found at global.penguinrandomhouse.com.

Penguin
Random House
UK

First published in Great Britain by Century in 2007
First published in paperback by Arrow Books in 2008
This edition reissued by Arrow Books in 2019

www.penguin.co.uk

A CIP catalogue record for this book is available from the British Library.

ISBN 9781787461468

Typeset by SX Composing DTP, Rayleigh, Essex
Printed and bound in Great Britain by Clays Ltd, Elcograf S.p.A.

For the late A. J. Hogan,
recently departed this world.
Rest in peace.

ACKNOWLEDGEMENTS

Special thanks to my agent Andrew Lownie for sharing a maverick sense of adventure in the literary world; to my editors, Tim Andrews and Mark Booth – whose boundless enthusiasm for this story helped propel it to completion; to Ron Beard, Robert Nichols, Neil Bradford, Jonathan Sissons, Rina Gill and all the production team at Random House. Special thanks to Mike M ('The Kiwi'), Kev S and Andy E for your input into the story. Special thanks to Tara Wigley, for the inspirational read. My thanks to Burt Joubert, for his advice on the aeronautical elements of this story; my gratitude to Fran and Alan Trafford, for his comments on the manuscript from a submariner's perspective, and more generally. Special thanks to Lisa Canty, my PA and assistant, for the research; very special thanks to Steve Clarke, for commenting on the dog-related sections of the early drafts whilst sharing a cold Whitstable Ale or two. My thanks to Clara McGowan and all the pupils at Saint James National School, for the inspirational visit on World Book Day. My thanks once again to Adrian Acres and Sinead Brophy, who read early drafts and provided invaluable critical comments. My gratitude to Tim Bailey for his advice on the sub-aqua elements of the story. Again my thanks to Don McClen for reading early drafts and for your comments and support. Very special thanks to Theodore Gray, for sharing with me his expertise and powers of lateral thinking in the field of metallurgy, in particular regarding tungsten and gold. To his colleague Max Whitby, and all at RGB Research – special thanks for the precious golden cylinder, and the advice that came with it. Lastly, special thanks to my wife Eva, for putting up with excessive bouts of crankiness during the months spent writing: it can't have been much fun. I hope the results are worth it.

'Cry "Havoc" and let slip the dogs of war.'
William Shakespeare

'Fine talking of God to a soldier, whose trade and occupation is cutting throats.'
Private Jack Careless

'Beware of what you want, for you may end up getting it.'
Cherokee Indian saying

AUTHOR'S NOTE

The world's biggest-ever bank robbery took place in 1970s Beirut, in the midst of the Lebanon's bitter and bloody civil war. The target of the raid was a British bank that had its headquarters on Rue Riad al-Sohl – better known as 'Bank Street' – the heart of the city financial district. The main bulk of the valuables stolen was made up of gold bullion. Estimates vary as to the value of the heist, from fifty million dollars (approaching two hundred million dollars at today's value) to ten times that amount. Amazingly, none of this loot has ever been recovered and no one knows who carried out the raid.

At the time of the raid, the Christian militia forces in Beirut blamed the opposing Muslim forces. Predictably, the Muslim forces in turn blamed the Christian militia. Other theories then surfaced, including: (1) that the Christian and Muslim forces cut a deal to jointly carry out the raid; (2) that the Corsican or Sicilian Mafia did the bank job; (3) that the Russian mafia robbed the bank; (4) that the Israeli Secret Service did it; (5) that the Irish Republican Army (IRA) did it; (6) that the late Yasser Arafat's Force 17 did it.

In short, the world's biggest bank robbery remains shrouded in mystery.

The military hardware and technology depicted in this story exists in the real world today and is employed by the elite of the British and US armed forces. This includes the submarine and drone elements, the surveillance gear, the fixed-wing aircraft, helicopter and boat based scenes. Likewise, the historical, religious and political background of the Assassins is accurately portrayed. The Assassins were a real force that existed at the time of the Crusades and had considerable similarities with the mysterious Knights Templar.

All the characters in this book are entirely fictional, as are their units and troop designations. There is no Q Squadron within the SAS, and there never has been. No Q Squadron could have been in Cyprus at the time depicted in this book, or at any other time for that matter. All the characters in this book are invented, and their characters and actions are entirely imaginary. Any resemblance to real persons, living or dead, is purely coincidental.

PART ONE

PART ONE

CHAPTER ONE

06.00 Hours: Present Day, Eastern Mediterranean Sea

Fifty nautical miles off the coast of northern Syria a sleek black shape came to a halt beneath the grey-flecked swell of the oily sea. The stealthy form of the USS *Polaris*, an Ohio-class nuclear submarine, barely moved with the rise and fall of the ocean, such was the bulk of the vessel suspended some thirty feet below the waves.

Slowly, a black metal tube extended itself vertically from the submarine's conning tower, making barely a whisper of noise as it did so. At the same time the Captain of the *Polaris* grabbed his periscope and did a quick three-sixty-degree scan of the surrounding sea. By the faint glow of dawn he could see that not another ship was in sight – which was just as he wanted it.

The Captain downed periscope just as the mysterious black tube – a Universal Modular Mast – broke the surface. A metal cowling flipped open with a faint pop, breaking the watertight seal at the top of the tube.

3

Inside there were four separate vertical chambers. Seconds after the Mast had broken through the waves, and on an order from the sub's captain, a rocket ignited in the bowels of the tube.

Moments later a cylindrical object shot out of one of the chambers, rising vertically away from the sea. The launch rocket propelled the device some two hundred feet into the air, whereupon its upward momentum slowed. As it did so, four arms folded out from the core of the device like the wings of some giant mutant insect emerging from its chrysalis, each one terminating in a vertical fin.

At the rear of the aluminium–titanium fuselage of the Sea Strike unmanned aerial vehicle (UAV) a propeller started to rotate – slowly at first and then with increasing speed as the aircraft's fuel-injected engine took over from the spent rocket thruster. Beneath the foam-packed nose cone a surveillance cluster dome whirred as the aircraft's pan-tilt-zoom video camera and infrared imagery systems kicked into life.

As the Sea Strike gained altitude under the lift generated by the aircraft's 4.5-metre wingspan, it increased its speed to some ninety knots and set a course for Syria. Some one hundred and twenty miles away in the mountains above the ancient Syrian town of Aleppo the diminutive aircraft had an urgent rendezvous with an unsuspecting target.

In the ops room on board the giant submarine special-forces pilot Bob Kennard stared into the blue-green glow of his Combat System Console Interface – a computerised control panel that enabled him to 'fly' the Sea Strike remotely. A state-of-the-art GPS autopilot system was now guiding the aircraft towards its target.

But it was up to Bob to take control of the final stages of the mission – that was if it was green-lit by his commanders, back at Special Operations Command (SOCOM) in Florida – and carry out the final kill.

As soon as Sea Strike One was airborne, and Bob had confirmed to the *Polaris*'s captain that he had full interface with the aircraft, the giant submarine slipped quietly down into the depths. Now it had become a waiting game. The aircraft was an hour away from Aleppo, and upon arrival she would have six hours' loiter time over the target. It would then be a matter of luck as to whether the intended victim was present at the training camp. Only if Bob was able to acquire a clear image of the target would he launch the kill strike.

Bob had over a decade's experience as a special-forces pilot but this was his first remote combat mission. He settled back into his seat with a fresh coffee, being careful not to spill it over the rubberised computer terminal, and eyed the screen. A green line traced the course of Sea Strike One as she headed east and climbed towards her 25,000-foot operating ceiling. Weather conditions over the Syrian mountains weren't perfect but in recent exercises the Sea Strike had proven herself capable of flying blind through all but the worst of storms.

Bob Kennard had little idea who the target was, or why the man was being singled out for such a costly and covert hit. The mission's security clearance was Beyond Top Secret. Bob had been given the target's name: The Searcher. And he'd been told that The Searcher was a British ex-soldier based in a terrorist training camp in the Syrian mountains. And that was that: Bob had no need-to-know when it came to the full mission details. In fact he preferred *not* to know: it was far easier to assassinate someone if it was done from a distance without ever knowing their true identity.

As retrieval by submarine of the Sea Strike UAVs had as yet proved impossible, they were of necessity disposable one-mission aircraft. At the end of this flight Sea Strike One was programmed to self-destruct: she would blow herself to pieces over a remote Syrian mountain range, leaving no evidence that she had ever flown. But at one and a half million dollars per aircraft they were costly pieces of kit – so whatever this British ex-soldier was up to, the US military and their British allies had to want him real bad, Bob reckoned.

Fifty-five minutes after launch Sea Strike One slipped quietly into the airspace over a remote Syrian mountain valley. The aircraft automatically switched from liquid-fuel engine to silent electronic-propulsion mode, descended from 25,000 to 10,000 feet, and began to fly a set of search transects across the known coordinates of the training camp.

Bob would have preferred to operate at a higher altitude, but there was no way around it. He needed to capture a clear enough image of the target to ID him from his facial features alone, which he might just be able to do from 10,000 feet. They would only ever get the one chance to make the kill, so they had to be certain that they had got him.

Not for the first time that morning Bob glanced at the top right-hand corner of his computer screen. It showed a single, still image – an old dog-eared photo of a figure dressed in army fatigues. A pair of intense green eyes stared out of the screen and the man's head was topped off by a shaggy mane of sandy hair. The expression on the thin craggy face wasn't hostile, or unfriendly: all it revealed to Bob was a fierce intellect and a peculiar predatory alertness.

Bob had operated alongside British special-forces soldiers often enough. He knew of their maverick reputation and their unconventional ways, and this guy certainly had that look about him. For a second it crossed Bob's mind that the target might indeed be ex-SAS. But even if he did manage to kill him, Bob would never know.

Bob's gaze was drawn to the live data-feed beaming back from Sea Strike One. A faint movement had caught his eye. He felt a kick of adrenalin as the video feed revealed a distant group of figures, half hidden among the rocks. He leaned forward and grabbed the joystick flight control, flicking the master switch from autopilot to manual.

Bob sent the Sea Strike into a tighter orbit and focused the camera in on the group. He felt his pulse quicken. Some two dozen men were squatted around a central figure, receiving some form of weapons instruction. They were dressed in a mixture of Arabic robes and army fatigues, and each held an AK47 between his knees.

But it was the appearance of the central instructor figure that interested Bob the most. His light features contrasted markedly with the dark complexions of the other men. Bob zoomed in closer – as close as the telephoto lens would allow – and flipped up a microphone arm from his head unit. As he started his commentary on the mission he knew that the General would be listening.

'Okay, this is Sunray Zero Alpha and I now have manual control of the UAV . . . So we have a group of possible targets at what seems like a lesson under way. I'm zeroing in on what I guess must be the instructor.

Notice the lighter skin of his face. And seems like that's sandy hair I can see to one side of the turban thing he's wearing, but let's take a closer look.'

Bob zoomed in still further. 'Hold it, hold it . . . We just kinda need to see the face more clearly . . . Looks like he's glancing up at us – is he going to? – yeah! Got it! That's a clear image of the face of the instructor now captured on the video. Okay, we're going to freeze-frame several of those images so we can all take a closer look . . .'

Bob turned and glanced at the UAV technician to one side of him. He raised an eyebrow questioningly to check that the technician had copied the instruction, and was given a thumbs-up. Bob resumed speaking into his microphone.

'Okay, we're just processing those images . . . Okay, you should be able to see them now, displayed on the left-hand side of your screen. That's five images of the face of the target glancing up in the direction of the camera. Question is, do we have a positive ID? It kinda looks right to me. A little older, maybe, but there's no mistaking that face. I'd say we do have positive ID . . . General, sir, I am now asking if I'm green-lit to hit the target?'

Eight thousand miles away in US Special Operations Command, Florida, General Sam Peters was on his feet, staring into his computer screen. He flicked his gaze across the series of still video images. The sandy hair and green eyes marked the instructor figure out as a Westerner, that much was for certain. And the faint scar across the right cheek was encouraging: it was exactly what the General had been told to look out for.

The General turned to a figure at his side. 'You reckon we got our man?'

Nick Coles glanced at the General, then back at the computer. He scrutinised the images for several seconds. He wanted to be one hundred per cent certain that this was their target – that they were going to get their kill.

'Son, you reckon we got him?' the General repeated, impatiently.

'I think we probably have, General, yes,' Nick replied. 'I think it's our target.'

'Listen, son, "probably" ain't good enough,' the General growled. 'Unless I'm mistaken, this guy's still a Brit citizen, still ex-special forces. Now, if the US is gonna sanction the use of our top-secret technology to assassinate the son of a bitch we'd better make darn sure of what we're doing. Wouldn't you agree, son?'

Nick hated the way the General was addressing him as 'son'. He was ex-military himself and had risen to the rank of lieutenant colonel before joining the British Secret Intelligence Service, MI6. Nick felt certain that the General would have been fully briefed on his credentials. Peters was playing a power game with him, and right now he held all the cards in his hand. But Nick prided himself on always being the grey man, on being able to take the abuse and show no visible sign that he had been needled.

He kept his stare glued to the computer screen as he framed his reply. 'Well, from the records we've been able to dig up on him all the physical characteristics – height, eye and hair colour, physique – seem to be correct, General. Plus The Searcher has a scar running down his right cheek. You've noticed this man's scar, I take it? So yes, General, I'd say I am convinced. I believe it's him. That's our target.'

'You're certain we got the right man?'

'Absolutely, General. Absolutely.'

'Now that's more like it.'

The General pulled his radio mouthpiece up so that he could make voice contact with Bob Kennard, the UAV's operator.

'This is General Peters, calling Sunray Zero Alpha. Good work finding him so quickly, son. I am giving you the green light to proceed with Operation Terminal Search. I repeat, proceed with the operation. Go get him, son.'

'Well copied, sir,' came back Bob Kennard's reply. 'This is Sunray Zero Alpha proceeding with Operation Terminal Search . . .'

'God, *Operation Terminal Search* – who thinks up these names?' Nick muttered under his breath.

In spite of four decades of military service, General Peters's hearing on his left side was still sharp. Unfortunately, Nick was sitting at the General's left shoulder.

'Sorry, son, did you say somethin'?' the General growled. 'We're only having to proceed with *Operation Terminal Search* for one goddamn reason, and that's because one of *your boys* has gone over to the dark side. You hear me? And boy, is his shit dark.'

Nick nodded. He had regretted making that comment almost before it was out of his mouth. From the file he'd read on the General, he knew that Peters had a long and distinguished combat history and was famed for his robust temper. With a rogue SAS soldier training the world's newest terrorism outfit – the Black Assassins – to take out seven of the West's top leaders, it was hardly surprising that the General was displeased. It would be a terrorism spectacular the likes of which the world had never seen.

The General glared at Nick. 'Now, *Operation*

Terminal Search is about the best hope we got of stoppin' *your boy*. So, if you don't appreciate the mission name, son, maybe we can settle on a better one? How's about "Operation Terminate with Extreme Prejudice that Goddamn Traitorous Brit Son of a Bitch"? Sound better to you, son? Does it?'

'Probably . . . I'm not sure, sir.'

'Well, like I said, *probably* ain't good enough, son. So, don't you sit there with your oh-so-superior English attitude and take the rise out of my operation, you hear me?'

'Yes, sir . . . And sir, I apologise.'

'Apology accepted,' the General grunted. 'Now, let's get on with the mission and kill this bastard.'

The General glared into the computer screen as the UAV was brought around for another pass over the target, and Bob Kennard recommenced his commentary on the mission.

'Now starting transect five, bearing 0407 degrees. I'm aiming for a second overflight of the target area. Should be overhead that position in less than three, repeat three, minutes. This is the attacking run . . .'

'One thing, General,' Nick remarked as the two men stared at the live video feed. 'The Searcher was never a commissioned SAS officer. He was only ever an NCO.'

'Don't make a heap of difference, son, now he's gone over to the dark side. Still knows his stuff, don't he? Makes my goddamn blood boil. What kinda name is that for a soldier, anyways – The Searcher? Don't the son of a bitch have a proper name?'

Before leaving London Nick had been told not to reveal The Searcher's true identity. The US military was notoriously leaky, and the last thing Her Majesty's Government needed was a story breaking about an

11

ex-SAS operator training the world's most fearsome terrorist outfit. There were half a dozen of the General's men crammed into that stifling ops room, not to mention the assistants who kept buzzing in and out. Any one of them could have a contact in the media, and once they had the man's name then they had a story.

'The Searcher' was a nickname that had been given to the target by his SAS mates back in the 1970s, Nick explained. He was always seeking some greater cause or meaning in life. He'd gone through most of the major religions – Buddhism, Hinduism, Sikhism – before converting to Islam and training up the Palestinian resistance.

But in 1986 there'd been a raid by Force 17 terrorists on an Israeli yacht. Two of the gunmen were Palestinians, but the third was a British mercenary. That man was almost certainly The Searcher. At that time he'd made the crossover to direct involvement in terrorism. Since then The Searcher's name had been linked to operations by Black September, Hezbollah, Islamic Jihad, Abu Nidal, the Turkish Grey Wolves and more. And now he was with the Black Assassins, plotting a world-class terrorism spectacular.

In spite of the submarine's air-conditioning, Bob Kennard was sweating heavily in the bowels of the USS *Polaris*. The tension of the mission was getting to him. His hands felt lumpy over the computer terminal as he waited for the image of the target to reappear. Every atom of his consciousness was focused on that tiny aircraft as he willed it to seek out and find its prey. Even though Bob knew little about their fair-haired target he could sense the threat in his bones, and was determined to go get him.

Sea Strike One pushed onwards and the group of

stick-like figures reappeared in the video screen. As Bob zoomed in he noticed one of them glancing skywards. Something – perhaps the glint of sunlight on the camera lens – had alerted him to the UAV's silent presence. The figure detached himself from the main group and hurried across to an underground bunker.

Bob put the tiny aircraft into close-orbit mode and began punching buttons on his console. From the nose cone of the UAV an invisible beam fired earthwards as the aircraft began to 'paint' the target area with the hot point of its laser. Seconds later a pair of miniature bomb doors swung open beneath the fuselage, revealing a blunt-headed projectile some three feet long, its four guidance fins folded against its body.

Sea Strike One was ready to attack.

The video image was still now: internal gyroscopes in the camera's housing kept the lens focused exactly on target. All Bob had to do was hit the 'fire' button, and the silent, gliding Viper Strike munition would drop almost vertically, accelerating to some 250 feet per second.

It would reach the target area in forty seconds, giving the enemy scant time to take cover – that was if they ever saw the strike coming, for they certainly wouldn't hear it. The 2.5-pound thermobaric warhead would hit without warning, throwing out a vapour cloud of fuel–air explosive that would detonate in a terrible vortex of heat and flame.

Bob spotted the figure re-emerging from the bunker and recognised it as their target. He was carrying an indistinct bundle slung across his right shoulder. Bob punched the 'fire' button, there was an inaudible click within the belly of Sea Strike One, and the Viper Strike munition dropped silently away from the aircraft.

As the warhead dragged the bulbous nose of the Viper Strike downwards four fins unfolded from the bomb's tail end and it began its graceful, gliding dive towards the ground. Immediately it did so, the on-board guidance system picked up on the hot point of the laser and began to minutely adjust the Viper Strike's glide path so that it exactly homed in on the target.

Bob's eyes were glued to the digital read-out on his computer screen as it counted down the seconds to impact – 30, 29, 28, 27 . . . But all of a sudden there was an intense flash of light at ground level. Bob refocused the camera, only to find the target with a smoking missile-launcher balanced on his shoulder and the arrow-like form of a surface-to-air missile streaking upwards towards Sea Strike One.

Bob knew that he had only seconds in which to act. If the missile struck the UAV then the debris of the aircraft would tumble to earth in the midst of the training camp – in which case their ultra-secret mission would be blown wide open. Several of the UAV's parts were clearly identifiable as American military: it even had 'Made in the USA' stencilled across the experimental titanium airframe.

For an instant Bob vacillated, torn between hitting the self-destruct button to vaporise the UAV and hanging on to see the Viper Strike detonate. But then he punched a button on the computer terminal hard. There was a sudden belch of smoke in front of the camera lens and the screen went black.

Just as the image died on Bob's screen the Iranian-made Sayyad-2 missile went hurtling through the plume of fire and fine debris which was all that was now left of Sea Strike One. At exactly that moment the Viper Strike

14

bomb ploughed into the hard-packed earth of the training camp. The compact warhead impacted with a dull thud and a small charge threw a fine mist of fuel–air explosive high over the camp.

A split second later the weapon detonated, instantly transforming the air above the training ground into a seething white-hot fireball. As the raging fire-monster sucked in oxygen, the blast wave flashed outwards from the epicentre of the explosion. It tore across the open ground and slammed into the nearest bodies, ripping them limb from limb.

It was followed in an instant by the firestorm itself, like the breath of an avenging dragon that incinerated every living thing. A black mushroom cloud of smoke belched upwards and outwards from the point of impact. And as the firestorm raged onwards it tore the very air out of the lungs of anyone caught in its path.

At 11,000 feet above the training camp the Sayyad-2 missile started to hunt across the horizon, trying to reacquire its target. Deprived of its kill it burned itself out. By the time the spent projectile fell to earth on a distant mountainside, the survivors of the Viper Strike explosion were stirring.

They emerged from the camp's bunkers to be met by a scene from hell itself. Pulverised weapons, torn clothing and the odd shoe lay scattered across the camp. And mixed in with this smoking debris were contorted, blackened shapes barely recognisable as human – the bodies of those caught in the fearsome vortex of the Viper Strike's blast.

'He hit the goddamn destruct button!' General Peters yelled for the umpteenth time, as he stared

15

dumbfounded at the blank computer screen. 'He hit the goddamn destruct . . .'

The General turned away, cursing in frustration. He had been replaying the last few seconds of the video over and over, but it seemed to lack the final moments when the Viper Strike hit. Deep down the General knew that the aircraft's operator had been right to send the self-destruct signal. But it still galled him.

The General glanced at Nick Coles, searching his face for some kind of confirmation that they'd made the kill. But Nick just shrugged his shoulders. He wasn't about to stick his neck out and say that they had.

'Sergeant Ames, I want you to grab that last image,' the General barked out an order. 'The very last frame before the screen went black. You got me?'

'Yes, sir!' came the reply from a bank of computers to the General's right.

'Let's just hope and pray we hit the bastard where it hurts,' the General growled, more to himself than to anyone else.

An image appeared on the General's computer screen. It was a fuzzy picture of the Viper Strike, guidance fins outstretched like the wings of a bird of prey, streaking downwards. It was the very last video frame filmed by Sea Strike One, and it showed the warhead still some 300 feet or more above the target area. And there, at the corner of the video frame, was the target – The Searcher himself – running hell for leather for the nearest cover.

'Dammit,' the General cursed to himself. 'We got no video of the point of impact.'

General Peters turned away from the computer terminal and spoke into his radio mouthpiece. 'Sunray

Zero Alpha, what d'you reckon, son? Tell me, you're the operator – you reckon we got him?'

'Sir, I just dunno, sir,' came back Bob Kennard's reply. 'It was a damn good Viper Strike hit, sir, just like we trained for in exercises. That's a thermobaric munition we used, sir – pretty much incinerates everything . . . But I just can't say for certain, sir, that we got our man.'

The General grunted. 'I'd like to say "Mission accomplished", son, but I can't . . . What I can say is a real warm thank-you, 'cause you did us proud. And pass my congratulations to the captain and crew of that boat, son. The mission couldn't have been done without them . . .'

The General squared his shoulders and pounded a balled-up fist into the palm of his hand.

He glared at Nick Coles. 'On balance, I reckon we got him. But this is a goddamn war, and you know what they say: presumption is the mother of all fuck-ups. You'd be amazed what people just walk away from. So you'd better get onto your people, son. It was your Humint that found this guy in the first place. Whoever you got out there on the ground in your local networks or whatever, they'd better put their feelers out again. See if they can pick up news of your Searcher – find out whether he's dead or alive.'

'Of course – I'll see what we can do, General.'

'Appreciate it. You know, we should've had a man on the ground. All it takes is one good operator up on one of them ridge lines and we'd have confirmation of our kill. You know what worries me most? Those moments after the UAV self-destructed there was no laser guiding in the Viper Strike. When you self-destruct the aircraft, you self-destruct the laser guidance system 'n'all. Just have to hope we were close enough to fry the son of a bitch.'

17

'Why didn't you have that man on the ground, General?' Nick asked. He knew that he held the trump card on this one, although he wasn't about to reveal it to the General.

'Goddamn politicians, that's why,' General Peters spat out. 'Wouldn't risk having one of our special operators dropped in country, just in case he got compromised. Political fallout with Syria would have been "too hot to handle", according to them pansy-assed bastards who sit up there in Washington scratching their backsides all day long.'

Nick saw an opportunity to needle the General and get a small piece of revenge. 'I suppose you have to see things from their perspective.'

'Nope, son, I *don't* have to see things from their perspective. Period. Haven't done for forty years, and I ain't about to start now. From where I'm sitting we've got us a bunch of murderers training for the greatest kamikaze mission of all time. Way I see it, we've got our President and your guy menaced by a bunch of crazies.'

The General fixed Nick with a steely eye. 'And as if that ain't enough we discover they're getting training from one of your best ex-operators. You don't fuck around with that little lot. You do whatever it takes – whatever it goddamn takes – to get the job done. We should've had a man on the ground, son, simple as that.'

Half an hour later Nick Coles left the entrance gates to the SOCOM building and got into a waiting taxi to take him back to his hotel. As he pulled away from the vast military complex he breathed a sigh of relief. Nick hadn't been sad to say farewell to General Peters. As far as he was concerned the next American who had the temerity to call him 'son' was going to get an earful.

Even his 'grey man' persona had its limits, and the General had just about overstepped them.

As he settled back into his seat, Nick allowed himself to feel just a little smug. He felt certain that they'd hit The Searcher, which meant that it was mission accomplished. Either way, he knew he would be getting absolute confirmation of the kill in the next hour or so. Whilst the Americans mightn't have had a man on the ground, the British had – only the General and the rest of the US military had been kept in the dark about it.

Nick punched a number on his mobile phone. It was time to check what their man on the ground had witnessed of the Viper Strike attack.

CHAPTER TWO

19 January 1979: UK Armed Forces Base, RAF Akrotiri, Cyprus

The air of the mess tent was thick with cigarette smoke, stale sweat and the reek of frying food. The fifty-odd men of Q Squadron SAS leaned back in their canvas chairs, taking it easy. It was nearly lunchtime, and they were far more interested in getting a good feed than they were in the briefing. Most had already been deployed to the Lebanon, so the MI6 liaison officer could tell them little new about the vicious little civil war that was going on there.

Since the outbreak of the fighting some six years earlier, Lebanon's capital city, Beirut, had been devastated. It was now divided into a Christian east and a Muslim west, with a shattered and depopulated no man's land in the middle. In recent months the men of Q Squadron had been tasked with inserting operators from the CIA and the US Intelligence Support Agency into Beirut, on a series of hostage-rescue operations.

As the MI6 officer finished his briefing, Major Marcus Thistlethwaite, Q Squadron's Officer Commanding (OC), stood up to speak. An audible groan went up from the tent. The Major had been barely a month with The Regiment. He was a humourless individual who lacked the common touch, and everyone knew he loved the sound of his own voice far too much.

'So that, gentlemen, is the Lebanon,' the Major began. 'Not a pretty picture. Now, yesterday morning I asked each troop for your plans on four mission scenarios. Well, I have your plans before me and I have read them all, and I can't say I'm impressed.

'Shall we start with the Lebanon bank raid?' the Major continued. 'To recap, your mission was to gain access to the vaults of the Imperial Bank of Beirut and seize papers that are of high intelligence value to Her Majesty's Government. The bank lies in the middle of the Beirut war zone, so such robberies are not unheard of. You have all been on the ground in Beirut, I believe?'

Major Thistlethwaite glanced up from his notes, seeking confirmation of their previous Lebanon ops from the men. The British Government had green-lit these missions, but only begrudgingly. Increasingly, the Commanding Officer of the SAS was being forced to fight tooth and nail to secure such work. On several occasions in recent years the SAS had come perilously close to being disbanded.

The ruling Labour government was strongly opposed to covert operations, and even the military high command was questioning the need for special forces and the maverick men they attracted. New officers kept being foisted upon The Regiment, tasked with bringing the more unruly elements into line. The men of Q Squadron were certain that Major Thistlethwaite was one of these. Nothing else would explain how he'd made it into the SAS.

The Major glanced enquiringly at his men. All he got in return was a series of blank stares. The mess tent was silent for several seconds as he waited for one of the men to speak. If only the Major had been able to, he would have learned an important lesson from their silence: it was impossible to command an SAS squadron without the support and respect of the men.

'No one got anything to say?' the Major snapped. 'Then I'll take your silence as a tacit recognition of your previous Lebanese ops. So – the bank raid. Up-to-date intel suggests that the bank is continuing to do business five days a week . . .'

The men were bored. The Major had been through all this once already, so why the need to repeat it?

'The bank vault remains operational,' the Major droned on. 'We understand that some fifty million dollars in gold bullion is held there, alongside the papers we are after. Those documents detail the financial holdings of Arab terror groups worldwide, so security will be tight. Now, as I said, I briefed you yesterday morning and asked each troop to come up with a mission plan.'

This wasn't the first time that the men of Q Squadron had been tasked with preparing a plan for a bank raid. In fact, banks were one of the favourite theoretical objectives of The Regiment. They provided a distinct target opportunity, one where security would be tight and ease of entry for the uninvited was particularly difficult. As an exercise, a bank job tested the men's ability to plan out an assault on a well-defended building, and get in and out again without being compromised.

On a practical level, if hostile regimes or terrorist

groups had sensitive documents that they needed to keep hidden, banks were one of the commonest places of concealment. Most of them offered blanket client-confidentiality, which meant that the SAS had to be ready to physically assault and burgle them whenever necessary.

'These are the mission plans that you came up with,' the Major announced, waving a bundle of written papers around. 'Now, I may be new to The Regiment, but I have many years' military service behind me and I have never set eyes upon such an abysmal set of documents. My mother could have done better, and needless to say she is not a member of your elite fraternity. One in particular is a complete joke . . .'

The Major glanced around the room. Q Squadron broke down into four fighting units – One, Two, Three and Four Troop. His gaze came to rest on Lieutenant Luke Kilbride, the leader of Four Troop. The Major stared across at the Lieutenant with open hostility: this wasn't the first time that they had crossed swords. Kilbride gazed back at him uninterestedly, his expression betraying not a hint of concern.

'Not for the first time,' the Major continued, 'it is Four Troop's plan that really takes the biscuit. I shall read it to you, shall I? It won't take me long, that's for certain. Oh, and I presume this is *your* writing, Lieutenant Kilbride, and chiefly *your* handiwork?'

The Major glared at Kilbride, but received no answer. Luke Kilbride was in his late twenties, and although he tried his best to hide it he was classic officer material. He was public-school-educated and came from a family with a long military pedigree. His parents were seriously wealthy, hence the nickname given him by his mates – 'Loaded'.

In part due to his moneyed background and boyish good looks he'd gone seriously off the rails with drugs, drink and girls. He'd joined the SAS at age nineteen, as a lowly trooper, in a last-ditch effort to sort himself out. That had been nine years ago. Since then he'd been in the forefront of the toughest operations. Northern Ireland, Malaysia, Borneo, Oman, Yemen – you name it, Kilbride had been there.

He was totally in his element in The Regiment. His wild, maverick spirit had proven to be an asset, not a liability. In 1972 he'd been on a mission known as the Longest Patrol. A four-man unit had gone missing in the Malaysian jungles for seventy-two days. It had been the longest unsupported operation in special-forces history and Kilbride was one of those who had made it out alive.

His recent promotion to lieutenant had come unasked for, and Kilbride cared little for status or rank.

'Nothing to say for yourself, Lieutenant?' the Major sneered. 'Very well. Your plan reads, and I quote:

Ground: Lebanon, Beirut.
Situation: documents and gold stored within bank vault; four security guards.
Mission: enter city and raid bank to liberate documents.
Execution: head into conflict zone disguised as guerrilla fighters. Set up OP in no man's land and observe guard force. Under cover of darkness mallet both front lines with mortars, blow up bank and rob vault. Grab documents, commandeer trucks and drive out of Beirut.
Service Support: bugger-all. End of story.'

With that last phrase, 'end of story', a ripple of laughter went around the room. Five years earlier an Irishman called Pat Moynihan had joined Q Squadron. Moynihan hailed from County Cork, in Ireland. But at age eighteen he'd crossed the border into the North, enlisting in the Royal Irish Regiment. It was a common enough route for an Irishman who wanted to get into the British army, especially when his parents had worked in Britain and held both Irish and British passports. From there Moynihan had gone on to do SAS selection.

Despite the ongoing Troubles in Northern Ireland, Moynihan had proven an instant hit in The Regiment, being blessed with a sharp Irish wit. He was a natural at demolitions work and could do just about anything with explosives. Moynihan was one of Kilbride's Four Troop men, and in everyday conversation he concluded just about every sentence with those words – 'end of story'. It had become something of a Regimental catchphrase.

'Think it funny, do we?' the Major snapped. 'Well, why don't you share the joke, Kilbride? Or is it your plan that's the joke? Because you can't really be suggesting that a plan like that would *work*, can you, Kilbride? Using your cunning disguise as "guerrilla fighters" you're just going to deliberately attack both sides in the war, is that it? Then blow the bank vault without either side retaliating? And drive right out of there without anyone stopping you? Is that it? Is that really your entire plan? Or have I missed something?'

Kilbride stretched and yawned and glanced around the room. As he started speaking his voice was measured and quiet, almost bored-sounding. But there was something about it that was menacing, conveying a barely suppressed violence.

'How long have you been with us, Marcus?' The use

25

of the first name was a deliberate provocation. Regardless of rank SAS soldiers addressed each other by name, but Major Thistlethwaite hated the tradition and was trying to stamp it out. 'How long, Marcus? In The Regiment, I mean?'

'"Sir" to you, Lieutenant Kilbride! When you address a superior officer, you do so as "sir"!'

'Not here I don't. Didn't you do your SAS induction, Marcus? If you did you've learned nothing from it. We do things differently: it's merit regardless of rank, Marcus, that's what matters. Merit regardless of rank. You've been with us long enough to know that . . .'

'I've been here long enough to know a piece of shit when I see it,' the Major countered, leaving his words hanging in the air.

On the rare occasions when he was driven to real anger, Kilbride's dark eyes turned a murderous black, which was just what they had done now. He was one of the hardest men in the Squadron to wind up, but once provoked he made a vicious adversary – as many an enemy had discovered to their cost. That, coupled with his maverick nature and innate cunning, made him an excellent SAS soldier.

'. . . And let me tell you, Kilbride, that's what your plan is,' the Major blundered onwards. 'Shit. An unworkable, unusable dollop of crap.'

'You're new here, Marcus,' Kilbride continued evenly. 'Six weeks – is it? – you've been with us. A word of advice: you don't stand there after six weeks and tell me that my plan is shit. Not if you want to breathe easily. Not if you want to sleep well at night.'

'Are you threatening me, Lieutenant?' the Major spluttered. 'Because if you are—'

26

'If I am, then what? I don't need to threaten you, Marcus. You're the biggest threat to yourself that there ever was.'

'You think you're so smart, don't you, Kilbride?' the Major shot back at him. 'The lean, mean SAS fighting machine. Well, let me tell you – I'm here to shake you up. Teach you a thing or two; show you some bloody discipline. That's every man in this room, yourself first and foremost, Kilbride. You think your plan's so clever? Well, let's see you prove it. Let's send you into Beirut and see how your wonderful bloody plan works then.'

Major Thistlethwaite pulled an envelope out of his pocket and waved it in Kilbride's direction. 'These are your orders. You are to deploy on a close target recce of the Imperial Bank of Beirut, keeping it under close twenty-four-hour surveillance. And let's be absolutely certain – I don't want anyone breaking wind in there without my knowing about it. Sergeant Jones will brief you on the details. Is that clear?'

Kilbride stared at the Major, the only sign that he had heard him being a slight inclination of the head.

'This may be an exercise only at this stage, Kilbride, but HMG may decide at any moment that we really do want those terrorist documents. And then you'll be forced to put your wonderful plan into action. So, God help you, you'd better be ready.'

'Beats me what you're getting so worked up about, Marcus. If that's all, me and my men will be leaving.'

The Major jabbed a finger in Kilbride's direction. 'Correction, Lieutenant, *you* will not be leaving. I am not having you leading your troop into that war zone with a plan that is bound to fail. Once I have briefed the other troops I will be instructing you on a completely

27

new plan for your Beirut bank operation. It is one that I have drawn up myself and—'

'Sorry, Marcus,' Kilbride cut in, 'but you obviously haven't been listening. *Merit, regardless of rank*, Marcus. *Merit, regardless of rank*. You don't tell me how to do things, any more than I tell my own men. All the men in my troop came up with that plan. And if we are called upon to risk our lives for this, or any, mission, we do so on our own terms.' Kilbride rose to leave. 'Come on, lads, we've a bank raid to prepare for.'

'Kilbride, if you step out of this room . . .' the Major bellowed. His face was glowing red with a mixture of rage and embarrassment.

'You'll what? Report me, is that it? Think how that'll look on your record, Marcus – that you can't control your own men. Take my advice. I'm trying to help you. Don't do it.'

Jimmy Jones, the squadron sergeant major, placed a restraining hand on the Major's shoulder. 'It's best you let your man go. I'll have a quiet word with him later. It's best you get on with briefing the rest of the men.'

Keeping a bank up and running in the midst of a civil war wasn't the easiest of tasks, but Timothy Cuthbert liked to think that he had risen to the challenge with typical British phlegm. Over the weekend four masked gunmen had stormed into his villa on the northern side of Beirut and had ransacked the place. Luckily, his prize collection of rare butterflies had survived untouched and, apart from the soreness in his ribs caused by some insistent prodding with the muzzle of one of the raiders' automatic weapons, he and his wife were unhurt. Then, on the Wednesday evening, his driver had been polishing the bank Rolls when three heavily armed men had kidnapped him and driven the car away. Fortunately, Timothy had been able to negotiate the return of both car and driver largely unharmed.

But this morning's goings-on had been decidedly troublesome, and he was starting to wonder for how much longer he could keep the Imperial Bank of Beirut open. First there had been the journey to work, which had proven largely uneventful until they had reached Rue Allenby. There a chunk of shrapnel from a stray shell had struck the Rolls, and Timothy had been forced to continue his journey by foot. Half an hour after arriving at work a van parked outside the bank had blown up, the explosion spraying flying glass and debris over several of his employees on the ground floor.

To cap it all he now had to receive a visitor – one of the bank's most wealthy clients – with the lobby looking like a bombsite. Luckily, his office was on the third floor of the five-storey building, so it had been largely unaffected by the blast. Over the years Timothy Cuthbert had never been able to establish the exact source of Abdul Sali al-Misri's immense wealth. As things presently stood this one client had one hundred million dollars' worth of gold deposited in the bank. It made the Imperial Bank of Lebanon one of the richest in the country – far outstripping the American banks.

There was a gentle knock at the door. Timothy glanced at his watch. It was 11 a.m., and just like his client to be precisely on time.

'Come in, come in,' Timothy said, rising from his desk.

'Timothy. Timothy. How are you?' Abdul Sali greeted the bank manager in faultless English.

The two men shook hands.

'Bang on time, I see, despite the tiresome war,'

Timothy remarked warmly. 'Take a seat. Coffee? I'll order some coffee. A cigar, perhaps?'

'Ah, the war, the war, my friend,' Abdul Sali replied, waving a hand disdainfully. 'Coffee, black, four sugars, would be simply wonderful. And a fine Cuban cigar, if you have one.'

Timothy Cuthbert leaned across his desk and offered his visitor a fat cigar from a richly inlaid wooden box. One of the most reassuring things about his client, Timothy reflected, was his dress sense. In contrast to some of his other *Arab* clients, Abdul Sali was always impeccably dressed in a Western-style business suit.

'Would you believe it, Abdul Sali – armed intruders in the villa garden, a lump of shrapnel in the Rolls engine, a truck bomb across the street – and all before coffee this morning. You'll excuse the mess in the lobby, won't you? Explosion broke some of the windows, you see.'

'Of course, my friend, I understand completely. This trouble unites us all, you know, draws us all closer together.'

'Indeed. And it won't be affecting the bank, let me assure you. The opening times remain the same – ten until five, Monday to Friday, every week apart from holidays.'

'Certainly – your bank has a most excellent reputation for reliability, Timothy.'

'Glad to hear it. So what exactly did you want to discuss? I trust the coffee's to your liking . . .'

'Delicious.' Abdul Sali paused for a second. He took a sip of his coffee, and a luxuriating pull on the cigar. 'It's security. I wanted to discuss the delicate matter of the bank's security. Of course, the Imperial Bank has an impeccable reputation. But with the war worsening I wanted you to put my mind at rest on the sensitive issue of security.'

'We've never had an incident yet, not in thirty years of operation.'

'I know, I know. But we have rarely had such sustained fighting. And with such a large amount of funds deposited with you, I sought to be reassured.'

'Abdul Sali, you and I have known each other for, what, ten years is it now? You will remember the run on the Beirut banks, back in the late 1960s. For forty-eight hours we were besieged by customers seeking to withdraw their funds. You will remember how we reacted. We held our nerve.'

'Indeed, Timothy, you did.'

'And you, you held your nerve alongside us. You didn't withdraw even one ounce of gold. And by the end of that week the same customers who had left were once again besieging the bank, only this time trying to pay their money back in. The Imperial Bank does not lose its nerve. Not when there's a run on the bank, nor in the midst of a civil war.'

'That is most reassuring to hear, my friend. But—'

'And one more thing. It should be no secret amongst our most treasured clients that the Imperial Bank holds the funds of *all* parties to the war. The Christian forces bank with us, just as the Muslims and Palestinians do. Even the Druze militia holds funds in our vaults. So who in their right mind would ever want to attack us? In this we have been very astute, I think you'll agree. We hold the money of all the factions and that constitutes the ultimate insurance policy. Do you see?'

'Aha, my friend! Now this brings a smile to my face. This is what I was looking to hear from you, Timothy. You English are smart, we know – always the

31

diplomats, always playing to all sides. I suspected this, but I just wanted to hear it from you directly.'

'I trust I've put your mind at rest? And if it helps, I'll also double the guard contingent on the bank vault . . . Now, I'd like to move on to more pleasant matters if I may – like the social gathering Fiona and I are having at the villa this Sunday. Drinks on the lawn from two o'clock onwards, everyone who's anyone invited.'

The SAS's makeshift Cyprus base occupied one end of RAF Akrotiri, which itself was part of the British Sovereign Base on Cyprus. It was made up of little more than a cluster of canvas tents, with a series of shipping containers providing a weatherproof storage area and armoury. Following his heated confrontation with the Major, Kilbride and his team had retired to the mess tent. Due to injuries, Kilbride's troop was down to nine men which meant that they were under strength. But Kilbride wasn't unduly concerned: a smaller unit might be better suited to a covert mission like the Beirut bank job.

Over a brew he and his men had a good moan about Major Thistlethwaite and placed bets on how much longer he would last in The Regiment. The maximum anyone gave him was another couple of months. Either one of the lads would end up punching out his living daylights, or the Commanding Officer of The Regiment would find a way to remove him.

Kilbride steered the conversation away from their hated squadron commander and onto the task ahead. However much personal enmity he might feel towards the Major, they now had a bona fide mission to prepare for. That mission would have been passed down from SAS headquarters in Hereford, and would have

32

emanated from somewhere deep within Whitehall. Kilbride was first and foremost a professional soldier and a leader of his men. If, as it seemed, he was about to take them into the heart of the vicious Beirut civil war, he wanted them going in doubly well prepared.

At present there was woefully little intelligence on which to base those preparations. All Kilbride did know for certain was that they were scheduled to depart for Beirut in a little over forty-eight hours' time. HMS *Spartan*, a British Swiftsure-class nuclear submarine, would leave its temporary berth off Cyprus and take his men to within striking distance of the Lebanese shoreline. They would be dropped at sea and make their way towards the coast under cover of darkness, or at least so Kilbride presumed.

'Right, heads up, lads,' Kilbride announced as he drained his mug of tea. 'Forget the Major – he'll never last. Let's focus on the mission. We pull this one off and we'll prove the Major wrong, which'll be one more nail in his coffin . . .'

'Won't be a moment too bloody soon, boss,' Sergeant Smith interjected. 'Where's he come from, *Dad's* bloody *Army*? The sooner he bloody well goes back there the better.'

Sergeant Phil 'Smithy' Smith had served under Kilbride as his second-in-command (2iC) for four years, and over that time the two men had become inseparable. It was an odd partnership – Smithy, the punchy, barrel-chested, shaven-headed cockney sergeant, and his rangy public-school boss who wore his hair too long for Major Thistlethwaite's liking. Smithy had spent his youth skiving off school and hunting rabbits in the Kent woods, and he had the cunning of a born tracker. And despite his lack of formal education

Smithy was an excellent sounding board for some of Kilbride's more maverick ideas.

Six months ago Smithy's role as second-in-command had been taken over by Captain Bill 'Bronco' Berger, an American operator on secondment to the SAS. Captain Berger was a towering six-foot hunk of muscle and bone, with a massive hook of a nose and deep laughter lines around his eyes. As a captain he held a rank senior to Kilbride's but an American operator had never commanded an SAS troop so Smithy had volunteered his 2iC position. As far as Bill Berger was concerned, he didn't give a rat's shit what place he got within the unit. Every man was treated pretty much as an equal.

Captain Berger was the oldest man in Four Troop, being in his early thirties, and had more accumulated combat experience than any of the others, Kilbride included. He was a veteran of the Green Berets Mobile Strike Force in Vietnam. For six years he had led a unit of local Motagnard tribesmen in behind-the-lines action against the Vietcong. He had taken part in the ultra-secret Project Delta, fought a desperate rearguard action during the Tet Offensive, and led a daring strike into the A Shau Valley.

The end of the Vietnam conflict was less than four years back, and the war was still raw in people's minds, especially Captain Berger's. He rarely if ever talked about it. Recently he had become the first US soldier ever to undertake SAS selection, which he had passed with flying colours. He was now spending a year with them so that he could return to the US and advise their own equivalent unit – Delta Force.

'The goddamn Major can blow it out his ass,' Captain Berger remarked, picking up on Smithy's comment.

Kilbride smiled. 'What worries me most is the lack of time we have to prepare for this Beirut mission. I suggest we break into three groups, each assigned a different area of responsibility for mission preparations. Okay?'

Kilbride glanced around the faces of the men in his unit. Six were regular SAS (including himself) and one was the big American. Then there were two lads from the Special Boat Service (SBS), the sister regiment to the SAS. As the first part of this mission was going to involve a sea assault, Kilbride was glad to have the SBS guys with them. He had a sneaking suspicion that their specialist fighting-on-the-water skills just might come in handy.

'Bronco and I will deal with the intel side of things,' said Kilbride, nodding in the US captain's direction. 'We'll be trying to get some answers about what it's like on the ground in Beirut. I'm presuming we'll need to blend in and make like locals, so I want everyone wearing unmarked combats and taking Arabic headscarves with them. Smithy, I want you and two others to deal with weaponry. I want maximum firepower, and you'll have to beg, borrow and steal whatever we don't have in the stores. Take Paddy Moynihan with you on the explosives side, and bear in mind that we may have to blast our way into a steel bank vault. So we'll need a shed-load of plastic explosives.'

Smithy rubbed his hands together excitedly. 'No problem, boss.'

'Sure, I've precious little experience blowing up banks,' Paddy Moynihan remarked. 'Not a lot of call for that in the Irish Republic, end of story.'

Smithy snorted. 'End of bloody story! Fairy tale,

more like. Every man and his dog knows the IRA funds itself with bank jobs.'

'Mortars are an issue,' Kilbride continued. 'No way are we going to lug a bloody great eighty-one-millimetre tube and baseplate in there. Smithy, take Jock McKierran and see if you can't frighten the regular-army boys into letting us have something smaller and more useful.'

'How about a couple of wee sixty-millimetres?' Jock McKierran volunteered. 'That should do the trick.'

Matt 'Jock' McKierran was a real man-mountain – six foot four tall and eighteen stone of Scottish beef, all topped off with a shock of red hair. He played rugby for the British forces and had on occasion sat on the reserve benches for the Scottish national team. Being the strongest man in the Troop, he was usually saddled with carrying the eighty-one-millimetre mortar's baseplate strapped to his rucksack. An easygoing giant of a man, he never seemed to complain about being used as the unit's packhorse, which endeared him to Kilbride no end.

'A pair of sixty-millimetres?' Kilbride queried. 'Like where from?'

'Och, the Israeli Soltam's used by both sides in the Lebanon,' McKierran replied, with a wicked grin. 'A canny piece of kit if you can get yer hands on one. Weighs in at a fraction of the eighty-one-millimetre.'

'Sounds perfect,' said Kilbride. 'Right, next I want a team pulling together all the non-lethal gear. Think about the operating environment: apart from the infiltration by sea, it's going to be entirely urban. We'll be operating in a built-up area, so it'll be very different from roughing it in the middle of an Irish bog – no offence intended, Paddy.'

'Sure, and none taken.'

'The bank is in the heart of Beirut's Green Line, a total no man's land. I presume we'll be basing ourselves in a bombed-out building, which means no electric lighting, clean water or food. What are we today, the nineteenth of January? That means we'll be leaving here the night of the twenty-first, which is a Wednesday, arriving off the coast of Lebanon on the twenty-second. The best time to hit the bank is going to be at the weekend, when it'll be closed. Beats me how they're keeping it up and running, but that's what the Major told us . . .'

Smithy snorted. 'The bloody Major wouldn't know his arse from his elbow, not even if he was playing tennis with the one and shitting out the other.'

Kilbride smiled at his sergeant's turn of phrase. 'If we don't hit the bank at the weekend, I reckon it's a no-show. In which case they'll pull us out. So we need to be prepared for a five-day op – let's say rations for a week, just to be on the safe side. I can't see us risking hot drinks or food, not with Christian and Muslim militias hunting each other down across the city. They'll smell us a mile off if we start brewing up. So it's hard routine, I'm afraid, lads.'

'Sure, your British army rations are feckin' shite, whichever way you take them,' Paddy Moynihan remarked. 'Hot or cold it makes no difference – end of story.'

'Better than bleedin' potatoes, though, ain't it?' Smithy retorted. 'Which is all you Paddies ever eat . . .'

'Okay, other non-lethal kit,' Kilbride announced. 'We're hitting a civilian bank with four security guards: so we want maximum surprise and minimum casualties. I want two dozen thunderflash grenades made up, and a couple of Mossberg shotguns so we can blast the hinges off the doors. Plus I want tear-gas grenades and respirators.

'Surveillance gear,' Kilbride continued. 'We'll need night-vision units, but that's big and bulky kit so we'll take just two in case one goes down. We'll need a couple of pistol-grip microphones – they're good for up to three hundred yards and should give us the range we need. Ron, you did a lot of surveillance work with the South African military – this kit's your baby, along with Tony Knight. Take the microphones with the collapsible umbrella cone, 'cause they'll pack down smaller, okay?'

Ron Boerke glanced up from where he was fiddling with a Rubik's Cube. They had recently become all the rage and Boerke seemed addicted to the plastic puzzle.

'Not a problem,' he confirmed, in his clipped South African accent. He looked across at Tony Knight. 'Leave it with us.'

Ron 'Bushman' Boerke was the sixth man to be allocated a task, and Kilbride had teamed him up with Tony Knight for a reason. Boerke was a hard man, brought up in the harsh environment of the Transvaal. He was a quiet, taciturn individual, with pale skin and pale blue eyes. He was only slightly smaller than the big Scot, McKierran, but his frame was lean and wiry and he was renowned as a bush fighter. Boerke was known to be a loner, a man of few words whom no one crossed lightly. Kilbride felt certain he would keep Tony Knight in hand – at least until they departed for the Lebanon.

If there was a troublesome member of Kilbride's unit Tony Knight was it. Small in stature, sandy-haired and prematurely balding, he had a big chip on his shoulder.

He resented anyone senior in rank, and especially those – like Kilbride – who came from a more privileged background. He was the least popular man in the unit, and no one knew much about his upbringing, except that he'd had a troubled Essex childhood. He had a face pitted with the scars of adolescent acne, and the lads joked that he still had a squeeze before bed each night. That had earned him the unfortunate SAS nickname 'Nightly'.

'What's the deal with the night-vision units?' Tony Knight queried. 'They get whited-out by a car's head-lamps and weigh a bloody ton. Nothing wrong with the British Army Mark One Human Eyeball, is there?'

'Ron's the surveillance expert,' Kilbride replied. 'What d'you reckon, Ron – worth having the NVGs?'

'There's no question. We take 'em, man,' said Boerke, which put an end to the matter.

Like many South Africans, Boerke added a clipped, staccato 'man' to the end of most of his phrases. This was not the drawn-out, laid-back 'man' of the hippie 1960s: it was more a pointer to the manhood he shared with whoever he was talking to.

'We're operating at close quarters in an urban environment,' Kilbride continued. 'So we need to concentrate on brute force rather than accuracy. I want each man with an M16 and underslung grenade launcher, which as a combo packs an evil punch. And I want one person with a GPMG, just so we've got some heavier firepower. Bronco, that's you – if you're okay with the big machine gun?'

'Sure thing, buddy,' Bill Berger replied, giving a wide, gap-toothed grin. 'Boy, the number of times I wished we had the Gimpy in Vietnam . . .'

'Last thing, I want some sixty-six-millimetre antitank rockets,' Kilbride added. 'Let's say one for each man if we can carry that many.'

'Jesus, nine of 'em. Why so many, buddy?' Bill Berger queried. 'That sure is one hell of a lotta firepower.'

'In case we're not invited into the bank and we have to blast our way in,' Kilbride replied. 'I'm presuming we can break in quietly. But if we *do* have to blow that bank apart I want the kit to do it. Plus both sides of the conflict have a few old Soviet tanks, so we want to be able to take one of those on if it comes looking for us.'

'Buddy, us nine guys are gonna be packing a bigger punch than any unit I ever served with. And that includes the Mobile Strike Force when we hit the Vietcong in the A Shau Valley.'

Kilbride gave a wicked smile. 'But I bet the Vietcong weren't holed up in a bank vault with a steel door twelve inches thick.'

Sergeant Smith eyed Kilbride. 'Boss, you seem pretty certain we'll be hitting that vault.'

Kilbride shrugged. 'If the order comes through for us to hit it, then we'd better be ready for anything . . .'

Smithy held Kilbride's gaze. 'Like getting our hands on fifty million dollars' worth of gold? Is that what you mean, boss?'

'You said it, Sergeant,' Kilbride replied, giving nothing away. 'Anyone got any idea how much fifty million in bullion weighs? Come on, Paddy, that's your area of expertise, isn't it?'

'Sure, are the jokes about Irish bank robbers going to last the whole feckin' mission?' Moynihan replied. ''Cause they just get funnier and funnier each and every time—'

'Less of the blarney, Paddy – just tell us how much it bloody weighs,' Smithy cut in. 'Every Irishman I ever met was a robbing, thieving bastard so you're bound to know.'

'Sure, well, let me think now. When was the last time I stole fifty million in gold? It was that bank in Limerick, wasn't it now? Or was it that one in Dingle? Either way, I think me and me brothers managed to carry it out of there in a couple of wheelbarrows . . .'

'Bet you had to get rid of the bloody potatoes first, though.'

Bill Berger spluttered into his tea. 'I gotta come to Paddy's defence here . . .'

'Must've been a tough decision,' Smithy continued, ignoring the big American. 'Wheelbarrow full of potatoes, wheelbarrow full of gold . . . Now, which do I bloody go for?'

'Hang on a goddamn minute,' Bill Berger cut in. 'My ancestors are Irish, and when the folks go home to Kilkenny they reckon the food's real fine over there. Darn sight better than your English chow, that's for sure.'

Smithy stared at the big American in mock disgust. 'Just goes to show how much you bloody Yanks know about real food.'

Kilbride held up his hands to silence them. On one hand he liked to see all the piss-taking – it meant that his men were relaxed despite the pressure of the coming mission. On the other, he knew that a clock was ticking, and there was one hell of a lot to do before their departure for Beirut.

'Right, back to the job in hand. On arrival in Beirut we've got a Lebanese contact who'll guide us in to the bank. So the two biggest challenges are these: one, the route in from the submarine drop-off point to Beirut itself; two, how we get in and out of the city without being rumbled by either side. The plan we put to Major

Thistlefuck has us going in disguised as a guerrilla force, but I'm open to anything on this one . . .'

Ron Boerke plonked down his Rubik's Cube on the mess table. He'd just solved it by arranging each face into a distinct block of solid colour.

'We had a similar situation in Botswana, when I was with the South African Defence Force,' he announced quietly. He glanced at Kilbride. 'We had to hit a high-value target. Diamonds, man. A big stash of diamonds in the hands of the rebels. We "borrowed" some Red Cross vehicles and used those as our cover. I say we do the same thing here, in Beirut.'

'You really think no one's going to notice?' Tony Knight demanded in disbelief. 'Course they fuckin' are. A load of hairy-arsed blokes sat there in their combats and armed to the teeth, claiming to be Red Cross doctors. Or is it nurses we say we are? Get real.'

'Think about it, man, before you open your mouth,' Boerke replied coldly. 'It's not difficult – you engage your brain before speaking . . . You don't wear combats, you wear white medical gowns. Someone acts dead, and lies in the back. Maybe that's your job, Nightly – you wouldn't find it difficult. There's not much difference between that and the way things are now, is there? You keep your weapons and whatever you've stolen from the bank hidden with the dead man, where no decent soldier will ever start looking.'

Smithy shook his head and grimaced. 'What, we load up a bunch of meat wagons with gold bullion instead of corpses? You're a real sick bastard, Bushman, you know that?'

Boerke narrowed his eyes. 'You can't stop talking about that gold, can you, man? If the Red Cross ruse works, who gives a damn?'

'It's a pretty evil idea but it does have merit,' Kilbride remarked. All of a sudden the situation had the potential to get ugly, and he wanted to move things along. 'It depends on the availability of Red Cross vehicles in Beirut, and that needs checking.'

'They have the vehicles, man,' said Boerke. 'Beirut is crawling with Red Cross – and with the Red Crescent, for that matter.'

Kilbride eyed the lean South African. He had a sneaking suspicion that Boerke had deep connections with South African intelligence, which had to mean with the Israelis, too.

'How do you know?' he asked.

Boerke reached out for his Rubik's Cube and started to mix up the coloured faces. 'I make it my business to know.'

'Y'know, if we're gonna go for it maybe it'd be better to be Red Crescent,' Bill Berger volunteered. 'Kinda more acceptable to the Muslim side of the conflict.'

'What is it with you Yanks and the bloody Muslims?' said Smithy. 'You want to be one, or something?'

'Way you Brits jerk the other guy's chain all the time it's a wonder you ever get any fightin' done,' Berger growled. 'And one more thing – what Boerke's proposing has gotta be unlawful. I mean, the Red Cross wrote the goddamn rules of war. There's sure as hell gotta be a clause in there somewhere saying the military shouldn't go impersonatin' doctors.'

Boerke levelled his cold gaze at the American. 'What are we, man: special forces or the United bloody Nations? In war you do what you have to.'

Berger held the lean South African's stare. 'You think we pussyfooted around in 'Nam?' Whilst he respected the South African as a soldier, he'd never warmed to

43

him. 'We broke more rules than you guys ever dreamed of, and broke more heads whilst we was at it.'

'I don't scare easily, Captain,' Boerke retorted. 'And what you did in Vietnam is your own affair. All I'm saying is the Red Cross ruse will work, so let's use it.'

'And I ain't tryin' to scare you, buddy,' Bill Berger growled. 'If I was, you'd know about it. In fact, I appreciate your plan. I'm just making us aware of some of the pitfalls, that's all.'

'There are no pitfalls. Let me tell you something, man. In Beirut neither side takes any prisoners – not even women and children. You want to steal a load of gold bullion from under the noses of the Beirut militias, you'd better have a plan that works.'

'Now who's going on about thieving the bloody gold?' Smithy cut in. 'You got gold on the brain, Boerke.'

'I take my cue from you, Sergeant,' Boerke replied, without missing a beat. 'One more thing. The Red Cross use foreign medical staff – always. It's one of their principles. So no one will suspect anything if a group of foreign Red Cross medics pitch up in Beirut. It's about the only cover that will work for us. Posing as a guerrilla force is fine – until you open your mouth, that is. Then it'll get us all killed.'

'With an accent like yours I wouldn't be bloody surprised,' said Smithy. 'Still, it'd be one less person to share the gold with, eh?'

The South African stared at Smithy in silence for a few seconds. 'You ever been in a war, man? A real war? A nasty, dirty, vicious little war with no rules – like we had in South Africa. And like they have now in Beirut.'

'Only nasty, dirty little war I ever been involved in

is with the wife,' Smithy replied, with a fixed grin. 'And—'

'Yeah, don't tell us – she goes for the nuclear option every time and grabs you by the balls,' Kilbride interjected. 'The joys of domestic bliss. Right, there's a lot to get sorted so let's move on . . .'

Things were starting to get out of hand, and Kilbride had a strong suspicion why. Each of his men had to be thinking the same thing: was there some way in which he could get his hands on some of the fifty million in gold bullion in that vault? It was unsettling his troop and causing friction, and he needed to get the men firmly focused on the job in hand once again.

'Boerke's plan has got a lot going for it,' Kilbride continued. 'I'll talk it over with the intel people and see what comes up. If there's a Red Cross depot we can access in Beirut, or some other way of getting hold of those vehicles, then let's do it.'

'What about the infiltration, boss?' Smithy asked.

'That's the first thing I'm off to investigate once we're done here. We need a drop-off point at sea that works for us and the submarine, plus a safe route into Beirut. Which reminds me. Ward. Johno. I want you two SBS lads to head down to stores and get us three eight-point-five-metre RIBs. No one else touches them from now on. Got it?'

'Sure thing, boss,' John 'Johno' Hare replied.

Johno was a lanky, laid-back operator who came from a Cornish sheep-farming family. Joining the SBS had been his ticket out of the lonely grind of the farm. The SBS always had a couple of their lads on exchange with the SAS, and vice versa. Johno had been with Kilbride's unit for three months now, and in his quiet way he was blending in well with the team.

'Just on the route in – there was an option Andy and I was thinking might work,' Johno ventured. 'It's something we recced with the SBS several months back.'

'What is it?' Kilbride asked.

'Andy, you spent longer in there 'n I did,' Johno prompted, turning to his fellow SBS operator.

'We reckon we may have a route into Beirut,' Andy Ward volunteered. 'Several months back we had to get some CIA agents into and out of Lebanon. There's a group of islands off the coast at Tripoli, forty miles north of Beirut – the Palm Islands. They're on the twelve-mile limit of Lebanon's territorial waters, so it'd be easy for the sub to drop us nearby . . .'

Andy 'Shagger' Ward was a fair-skinned, blue-eyed boy in his early twenties. He came from Bournemouth, in the south of England. He was a smart dresser and a real hit with the ladies – hence the 'Shagger' nickname. He'd joined Four Troop at the same time as Johno, but Kilbride felt he had yet to fully get the measure of this young SBS soldier. He was a bit of a smooth operator for Kilbride's liking.

'We recced all three islands – Palm, Sanani and Ramkine,' Ward continued. 'They're completely deserted, which is a rarity for the Lebanon as the coastline's heavily populated. There's no fresh drinking water, so they don't exactly get a lot of visitors. It's the last one, Ramkine, that interests us the most.'

'In what way, exactly?' Kilbride asked.

'All three islands are eroded limestone outcrops. Ramkine is furthermost from the shore, and it's small, less than forty thousand square yards of surface area. It only rises to about fifteen yards above sea level, but it's what's under the sea that interests us. What led us to it was the barking of the Monk seals . . .'

Ward paused for a second to catch his breath – and for dramatic effect, Kilbride figured. He had all the men of the unit gripped.

'There's a series of caves that remain half-submerged most of the time. Apart from the seals, they're totally deserted. Where the sea action has scoured out the caves they go down to considerable depth. They're big enough to sail a dozen RIBs into, and they'd be totally hidden from view. There's only one drawback: the whiff's a bit much from all the accumulated seal shit. But if you SAS lads can handle that, it's the perfect hideaway.'

'If we can put up with the smell from your tent, I reckon we can handle bloody anything,' Smithy grunted.

'So what're you suggesting?' Kilbride prompted.

'Well, back in 1289 the islands were the scene of a bloody massacre,' Ward continued. 'The Muslim Mamelukes were advancing on Tripoli, which was a big Crusader outpost at the time. The Christian inhabitants fled by boat to the islands. They hid in the church of Saint Thomas, on Palm Island, but the Mamelukes found them, tore down the church and slaughtered them all. Ever since then the islands have been cursed. Even the local fishermen avoid the place, which is a blessing for us, really.'

Bill Berger yawned. 'Jesus, buddy, enough of the history lesson. Get to the point . . .'

'The point is that they're deserted and shunned by everyone, which makes them the perfect forward mounting base for us lot. I'd say we deploy from HMS *Spartan* to Ramkine Island and lie low while the sub disappears. We can dump any surplus supplies in the cave and head on to Beirut from there. That way, if the mission goes tits-up at any stage we can make for

47

the islands until it all dies down again. No one knows those caves exist – I'm certain of it. So we'd be safe as houses in there.'

'How long did you spend checking them out?' Kilbride asked.

'We did a three-day recce. We got a feel for the best access routes, and I did three dives on the main cave. There's tunnels going back into the limestone that probably end up in Syria, for all I know. Only sign of human life we ever saw was a few distant fishing boats, and no way in the world were they ever going to notice us.'

'Nice work, Ward,' Kilbride announced. 'Right, unless someone comes up with a better plan we'll be paying a visit to the Palm Islands. Don't forget to bring your deck chairs and sunscreen. We'll meet back here same time tomorrow evening for a heads-up. I want to see real progress on all fronts by then.'

The men broke up into their groups and headed off to their various tasks. As Bill Berger made to leave the mess tent he felt a hand on his shoulder. He turned to find himself face to face with Boerke. He and the lean South African were the same height, and they were eye to eye with each other.

'I meant no offence, Captain,' Boerke remarked, quietly. 'I have a great respect for the US military – what you did in Vietnam. I don't know if it was the right war exactly . . .'

'It started off being the right war,' Berger replied, a hint of bitterness in his voice. 'But by the time we left, the media and the politicians had made darn sure it was the wrong one.'

'Isn't it always thus? Just look at South Africa, man.' With a thin smile, Boerke offered his hand to the

48

American captain. 'There are few units I rate alongside the South African special forces. The SAS is one; your Mobile Strike Force is another. It's an honour to serve alongside you.'

Berger took Boerke's hand and gripped it. 'Appreciate it. And less of the "Captain": it's "Bronco" to my buddies.'

Seeing that Bill Berger had been waylaid, Kilbride grabbed Ward, the young SBS operator, and led him away to a deserted corner of the mess tent.

'A quiet word,' Kilbride said. 'How deep did you say the water went in that main cave?'

'About thirty-five to forty feet. Imagine a horizontal tunnel going back into the cliff face, a tunnel that ends in a deep pool. What with all the sediment we stirred up it was pea soup down there, but I could feel an inrush of water. I reckon that's an underground stream venting into the cave, and it's that which has carved out the deep pool. Why d'you ask, boss?'

'Just curious. You seem to know a lot about Lebanese geography and history.'

'I like to know the enemy territory, the lie of the land. Lebanon basically doesn't have a coast in the normal sense – the mountains just rise straight out of the sea. They're supposedly honeycombed with underground rivers. That's what I reckon we have with these caves.'

'Thanks,' Kilbride remarked. 'I'll go and check it out on the charts.'

'The caves are unbeatable, boss,' Ward added. 'Oh, and in case you were wondering, they're the perfect hiding place. If you were looking to hide anything, that is . . .'

'I wasn't,' Kilbride retorted, evenly. 'Should I be?'

CHAPTER THREE

That evening, Kilbride and Berger went to work on the two military-intelligence officers who had been assigned to Q Squadron's Cyprus operations. They had many questions to which they needed answers, with scant time. Luckily, the MI6 boys had at their disposal a tame journalist in Beirut. Within twenty-four hours they could have him check out the Imperial Bank's guard strength and security systems. They would get him to open a safety-deposit box with the bank so that he could check out in person the way in which the vault operated. They also had a trusted Lebanese fixer, who was perfect for checking out the Lebanese operations of the Red Cross and the availability of suitable vehicles.

The MI6 officers proceeded to brief Kilbride and Berger about a recent SAS mission. A four-man team had entered Beirut city from the sea, using the Beirut River as their route in. They had done so using one-man Rigid Raiders, flat-bottomed rapid-assault craft similar in design to a jet ski. Fast, silent and compact, they were great over short distances in sheltered coastal waters.

But they were useless over long stretches in the open sea with a heavy load of weaponry, which ruled them out for Kilbride's mission.

But if that four-man team had got up the Beirut River using Rigid Raiders, maybe Kilbride's larger force could do the same with their Zodiac Rigid Inflatable Boats (RIBs). Kilbride knew better than to ask about the objective of the previous mission. If it had already happened and he knew nothing about it, then there would be good reason for that secrecy. All he wanted to know was the ease of access up the Beirut River. It turned out that the leader of that previous mission had been a fellow Q Squadron operator – John Knotts-Lane, the commander of One Troop.

'Best we go and find Knotts-Lane,' Kilbride remarked to Berger as they left the meeting. It was getting late, but both men were fired up with the excitement of the coming mission. 'He usually hangs out in the ops tent, just in case there's any juicy intel coming in. He likes to be the first to know, if you get my meaning.'

Bill Berger nodded. 'We got the same types in the Green Berets. Say, you reckon those intel guys will come up with the goods? That's a lot to ask of them in twenty-four hours.'

'They'll have the answers for us,' Kilbride confirmed. 'They get a kick out of this sort of thing.'

'What kinda name is Knotts-Lane, anyways?' Berger asked as they threaded their way through the tented sleeping area of the camp. 'We just don't do this two-surnames shit in the States. I feel kinda sorry for the poor bastard going through life with a name like that.'

Kilbride laughed. 'I wouldn't tell him that if I were you. He's sort of touchy about it.'

'Who wouldn't be?'

51

'It's a double-barrelled surname. Means he's got class. Breeding. Or so he thinks.'

It was Bill Berger's turn to laugh. 'What is it with you Brits and all this class crap? Only thing that matters in the US is whether you got money – and balls.'

Sure enough, the two men found Knotts-Lane hunched over a desk in the ops tent. He was playing a game of chess with himself and seemed lost in a world of his own.

'Knotty,' Kilbride announced, using the man's nickname. 'Need a word. You got a minute?'

Knotts-Lane glanced up, a faraway look in his eyes. Kilbride registered an angry red cut to his face, and wondered if he'd sustained an injury on the recent Beirut mission.

'I suppose I can spare you just the one minute, Kilbride. That's unless you want to stay and have me massacre you at chess again? I seem to remember the last time it took about half a dozen moves.'

'Something like that,' said Kilbride. 'You know Captain Berger? He's over from the States, attached to my troop.'

Knotts-Lane flicked his gaze towards Bill Berger, and barely grunted. 'So what is it you want?' he asked Kilbride.

'You were on a mission into Beirut recently, up the Beirut River. I need to know if we could get some RIBs up the same route that you blokes used.'

'Ah – your little bank robbery,' Knotts-Lane replied. 'Well, I'm sorry but I can't tell you, Kilbride. I'm afraid our little op was need-to-know stuff only. It's restricted.'

'Well, it *is* my need-to-know, mate,' said Kilbride.

'And the Yank?' Knotts-Lane remarked, nodding in Berger's direction. 'What about *him*?'

'The MI6 boys just briefed us *both* on your mission. Anyway, we don't want to know the classified stuff, just the state of access via the Beirut River.'

'Best you pull up a chair,' Knotty said, indicating the space beside him. 'And your Yankee sidekick.'

Bill Berger grabbed himself a chair, straddled it so that he faced Knotts-Lane across its back and eyeballed him. 'You got a problem with Americans, buddy?' he demanded. ''Cause it sure as hell looks that way from where I'm sittin'. If it makes things easier I can make myself scarce, and you can talk to my buddy here alone . . . Once you're done I'll be waiting around the corner, and you can get what's coming.'

Knotty held Berger's gaze without a hint of fear in his eyes. 'Is that right? Just the way it happened in Vietnam, when you kick-arse Yankee tough guys took on the Vietcong? Let's knock the shit out of the slanty-eyed bastards, just 'cause they're Commies and for the heck of it.'

Bill Berger pushed his chair away angrily and rose to his feet, knocking over the chessboard as he did so. 'Ain't you the bleedin' heart?' he growled. 'From where I'm standin' seems like you're in the wrong goddamn business, but I hear Mother Teresa's got some vacancies. I'll be waiting for you outside, Kilbride.' He turned to leave. 'Oh, and sorry about the chess game, buddy.'

Knotts-Lane stared after the big American, resentment burning in his eyes. 'Fucking Yanks . . .'

'Better not let me catch you alone in the shadows, boy,' Berger called over his shoulder. 'If I do, you'll be getting another scar on your face to match the one you've already got.'

Knotts-Lane sneered. 'Real tough guy, eh? Beats me

how come the Vietcong took Uncle Sam to the fucking cleaners, with blokes like you on their side . . .'

Kilbride had known Knotts-Lane for the seven years that he'd been in The Regiment, and he'd learned as much about his background as anyone. The man's father was an international businessman, and Knotts-Lane had spent the bulk of his childhood growing up in the Far East. Whilst there, he'd become an expert in martial arts – which was why he seemed to fear no man, Bill Berger included. He'd tried a career in business but had been bored senseless. Then he'd found his way into The Regiment.

Kilbride was about as close as anyone came to being his friend, which wasn't saying a great deal. Pretty quickly he'd realised that somewhere there was a serious disconnect with Knotty. He seemed incapable of forming genuine, close friendships. He led his troop by virtue of his position, as distinct from any sense of comradeship with his men.

Nevertheless, Knotts-Lane had confided to him something of his troubles. Two years earlier they'd been on Arctic exercises, and Kilbride and Knotty had spent twenty-four hours holed up in a snow cave. Over a shared flask of whisky Knotty's story had emerged. When he'd been fourteen he'd gone trekking in Yellowstone National Park, in the States, and his sister had fallen from a cliff.

His father had called in an emergency chopper, but the hospital had demanded proof of medical insurance before they would treat the girl. She'd died on the operating table, and that was the moment when Knotty's hatred of Americans had begun. He'd been very close to his sister. They'd been soul mates. And, over time, he'd realised that he found it difficult to get close to anyone else, in case the same thing happened again.

He still felt that his sister's spirit was with him, Knotty had explained. She was an angel sitting on his shoulder, watching over him and waiting for the perfect moment for revenge.

'Wanker!' Knotts-Lane spat out, as he jerked his head in the direction of the American captain.

Kilbride ignored the remark. He needed to get some information out of Knotts-Lane. 'So, the Beirut River – what's it like?'

'It's a cesspit,' Knotty replied. 'It's full of offal from the slaughterhouses and polluted as hell. But this time of year, with the river in spate, you shouldn't have a problem. Take it slowly and watch out for underwater snags – you know, old motorbikes, rotten prams, decomposing corpses, that sort of thing. You'll make it all right. I just hope the big Yank takes a fall and swallows half the river – that'll finish him.'

Knotts-Lane sketched out a rough map of the route that Kilbride should take up the river, plus the landmarks to look out for. Two converging lines marked the river estuary; a series of dots at the estuary mouth marked the oil-storage depot; a pair of ruler-straight marks depicted the path of the river as it was channelled through a massive concrete culvert; a line across the river's route marked a road or rail bridge; a group of squares on the riverside showed the location of the sprawling Karantina slaughterhouse complex.

When he was done, Knotty handed Kilbride the map. 'Follow that and you'll be okay.'

'Thanks. What happened to your face?'

'That?' Knotty touched a hand to the cut on his cheek. 'Last leave I did a solo crossing of the Darien

55

Gap. You know where that is? It's in Panama, one of the largest unexplored tracts of jungle in the world. Met some native Indians who took me in and fed me up for a few days. I was pretty much starving by then. They gave me this hallucinogenic drug made from the bark of a tree. They got this wooden pipe about five feet long, packed one end with the stuff and blew it up my nose. It's literally mind-blowing stuff—'

'Remind me to try some,' Kilbride interjected dryly.

'Well, the Indians believe you are possessed by their gods once you take this stuff – so whatever you do when you're under the influence they won't intervene. I went on this mind-bending trip for forty-eight hours. When I came to I'd had half my face ripped open. The Indians told me that I'd tried to kill one of their dogs – a savage little mongrel that they had running around the place. It's feasible: I never have liked dogs. Too blindly loyal for my liking. Anyway, the dog fought back and ripped my face open . . .'

'Thanks again for the info on the river,' Kilbride remarked, as he rose to leave. 'I appreciate it. And you'd better get the medic to take a look at that cut. It could turn nasty.'

Knotty grunted a reply, turned back to his chess-board and started to replace the pieces.

'By the way, whatever happened to the dog?' Kilbride added.

'The village dog?' Knotts-Lane gave a thin smile. 'I slit its throat. The Indians weren't too happy at first. But I was under the influence of the drugs and their gods, so what could they say? We cooked it and ate it. Ever tried dog, Kilbride? You should. It's not so bad.'

'I'm pretty fond of them myself – man's best friend

and all that. I appreciate the loyalty. You won't be finding any on my menu.'

Knotts-Lane glanced up at Kilbride, a strange look in his eyes. 'You're going to hit that bank, aren't you? Take it for all it's worth. See, I know what makes you tick, Kilbride. Fifty million in gold bullion: you just won't be able to resist it.'

Kilbride's face remained a blank mask. 'Don't know what you're on about, Knotty.'

'A word of advice for when you do: hide the gold at sea. No one will ever think of looking for it there. Gold is almost a hundred per cent indestructible – and it never corrodes in sea water. Never – not in a million years.'

'*Assalam alaikum* – peace be with you,' Abdul Sali al-Misri intoned. He reached out to touch the hand of the old man who sat cross-legged before him.

'*Alaikum assalam* – and unto you, peace,' the old man replied.

He took Abdul Sali's proffered hand, shook it gently, and then placed his palm over his own heart. It was a traditional Muslim greeting, showing that he brought the peace of the other into his being.

The old man indicated that Abdul Sali should sit. There were no chairs, so he squatted on the floor. As he waited for the old man to speak, Abdul Sali glanced around the sparsely furnished room. This part of Beirut had lost its electricity many months ago, but by the light of a sputtering gas lamp he could see a dog-eared poster. It announced the 'Never-ending struggle of the Popular Front for the Liberation of Palestine.' Next to it hung a gold-embossed verse of the Koran on a plastic backing hung in a cheap picture frame: 'They fight in Allah's name, so they kill and are killed.' There was nothing about the room to suggest the immense power and wealth that was at the old man's command.

The silence deepened as they waited for the tea to be brought. It was always thus whenever Abdul Sali came to visit, and he had got used to the slow pace of the ritual. Eventually, there was a tap at the door and a young man came in, carrying a tray: on it was a cheap brass tea pot, two small tea glasses and a bowl heaped high with sugar. In the austere atmosphere of the old man's office, sugar was one of the few permitted indulgences. As the young man backed away his Kalashnikov clunked against the door frame. The old man glanced up, gave a thin crack of a smile and waved him out of the room.

He leaned forward and spooned four sugars into Abdul Sali's glass – always four sugars, always no asking. As he poured the tea he raised and lowered the brass pot several times in quick succession, so that the hot liquid splashed and foamed into the glass. It was supposed to aerate the brew, so making it more agreeable to the palate. Once he had served both glasses, the old man would be ready to speak. No matter what Abdul Sali had been called to the old man's office to discuss, the routine was always the same.

'Your mission was successful, by the grace of Allah?' the old man asked, handing Abdul Sali his glass.

'Indeed, Sheikh, I believe it was.'

'The brothers' and the sisters' money is secure?' the old man queried, his eyes like hot coals beneath fearsome brows.

'As secure as it can be anywhere in Beirut, of that much I am certain.'

'No one suspects who you really are? No one suspects the source of the funds?'

'I don't think they have any idea, Sheikh. And I don't think they would care that much, even if they did. The Englishman who runs the bank is an infidel and a capitalist. Like all of them, he is greedy and blinded by money. He has never so much as asked.'

'It is good,' said the Sheikh. 'That gold may come from Syria and Iran – but it is the people's money, Abdul Sali. It is the money to fund our struggle, to repulse the Jews and their Crusader allies. To retake our lands, our Holy Lands. To wage the eternal Jihad . . .' The old man took a sip of his tea. 'You have heard about the hijacking, Abdul Sali? A cruise ship. Ingenious, wouldn't you agree?'

'*Al hamdu lillah* – praise be to God,' Abdul Sali muttered. 'Only one American infidel killed, but it sends the right message . . .'

The old man paused for a second. 'You know, this war has brought great instability to the Lebanon, Abdul Sali. We should be fighting in Israel, in America, in Europe, not here on our own doorstep. The city lies in ruins. Several banks have been robbed. Heaven forbid that anyone should steal the people's money. This is my great worry, Abdul Sali, my great fear . . .'

'Sheikh, I spoke to the manager of the Imperial Bank . . .'

'As I asked.'

'As you asked. The Englishman assures me that he banks the funds for all sides of the war – Muslim, Christian, Druze, whoever. He actively encourages it. As he says himself, it is the Imperial Bank's greatest insurance policy – for who in their right minds would attack them, this being so?'

'Keep always your friends close and your enemies closer,' the Sheikh murmured. He permitted himself a thin smile. 'This Englishman, he is a clever dog, like the whole breed . . . That gold represents our war chest, Abdul Sali. Let no one try to take it from us.'

'Rest assured, dear Sheikh, if it is safe anywhere—'

'It is on your head, Abdul Sali,' the Sheikh, interrupted softly. 'This is your Holy Duty. This is your duty to the Struggle, to your People, to your God. It is on your head, Abdul Sali – and the heads of your children and their children if you fail . . .'

Kilbride had found it more than a little difficult to sleep, with all the mission details seething around in his mind, and he was awake with the dawn. That evening they would be departing for the Lebanon, and he was keen to get the operation under way. The planning stage was complete, and all that remained for the men to do was to get out on the ranges and zero in their weapons. That afternoon they would ferry their kit out to the submarine, HMS *Spartan*, and be shipshape for departure.

Kilbride glanced at his watch. It was not yet 6.15 a.m. and he could afford a few minutes of relaxation before starting the day. He stared up at the canvas ceiling of the tent that he shared with Berger, Smithy and Moynihan. As he did so, he ran through the mission plan one last time in his mind. The *Spartan* was scheduled to drop them seven miles off the Palm Islands, at last light on the following day. They would head directly for Ramkine Island at twenty-five knots, which should take them less than a quarter of an hour. Once safely hidden in the cave, Kilbride would brief his men – and he was looking forward to this with a mixture of exhilaration and trepidation, he reflected to himself.

Still, presuming all went well with the briefing they would be back on the water by 11 p.m. The run to

Beirut should take no more than two hours, so they would reach the mouth of the Beirut River at around 1 a.m. The three boats would head up the river in line astern at dead slow. The city was under a de facto curfew at night, so no one would be out on the streets. With the electricity off in most of the suburbs the boats would be all but invisible. Some twenty minutes upriver their Lebanese fixer, Emile Abdeen, would be waiting for them and he would signal them in with three flashes of a red torchlight.

They would tie up the boats and camouflage them in an old shack on the riverside. In the compound of a nearby safe house, Emile would have the Red Cross vehicles ready and waiting. Kilbride hadn't pried too deeply when the MI6 officers had outlined this part of the plan. How they'd managed to get hold of the Red Cross vehicles wasn't his need-to-know, although he felt certain that money had changed hands. Emile had identified a route that would take them directly into Rue Riad al-Solh, more commonly known as Bank Street, the location of the target. They would pass via one checkpoint only, which was manned by the Christian militia, so they should face few problems there.

Kilbride kicked his legs over the edge of the camp bed and wriggled his toes into some flip-flops. He and the rest of the Troop had a week of unwashed days ahead of them, and it was time for a last shower. As he shuffled across to the concrete shower block, Kilbride racked his brains as to what could conceivably go wrong with the plan. He entered the shower and stood beneath the lukewarm stream of water, soaping himself all over. It seemed like the perfect plan of attack, yet still he couldn't shake off the uneasy feeling that something *had* to go wrong.

Ten minutes later Kilbride came out of the shower block and almost stumbled into Sergeant Smith.

'A word, boss,' Smithy remarked as he jerked his head in the direction of the now-deserted shower block.

As the two men stepped inside, Kilbride had a strong suspicion that he knew what was coming.

'Boss, are you thinking what I think you're thinking?' Smithy hissed. ''Cause knowing you like I do, I wouldn't be surprised. I haven't slept a wink worrying about it . . .'

Kilbride feigned ignorance. 'You've lost me, Smithy.'

'Are you thinking of pulling off this bloody bank job for real? I'd be buggered if you're just going to walk away from fifty million dollars. I got to know, boss, I just got to know.'

'Of course not, Smithy,' Kilbride replied, a twinkle in his eye. 'Nothing could be further from my mind . . .'

'Bloody level with me, boss. I won't breathe a word to the others.'

For a moment Kilbride was tempted to reveal to his trusted sergeant what he really had in mind. But he let his instinct rule him – for now at least he would keep it to himself.

'Smithy, if there's anything like that going down you'll be the first to know. Trust me.'

'I can feel it in my bones, boss, and I just want you to know to count me in . . .'

Kilbride grinned. 'Whatever happens on this mission, Smithy, I'm counting you in.'

Kilbride made his way over to the mess tent for breakfast. At this early hour the place was all but deserted. The only other person present was the squadron sergeant major (SSM), Jimmy Jones, who was tucking into a massive fry-up. Like Kilbride, Jimmy Jones was a bit of an early bird.

'Kilbride!' he called out, jabbing a fork with a sausage speared on it in his direction. 'Lovely nosh. Come 'n join me, lad.'

The SSM was in his mid-forties and was affectionately known to the men as 'Spud'. He was a bit of a father figure to the younger soldiers, Kilbride included. The two of them had an instinctive liking for each other, and Kilbride felt he could trust the SSM on most things.

Kilbride loaded his plate and made his way over to the SSM's table. 'Morning, Spud. You want to give me an ear-bashing over the Major . . .'

'Thistlebollock?' the Sergeant Major cut in. 'The bloke's a bloody moron. Made my life a bloody misery, he has. He'll never last.'

'Glad to hear it.' Kilbride attacked his breakfast. The thought of the coming mission gave him a fierce appetite. 'He's a stool-pigeon, Spud. An agent provocateur.'

'An agent bloody what? What you on about, Kilbride? You don't half talk a load of bollocks. That's what I like about you, lad.'

'The Major's a bloody stooge, Spud. He's been sent here to teach us the three Rs: Rules, Rank and Regulations. It's all bullshit. He's trying to mess us up, Spud, to mess with the only R that matters – The Regiment.'

The Sergeant Major stopped chewing for a second and fixed Kilbride with a beady eye. 'No one fucks with The Regiment, lad, no one. Like I said, the bloke's bloody history. So, don't you worry none . . .' He rapped his knife on Kilbride's plate, which was piled high with fried eggs and bacon. 'You get a good feed down you, lad. You've got a week on cold rations in

63

Beirut, which is more 'n enough for anyone. Talking of which, I got something for you.'

The Sergeant Major scrabbled around in his pocket and pulled out a scrap of paper. He handed it to Kilbride.

'What's this?' Kilbride asked.

'Well, seeing as you're supposed to be stealing some *documents*, I thought you'd better have the numbers of the safety-deposit boxes that they're stored in. Remember? The terrorist documents? You haven't forgotten about them, have you, lad?'

Kilbride smiled, sharing the Sergeant Major's implied joke, and the two men ate in silence for several seconds. Finally, the SSM stopped shovelling food into his mouth and glanced up at Kilbride.

'Listen, lad, word of advice. Whatever we all think of Thistlebollock, he's gunning for you big time. Step out of line on this mission and you could be finished with The Regiment. And that'd be a great loss, 'cause you're a good soldier, Kilbride.'

Kilbride nodded. 'Tell me something, Spud – who owns the gold in that vault? I mean, there's a load of terrorist documents in there, and it sort of makes me wonder who owns the gold.'

The Sergeant Major glanced around the mess tent, checking that they were alone. Then he leaned closer across the table. 'You're a smart lad, Kilbride, so work it out. You put two and two together, what d'you get?'

'Four.'

'You put terrorist documents in a vault along with a shed-load of gold, so who owns the gold?'

'The terrorists.'

The Sergeant Major nodded. 'You said it, lad. You said it.'

'So why the hell aren't we lifting the gold? I just don't get it, Spud. I mean, you can do a lot of damage with fifty million dollars. That's one hell of a lot of hijacking, hostage-taking and car bombs.'

'Don't I know it,' the Sergeant Major snorted. 'Listen, lad, back in the good old days before Thistlebollock and his like, that's exactly what we would've done. You remember Oman – the Jebel Akhdar mission?'

Kilbride shook his head. 'Before my time.'

'Well, here's the short version. 1959. Bunch of rebels trying to topple the Sultan of Oman. He was a friend of Her Majesty, wasn't he, so the lads got sent in. They did the bloody impossible and scaled the Jebel Akhdar, the highest mountain in the Gulf. The rebels had a stronghold on the summit, but the lads took 'em by surprise. Dawn assault, couple of three-point-five-inch rockets bang into the cave entrance – blew the fuckers away. They seized the cave, thinking it was full of ammo and stuff. Sure enough, they found a load of wooden crates. They levered the lid off the first one. Guess what they found inside?'

Kilbride shrugged. 'A load of Liverpool FC T-shirts.'

'A load of Liverpool . . .' The Sergeant Major shook his head. 'What're you on, Kilbride? It was full of Maria Theresa silver dollars, that's what. The cave was full of crates and crates of silver. It was the rebels' frigging bank. It was riches beyond their wildest dreams. So what did the lads do? What the fuck d'you think? They emptied their packs, filled them with the loot and the rest is bloody history.'

Kilbride smiled. 'Not bad. So why aren't we doing the same?'

'Good question.' The Sergeant Major took a swig of tea. 'Think what they pulled off in that one mission, lad:

they busted the rebel stronghold, put the fear of God into 'em, and bankrupted 'em, all in the one hit. And that was it – pretty much curtains for the war in the Oman. You take the terrorists' money away, lad, and they ain't got a hell of a lot left to fight with.'

Kilbride eyed the SSM. 'So why aren't we nicking that fifty million dollars in gold bullion?'

The Sergeant Major frowned, heavy lines creasing his forehead. 'I don't have an easy answer for you, lad . . .' He scratched his head thoughtfully. 'Well, first, Thistlebollock doesn't have the balls for it, that's for starters. And second, it's not the sort of shit The Regiment gets up to these days, not with wankers like him in charge.'

'It's bollocks, Spud, complete bollocks. We should be lifting the bullion. We'll only get the one chance. Once they realise the papers are missing they'll move that gold.'

The Sergeant Major nodded. 'Sure as eggs is eggs they will, lad. Fancy another brew?'

Sergeant Major Jones went to fetch two mugs of tea, leaving Kilbride brooding over the gold in that bank vault. There was an unspoken subtext to their conversation, which both men were well aware of. Ten years of a flaky Labour government had knocked the wind out of the British military, and special forces had taken the worst of the hit.

'Thistlebollock's still whining on about your mission plan,' the Sergeant Major remarked as he plonked the brews down on the table. 'Seems like he thinks he's got a better way of doing things.'

'Well, he can stick it up his fucking arse . . . In any case, no plan survives first contact with the enemy. That's what you're always telling us, isn't it, Spud? So

66

there's no knowing what might happen when we hit that bank, is there?'

The SSM grunted an affirmative. 'Too right. Anything's possible, ain't it, lad? But whatever you *do* get up to in there, don't let Thistlebollock catch you at it. He'll have your fucking guts if he does, you mark my words.'

Kilbride looked the SSM in the eye. 'So, you'll cover for me, will you, Spud?'

The SSM held his gaze. 'Listen, lad, I don't know what you're up to and I don't want you telling me.' He winked, slowly. 'But if there's any way Spud Jones can cover your arse, then I fucking will.'

The rest of the day passed in a whirlwind of activity as arms, ammunition, personal kit and boats were ferried out to HMS *Spartan* at her anchorage. There was nothing sophisticated about the way in which the three Zodiac RIBs would be carried to their drop-off point. They were deflated and lashed to the deck just aft of the conning tower, and would remain there until they reached the Lebanese coastline.

By the time the men of Four Troop had gathered in the mess tent for their last hot meal before deployment they were all dog-tired. The sub's crew had volunteered their bunks, and Kilbride's men were looking forward to getting a good sleep before going into the unknown.

'Everyone's knackered,' Kilbride announced, once the men had finished eating. 'So if you want to forgo the pre-mission send-off, I'll understand.'

'No bloody way, boss,' Smithy protested. 'Never has a mission gone down under your command without one.'

With that, Smithy pulled out a bottle of Johnnie Walker Red Label from his kitbag. Mess mugs were passed across to him and each soldier received a generous shot. It was totally against army regulations, of course. Drinking alcohol was seen as a dereliction of duty. But The Regiment had never been big on rules, especially those of the dumbest sort. Smithy proposed a toast to the coming mission. The men raised their mess mugs and drank to it.

Over in one corner of the mess tent a lone figure watched Four Troop with something approaching burning resentment. John Knotts-Lane had never been able to reconcile himself to Kilbride's unforced popularity. And seeing the big American taking an easy place amongst his men made his blood boil. Knotts-Lane wondered how it was that Kilbride had such a close, instinctive bond with the men of his unit. Part of him hated Kilbride for it – and envied him, too.

CHAPTER FOUR

Some twenty-four hours later the massive slab form of the *Spartan*'s conning tower slunk away into the night and was soon lost in the slap of the sea and the inky shadows. The last that Kilbride and his men had seen of the sub's crew were their ghostly white faces peering out of the darkness. The three 8.5-metre Zodiac RIBs set out towards the Lebanese coastline in a tight V formation, showing no lights. Kilbride was in the lead boat, along with Ward, the young SBS operator. Ward was navigating using a DECCA radio direction finder. It was accurate to within ten metres, and would steer them in to the cave entrance itself.

As they drew away from the submarine drop-off point, Kilbride scanned the surrounding ocean for any sign of trouble. In the far distance he could just detect a faint line of lights, twinkling on the pencil-thin horizon. That had to be downtown Tripoli, the brighter glow that of the Al Mina port area. So far, Tripoli had remained largely unaffected by the war. But for how much longer that would remain so was anyone's guess.

As far as Kilbride could tell there were no other craft out on the night-dark sea, which was just as he had hoped.

The throaty roar of the Zodiacs' engines and the whip of the sea wind made talking all but impossible. But Kilbride decided that he had to seize the moment for he might not get another chance. He grabbed Smithy by the arm and leaned across to have a word in his ear.

'I said if there's anything going down, you'd be the first to know,' he yelled. 'Well, there just might be.'

'Like what?' Smithy yelled back.

'I've got an alternative plan to present to the lads, when we reach the cave. Whatever happens, I want to hit that gold.'

'Bloody A-okay with me, boss,' roared Smithy.

'I don't trust Nightly. Plus Boerke's an odd one. That's why I didn't mention it back at base.'

'Bushman's okay – he's just a thick-skulled Afrikaner. I dunno about Nightly, though.'

'When I present the plan, I want back-up, okay? If you come right out and support me, I reckon the other lads will follow . . .'

'Fine by me, boss. Like I said, count me in.'

As the boats nuzzled in closer to the Lebanese coastline a squat dark shape loomed out of the swell. It was the island. Ward brought the RIB in under the low cliffs, throttled back the engine and began searching for the cave entrance. Kilbride soaked up the night atmosphere. There was the slap of the waves on the rocks, and the strong iodine smell of the sea. It was good to be out on the ocean, preparing to go into action again.

'There she is,' Ward announced softly as he pointed out a darker shadow amongst the grey cliffs.

70

Ward brought the craft around, lifted the outboards from the water using the on-board hydraulic tilt mechanism and edged her into the blackness of the opening. The other two boats fell in behind, in line astern. The lead RIB glided forward for several seconds, propelled by little more than her momentum, the noise of the sea muffled by the massive rock walls. Quite suddenly, she scraped across a shallow ledge and came to rest against the back wall of the cave. It was dark as pitch in there, but at least the men's natural night vision had had time to kick in during the journey across the sea.

As Smithy held the boat steady Kilbride made a leap for the rock ledge, a mooring rope in one hand. He landed safely a few feet above the water level and pulled the RIB in towards him. He tied her off so that Smithy and Ward could unload the gear. As he did so, he heard the soft rubbery squelch of the other two boats nosing into the rock wall behind him. They had all made it safely into their cave refuge.

Kilbride lit a battered oil lantern and took stock of his surroundings. The cave was largely as Ward had described it and there was ample space on the ledge for the nine men and their gear. The place certainly smelled as if it was occupied by some pretty unsavoury beasts, Kilbride reflected, as he wrinkled his nose. All the same, it was an excellent forward mounting base for the mission. As to the cave's features *below* the waterline, Kilbride would have to trust to the accuracy of Ward's word on that. There would be no time to check before their onward deployment to Beirut.

His inspection of the cave complete, Kilbride gathered his men around him. The plan he was about to propose was pretty bloody crazy – and he knew it. He steeled himself, breathed deeply and began speaking, his voice echoing weirdly around the cavernous space.

'Right, lads, I'm not going to fuck around: prepare yourselves for a major change of plan. We're going into Beirut but with a very different mission objective – or at least we will be if the rest of you are with me. If you are, I can promise you this will be the mission of a lifetime.'

All eyes were on him now, and he let his words hang in the air for a second.

'There's fifty million dollars' worth of gold bullion in that bank vault. Now, Major Thistlebollock wants us to steal some documents – and nothing more than those documents. So, we either do what the Major's ordered or we don't – *we disobey orders*. If we do the former, things will be the same at the end of this week as they are now. If we do the latter, we'll be fifty million dollars better off by this coming weekend.'

Kilbride glanced at the figures around him. Eight pairs of eyes stared back at him from the gloom, eight faces half lit by the dancing light of the lantern.

'I say we go in and get that gold. I've been planning this ever since Thistlebollock did his speak-and-be-heard number back on Cyprus. But let's be clear – if we do this, it's not out of any spite we might feel towards the Major. No fucking way. We're doing this because it's a once-in-a-lifetime opportunity. Think about it. When will any of us ever get another chance like this – to steal fifty million in gold bullion? With up-to-date intel, a perfect cover story, a pile of weapons and eyes on target? Plus it's in the middle of a war zone, which is where we work best. This is the dream bank job just waiting to happen.'

Kilbride paused to let his thoughts catch up with him. As he did so there was an eerie silence in the cave. It was as if every man was holding his breath in case they missed whatever was coming next. No doubt about it, Kilbride reflected, this was a wild, crazed situation. But right at this very moment there was nowhere else in the world that he would rather have been, and nothing else he would rather have been proposing.

'This is a freelance operation,' Kilbride continued. 'Everyone has to be a volunteer. I'd like you all to be with me – every last man amongst you. But I'll understand if any one of you opts to remain behind, and I'll think nothing less of you for it. Anyone who decides not to join the party will be left here as a guard force to protect our rear. They will have taken no part in the operation, and no discredit will reflect upon them if we who proceed get nobbled.

'Now, before you make your decision consider the risks . . . I have every confidence we will pull this off, but I want none of you to underestimate the hazards. They are significant, and very real. We are heading into a major war zone to rob a bank of an enormous sum of money. For those of you who do decide to join me, I have to say that whilst I have tried to plan for every eventuality we may well fail. Any one of us could be injured, captured, or killed . . .

'And one more thing,' Kilbride added. 'I have it on good authority, very good authority, that the gold in that vault is terrorist gold. If we don't empty that vault, rest assured that it will be used to finance more mayhem and bloodshed. So, if greed doesn't get the better of you, maybe your consciences will. Right, it's make-your-mind-up time. Do I have any volunteers?'

Almost before Kilbride had finished speaking Smithy was on his feet. 'You can bloody well count me in, boss! I wouldn't miss it for all the tea in China.'

'Same goes for me, buddy,' said Bill Berger, stepping forward to join Kilbride. 'I had a feelin' you was up to somethin' and I ain't been disappointed yet.'

'Sure, I'm a thieving, robbing Irish gobshite,' Moynihan announced. 'So you may as well count me in. I'll tell you, Kilbride, you'd live well without your mother.'

Smithy scowled. 'What the hell does that mean, you thick Paddy bastard?'

'Sure, it means the boss man there's a feckin' survivor, which is more than I can say for a lump of brainless British beef like you.'

'I've got an Englishman, an American and an Irishman,' announced Kilbride. 'As a multinational force it's a start. Any more?'

McKierran stepped forward from the gloom. 'Ye'll be lost without a bloody Scot . . . In for a penny, in for a pound. I'm with ye.'

Ward shifted his position, bringing himself more into the light. 'One question. Fifty million in gold bullion weighs a ton, I would imagine. And we're not going to be taking it back to Cyprus to present it to Major Thistlebollock. So, what are you planning to do with it?'

'Fifty million in bullion weighs eight-point-seven-five tons, to be exact,' Kilbride replied. 'You know that deep pool at the back of this cave, the one you discovered? Well, we're going to sink the gold and leave it there. That way, we return to Cyprus clean as a whistle. This war can't last for ever, can it? And when it's over we'll come back and collect our loot.'

Ward grinned. 'I thought as much . . . Okay, silly question – does it rust or anything?'

'Gold doesn't tarnish or rust in sea water,' said

74

Kilbride. 'Not if we left it here for a hundred million years.'

'Which we won't, will we?' Ward replied. 'Sounds good enough for me. I'm in. Johno?'

'What've we got to lose?' said Johno. 'If anything goes wrong we can just blame it on you SAS lot, say you led us SBS lads astray.'

Smithy snorted. 'That'll never bloody work. You SBS lads may fight on the water – we bloody walk on it.'

'Right – Boerke? How about it?' Kilbride prompted.

'South Africa is the biggest producer of gold in the world,' Boerke announced as he stared into the lantern flame. 'We have had a long love affair with the stuff. But there's not much you can do about it on a soldier's wage. You think I would miss out on this, man? *I'm in.*'

Boerke stood up to join the group, leaving only Tony Knight crouched on the cave floor. All eyes turned to him.

'Nightly,' said Kilbride. 'Come on – you're with us, aren't you?'

'Why didn't you tell us about this back on Cyprus?' Nightly asked, the resentment clear in his voice. 'Who don't you trust?'

'The walls have ears, Nightly,' Kilbride replied. 'Anyone could have been listening. Word could even have got back to the major. That's not a risk I was willing to take.'

'That's bullshit,' Nightly muttered. 'Truth is, you didn't trust us enough to share it with us. If you'd done so we could have planned for it properly . . .'

'I've done all the planning that's needed, Nightly.'

'Anyhow, it'll never work. We'll get nobbled. Beirut's crawling with Brit and American spies. Just as soon as we hit the bank every man and his dog will know about it.'

'Possibly,' Kilbride conceded. 'But even if they do, they'll never prove it was us. The gold will be safely hidden here, where no one will ever find it. That's the beauty of the plan – we pitch up in Cyprus totally clean. If anyone accuses us – we'll be outraged. As the Major himself pointed out, two Beirut banks have been robbed already since the civil war began. No one can pin it on us – end of story.'

A ripple of laughter echoed around the cave as the men reacted to Kilbride's use of Moynihan's catch-phrase. For a second or so the tension eased a little.

'Yeah, okay, maybe,' said Nightly. 'But what if someone talks? What about if one of *us* talks?'

'No one's talking,' Smithy growled. 'And if you don't bloody fancy it, Nightly—'

'No one will talk,' Kilbride cut in, stopping Smithy from completing the sentence with what he knew was coming – '*you can bloody well stay behind*'.

'It's very simple,' Boerke added. 'We deny it, man. Bank raid, we say, what bank raid? Try it. It's not so difficult, is it?'

'How do we divide the loot?' Nightly asked, glancing up at Kilbride. 'At the end, when we come to retrieve it, how do we divide it between the nine of us?'

'Equal shares,' Kilbride replied. 'How else could it be?'

Bill Berger shifted his weight impatiently. 'Come on, buddy, the clock's tickin'. We gotta go blow a bank vault.'

'All right,' Nightly announced, getting to his feet. 'I don't suppose I have much choice. I'm with you blokes, then.'

Kilbride breathed a sigh of relief. They were one hundred per cent on to hit the Imperial Bank of Beirut for fifty million dollars.

'One more thing, buddy,' Bill Berger said. 'What's the mission code name?'

Kilbride scratched his head, sheepishly. 'No idea, mate.'

Bill Berger grinned. 'Well, we gotta have one, if only so's we can tell our grand-kiddies about it after . . . Couple of years back we did this exercise on the Vietnam border with the Thai special forces. We called it Cobra Gold. I think some of you guys was there too?'

Kilbride nodded. 'Most years some of the lads from The Regiment do it.'

'Dunno why, but it just came into my head. It's kinda appropriate . . .'

'For the mission code name? Cobra Gold?' Kilbride smiled. 'It's perfect.'

Kilbride spent the next half-hour running over the logistics of Operation Cobra Gold. It was now 8.45 p.m. on Thursday, 22 January. They would hit the bank under cover of darkness the following night, when it would have been shut down for the weekend. Kilbride reckoned that they ought to be able to load the gold into the Red Cross vehicles and get on the road by early Saturday morning. They would drive directly back to the safe house, load up the RIBs and head for the Palm Islands.

Each 8.5-metre Zodiac RIB had a cargo capacity of 2,500 kilos, so that meant 7,500 kilos between the three boats. With 8.75 tons – or 8,846 kilos – of bullion, plus the men and their weapons, each craft would be overloaded by some 500 kilos. But as long as the weather held good Kilbride had every confidence that the boats would be up to the job. Presuming they made Ramkine Island on schedule, they would spend the rest

77

of the weekend sinking the bullion in the cave's depths and be ready to rendezvous with the sub on the Monday evening. It was a simple plan that relied heavily on the cover of using the Red Cross vehicles. If the ruse worked, so would the plan. If not, they were in trouble. But Kilbride could see no way around that.

By 11 p.m. the men were ready to depart. Kilbride's boat led the force out of the cave hideaway, and Ward set a course on a bearing for Beirut. Relieved of the weight of the extra kit, the RIBs were quickly up on the plane and slicing through the seas. Each craft was powered by a pair of Johnson 150-horsepower engines, extensively modified to suppress sound emissions. The RIBs had a range of one hundred miles on a set of full fuel tanks and were durable and sturdy in open seas. The run into Beirut was being done in coastal waters and would be like child's play to the powerful craft.

The three RIBs flitted across the darkened waters, as invisible as black shadows on the charcoal sea. Each man sat alone with his thoughts. Each in his own way had suspected that Kilbride was up to something. And as each reflected on what he was about to do, he knew that he had passed the point of no return. All nine of them – Nightly included – were now committed to Kilbride's fifty-million-dollar bank job. And each one of them had done their calculations: they stood to gain five and a half million dollars each, should the mission be successful.

An hour out from Ramkine Island Smithy leaned across to Kilbride. He had to yell to make himself heard above the smacking of the hull against the waves.

'Why you doing this, boss? It's not as if you need the bloody money.'

'How so?' Kilbride replied, his teeth showing white in the darkness.

'Your family's bloody loaded. That's what everyone says.'

'Not to the tune of five million dollars they aren't.'

'But they ain't short of a bob or two, are they?'

'I'm doing it for the craic, as that mad Irishman Moynihan would say. I'm doing it because it's there. Because we can. For the rush. And 'cause it's terrorist fucking gold. You?'

Smithy grinned. 'I'm doing it because it's your bloody idea and you're the boss.'

'Bollocks you are.'

'All right, then, I'm doing it to shut the missus up. I'm tired of hearing her – "When are we ever going to have any money? Blah, blah, blah . . . You care more about that bloody Regiment than you do about me." I'm doing it so there won't be any more nasty, dirty little wars with the wife. She's always said I'll never amount to anything. This'll learn her.'

'I've never asked – how long have you been married?'

'Five years. Feels like a bloody life sentence.'

'Why no children? You strike me as the sort who'd make a good dad.'

'I'd like them, but the missus won't go for it – not as long as I stay in The Regiment and keep fucking off to foreign parts with the likes of you.'

'Sorry.'

'I reckon this might just swing it, though. I've been rehearsing what I'm going to say to her. Listen, love, here's a cool million – no strings attached. All I want is for us to have some kids and me keep doing what I'm doing. Deal? She's got to go for it, hasn't she, boss?'

'What woman wouldn't? But what about the other four and a half million?'

79

'Ah, now that's what I bloody well keep for myself – in reserve, like.'

The two men lapsed into silence as the boat powered onwards. Like many in The Regiment, Kilbride didn't talk about his family background much. It was something the men tended to keep to themselves, and in Kilbride's case he had more than the usual reasons to do so. The men attracted to the SAS generally tended to be independent and spirited and questioning of organised religion. Rather than God binding The Regiment as one, it was the bonds between men that were the glue that held things together. They fought for each other, for their mates in their troop. Kilbride's great secret was that his father was a priest, and that he had been expected to follow him into the priesthood.

Kilbride's dad had been the vicar at Bryanston, a minor public school in Dorset, and that was where Kilbride had himself been educated. From his earliest years Kilbride's father had groomed his eldest son for a career in the Church. But Kilbride had had different ideas. He had always found himself inspired less by his father's pious ways and more by those of his grandfather George, a twice-knighted general and one of the best commanders the British army had ever had. Kilbride shared his grandfather's dark good looks, and his boyhood games had been full of bloody woodland skirmishes, with half the village boys acting as the German enemy.

It had been the last straw for his father when Kilbride had openly declared his ambition to follow his grandfather into the military. His choice of the SAS had been inspired by a visit of the Commanding Officer (CO) of The Regiment to inspect the school's Combined

Cadet Force. As an adolescent boy standing in rank in his khaki uniform, with a .303 Lee Enfield rifle held in the present-arms position, Kilbride had been awed by the man's easy good nature and his stylish uniform. Having no idea what it might mean, Kilbride had asked the CO how he might get to wear the same beige beret and winged-dagger cap badge.

'Ah, well, sonny, that's the SAS,' the CO had responded. 'I'll set you a little challenge: if you can find out any more about us, and where we're headquartered, come and see about joining.'

The more Kilbride had learned about the SAS the more he had been drawn to the unit, rising to the challenge to do the impossible. Ever since then he had found himself driven by that same maverick desire to achieve the unachievable. And it was that which lay behind the present mission. The fact that it was terrorist money added a touch of moral conviction, but the driving force behind Operation Cobra Gold was the sheer bloody-minded challenge that it posed.

True, an SAS trooper's wage was less than £2,500 a year. And the gold in that bank vault was worth a fortune beyond their wildest dreams. But it wasn't money that drove Kilbride: if it had been he'd never have joined the SAS. Back at home he drove a knackered Austin Princess, and he didn't have a mortgage or a family to support. Falling off the wagon when he was a kid had made him even more determined to succeed. But he would do so in his own way, facing the challenges he chose – like the present mission to rob the Imperial Bank of Beirut of fifty million dollars in gold bullion.

As they approached Beirut from the open sea Kilbride

felt his pulse quicken. It was an unearthly sight. The high-rise section of the city clustered along the shoreline – fine hotels, casinos and restaurants – but all of it was lying in darkness, the humped silhouettes of a dying city whose people were at war with themselves. Here and there a window was aglow with the flickering light of a gas flame, but even these were shuttered and blanketed, as if to keep the city's bloodlust and hatred barricaded outside in the dark. During the long night of Beirut's civil war, light had come to mean death for the city's inhabitants – Muslim and Christian alike. It brought a sniper's bullet, the fiery trail of an RPG, or the thump of the killer's boots on the stairs.

Kilbride had done his research and knew all this. He was expecting it. But the sight of a whole city like this – eyeless and entombed and dark as the grave – was deeply unsettling. He raked the skyline with his eyes, searching for a landmark that would point out the location of the Beirut River estuary, their entrance into a city peopled by ghosts. Kilbride searched to the east and could just make out a long, low silhouette rising barely above the sea – the breakwater that sheltered the Beirut port area. Two kilometres to the east of that lay a sprawling oil terminal, which marked the entrance to the Beirut River.

Kilbride scanned along the faint phosphorescence of the shoreline for the cylindrical fat black shapes of the giant oil tanks. But it was Ward who spotted them first.

'There!' he hissed, stretching out an arm across the dark water.

Ward readjusted the trim of the RIB until she was heading for a point just to the west of the oil depot, the mouth of the Beirut River. Kilbride glanced behind him and was relieved to see the squat forms of the other boats falling in line behind. Ward throttled back to dead slow and they crept past the oil depot, some hundred yards distant off the port beam. Gradually, the mud banks of the estuary closed in on them. Kilbride glanced at his watch: it was 1 a.m. – they had entered the Beirut River and were bang on schedule.

Smithy broke out one of the night-vision units. The technology was still in its infancy, and the device was unwieldy, being some twelve inches long and over two pounds in weight. He crawled forward to the prow of the boat and began to scan the waters ahead for any hidden obstructions. Every now and then he used a hand signal to steer Ward to the right or left of the central line of the river.

As they crept into the city, Kilbride kept watch on the banks to either side of him. There was a temporary ceasefire and it was eerily quiet. Over the past year there had been several such truces, but none had lasted. Within days the hatred had always proved too strong, the city's desire to devour itself too insatiable. A dog barked on the right-hand bank – once, twice, three times, and then there came the muffled cursing of the owner. Kilbride doubted that the dog had heard them: the boat engines were all but inaudible, and not a word was being spoken by the men. Since entering the river estuary they had been on silent routine, and the roar of the swollen river beneath the boats was louder than any noise from their passing.

Kilbride was convinced that the dog couldn't have smelled them, either. The stench from the putrid water was overpowering, in spite of it being January and the river being in full flood. They passed by the rectangular bulk of the Karantina slaughterhouse, and Kilbride was hit by the smell of decomposing animal carcasses. It

83

mingled with the reek of raw sewage, the overall effect being doubly sickening. Whatever else the inhabitants of this cursed city might have stopped doing – partying, holding tidy neighbourhood competitions, *tolerating each other and living in peace* – shitting certainly wasn't one of them. Knotty had been right: the Beirut River was a festering sewer.

They passed under a small road bridge. From there on the Beirut River was channelled through a massive concrete culvert some three hundred yards wide as it flowed through the normally busy suburbs of Ashrafieh, Burj Hammoud and Sin El Fil. Despite having to navigate a series of semi-submerged obstructions, Kilbride reckoned they were making a good five knots – which meant that they would be at their destination in under twenty minutes. He settled back in the RIB to enjoy the ride.

The riverside market of Souk el Ahad was one of the few Beirut institutions that seemed to have survived the war. It was held every Sunday on a derelict section of the river bank, itself part of this forgotten and poisoned artery of the city. Where the market reached down to the water, a series of decrepit wooden jetties groped out into the current. Over the years most had been washed away by the winter floods, but a few were stubbornly holding on. It was on one of these that Emile Abdeen was waiting. He gazed out over the river, an extinguished torch in his right hand. At any time now he was expecting to see the three British boats round the bend below him, at which time he would signal them in to land.

He glanced across at the makeshift bed that lay beneath the wooden jetty. It was made up of an old door, propped up at one end by a desk, at the other by an upturned fridge. On top of the bed was a battered length of foam, an old blanket and some tattered clothes. Until the war had come to this ancient city, Beirut had been a magnet for casual workers from Syria and further afield. The bed would belong to one of them, Emile reflected. And maybe he still slept there, scratching a perilous living from the Souk. Emile wrinkled his nose: it certainly smelled as if he was still around and that his toilet was somewhere nearby.

As he stared out over the water Emile reflected on what he was doing here. The son of a French Catholic mother and a Lebanese Muslim father, his was an unhappy union of the two sides of hatred that were tearing this city apart. It made him a loner and a refugee in his own country, and a misfit in these hate-filled times. He had been conceived in a moment of hopeless optimism, thirty-three years earlier, and the marriage between his liberal parents had failed to last. Since then he'd been educated at a top Beirut school, grown up an atheist, and had no allegiance to either side in the war.

Emile could see what religion was doing to his country – who couldn't? The orgy of fighting – all in the name of religion. The massacres of the women and children – all in the name of religion. The looting of this once beautiful city – all in the name of religion. And if the British were happy to pay him well for his services, then so be it. It was a damn sight less dangerous than some of the alternatives – like joining one of the militias, or working in the souks, like his absent Syrian bedfellow. And working for the British somehow made Emile feel like he *belonged*. The British were outsiders, just like him. In spite of his mongrel roots, they seemed to have had little trouble accepting him.

They also seemed to have little shortage of funds. They certainly paid him well enough, but it was in the spin-offs from his activities that Emile was making real money. Of course, it had been necessary to bribe the guards at the Red Cross compound to let the vehicles go missing for a long weekend. And of course, the British had been happy to pay the bribes. And the difference between what the British had given Emile and what he had paid the guards was his cut, his share of the deal. It was always like this doing business in Beirut, and Emile saw no reason why it should be different with his own dealings. Soon he would have enough money to leave this blighted city. Maybe he would take his family and head for a new life in London, where he would have no problem melting into the crowd.

Kilbride glanced to his right: something had caught his attention. He scanned the rooftops, and then, as the RIB shifted in the current, he spotted a figure silhouetted in a spray of light. He brought his M16 into the aim, bracing the weapon on the black rubber side of the RIB. He watched as the light behind the dark figure shifted slightly, and then there was the throaty roar of a powerful engine, thick fumes drifting into the pool of light, tingeing it a ghostly blue. Only the militia would be moving around this city at night. As he scrutinised the backlit figure, it struck a contorted pose: it was staring out over the river, totally unmoving, with something thrust skywards from its right hand.

As the RIB drew level with the bizarre scene, Kilbride recognised the figure for what it was: a body carved from stone, an ancient statue of some sort suspended on a Roman column high above the mass of the city. The history of the Lebanon stretched back some seven thousand years, and the country was crammed full of Roman, Phoenician and more ancient ruins. Smaller figures clustered around the base of the Roman statue, but these ones were alive and were dressed in a motley collection of military fatigues.

To the rear of the statue, an army truck cut its engine. A figure jumped down from the cab and strode through the headlights, a guitar clutched in one hand. Kalashnikov assault rifles were propped against the base of the statue as a bottle was passed around. The militia were having a street party, and by the looks of her shapely figure and the hair spilling out from under her khaki cap, Kilbride could tell that at least one of the fighters was a woman.

Kilbride rolled away from the side of the RIB and lowered his weapon. But as he did so there was a sudden burst of gunfire. He tensed for a second, bracing for an attack, before realising that it was one of the party-goers loosing off a salvo of rounds into the night sky in a fit of high spirits. What they had to celebrate in this blackened urban wasteland Kilbride couldn't imagine. Maybe it was the fact that they had finished the killing for the day.

They pressed onwards upriver. Twice Ward had to throttle the boat's speed back to zero as he and Kilbride leaned over the stern to cut an obstruction free from the propeller. But eventually they reached the intricate latticework of the iron railway bridge beyond which lay Souk el Ahad. So far, so good, Kilbride told himself: very soon they would be meeting their contact and setting foot in the dead city.

He swivelled his eyes to the right and began searching the river bank. It was dark and empty here where the city's only green space groped its way down to the flanks of the sick river. A point of red light blinked just ahead – once, twice, three times. Kilbride watched intently: there it was again. He pulled a small torch out of his camo smock and gave the answering signal. Kilbride glanced behind him as Ward brought the craft around, and slowly the RIB felt its way in towards the river bank. As it did so, a skeletal wooden structure reared out of the water. This was the jetty on which they would rendezvous with their Lebanese fixer.

Kilbride and Emile greeted each other wordlessly, with a rough handshake. The boats were drawn in under the jetty and hidden beneath its rusted galvanised sides. The men hoisted their weapons and gear and walked up the grassy bank. Emile led them to a metal door in a high brick wall. He unlocked a padlock, pushed it open and they disappeared inside.

By the faint light of the night sky that filtered into the compound Kilbride could tell that the safe house had seen better days. The windows on the ground and first floors were secured with iron bars, and most were glazed only with polythene. Kilbride wondered if the glass had been shot out during the war, or deliberately removed to prevent damage from flying shards. They rounded a corner of the house and his gaze was drawn to a group of vehicles parked towards the centre of the compound. There were two Toyota Land Cruisers and a large Bedford truck. All displayed the distinctive colours of the Red Cross: clear white, with a large red cross symbol painted onto doors, bonnets and roofs.

Emile led Kilbride inside the house. He gestured to a bare concrete-floored room with a few battered armchairs lying around. 'Welcome.'

'It's Emile, right? I'm the boss. Quick introductions,' said Kilbride, deliberately opting to use the men's nicknames. 'This is Bronco, Smithy, Paddy, Jock, Bushman, Nightly, Johno and Shagger.'

Emile nodded a greeting at Kilbride's men. He pointed to a couple of cardboard boxes lying on the floor. 'Your uniforms. I hope I have your correct sizes.' He glanced at McKierran and Berger. 'We Lebanese often tend to forget how large of build you English can be.'

'Hey – I'm no goddamn Brit, I'm an American,' Bill Berger remarked, with a grin. 'And they make everything big where I come from – even the goddamn noses.'

'I hadn't noticed,' Emile countered, with a smile.

'And if ye want to know what they make that's extra large in the glens, check under my kilt,' McKierran added.

There was a ripple of laughter.

'Right, lads, it's two-fifteen a.m., so we're ahead of schedule,' Kilbride announced. 'We've got to make like doctors and nurses and load up the vehicles. Let's try to be on the road by, say, an hour from now – so three-fifteen a.m. Okay by you, Emile?'

'Okay,' Emile confirmed. 'There is just one checkpoint, manned by the Lebanese Forces militia, on the route that we will be using. They see the Red Cross as being their ambulance service, whilst the Muslims on the west of the city see the Red Crescent as being theirs. So you will have little trouble. Riad al-Solh is your intended destination?'

'It is,' Kilbride confirmed, giving nothing away.

'Just checking . . .' Emile replied. 'If anyone asks, tell them you are taking medical supplies to the Red Cross centre in Ein-el-Helweh. It is some distance south-east of the city and in Christian territory. They will like you all the more for it. There is little point in saying that we are carrying wounded as there is at present a ceasefire. It won't last, of course. They never do. But ferrying medical supplies is our best cover story . . . Where exactly in Riad al-Solh are we headed?'

'Our interest is in the Imperial Bank of Beirut,' Kilbride replied. 'You know it?'

'Everyone knows the Imperial Bank.'

'We need to get eyes on the bank for twenty-four hours or so, preferably from good cover – so a deserted tower block, or something. How doable is that, Emile?'

'Half of Riad al-Solh lies in ruins. Every other building is deserted.'

Kilbride grabbed one of the uniforms. It consisted of a white medical tunic and trousers, with the Red Cross logo sewn onto one arm. He had no doubt that it was a genuine Red Cross original.

'How busy is it likely to be in there?' Kilbride asked.

'Quiet as death,' Emile answered. 'It is in the very heart of the Green Line. On the one side sit the Christian militia, on the other the Muslims. In between it is mostly a wasteland. Only the foolish or the desperate go there. Maybe those wishing to withdraw their funds from the Imperial Bank, or those wishing to make a deposit. But how do you decide? In a city as crazed as this, do you keep your money in the boot of your car or under the bed, or in the vault of a bank in the very heart of the war zone?'

'So no one's going to be disturbing us?' Kilbride asked, ignoring Emile's last remark.

'No, certainly not after dark. And come the weekend it will be empty. Not a soul will be moving in there.'

Kilbride knew that he would have to put Emile in the picture at some stage. But he seemed a sensible enough individual, and Kilbride figured that an offer of a share

90

in the loot should buy his cooperation and silence. He would level with Emile once they were through the roadblocks and had reached their destination – which was pretty much the point of no return.

At 3.30 a.m. the convoy of vehicles revved up their engines and prepared to depart. Trying to hide all the team's weapons and ammo had taken slightly longer than anticipated. Luckily, Emile had had the foresight to fill the Bedford truck with boxes of medical supplies, and the larger weapons had been buried beneath this pile of kit.

Once he had checked that the way was clear, Emile swung open the large metal doors that led out of the compound. He waved the convoy forward onto the war-torn streets of Beirut.

CHAPTER FIVE

Kilbride was driving the lead vehicle, one of the Land Cruisers, together with Ward, Moynihan and Emile. Behind them came the Bedford truck, with Smithy at the wheel and McKierran and Johno as passengers. The second Land Cruiser brought up the rear, with Berger driving and Boerke and Nightly riding shotgun. As the last vehicle pulled away from the safe house, Boerke glanced at a sticker on the dashboard and shook his head in disgust. It showed the silhouette of an AK47 assault rifle with a red line running though it. It was the only time in his life that he had ridden in a vehicle that expressly forbade the carrying of weapons.

The lean South African patted his pocket, just to make sure that his handgun was there. All the big guns were hidden in the vehicle's rear. But at least his pistol was a 9mm Browning HiPower, with a staggered-row thirteen-round magazine – the personal weapon of choice for elite forces. With each man carrying a Browning they at least packed a little firepower, and stood half a chance if they did hit trouble. But since the pistol's effective range was no more than thirty yards it had better be up close and personal, Boerke reflected.

The convoy pushed ahead using full headlights, and making little effort to avoid being spotted. They were posing as an official Red Cross convoy now, which had a free right of passage across all parts of the war zone. Apart from the odd militia vehicle, nothing was moving on the streets. Those militia they did pass paid little attention once they had spotted the distinctive Red Cross insignia on the vehicles. As they trundled through the deserted city the extent of the devastation was breathtaking: whole streets lay in blasted ruins, with broken furniture, burned-out cars, shattered glass and rubble strewn across them.

As they neared the city centre the reek of decay caught in Kilbride's throat. He wound up his window, but the stench of rotten death was everywhere, even in their vehicle or so it seemed. Out of the corner of his eye he caught a movement to his left, down a darkened alleyway strewn with rubbish and the discarded debris of war. A pack of emaciated hounds snarled and fought, tearing at something sacklike on the ground. For a second Kilbride mistook it for a dead dog, before the rabid pack began a tug-of-war with what was unmistakably a bloated human limb. One of the dogs paused to stare at the passing vehicle before turning back to its putrescent feast. Kilbride shuddered. Welcome to Beirut, he told himself.

Finally, the three-vehicle convoy approached the limits of Christian-held east Beirut and the crossover point into the Green Line. Up ahead a roadblock hove into view, a wooden pole counterbalanced with a lump of concrete at one end. To one side there was an American pick-up, with a Soviet Dushka heavy machine gun mounted on its rear. A soldier with a wild Afro hairdo and a white bandanna tied around his forehead manned the massive machine gun. Kilbride knew the Dushka well: it was an awesome piece of weaponry, which could make mincemeat out of any of their vehicles.

To the other side of the roadblock half a dozen soldiers lounged around in a sandbagged position. They were wearing an odd assortment of combats and carried AK47 assault rifles. Each one had the lower half of his face covered by a khaki scarf, leaving just the eyes visible. A battered radio set was perched atop the sandbags, and Kilbride could just make out the beat of some Western-style pop music. It sounded oddly out of place in the midst of this blasted city, and the overall effect was unnerving.

He slowed his vehicle to a stop in front of the barrier and wound down the window. As he did so Kilbride recognised the sound of Blondie's hit single 'I'm Always Touched By Your Presence, Dear' blaring out from the radio. But barely had he registered the song when he got the shock of his life. One of the soldiers had emerged from behind the sandbags only to reveal a shapely set of legs ending in a pair of high-heeled shoes.

As she strolled across towards him, moving in time to the pop beat, Kilbride couldn't help admiring the lady soldier's svelte figure and her obvious grace and poise. Emile leaned across from the passenger seat and called out a greeting in Arabic. There was a quick exchange between them, of which Kilbride understood not a word, but all the while he was transfixed by the beautiful brown eyes above the mask. As she waved him through the roadblock the girl tugged down her khaki cloth, and offered Kilbride a brief smile.

'Hello, my friend,' she called after him. 'Welcome to the Green Line.'

Kilbride almost stalled the vehicle, and he cursed inwardly. A beautiful young lady soldier in high heels and carrying a Kalashnikov assault rifle was the last thing that he had been expecting on this mission. For once he had found himself lost for words with a woman. Behind him the Bedford truck pulled through the roadblock, with Smithy giving the girl a wave. But the last vehicle ground to a halt. The big American, Bill Berger, leaned out of the window of the Toyota with a beaming smile on his face.

'Hello – you need help?' the girl with the eyes asked.

'Just wondered if y'all needed anything,' Berger announced, his eyes dancing. 'We got us a load of cigarettes, some food rations – but no silk stockings, I'm afraid.'

The girl accepted a carton of Marlboro. 'Next time, some stockings,' she scolded, giving him a coy smile. 'Or else big trouble.'

Bill Berger laughed. 'No problem. I'll see if I can't pick some up for y'all in the Green Line.'

'You're supposed to be a Red Cross doctor,' Nightly muttered, as they pulled away from the roadblock. 'Not her bloody pimp.'

'Never admired a beautiful woman before?' Berger drawled. 'Women with guns – boy, I gotta tell you . . . Never wondered what it'd be like to peel off that khaki uniform with your teeth? You'd better lighten up, buddy, before you shrivel up and die of old age.'

Ron Boerke let out a thin laugh. He was hardly a ladies' man himself, but he was warming to the big American's ways. And by the end of this mission he just might have five and a half million dollars in the bank. In

95

which case he reckoned even he could be a hit with the fairer sex.

Ten minutes after passing through the checkpoint the convoy rumbled into Rue Riad al-Solh. Glass crunched under tyres as the lead vehicle ground to a halt. It was dark as pitch here in the ruined wasteland of the Green Line, and not a soul stirred. Emile pointed right up the street to where a building lit up by a faint glow was just visible. It stood by itself some five storeys high, an island of light in a sea of darkness.

'The Imperial Bank,' Emile announced. 'One of the few buildings that still has a working generator, hence the illumination.'

'The main entrance is on the corner, right?' Kilbride asked. 'What about the rear – is there a back way in?'

'I am not that familiar with the building,' Emile replied. 'What little money I have I chose to keep elsewhere.'

'Right, let's park up at the far side of the building, off of the main drag,' said Kilbride. 'Then take a look at the terrain.'

'I think maybe soon you are going to tell me why we have come here?' Emile ventured.

Kilbride glanced at him. 'Once we're safely established in one of the empty buildings, you and I need to talk.'

The convoy proceeded up Riad al-Sohl at a dead-slow pace, then swung right onto a side road that led down towards Place de l'Etoile. Kilbride scanned the buildings to either side of the Imperial Bank and picked out one that was totally gutted. It offered a perfect vantage point from which to keep watch. He pulled out a walkie-talkie from his pocket. For a second he considered radioing the other vehicles, but then he thought better of it. Both sides in the civil war were known to scan the radio traffic as a way of sussing out what the enemy was up to. Kilbride knew that he and his men should keep their radio use to minimum.

He turned to Moynihan. 'Take Boerke and McKierran and check out that building. I want confirmation that it's unoccupied. If it is, that's where we'll establish the OP.'

As Moynihan disappeared up the darkened street, Kilbride turned to inspect the target. The Imperial Bank of Beirut was constructed of a light yellow chiselled stone. It had once been a truly imposing building and would not have looked out of place in the City of London. But now . . . Kilbride glanced upwards: '—perial Bank of Beiru—' a sign running above the entrance announced. The beginning and end of the lettering had been blown away, the stonework pockmarked by heavy gunfire. Several of the windows were smashed, and scorch marks from a recent blast disfigured the whole front of the bank. Kilbride could hardly believe that there was fifty million dollars in gold bullion stored in that building's vault. But where else in this warring city did anyone have to stash their money?

Moynihan returned. Apart from the odd pigeon or two, he reported, the building was completely empty. Inside it stank of stale urine and staler smoke, and not a window remained intact. But it would serve their purposes well, the Irishman reckoned. Kilbride staged a breakdown of the Bedford truck by removing the rotor arm, and left it with the bonnet open. To the casual observer it would appear as if a Red Cross convoy was parked up off Riad al-Sohl, waiting for a mechanic to arrive. The men unloaded their gear. Weapons, explosives, food rations, water and surveillance kit – all of it was piled into the deserted building.

'Right, lads – you know the drill,' Kilbride announced once they were gathered on the first floor. 'I want one man watching each end of the street at all times, so start a rotating stag. Get a Claymore ambush set up covering each approach to this building and prepare your arcs of fire. By rights, we shouldn't be getting any unwanted visitors, but if we do we're going to need to deal with them. Get the mortars set up on the roof, and get some jerrycans of petrol from the vehicles, in case we have to boost their range. Grab some galvanised iron from somewhere so you can disguise your signature if you have to fire from up there. Smithy, I want you to organise that lot, okay?'

'Boss,' Smithy confirmed.

'Right: Berger and Boerke, I want you guys on the listening device and the night-vision unit. We've got about three hours left until daybreak and I want all the intel we can get on the bank's night operations. Take Emile with you, and rifle-mike the guards' conversations. I want to know numbers, locations, patrols, how they're armed, and any security systems that may be in operation, plus the location of that generator. The vault is below ground – in the basement – and I want to know if they've done anything stupid like lock up a guard in there. You never know – this is one fucked-up war. You got it?'

'Sure thing,' Berger replied. Boerke nodded.

'Okay, the rest of you are on guard duty. Keep your eyes peeled. Meanwhile, I'm going to give our friend Emile a short briefing.'

'Boss, one question,' said Nightly, nodding in Emile's direction. 'What's his share of the loot?'

'Keep your mind on the job at hand, Nightly,' Kilbride replied. 'Get to it.'

'But—'

'Just shut it!' Boerke snapped. 'There's work to be done, man.'

Kilbride turned to their Lebanese fixer. 'Okay, Emile, I figure you've got every right to know what we're up to. Plus, we need you on side for the rest of the mission . . . Believe it or not, there's fifty million in gold bullion hidden in that bank vault. We're going to remove it, starting tonight. We'll use the Red Cross convoy to move it across Beirut to the safe house. Then we load it onto the RIBs and we're gone. You get your share before we depart – that's if you're on for it. All I expect in return is for you to carry on doing what you've been doing so far, and guide us the hell out of here.'

Emile gave a wry smile. 'I am not entirely surprised. It is what I suspected you might be doing. But fifty million dollars' worth of gold – that I *am* surprised about.'

Kilbride grinned. 'You'd never have believed it, not looking at the state of the place. I reckon we can have the gold loaded and be ready to depart by sundown tomorrow, latest. That's less than twenty-four hours away, Emile, by which time you should be very rich indeed.'

Emile smiled. 'Or dead, my friend . . . How rich? I think I have to ask.'

'Two and a half million dollars, Emile,' Kilbride announced, softly. 'Our share of the gold is twice that, but you'll appreciate we've planned the whole thing and we'll be doing the fighting. It's a fair share, don't you think?'

'It is more than fair, my friend.' Emile paused for a

second, seeming uncertain of what to say next. 'In fact, it seems very generous . . .'

'Anything troubling you, Emile?' Kilbride prompted. 'Feel free. Ask away.'

'I think I know the answer, my friend, but is this a British Government operation, or a . . . private initiative?'

'Private. We've been sent in to get eyes on the bank, that's all. So robbing it is where this becomes a wholly freelance job.'

'Then it will be doubly dangerous. For all of us.'

'Don't worry, Emile. We aren't planning on leaving anyone behind.'

Emile stared at the floor. 'No Englishman, no Scotsman, no American . . . not even a Lebanese?'

'No one, Emile,' Kilbride confirmed. 'Regardless of their nationality, flag, race, religion or football team. We go in as one: we come out as one. End of story.'

Emile thrust out a hand to Kilbride. 'Then I am on for it. It will be my ticket out of this godforsaken city . . .'

For the rest of that morning Kilbride's team lay low and kept their eyes fixed on the battered façade of the Imperial Bank of Beirut. At 10 a.m. the bank manager pitched up in a Mercedes pock-marked by shrapnel. He was dressed in a well-pressed blue pinstripe suit, and carried a leather attaché case in one hand. He would not have looked out of place in the Square Mile of London's banking district or on Wall Street in New York. Kilbride had to admire the man's nerve. The day staff started to arrive, and as the morning wore on there were even some furtive customers. But other than that there were few visitors to Rue Riad al-Sohl, and no one showed any interest in the gutted building where Kilbride and his men were hiding, or the broken-down Red Cross convoy.

By 4.30 p.m. the bank was shutting down, its staff looking forward to a weekend away from the city's empty quarter. As dusk descended on the city the four security guards took over for the weekend shift.

And Kilbride prepared to strike.

He called his men together for a final assault briefing. 'Right, lads, this is it. We've learned a lot from today's observations, and the assault plan we've come up with is based upon minimum firepower and maximum stealth. We should be in and out of the bank building without anyone noticing. Well, all apart from the four security guards, that is.'

Kilbride pulled over an old cardboard box and turned it on its lid. 'Imagine this is the bank: this – the front; this – the back. Stage One of Cobra Gold is the assault itself. At eight p.m. sharp Smithy and Johno disable the generator, here, at the rear of the building. At that moment the bank should go dark. There's two separate alarm systems, as far as we can tell, one of which is rigged to a series of metal cages. If that system goes off, then metal bars drop from the ceiling, closing off the vault. But with the generator taken out, that shouldn't be a problem for us.

'Of the four security guards, two are located here, at the front entrance, one here, at the rear, and one is stationed in a central security room on the first floor. As soon as the building goes dark I want four men hitting the lobby with thunderflash grenades and disabling the guards. Boerke, Nightly, McKierran and Ward – that's you lot. Smithy and Johno, as soon as you've hit the generator at the rear you take out the guard there. Then

McKierran and Boerke, you hit the central security room. By the end of Stage One the bank will be in our hands, and no one apart from the guards should have seen or heard anything.

'Berger, Moynihan, Emile and I will remain here, as command and back-up. I'll be eyes on the building and monitoring your radios at all times, in case of any trouble. Berger will be on the roof with the GPMG, keeping you covered. And Paddy will be fingering his PE4 charges, saying a few prayers and preparing to blow the vault.'

Moynihan grinned. 'Amen and end of feckin' story.'

Kilbride glanced around the faces of his men. 'Soon as Stage One – the assault – is complete, we move on to Stage Two: the robbery. Bronco, Johno and Ward, you set up watch on either side of the building, whilst Boerke and Nightly, you relocate the Claymores to cover the bank. I'm allowing an hour for Stage One and Moynihan reckons he'll need three hours maximum to blow the vault, so by twelve midnight we should be in there. That still leaves us seven hours until daybreak.

'Right, by my calculations the gold weighs eight thousand, eight hundred and fifty kilos. Each bar weighs twelve-point-five kilos, so that's seven hundred bars, give or take a few. That's a hundred bars an hour we've got to get out of the vault and into the truck. If we have seven people loading the gold – Emile included – and three keeping watch, that's fifteen bars per person per hour, or one every four minutes. That has to be easily doable, which means we can be in and out of there *tonight*. If we're all loaded by seven a.m., then it's time for Stage Three of the operation, the exfil. We retrace our route across the city, hit the safe house and lie up for the day. Saturday night we load up the RIBs, head down the river and get the hell out of Beirut. Any questions?'

'What about the guards, boss?' Smithy asked.

'Tie them up and lock them in one of the rooms out the back,' Kilbride replied. 'Leave them enough water to last until Monday morning, plus some ration packs.'

'What about the guards getting relieved, boss? Like, do they send in a fresh guard force Saturday morning, or anything?'

'They don't. With Emile's help we listened in on the guards' chat and there's no change over the weekend. They just rotate during the day, with two on and two off. There's a makeshift kitchen out the back, with a couple of sofas for them to get some kip.'

'Is there a back-up generator?' Ward asked.

Kilbride glanced over at Emile. 'Not that we know of.'

'There is a great shortage of generators in Beirut,' Emile volunteered. 'They are lucky even to have the one.'

'If there *is* a back-up generator, what then?' Ward insisted.

'If there is one it must be hidden somewhere inside the building, probably in the basement. We'll hit the generator we know about first and see what happens. No one hits the bank unless and until it goes dark. If a back-up generator does kick in, then it's time for Plan B.'

Ward glanced at Kilbride. 'Plan B?'

'Plan B is we mallet the fucking place with all we've got . . . It's not very sophisticated, but we reckon that if we wreck the bank's central security room, then the alarm systems won't have time to cut in. They're designed to deter a straightforward robbery, not a full-scale military assault by the likes of us.'

103

'What about all the racket?' asked Ward. 'There's a ceasefire, so it'll be obvious a major shit-fight's going down. That'll alert both sides, won't it?'

Kilbride was silent for a second, and he glanced uneasily at their Lebanese fixer. 'Not if we hit both front lines first with a barrage of mortars – just like we outlined in the original plan of attack. We provoke both sides, the ceasefire collapses and we go in under the cover of a bloody great battle.'

'Don't worry so much, my friend,' Emile volunteered. 'This ceasefire, it will never last. They never do. All you are doing is bringing the inevitable a little closer . . .'

'Anyone of you guys know the gross vehicle weight of the truck?' Bill Berger asked, seeking a rapid change of subject.

Smithy nodded. 'She's got a six-'n-a-half-ton cargo capacity, mate.'

'So we'll be two tons overweight. That a concern for us, you reckon?'

'She's a bloody Bedford, mate. That means she's built like a brick shithouse. Nothing to worry about.'

'Anyone know what the guards are carrying?' Nightly asked. 'Shorts, longs, grenades, or what?'

'AK47s,' Boerke replied. 'And I overheard one of the guards saying how he's been selling off his ammo to the militias. There's nothing to worry about, man.'

'No one's worried,' Nightly retorted.

'Right, you've all got your Arabic headgear?' Kilbride cut in. 'Wear it when you go in. And make sure no one speaks in front of the guards. That way they won't have a clue who we are, and hopefully they'll take us for one or other of the militias.'

As he briefed his men Kilbride was trying to project an aura of calm professionalism, a keenness to get the job done. But inside, his guts were twisted into knots. He was always like this before an attack, and fine just as soon as it got started. But this time it was far worse: this time, if any of the men were hit then he would be responsible. They were all volunteers. But Operation Cobra Gold was his mission and his alone, with no one from headquarters ordering them in.

'One last thing,' said Kilbride. 'If we are driving out of here by tomorrow morning, I want one man in the rear of the Bedford, on a stretcher, looking like death. That's you, Bronco. Have the GPMG with you, hidden under your blanket. If anyone opens that truck without yelling out the password, you mallet the fucker, okay?'

'Fine by me, buddy. What's the password?'

'Gold fever?' Kilbride ventured.

'Gold fever,' Berger growled. 'I like it.'

Night crept silently into Rue Riad al-Sohl, leaving just the warm glow from of the Imperial Bank of Beirut to offend it. The men waited, poised in the empty shadows between windows and doors. Kilbride gazed eastwards. A fog of darkness lay across the city like a death shroud. He thought of the young militia girl with the brown eyes above the mask. There was a burst of distant gunfire, with no answering shots. Kilbride thought of the girl again, this time letting loose her thick auburn hair from beneath her khaki combat cap. Being passed a bottle, taking a drink, passing it on. It seemed that they started partying early on Friday nights in Beirut. That was one party to which Kilbride would have liked an invitation some day.

Somewhere out at the back of the bank the generator coughed, then resumed its steady rhythm. It caught Kilbride's attention. He glanced at his watch: 7.45 p.m. Fifteen minutes to zero hour. From the first floor of the deserted building he watched as Smithy and Johno slipped across the street and disappeared around the corner of the Imperial Bank. They were moving into position to take out that generator. Otherwise, the street was deserted. He glanced across at Moynihan, who gave him a silent thumbs-up.

Above them on the roof, Bill Berger trained his GPMG on the front of the bank. He could just make out one of the guards flicking through a dog-eared girlie magazine. For a second, his mind wandered and he thought of the doe-eyed girl at the checkpoint. He daydreamed about her warm brown eyes and tawny skin, and about the lingerie that she might be wearing beneath the khaki uniform. Then he pushed the thoughts to the back of his mind, and pulled the cold metal of the big machine gun closer into his shoulder. There'd be plenty of time for girls like her once he'd banked the five and a half million dollars.

Down below on the ground floor, Boerke, Nightly, McKierran and Ward readied themselves in the cover of the darkness. They checked their M16s, making sure they had a 40mm grenade snugly in the weapon's stubby underslung M203 launcher. It was the first time the men had gone into action wearing white medical uniforms, and they had improvised grenade pouches and webbing wherever possible. As soon as the bank went dark Boerke would put a 40mm smoke grenade in through the front door, blowing out the windows and stunning the two guards. A muffled *crump* as the round exploded and they would be inside, lobbing around the thunderflash stun grenades, by which time the lobby would be pretty much theirs.

The hands of Kilbride's watch crept slowly forwards and he found himself holding his breath, transfixed by

106

the dial's faint luminosity. As the second hand hit 8 p.m. there was a faint thud from the rear of the bank. Smithy and Johno had just hit the generator. For a second the lights dimmed and the bank almost went dark. But then there was a muffled roar and a splutter, and somewhere a second generator kicked into life. Kilbride stared at the bank, willing it to go dark again, but it remained stubbornly illuminated, a bright ship in a sea of darkness.

There was a faint burst of static on Kilbride's walkie-talkie, and Smithy's voice came up over the radio.

'We hit the genny, boss,' he whispered. 'No joy.'

'Stand by for Plan B,' Kilbride replied. 'Stay in your positions. McKierran, Ward – on me.'

Kilbride heard the big Scot and the young SBS soldier pounding up the stairs below him. Together with Moynihan and Emile, the three men headed up onto the roof. The night air was chill and Kilbride found himself shivering in his thin cotton uniform. They had to move quickly now. Sooner or later, one of the guards would go to investigate the faulty generator, and Smithy and Johno would be forced to take him out. And that in turn might alert the other three guards.

'Right, McKierran, you're on one mortar tube, with Moynihan as loader,' Kilbride ordered. 'Bronco, you've drawn the short straw – 'cause you're on the other one with me. I want twelve rounds onto either side of the Green Line. McKierran, you take east Beirut. Bronco, we'll take the west. What is it, seven hundred yards or so to get in among them? Right, set your elevation and add some petrol to boost the charge. And don't worry too much about accuracy: they're smoke rounds, remember, and the aim is simply to convince each side that it's being mortared by the other.'

McKierran grabbed one of the mortar tubes, directed the muzzle towards the east of the city and rammed a foot down onto the baseplate to hold it firm. He'd watch where the first round fell and readjust his fire from there. Berger grabbed the other tube and did a repeat performance, pointing west. Kilbride and Moynihan made a pile of mortar rounds next to each of the mortar tubes, and hauled across a jerrycan of fuel each.

'Ward, grab that sheet of galvanised iron and improvise a flash deflector in front of McKierran's mortar,' said Kilbride. 'Emile, see if you can't do the same with the other lump of galvanised. Just copy what Ward does, okay?'

Emile nodded. He dragged a sheet of galvanised iron across the roof, and held it bent into a half-circle in front of the mortar's muzzle.

'Keep your bloody head down,' Kilbride added. 'Don't go getting it blown off before you can get us the hell out of here.'

Kilbride heaved up the jerrycan and glugged a slurp of petrol down into the mortar tube. To his left, Moynihan did likewise. Kilbride took one last look around him to make sure that everyone was ready. By operating the mortars on the roof they would be invisible from street level. All the bank guards would detect was the indistinct thump of each weapon firing. And the galvanised iron would help shield the white muzzle flash from any watching eyes across the city, plus it would deflect the sound signature.

'Now!' Kilbride announced as he dropped a round down the tube.

There was a massive *whump!* from the petrol-boosted detonation, and the first two mortars were

108

away. Each man counted the seconds, using the time to refuel and rearm each mortar, as the smoke rounds flew across the darkened city. Nine seconds after the flash of the tubes firing the first shell hit, the crack of the explosion illuminating the dense plume of smoke that it threw up. It was followed almost instantly by the second.

'Bang on,' McKierran growled. 'Fire for effect.'

Moynihan dropped in another round and away it flew. He grabbed the petrol can and another mortar shell, settling into a rhythm. To the right of him Kilbride and Berger were doing the same, having adjusted their fire to hit the front-line positions to the west of the city. Two minutes after the first mortar round had struck the final two were away.

After the muffled *crump-crump* of those last two exploding a deathly silence descended over Beirut. Two clouds of smoke drifted over the blackened city, one to either side of the Green Line. They were barely visible against the grey smudge of the sky. Now the wait for the response, Kilbride thought to himself grimly. The calm before the storm.

Kilbride could just imagine the panic on both sides as radios went haywire and front-line commanders requested orders from their back-room chiefs on how to respond to the unprovoked attack. The Muslim and Christian militias would each be thinking the same thing now. Ceasefire? What ceasefire? The cursed enemy could never be trusted.

Kilbride heard a sudden burst of shouting to the east of the city, and then the grunt of a heavy engine firing up. Moments later there was a blinding flare, and a barrage of rockets went flashing into the night sky.

'Goddamn Katyushas!' Bill Berger growled as he

watched the fiery ejections from the Soviet multiple-rocket-launcher.

The first of the rockets smashed down onto the Muslim side of the Green Line, the white flash of the blast lighting up the western side of Beirut. Then there was the answering roar of a diesel engine followed by the crunch of a big gun firing out of that part of the city.

'Sounds like a tank with a one-oh-five-millimetre,' Kilbride remarked. 'They're answering fire with fire from both sides . . .'

Kilbride ordered his men down from the roof and back to their original positions. The firefight was growing in intensity, salvos of mortars rippling across the night sky. It sounded as if one long drawn-out eruption was consuming the city, and for a moment Kilbride wondered what terrible destructive power he had unleashed on Beirut.

'It would have started soon enough,' Emile yelled, as if he was reading Kilbride's thoughts.

Kilbride gave a shrug and grabbed an M72 66mm light anti-armour weapon (LAW). It was too late for any second thoughts now. He flipped off the end covers, extended it into its firing position by telescoping the inner tube outwards, and signalled for Moynihan to do likewise.

'Fourth window from the right,' Kilbride yelled at Moynihan. 'That's where the security room is.'

Kilbride grabbed his walkie-talkie. 'Lads: on me – give it all you got.'

From Smithy, Berger and Boerke he got a one-word acknowledgement: 'Boss.'

With the LAW on his shoulder Kilbride took aim on the target. The rocket motor would be fully burned out just as soon as the missile exited the tube, causing a large back-blast. Kilbride checked to make sure that Emile was safely out of the danger area, turned back to the bank and squeezed the trigger. There was a sudden gout of flame, which momentarily blinded him, and a split second later the one-kilogramme warhead tore through the window of the Imperial Bank. It ploughed into the back wall, detonating as it did so, throwing a powerful blast wave into the centre of the building. A split second later Moynihan's rocket hit, blasting its way even further into the bowels of the bank.

Down below on the ground floor Boerke took the roar of the rockets as his cue to attack. He squeezed off a 40mm grenade, and there was the loud *bloop!* of the other lads doing likewise. The four rounds smashed through the glass of the bank's lobby and hit the back wall, exploding in a sheet of debris and smoke. An instant later the blast wave blew out the windows all along the front of the building, spraying shards of glass into Rue Riad al-Solh. With a signal to the other lads to follow him, Boerke sprinted across the street, heading for the bank's blasted interior. Thick smoke billowed out of the shattered doorway, but without a moment's hesitation Boerke charged inside.

At the rear of the building, Smithy and Johno blasted their way through the bank's back doorway with two 40mm grenade rounds. As they stormed through the scorched ruins of the back entrance they could hear the harsh clamour of the bank's alarm system rising above the noise of battle. Up on the roof above Kilbride, Bill Berger was covering the men with his big machine gun. He too heard the ringing of the bank's alarm as it built to a deafening crescendo, and he did so with a sinking feeling. Whatever Kilbride's rocket attack had achieved, it didn't

111

appear to have shut down the bank's security systems.

Moments after he'd disappeared into the smoking lobby Boerke re-emerged, coughing and choking his guts up and dragging one of the guards by his feet. Seconds later, big Jock McKierran came charging out onto the street after him, the second guard held in a fireman's lift across his broad shoulders.

'Ward! Nightly!' Boerke yelled as he wiped a glob of spittle from his mouth. 'You got first aid, man? Stabilise these two, and stay on them.'

Boerke turned to face Jock McKierran. 'Security room – let's do it, man.'

The two big men headed back into the grey haze of the shattered lobby. As they did so the whole of the building went dark, the wail of the bank's alarm systems dying with the light. In the echoing silence that followed, Boerke reached forward and hit the switch on the torch that he had gaffer-taped to the barrel of his M16. McKierran did likewise. They moved forwards, their torch beams probing the darkness, the light diffusing in the thick, swirling dust. They pressed onwards towards the rear, stepping carefully over upturned furniture and buckled floorboards. The bank's long polished-mahogany counter had collapsed with the blast, and it lay at a crazy angle to the floor. Boerke and McKierran skirted around it and made for the doorway to the rear.

Through the blackened door frame a wooden staircase could be seen leading up to the first floor. Boerke and McKierran made for the start of those stairs, balancing on the balls of their feet. They paused and swept the darkened stairwell ahead of them with their torch beams, their weapons at the shoulder and in the aim. It appeared to be totally deserted, with no sign of life coming from the floor above. As they went to advance there was a burst of static on Boerke's radio.

'Sitrep,' came Kilbride's voice, demanding an update on the assault.

'Two down,' Boerke intoned into his walkie-talkie. 'Going up to deal with third.'

'One down,' Smithy added, from his position at the rear of the bank. 'Going down to deal with the genny.'

Boerke and McKierran reached the top of the stairs and a corridor opened out in front of them. Smoke was billowing out of a room halfway along it, and there was the acrid smell of burning rubber. Boerke signalled to the big Scot that he was going forward. As McKierran covered him the lean South African pushed ahead, a hunter silently probing the shadows. He reached the smoke-filled doorway, choking on the bitter smell of an electrical fire. He dragged his Arabic headscarf up over his face to try to filter out the fumes, and took up position on one side of the doorway.

Above it was a sign:

> Imperial Bank of Beirut.
> Security Control Room –
> Authorised Personnel Only

Boerke grinned to himself behind the headscarf. *Authorised Personnel Only.* That was good.

He sensed McKierran join him at his left shoulder, and signalled that he was going in. Boerke stood back, levelled a boot at the wooden door and gave it a savage kick. The door panels splintered, it caved inwards and Boerke leaped through the opening. His weapon at the shoulder, he did a quick scan of the room: a crackling fire to his right, in among a series of metal boxes and

113

wires, throwing out a cloud of black smoke; up above him, a jagged hole blasted through the roof, which had to be where Kilbride's rockets had hit; to his front, a desk covered in chunks of plaster and a thick layer of dust, plus an upturned brass teapot and some shattered glasses; to the left of that a chair on its side – and a figure lying slumped in one corner, half lost in the shadows.

As Boerke's torch beam probed the darkness around the fallen man, the wiry South African spotted the shape of a weapon rising from the floor and turning towards him. Instantly he pulled his trigger. The M16 barked, three bullets shattering the hand that gripped the gun. The guard let out an agonised cry, and his bloodied AK47 clattered to the floor. Three quick strides and Boerke was over by his side, kicking the weapon away from him.

Behind him McKierran did a quick scan of the room. The priority had to be to put out the fire before the whole of the bank went up in flames. He glanced across at Boerke, giving him a T-sign, with the tips of his fingers held against the palm of his hand, and disappeared into the corridor. McKierran headed back to the junction with the stairs, where he found what he was looking for. Once back in the security room, he emptied the fire extinguisher in several long bursts, its contents dousing the burning fuse board and the frazzled electric circuitry in foam. When the flames were extinguished, all that was left was a smoking mass of scorched wiring and blackened terminals.

Boerke grabbed his radio. It was time to report in to Kilbride. 'Fourth man down. All areas secure. Come and join the party, man.'

CHAPTER SIX

Twenty minutes later and Boerke had the four guards locked up in a secure room at the building's rear. They had suffered blast wounds, shock and loss of hearing, and the guard from the security control room had a badly shot-up hand. But Boerke reckoned they would all live, which was saying something after the ferocity of the assault. Ward, the young SBS soldier, was proving to be an excellent medic. He'd got a saline drip into each of the guards, and he'd strapped up the fourth man's smashed hand. For now at least there was little need to restrain them. None of them were capable of going anywhere, let alone trying to escape.

While Ward tended to the wounded guards, Boerke, Berger and McKierran went about strengthening their hold on the bank. A daisy chain of Claymore anti-personnel mines was established on Rue Riad al-Solh, to either side of the building. Three of the tripod-mounted mines were connected together with detonation wire – one angled towards the left of the street, one up the centre and one to the right. When triggered, each mine would fire out a charge of seven hundred steel ball-bearings in a sixty-degree arc, scything down anything in its path. Once the Claymore ambush was set, the men concealed it with war debris: chunks of wood and shattered masonry that lay scattered along the street. And then they began their first watch.

To the rear of the bank Johno and Nightly took up their guard positions, although no surprises were expected there as the back-access alleyway ended in a cul-de-sac. This left Kilbride, Smithy, Moynihan and Emile free to investigate the vault. At the inner end of the blasted lobby a staircase descended below ground. Under normal circumstances, customers would be taken down to the bank's vault using the lift. But with the whole place bereft of all power the stairwell now offered the only access to the bowels of the building.

At the top of the stairway Kilbride encountered the first security gateway. As soon as the bank's alarm had been triggered, metal bars had started to descend from the ceiling. The steel barrier had dropped to within just two feet of the floor, and had then stopped dead as the bank's electricity died. Kilbride stared at it in amazement, realising just how close the assault had come to a total fuck-up. They had managed to fry the bank's circuitry with just seconds to spare before those steel gates closed completely.

Kilbride ducked down and thrust his M16 under the obstacle, rolling through the narrow gap after it. Smithy, Moynihan and Emile followed, until all four men were standing on the far side of the partially lowered metal gate. At the bottom of the flight of stairs was a second security barrier, and they had to repeat their rolling manoeuvre to get past this one as well. Kilbride shone his torch into the gloom on the far side.

A main corridor stretched ahead, leading to the vault. A small service passageway branched off to the left-hand side.

Smithy jerked his head in that direction. 'Leads to the back-up genny room, boss.'

Kilbride glanced towards the side passage, then turned back to the main corridor. Some twenty yards beyond where he was standing he could see a massive shape blocking their way. It glinted dully in his torch's beam, a faint bluish tinge betraying the fact that it was made of solid steel. It was time for Moynihan to go to work with his bag of tricks and blow the door to the vault.

'Smithy, we're going to need some light,' Kilbride announced. 'Take Emile and get the lanterns from the truck. Put a couple on the stairs to light the way and bring the rest down here.'

'Boss,' Smithy replied.

He and Emile disappeared up the stairwell, and Kilbride turned to face Moynihan. He nodded in the direction of the vault. 'Shall we?'

Moynihan raised one eyebrow. 'Sure. It should be age before beauty, shouldn't it, boss?'

Kilbride shrugged and moved towards the massive steel structure. As he got closer, details became clearer. The passageway was some six feet wide by eight tall, and the door to the vault filled most of it, apart from the solid steel door frame. The smooth brushed-metal surface of the door itself was interrupted by a series of large rivets that ran around the edge. Set in the centre-left of the door was a steel wheel of the type used to seal off bulkheads on a submarine.

Kilbride played his torch beam on the walls to either side of the door. To the left lay a black panel, inside

117

which was a dial for keying in the combination of the lock. If the right sequence of numbers was entered the metal wheel would free itself, allowing the internal steel locking bars to be rolled back, at which point the giant door could be swung open.

Kilbride took hold of the cold steel spokes of the wheel and tried to spin it anticlockwise. It didn't shift one inch. He put his weight against it and tried again, this time in the opposite direction, just in case it had a reverse thread. Again, it didn't budge.

Kilbride turned to the Irishman. 'Paddy?'

Moynihan ran his hand over the cold steel surface of the door. 'Sure, there's an old saying: "A golden key will open any door." And when you don't have a golden key, Paddy Moynihan says a little bit of plastic explosives will work wonders.'

'You reckon?'

'Sure, she's a big fecker all right. Must weigh all of four tons. But there's two weaknesses to any door: the lock and the hinges. Now, the hinges on this one are pretty massive and they're no help . . . But the lock . . . If we can hit the door with a shaped cutting charge and blow a hole in her, we should be able to reach in, fiddle with the lock and retract the pins manually. End of story.'

Kilbride slapped the Irishman on the shoulder. 'Get to work, Moynihan.'

Moynihan dumped his bag on the floor and rooted around, pulling out a shaped charge of PE4. The plastic explosive was rolled into pencil-thin lengths, several of which had been wound together to make up a long sausage-shaped charge. Using gaffer tape Moynihan started stringing the PE4 in a ring around the lock. Smithy arrived with the lamps and brought

118

one closer to light Moynihan's work. Finally, the Irishman affixed a length of detonation wire to a firing cap which he inserted into the charge.

'Either I'm a Chinaman or that'll never bloody work,' Smithy grunted. 'You should use four of 'em – one charge'll never do it.'

Moynihan kept his eyes glued to his work. 'Sure, Smithy, has no woman ever told you – it isn't size alone that counts, it's what you do with it.'

'You'll eat your bloody words when it fails to blow. There's fifty million in gold riding on this, Paddy . . .'

The Irishman ignored Smithy and talked to himself softly as he prepared to blow the charge. 'Sure, we'll roll out a length of wire this way, and maybe to the bend in the corridor and then down the service passageway – get us back away from the feckin' blast. For it's better to arrive ten minutes late in this world than ten minutes early in the next . . .'

Moynihan rolled out the detonation wire all the way back to the generator room, and got Smithy, Emile and Kilbride in there with him. Having half closed the door he glanced at the others and raised one eyebrow.

'You feckers ready?'

Kilbride and Emile nodded.

Smithy scowled. 'Ready for fuck all—'

The last words were lost in an almighty explosion as Moynihan hit the detonator switch. For a split second the air was punched out of their lungs as the blast wave rolled through the confined space, ripping along the corridor and the walls. It tore up the stairs and through the lobby of the bank, whipping up a storm of splintered wood and debris and spitting out the remaining glass in the bank's shattered windows. The noise of the blast echoed out across the Green Line,

119

losing itself in the rumble of battle that rolled on and on across the city.

At the front of the bank Boerke, Berger and McKierran raised their heads from the dirt and exchanged glances.

'Holy shit,' Bill Berger muttered. 'That Irishman sure ain't messin' around. Anyone left alive down there, you reckon?'

Boerke gave an evil grin. 'Who cares, man, as long as the door is blown.'

'You're a canny bastard, Bushman,' Jock McKierran growled. 'More gold for us, is that yer meaning?'

The three men laughed. They had every confidence in Moynihan's explosive abilities. But if the vault *had* been blasted open each of them was now itching to get sight of the gold. Boerke righted a battered armchair that had been blown over by the blast. It was one of the few pieces of furniture that had survived their assault on the bank. He climbed into it and pulled out the Rubik's Cube from the smock pocket of his medical tunic. Keeping one eye on the street up ahead, he started to manipulate the plastic puzzle.

McKierran glanced at Bill Berger, then nodded at Boerke in his green armchair. 'Aye, well, there's nothing like making yerself comfortable . . . Are we taking it in turns, laddie?'

Boerke carried on playing with the Rubik's Cube as if he hadn't heard him.

As the smoke in the basement cleared, Moynihan was the first to pop his head around the corner of the corridor. At the far end he could just make out the form of the giant door, still looking very much intact. The steel was scorched and blackened by the blast, but that

120

was about all . . . He groaned to himself, and went to give the lock a closer inspection.

While he did so he heard Smithy behind his back, muttering, 'Thick Paddy bastard . . . I said it'd never bloody work.'

Moynihan felt a sudden flash of anger towards the Sergeant, but he forced himself not to react. He needed to concentrate all his energy on opening the massive steel door. He felt certain that the problem was less the amount of explosive he'd used and more his ability to channel the blast in the right direction. He had to focus one hundred per cent of its destructive impact onto the steel surface of the door, and he had an idea how he might just do that.

Moynihan dropped his bag and began scrabbling around again. 'Sure, in case you feckin' English bastards was wondering that was just the dress rehearsal.'

He pulled out a handful of PE4, a couple of metal funnels, some wooden batons and a roll of black gaffer tape. As he set to work, Kilbride and Smithy glanced at each other in amazement.

'Couple of old gardening funnels like I keep in me garage to fill up me lawnmower,' Smithy remarked, incredulously. 'Okay, you mad Irish bastard, what're you up to now?'

Moynihan ignored Smithy's question and continued working on his new explosive device. As he did so, Kilbride did a quick walkabout of the bank, giving the men an update on the Irishman's activities. He paused in the bank's lobby, at the unit's long-range radio set. Every four hours Kilbride had been sending a one-word sitrep to their Cyprus base, signalling that all was fine with the mission. If he missed a transmission, then that would raise the alarm. Kilbride checked his watch: it was twenty minutes before another sitrep was due. As he turned away from the radio he heard the faint staccato bleeping of an incoming message.

He grabbed the headphones and started transcribing the Morse code onto a scrap of paper. 'Kilo One, Base. Heavy fighting in Golf Sector. Mission aborted. Return to base. Repeat, return to base. Acknowledge.'

Kilbride chuckled to himself. 'Kilo One' was the code name for his own unit and 'Golf Sector' was that for the Green Line. As if they didn't know already that they were in the middle of a bloody great big firefight. And what sort of bullshit reason was that to call off the mission, anyway? Kilbride sensed the hand of Major Thistlethwaite at work. He began tapping out a response to the message on the radio's Morse pad.

'Base, Kilo One. Radio malfunction. Repeat, radio malfunction. Do not copy your message. Await further update. Kilo One, out.'

Kilbride didn't believe that they would swallow it back on Cyprus, especially Sergeant Major Jones and some of the other old hands. But it was about the best he could manage in the circumstances. Once he'd finished sending the message Kilbride unscrewed the cover on the radio's battery compartment, removed the battery and bent a couple of the lug pins out of shape. He reassembled it and the radio stubbornly refused to power up. Now they really did have a radio malfunction. If they needed it at any stage, he could always bend the lug pins back into shape again.

Down below in the basement, Moynihan had filled each of the two metal funnels with a half-circle of plastic explosive. He inserted a detonator, attached the wire and gaffer-taped the whole lot up. Then he gaffer-taped a couple of one-inch wooden blocks onto the open end of each funnel. He attached a wooden baton to the neck of the funnel, and with a second baton taped to the first Moynihan had fashioned a wooden handle that was just the right length to jam against the wall.

He glanced at Smithy. 'Make your fat self useful and grab hold of that.' He indicated the free end of the wooden handle. 'When I have the feckin' charge in position I want you to jam that baton in tight against here.' Moynihan patted one of the vertical concrete stanchions of the corridor. 'Got it?'

Smithy grunted.

Moynihan manoeuvred the open end of the first funnel over the lower half of the lock. When he had it exactly in position Smithy jammed the baton in place, and the first of the funnel charges was held tightly against the door. They did a repeat performance with the second, jamming it in tight over the upper half of the lock.

Moynihan stepped back to admire his handiwork. 'Simple lesson of explosive physics,' he remarked. 'When the PE4 blows it takes the path of least resistance – the inch gap at the funnel's mouth – so placing the lock at the epicentre of the explosion. End of feckin' story.' He turned to Smithy. 'Sure, even you should be able to understand that . . .'

Smithy shook his head in disgust. 'Couple of gardening funnels . . . You're round the bloody bend, Paddy. It'll never bloody work . . .'

Moynihan ran the detonation cord back to the generator room, and the two men retreated inside. Five minutes later Kilbride rejoined them. He'd made the Irishman promise not to blow the funnel charges without him.

123

The noise of the second explosion had barely died away before Moynihan popped his head around the corner of the corridor to check. The two metal funnels had been blasted backwards like a pair of missiles, flattening themselves against the back wall of the basement. They lay there among the splintered remains of the wooden batons. But as far the steel door of the vault was concerned, it remained almost unchanged.

Moynihan uttered a string of curses. 'We could be here all feckin' night trying to feckin' blast our way through that feckin' thing . . .'

Smithy glared at the Irishman. 'We don't have all night, you thick Paddy bastard. I said it'd never bloody work—'

Moynihan rounded on him. 'So what does a feckin' gobshite Sassenach like you know about it? You have any better suggestions? Keep feckin' quiet if you don't.'

The two men eyeballed each other. 'Well, why don't we just bloody do like we do on training and blast a hole through the bloody wall?' Smithy demanded. 'It's only bloody concrete. Got to be a lot bloody easier than going through six inches of bloody steel.'

For an instant Kilbride, Moynihan and Smithy exchanged startled glances. Then there were smiles all round: why the hell hadn't any of them thought of that before?

'Sure, that's what I intended all along,' Moynihan announced as he clapped his arm around Smithy's shoulders. 'I was just testing you . . . It's third time lucky, so it is: stand back, while I blast my way into the feckin' vault!'

It was approaching midnight on Cyprus, a time of day that Knotts-Lane favoured. He could enjoy the quiet of the ops tent and the peace it afforded him to challenge himself on the chessboard. He had just started his third game of the evening: white versus black and himself as the only possible winner. Ernie Jones, the radio operator, was the only other person present, hunched over the comms equipment in the rear. Over the years, Ernie and Knotts-Lane had developed a familiarity that was based upon many largely silent hours spent in each other's company.

As he considered his next move on behalf of black, Knotts-Lane pricked up his ears. There was the distinctive beep-beep-beep of an incoming message. A couple of minutes later Ernie had it decoded.

'Bloody hell!' he snorted. 'Kilbride . . . He's a crafty bastard, or a mad one – depends which way you look at it.' He turned to Knotts-Lane, handing him the hand-scribbled message. 'Take a butcher's at that.'

Knotts-Lane grabbed the paper excitedly. He flicked his gaze across the message and whistled to himself in amazement.

He glanced up at the radio operator. 'Some radio malfunction . . . Kilbride put a bullet through it with his M16, no doubt.'

'More 'n likely. Shit's going to hit the fan good 'n' proper, especially when the bloody Major sees it.'

'Want me to run it across to the SSM?'

Ernie nodded. 'You do that. Rather you than me. The SSM's got a nasty habit of shooting the bloody messenger.'

Knotts-Lane glanced at his chessboard and made the next move: black rook to J4, to finish off the opposing side's king. Checkmate, he reckoned, in only six moves. Knotts-Lane preferred it when black won, and most evenings he tried gently to engineer a black victory. He jumped to his feet and strode out of the ops tent. He wondered how it was that Kilbride couldn't have come up with a better excuse. A radio malfunction was so obvious, so predictable. It was pretty brainless, really. It must have been Bill Berger's influence, Knotts-Lane reasoned. The dumb American Vietnam vet was dragging Kilbride down to his own level.

As he made his way through the camp, Knotts-Lane scratched at the scar on his cheek. He remembered Kilbride's caution that he should go and see the medic about it. Well, Kilbride ought to spend a little more time worrying about his own problems, Knotts-Lane reasoned. The Major was gunning for him anyway. With a stunt like this one – *a radio malfunction* – Kilbride was really in the shit. If he wasn't careful he could even get himself booted out of The Regiment.

Knotts-Lane gave a thin smile. He was going to get a real kick out of delivering this message.

There was a sudden crack like a thunderbolt, and Moynihan's cutting charges blasted into the wall to one side of the massive steel door. As the concrete burst asunder, a man-sized hole was opened up into the bank's subterranean interior. In the deathly silence that followed, Moynihan glanced at Smithy and Kilbride and then back at the breached wall.

'End of story?' Kilbride quipped.

Moynihan crossed himself. 'Never mind end of feckin' story – it's a feckin' miracle, it is.'

Kilbride shone his torch through the jagged-edged dust-filled opening. He could almost sense the glint of gold in there as the finger of light played among the coal-black shadows. The torch beam glinted on the dull metal surface of a safe, and to one side of it Kilbride

126

could just make out a wall stacked with safety-deposit boxes. He glanced at the luminous dial of his watch: it was 11.45 p.m. They had made it into the vault some fifteen minutes ahead of schedule.

'Who's first?' he asked.

Smithy nodded in Moynihan's direction. 'Got to be the mad bloody Irishman. None of us would be setting foot in there if it wasn't for him.'

Moynihan shrugged. He placed a foot through the opening. As he disappeared into the gloom, he turned back to Smithy. 'Sure, pass me the lamp, will you? There seems to be a problem with the feckin' lighting in here.'

The vault of the Imperial Bank of Beirut was of a simple rectangular construction, about fifty feet long by thirty wide. Along two of the walls there were banks of metal safety-deposit boxes arranged on shelves from the floor to the ceiling, and the third wall was dominated by the entrance hole that the SAS men had blasted. But backed up against the fourth wall were three iron safes, and it was these that drew the men's attention.

Moynihan strolled across to the first and gave it a quick once-over. 'Sure, after the feckin' door this'll be like child's play.' He turned to Kilbride. 'Shall I blow the feckin' three of them together, shall I, all in one go?'

Kilbride shrugged. 'Why not?'

Moynihan grabbed three ready-made PE4 charges from his pack and gaffer-taped one onto each of the safes. He strung the three charges together with a length of detonation wire, and then they all retreated into the corridor once more. Moynihan hit the detonator switch for a fourth time, and another, slightly smaller blast rocked the basement of the Imperial Bank of Beirut. Once the smoke and debris had cleared a little, Moynihan knelt before the first safe, fiddled with the broken lock and in seconds he was able to swing the door open wide.

His heart beating with anticipation, Kilbride peered inside. The shelves were stacked with grey hardboard containers, each about the size and shape of a shoebox and sealed with two thin strips of metal. He reached inside and pulled one out, and as it came free of the shelf he all but dropped it. It was massively, inconceivably heavy. He glanced across at the others and smiled. They gathered around excitedly as he pulled out his knife and sliced through the metal retaining straps. He levered up the lid and threw it to one side. Two beautiful golden bars stared up at him, glinting in the light of his torch beam.

Kilbride reached in and picked one up. It was wonderfully cold and smooth and so *heavy*. But the thing that struck him most was the maker's mark stamped into the middle of each of the bars. Kilbride stared at it in disbelief, then felt around in his pocket for his SAS winged-dagger cap badge. It was bad tradecraft, but he always carried it with him, even on a deniable operation like this one. He'd had the same cap badge ever since his first combat mission, in Malaysia, and it was his lucky talisman. He held it up against the golden bar. The maker's stamp showed a metal staff pointing downwards, set over a pair of wings at the top. It and the SAS cap badge were almost identical.

As Kilbride stared at the maker's stamp, he noticed that twined around the staff were two snakes, their heads pointing upwards towards the wings. And each had the unmistakable flattened hood of a cobra. Kilbride felt a shiver run up his spine. *Cobra gold.* That was their chosen mission code name. First a stamp remarkably similar to their own SAS cap badge; now

128

the two cobras. Somehow it felt as if the gold had been sitting here, just waiting for them.

Kilbride scrutinised the rest of the bar. Next to the maker's stamp was their name: Schone Edelmetaal BV of the Netherlands. Above that was what looked like a serial number: COBRA 405. Kilbride checked the other bar: it was stamped with a sequential number – COBRA 405. The golden bars were sisters, and they must have come one after the other off the company's Dutch production line. Below the maker's stamp was the number 400.095. That, he guessed, had to be the weight of the bar: four hundred ounces (as near as damn it), or 12.5 kilogrammes. Below that again were the words '9999 Fine Gold', which signified that it was 99.99 per cent pure gold – as if he'd needed to be told.

Kilbride shook himself out of his reverie and turned to the others. 'Right, it's time to load up. Smithy, get everyone in here but Boerke, McKierran and Berger. Tell them to keep their bloody eyes peeled: last thing we want is to be busted by the militia while we're removing this little lot.'

Smithy nodded, and disappeared out the doorway blasted in the vault's back wall.

Kilbride turned to the others. 'We're in luck: it all appears to be boxed. Two bars per box, twenty-five kilos per box, one box per man. Moynihan, Emile – time to get busy.'

As the men began ferrying the gold out of the bank and into the waiting truck, Kilbride went to inspect the other safes. Each one was stacked in a similar fashion to the first. Kilbride stepped away from the three safes and took in the wider scene. The loading was going well, and he reckoned they'd have all seven hundred bars on the truck within two hours. They should be ready to hit the road well ahead of schedule. But something was eating him, and he couldn't work out what it was.

He sat back against the wall and took a minute to think things over. As he gazed at the three safes with their doors hanging open, he suddenly realised what it was. Surely there was too much gold? He studied the first safe and did some quick mental arithmetic, working out how many boxes each shelf held. He then multiplied that by two to reach the total number of bars stored there. He came up with the figure of 714 bars – the exact number of 12.5-kilo bars that equated to fifty million dollars.

Kilbride shook his head and did the sums again, and came up with the same answer. But if there was fifty million dollars' worth of gold bullion in that *one safe alone*, then each of the other two safes had to hold a similar amount. In which case, he was looking at a cool one hundred and fifty million dollars across the three of them. The MI6 officers had assured him that there was fifty million in bullion in the vault, and no more. Their intel was some of the best, they had boasted. How could they have got it so badly wrong?

Kilbride ran his hand across the stubble of his jawline. However much he tried he just couldn't seem to get his head around this discovery. He glanced across at the first safe: pretty soon the lads would have all the gold from that one stacked onto the truck, which meant that the Bedford would be a couple of tons overweight already. At present rates of loading, and as no one was counting the bars going in, they'd just keep going until all the gold was on board. But by then the truck would be more than twenty tons overweight, which meant that it wouldn't be able to move one inch up Rue Riad al Sohl before it broke its back.

Kilbride called Smithy over. He needed to get

everyone together for a heads-up, he explained. Everyone, including the three men on guard. It was past midnight and quiet as death in the Green Line. So to hell with the risk – he needed to speak to them all. A couple of minutes later Kilbride stood in front of all nine of the men, eyeing them in the dim light of the bank vault. At his feet there was an open box, showing two of the golden bars.

'Right – d'you want the good news or the bad news?' he announced. 'There's no way to go about saying this without blowing your minds, so here goes . . . The good news is that there's twenty-one hundred gold bars in this vault. That's *three times* what we were expecting. Total value: one hundred and fifty million dollars. I repeat: *one hundred and fifty million dollars.*'

The men stared at Kilbride in a stunned silence. It struck him then that the situation would have been hugely comical, were it not for the very real dilemma with which this presented them.

'Now for the bad news: twenty-one hundred bars weigh in at twenty-six tons, give or take a few kilos. That's pretty much three times what the Bedford can carry. I'm as dumbfounded as you lot are. But I've done my sums and checked and double-checked: each safe holds seven hundred bars, that's twenty-one hundred in all. Total weight: roughly twenty-six tons. Total value: one hundred and fifty million dollars . . . So the question is – what the fuck do we do with it all?'

'Well, we can't bloody leave it here,' Smithy blurted out. 'I mean, one hundred and fifty million – that's a bloody fortune.'

'Fifty million; a hundred million; it's all a fortune,' Nightly snapped. 'But it's worth fuck all to us if we get nobbled while we're nicking it.'

Boerke picked up one of the golden bars COBRA 405. 'Listen, have you seen the stamps, the winged staff . . .' He had a feverish look on his face, as his gaze flicked from one man to the next. 'Take a very careful look. Now, have you ever seen anything more like our own cap badge?' He locked stares with Kilbride. 'It is like it was made for us, man. *Made for us*. We cannot leave one bar behind.'

Kilbride glanced from Boerke to Bill Berger. 'Plus the two cobras, climbing up the staff. *Cobra Gold*.'

Bill Berger reached out, took the bar from Boerke and stared at it for a second. 'I gotta admit, it's kinda weird. But even if it had our goddamn names stamped on it, we still got us a problem. I know you reckon they build them Bedfords strong, but twenty-six fuckin' tons? That's three journeys to carry that lot, no matter which way you look at it.'

Smithy glared at the big American. 'So you're for bloody leaving it behind, are you?'

Bill Berger snorted. 'Over my dead body! Just we gotta think how we get it outta here, that's all.'

'Let's try and simplify this,' said Kilbride. 'As I see it, there's only two possible options. First, we stick to the plan: we load seven hundred bars onto the truck and we're out of here tonight. Let's say we're fully loaded by two a.m. We'll be back at the safe house an hour later, loaded onto the boats by five-thirty a.m., which still gives us an hour's darkness to get out of the city. So, it's easily doable. By sunup tomorrow we'd be safely away, and each be five million dollars better off. That's option one, and it makes one hell of a lot of sense . . .'

Kilbride studied the faces of his men in the eerie light of the bank vault. None of them were giving much away.

'Option two: we go for all twenty-one hundred bars,'

he continued. 'That means three trips across the city, three trips by boat up and down the Beirut River, three trips back and forth to the Palm Islands. That's three times as much risk of being discovered and hit by one of the militias.' He glanced at his watch. 'We'd try for one trip tonight, two tomorrow – which means loading and unloading the truck twice tomorrow night. We should be able to manage it, but it's one hell of a lot of risk for an extra hundred million . . .'

Kilbride shrugged before finishing the statement. 'For an extra hundred million dollars.'

'What d'you reckon, boss?' Smithy asked.

'It's not up to me . . . But if you're asking would I go for the sensible option or the insane one – I'd go for the insane one, every time. I'd go for the one hundred and fifty million . . .'

'Yeah, and you'd get us all fucking killed,' Nightly muttered.

'No one's getting anyone killed,' Kilbride said evenly. 'That's why I called a Chinese parliament – so we could all make the decision. And don't forget, everyone here's a volunteer. You go getting yourself killed, you'll only have yourself to blame.'

'You're a big boy, Nightly,' Boerke added. 'Act like one, man. Take some responsibility. One hundred and fifty million dollars in gold . . .'

'It's still no use if you're fucking dead,' Nightly retorted. 'All the money in the world won't stop a bullet to the head.'

Kilbride took the gold bar from Bill Berger, placed it back in the box and shut the lid. 'The clock's ticking,' he announced. 'So if no one's got a better suggestion let's go to a vote. All those in favour of Plan B, the totally fucking insane one, raise their hands.'

Six hands shot into the air: those of Kilbride, Smithy, Berger, Moynihan, McKierran and Boerke. After a second's delay, Ward and Johno followed suit.

'Emile?' Kilbride queried.

'I am permitted to vote?'

''Course you fucking are,' said Smithy. 'It's a *Chinese*.'

Emile raised his hand. 'Then, of course, I too am one of the insane ones.'

'It's your fucking funeral,' Nightly muttered, keeping his hand stubbornly by his side. "Don't say I didn't warn—'

'Right, it's decided,' said Kilbride, ignoring Nightly's remark. 'Get that truck loaded with as much as she can carry, 'cause the more we take out tonight the less we have to do tomorrow.'

Boerke reached down and picked up the box of gold bars at his feet. As he did so, he had a look of wild elation on his normally stony features. He turned and carried it out of the vault. Behind him, lying beside one of the safes and completely forgotten, was his Rubik's Cube.

One very sweaty hour later the men had finished loading the vehicles with nine tons of bullion, give or take few bars. The gold made a tiny heap in the rear of the truck, and none of the men could quite believe it weighed so much, or that it was of such immense value. Smithy had had the bright idea of loading up the two Toyota Land Cruisers, and each of those had been packed full of a ton of bullion, or some eighty bars each.

At 1.45 a.m. the convoy of vehicles rolled out of Rue Riad al-Solh. In the back of each one man was posing as wounded: Johno and Ward in the two Toyotas, and

Berger in the Bedford. Each man had stripped down to his underclothes and wrapped himself in the bank security guards' discarded bandages. Johno and Ward each had an M16 hidden beneath their stretcher, whilst Berger was cradling the big GPMG under his hospital blanket. But all any curious militia member would see if he inspected the rear of the vehicles was an apparently badly wounded patient, swathed in dirty, bloodstained bandages. Even the smell – stale blood and iodine – was entirely convincing.

Kilbride had left Boerke, McKierran and a sullen Nightly to keep watch over the bank. Under Emile's guidance he retraced their route through the Green Line. The vehicle convoy reached the checkpoint without incident. Kilbride was so hyped up that he almost failed to notice the girl with the brown eyes above her mask. She asked Emile how their journey had fared, and he told her that all had gone well despite the renewed outbreak of fighting. They had picked up some wounded on the way, and they were in a hurry to get them to a hospital on the eastern side of the city. Sensing the urgency – if not the essence – of their mission, the brown-eyed girl let them through, saving a very special smile for Doctor Luke Kilbride.

Once back at the safe house the gold was unloaded and carried down the river bank to the waiting boats. By 4.30 a.m. each of the Zodiac RIBs had been loaded with three tons of gold, which was the maximum that Kilbride reckoned each craft could manage. The convoy of boats set off downriver in line astern, with Ward in control of the lead RIB and Kilbride stationed at the prow with the night-vision equipment. Johno took control of the rear boat, while Moynihan had volunteered to pilot the craft in the middle.

As the three boats were heavily laden and low in the water, Kilbride opted not to use the outboard engines. Instead, they allowed the current of the river to carry them through the dark city and down towards the open sea. By five o'clock that Saturday morning the flotilla had reached the estuary of the Beirut River without mishap.

Ward swung the engines of the lead craft down into the water and fired them up with a gentle roar. He set a bearing for the Palm Islands, on a calm and softly undulating sea.

Major Thistlethwaite was not in the best of moods. In fact, as he strode backwards and forwards behind his desk he was incandescent with rage.

'Twenty-four hours now and not a word from Kilbride. Not a word! What the devil can have happened to him?'

'Radios do malfunction,' Sergeant Major Spud Jones, replied. 'It does happen . . .'

'Not on my watch it doesn't,' the Major snapped. 'Don't they have a back-up unit? Twenty-four hours and a whole troop still missing. It's a disaster.'

'They're not missing, sir. It's a radio malfunction.'

'Not missing, Sergeant Major? Well then, why the devil don't you tell me where they are?'

'Radios do malfunction,' the Sergeant Major repeated, as if he were talking to a child. 'And Kilbride's unit will have a back-up set. But it's likely to be in their forward mounting base. When they get back to that location they'll call in.'

The Major stared at Sergeant Major Jones. 'You seem remarkably sanguine about all this, Sergeant Major. Remarkably so. Let's just remind ourselves of the situation, shall we? Fighting has broken out all over Beirut; the militias are knocking seven kinds of shit out of each other; we have nine men in the midst of all that chaos somewhere, and they've been out of contact for the last twenty-four hours; and to top it all we have no idea where they are. I'd say that is a fairly serious situation, Sergeant Major. They could be killed, captured or worse . . .'

'Kilbride's a survivor,' Sergeant Major Jones interjected. 'He's commanding a unit of fine men. They're all trained for this sort of thing. In the Congo, Kilbride was part of a unit that went missing for ninety-six days. We'd given them up for dead, but Kilbride and his three mates made it out alive. "The Ghost Unit", we called them . . . Like I said, Kilbride's a survivor and he'll bring his men out alive.'

'Yes, I've heard all about his *Ghost Unit*, Sergeant Major – let's just hope this isn't a repeat performance.' The Major stopped pacing and stared at the SSM. 'In any case, it's one thing going missing in the Congo jungles, quite another doing so in the middle of bloody Beirut. It's hardly uninhabited forest, is it? I mean, can't the man get to a telephone or something?'

'Kilbride wouldn't compromise himself by using voice comms, not unless it's a life-or-death situation. That's why we operate in Morse code . . . sir. He'll wait until he can make contact via the radio . . . When we was on operations in Malaya, Congo and Borneo, it was standard operating procedure that any patrol had to be able to lose itself for a fortnight without revealing itself to the enemy.'

'Well, you're not in Malaya or Borneo now, are you? In all my years in the military I've never known such lax procedures . . .'

'With respect, sir, this isn't the regular army. We work to a different set of rules. I said before, Kilbride's a survivor, and that's what makes him a good operator.'

The major glared at Sergeant Major Jones. 'He may be a good operator in your book, Sergeant Major, but in mine he is a menace . . . I want to ask a simple question of you, Sergeant Major, and I'd appreciate an honest answer. Do you really give any credence to this "radio malfunction" nonsense? Well, do you? Or might it not be one of Kilbride's little games . . . What I'm driving at is this: is Kilbride *really* a survivor, Sergeant Major, or is he more of a . . . dangerous liability?'

'I wouldn't want to speculate,' Spud Jones replied, stiffly. 'Like I said, radios do go down. Not often – the A41's a pretty bulletproof piece of kit. But it does happen. Anyhow, don't you worry about Kilbride and his men – he'll bring them out alive.'

'It's not that which worries me,' the Major muttered. 'Just imagine the fuss they'll make in headquarters, not to mention Whitehall, if we lose a whole unit of men in the Lebanon. I mean, for God's sake, Sergeant, officially we're not even supposed to be in Beirut . . . We have a decidedly shaky Labour government in power, and Lord only knows if this has been cleared with them . . . This has the makings of a career nightmare . . .'

CHAPTER SEVEN

At 6.30 a.m. on Sunday, 25 January an exhausted Kilbride found himself back at the Imperial Bank of Beirut overseeing the loading of the last of the gold. Kilbride had never felt so tired in all his born days, and the rest of the men appeared equally shattered. None of them had slept since being dropped by the submarine off the Lebanese coast some three days earlier.

He'd never quite believed that they would actually make it to this point, yet here they finally were. Eleven tons of bullion had been removed from the bank on the Friday, and ten tons had been taken out on the Saturday night, most of which had already been ferried across to the Palm Islands. Five more tons to go and they would be home and dry.

For this last trip Kilbride had divided his forces, which meant that his men were doubly overstretched. He'd left Johno and Ward on Ramkine Island, working with their scuba gear to sink the bullion in the cave depths, with Nightly lending them a hand. Kilbride was relieved to have got shot of the disgruntled SAS soldier:

so far on this mission Nightly had turned out to be something of a liability.

Taking all the gold had always been a crazy idea, and Kilbride hoped that they wouldn't end up paying for it with their lives. They just needed their luck to hold for one last trip across the war-torn city, and then they would be out of there for good. Kilbride had no desire ever to return, and even the allure of the brown-eyed girl at the checkpoint was starting to fade. The ceasefire had yet to be re-established and fierce firefights were raging up and down the Green Line. But at least this gave Kilbride and his men good cover for their ongoing activities: fresh fighting meant fresh wounded, and more work for the Red Cross medics who tended to the victims.

As the last gold bars were being loaded Kilbride went to check on the bank guards. They still had twenty-four hours until the bank's opening time on Monday morning, and he wanted to ensure there was enough food and water to last them. As he opened the door to the room, Kilbride had an ominous, sinking feeling. There was no sign of the prisoners anywhere. He noticed a smashed window, high up on one wall, with a chair propped against it. He jumped up and peered into the darkness outside, but the guards had disappeared.

Kilbride didn't know who was to blame and he didn't really care. They were all dog-tired, and when fighting men got overtired mistakes started to happen. None of them had realised the extent of the guards' recovery – that they were actually physically capable of making a getaway. Kilbride kicked himself for being so stupid. He hurried back to the front of the bank. Smithy and Berger emerged from the lobby carrying the radio set and the mortar tubes.

'The guards have scarpered,' Kilbride announced flatly. 'Let's hit the bloody road. And keep your eyes peeled.'

The men cursed their bad luck and made for the Bedford truck. Kilbride headed for the lead Toyota. But as he jumped inside he remembered something: *the terrorist papers.* There were documents in that vault detailing the financial holdings of Arab terror groups worldwide. He still had the number of the safety-deposit box that Sergeant Major Jones had given him. Could he live with his conscience – let alone Spud Jones – if he carted off the gold but left the papers behind?

He signalled to the lads to wait one, and sprinted back inside. A minute later he was back again, a thick wad of documents stuffed down the front of his medical tunic. But as he went to start the Toyota he heard the distant snarl of an engine from the southern end of Rue Riad al-Solh. He turned to see the familiar shape of a big American pick-up roaring around the corner. It accelerated towards him, its Dushka heavy machine gun searching for a target.

When it was still some five hundred yards away, the pick-up slowed to a halt and a dozen soldiers dismounted. They fanned out to either side of the street and began advancing towards Kilbride's position. These were clearly professionals doing a professional job, and they knew the location of their target.

Kilbride grabbed his walkie-talkie. 'Fuck it,' he snarled. 'Ambush positions.'

Smithy, Berger, McKierran, Moynihan and Boerke dismounted from their vehicles and filtered into the cover of the ruined buildings to either side of them. The men were tired beyond imagining, but the adrenalin was kicking in now and they were up for the fight. The

141

Claymores were still in position, which was the last thing the enemy would be expecting. The one thing Kilbride hoped was that the Dushka operator didn't open fire before they triggered the Claymore ambush.

Kilbride pulled out a 66mm LAW rocket from the rear of the Toyota. He scuttled across to the cover of a low wall and flipped it out into its firing position. Then he grabbed his walkie-talkie, held it to his mouth, and pressed the transmit button gently.

'On Boerke, open up,' he whispered. 'When he hits the Claymores.'

The enemy advanced in a classic fire-and-manoeuvre pattern, each half-dozen soldiers providing cover for the others as they 'leapfrogged' their way down the street. Four hundred yards; three hundred yards; two hundred yards: the force drew closer and closer. Kilbride's men were all but invisible in their positions, and the enemy had no option but to try to flush them out of hiding. At fifty yards, Kilbride could make out the features of the individual fighters. As they drew to within thirty yards' range, he began to worry that Boerke had left the Claymore ambush too late.

One of the soldiers leaned out from the cover of a building, momentarily sighting an assault rifle on Kilbride's position. Kilbride suddenly felt his blood run cold. He recognised the thick auburn hair spilling out from beneath the cap, the eyes above the khaki mask . . .

But the warm features of the brown-eyed girl from the checkpoint had now been transformed into those of a hunter. To either side of her were similarly feminine figures: the other girls from the checkpoint had come to hunt down Kilbride and his team.

There was a squish of static on Kilbride's radio.

'Now, man!' It was Boerke's voice, thick with the aggression of the imminent contact. Even had Kilbride wanted to, there was nothing he could do to stop him.

Boerke squeezed the clacker hand-held firing device three times, and a split second later a vortex of flying death erupted from the Claymore daisy chain. A wave of 2,100 steel ball-bearings tore up Rue Riad al-Solh, scything down anything in its path. The first half-dozen fighters – the doe-eyed girl included – were hit at point-blank range, their bodies pulverised, blood and shredded flesh thrown high into the air. An instant later, the second group of enemy fighters were ripped apart by the whirlwind of steel.

Behind them, several hundred spherical metal projectiles tore into the American pick-up, opening it up like a giant tin-opener. It slewed to one side, mounted the pavement and shunted its nose in through the window of a derelict shopfront, the driver slumped dead over the wheel. In the rear the Dushka gunner spun around, a smashed hand clutching his bloodied forehead, and keeled forward over the big machine gun. Kilbride let rip with the 66mm LAW, deliberately aiming for the vehicle's fuel tank. The moment the rocket struck there was an intense flash of flame and the pick-up exploded, turning the street into a blazing inferno, a plume of black smoke billowing above the stricken vehicle.

Boerke and Berger began firing off rounds from their stubby M203 grenade launchers, pounding the positions where there might be enemy survivors. In less than sixty seconds it was all over, and over a dozen militiamen – and women – lay dead. No one from Kilbride's force had suffered so much as a scratch, but he felt sick to his very bones. The brown-eyed girl from the checkpoint would be doing no more partying in Beirut, that much was for certain, and the same went for her warrior girlfriends. Kilbride wondered how many more of the militia would now be coming after them.

'Move out,' he grated into his radio. 'Follow my lead.'

He pulled Emile to his feet and dragged him towards the lead Toyota. Once inside, he gunned the engine, wrenched the wheel angrily around and did a spectacular U-turn, wheels spinning on the debris that littered the road. Behind him, Smithy did a more ponderous about-turn in the big Bedford truck. Kilbride led the three-vehicle convoy north along Rue Riad al-Sohl – in the opposite direction to the burning wreck of the militia truck that blocked their route out of there. He glanced across at Emile. Their Lebanese fixer had buried his head in his hands.

'Take us west,' Kilbride said in a voice dead with exhaustion. 'We're not out of here yet, Emile. Take us west, okay?'

Emile lifted his head and ran a tired hand over his dirty medical tunic. 'West?' he queried. 'West? West will bring us to the Muslims . . . to the Muslim militia.'

'You have a better idea? Word's out among the Christian forces about what we're up to, so that's our only chance.'

'Take a left on Rue Weygand,' Emile muttered.

They drove on in silence for several seconds, the only noise being the hum of the wheels on the road and the distant rumble of fighting across the city.

Emile turned to Kilbride. 'Has it really all been worth it, my friend?'

'Who knows?' said Kilbride, keeping his eyes on the road ahead. 'That's not my concern right now. In a few minutes we could all be dead. Get us the fuck out of here, Emile.'

Emile shrugged. 'All roads out of the Green Line lead to a checkpoint, my friend . . .'

Sure enough, five minutes later Kilbride found himself approaching a roadblock. He brought the vehicle's speed down to dead slow.

'Christian or Muslim?' Kilbride asked as they crawled forwards. To him it looked pretty much like 'Checkpoint Charlie', as they'd nicknamed their regular crossing point into the Christian side of the city.

'Muslim,' Emile replied, quietly.

'How d'you know?'

'Trust me – I know.'

They rolled to a halt before the barrier. It struck Kilbride that the Muslim militiamen didn't look entirely friendly. One of them approached the passenger door and rapped on the glass with the barrel of his AK47. Emile wound down his window and the militiaman began firing questions at him in Arabic. The Muslim militia knew that the Red Cross carried the Christian wounded, and the questioner was being far from friendly.

Kilbride felt a presence on his side of the vehicle. He glanced out of the side window. A second militiaman was jabbing his assault rifle at the Red Cross symbol on his driver's door, and miming as if to shoot it up. He grinned evilly at Kilbride, his teeth showing yellow and rotten as he did so. The first militiaman started yelling at Emile, motioning for him to get down from the vehicle. Emile glanced at Kilbride, terror in his eyes, then turned to open the door.

The militiaman prodded Emile in the back and began

145

marching him towards the rear of the convoy. The second militiaman went with them, and Kilbride kept watch in his wing mirror as they walked the length of the three-vehicle line. They paused at the canvas back of the truck, and Emile was forced to kneel down. Kilbride saw the first militiaman whip out a knife, and for a moment he feared that he was about to cut Emile's throat. But then he stepped out of view behind the truck, brandishing the knife as he went. Kilbride knew that it was about to kick off big time.

He glanced ahead of him at the sandbagged position to his right. Four more militiamen were lounging about and enjoying the show. He eased his Browning out of his pocket, slipped the safety off and wound down his window. He gave the four enemy soldiers a big smile, and got a series of hostile stares in return. Keeping the weapon hidden, he brought his left hand over to join his right on the pistol grip, so as to better steady his aim. The sandbagged position was no more than fifteen yards away – he had thirteen rounds in the Browning and four men to kill. It was all about timing now, about how fast and accurate he could be on the draw.

In the rear of the Bedford Bill Berger was lying on a makeshift stretcher under a medical blanket. His head was wrapped in a bloodied bandage, and he had done the best job he could to make himself look like an injured man in need of urgent medical attention. As he listened to the yelling outside he felt a growing sense of unease. Although he spoke no Arabic, he could tell by the militiaman's tone that he was cursing Emile and threatening him.

Like Kilbride, the big American sensed that it was all about to get very nasty. He eased the bulk of the GPMG onto his stomach, and double-checked that he had a

146

round chambered and the weapon cocked and ready to fire. If anyone came into the rear of the truck he didn't think they'd be doing so in friendship. And he didn't think they'd be using the code word 'Gold Fever', either. In which case they were already as good as dead.

Suddenly, a blade came slicing through the canvas back of the truck. There was a savage down thrust, and then a slash to the right, forming a large L-shaped rent. A hand grabbed the flapping material and pulled it aside, and then a face was peering in. For a split second the militiaman and the big US soldier locked eyes and then Bill Berger squeezed his trigger. The big machine gun exploded with a roar, tearing smoking rents in the medical blanket and spitting out rounds into the militiaman's chest. The force of the impacts hurled him upwards and backwards, and he landed on the windscreen of the vehicle behind with a soggy thud. As the body slid downwards, Moynihan levelled his pistol at the second militiaman and shot him in the head.

The instant Kilbride heard the noise of the GPMG he had his Browning in the aim. Time seemed to slow to a crawl as he opened fire on the nearest figure. He pumped two shots into his torso, punching a hole like a bloodied flower in his stomach. Moments later the second militiaman went down in slow motion, as Kilbride swept the Browning right and kept firing. The third and fourth enemy figures dived for cover behind the sandbags, and Kilbride wasted three more bullets following them down. And then he ceased firing.

He kept his weapon in the aim and breathed deeply to calm his nerves. He waited for the two surviving militiamen to show themselves. He was seven bullets down, with six remaining and two men left to kill. It was just about doable.

Behind him there was the thump of a door opening and McKierran rolled out of the vehicle onto the ground. He came up in a crouch, levelled his M16 and fired off a 40mm grenade into the centre of the sandbagged position. Kilbride dived for cover behind the engine compartment of the Toyota as the grenade exploded, the force of the impact slamming into the vehicle and rocking it wildly on its springs. Razor-sharp shards of shrapnel tore through the enemy checkpoint, the blast throwing fragments of shredded flesh high into the air. As smoke drifted away, the battle scene fell silent. All four militiamen from the sandbagged position lay dead on the ground.

Kilbride's Toyota was pock-marked by shrapnel and badly dented from the explosion. The windscreen was shattered into a crazy latticework that was held together only by the laminate sheeting. Luckily, the big diesel engine had sheltered Kilbride from the worst of the blast. He just hoped to hell the vehicle was still driveable. He leaned forward and smashed away the shattered windscreen with his pistol.

'McKierran, get the fucking barrier!' he yelled.

As McKierran strode across to free up the route ahead, Kilbride checked his wing mirror: Emile was still kneeling exactly where the militiaman had placed him.

Kilbride leaned across the vehicle and stuck his head out of the passenger window. 'Emile!' he yelled. 'In the fucking vehicle! NOW!'

The shout seemed to break Emile's trance. He jumped to his feet and stumbled towards the lead Toyota, falling into it at Kilbride's side. Kilbride glanced across at him but Emile refused to make eye contact. He stared straight ahead, hands clasped in his lap seemingly in prayer.

148

'Emile, get with it!' Kilbride yelled. 'Back to the land of the living. You got to get us out of here. Prepare to give me some fucking directions . . .'

Kilbride revved the Toyota's engine as McKierran heaved at the concrete counterweight that lifted the barrier. Slowly it began to rise. McKierran went to step away, but as he did so there was a sharp crack of gunfire. McKierran grasped at his groin, a look of shock and disbelief on his face, and an instant later blood was spurting through his fingers, a rich red stream arcing through Kilbride's headlights. For a second McKierran made a grab for the barrier, and then the big Scot slumped to his knees, his M16 still held upright in his hand.

Kilbride wrenched the driver's door open, rolled out of the vehicle and ran. There was a second burst of gunfire, bullets chasing his heels, and then he dived for cover behind the pile of blasted sandbags. He crawled across to McKierran and forced the big Scotsman onto his back. He had a balled-up fist thrust deep into his groin wound to try and stem the flow of blood, but his dirty white medical tunic was spattered with streaks of red. The bullet had to have severed McKierran's femoral artery, for nothing else could cause such heavy bleeding. He would bleed to death in less than five minutes unless Kilbride could save him.

'I got 'em!' a voice rang out from behind. 'Above the ruined shopfront! Four o'clock.'

Bill Berger had the big GPMG cocked against the side of the truck as he waited for the enemy gunmen to show themselves again. There was another savage burst of gunfire, this time from a different window in the same building, and the windscreen of the Bedford shattered. Smithy felt a round slam him back into his seat and he

149

cried out in pain as he clutched at his shoulder. Berger answered with a heavy burst from the GPMG, but the enemy gunmen were too quick. They kept changing position to avoid being hit.

Berger vaulted down from the truck and took cover behind the rear axle. 'Anyone get a grenade through them windows?' he yelled.

'I'm hit!' Smithy yelled.

Boerke lay in the cover of the wheel of the Toyota at the rear. 'Watch this, man.'

He levelled his M16 and took aim with the grenade launcher. Rather than using a standard high-explosive grenade, Boerke had armed his weapon with an incendiary round. His finger gently squeezed the trigger, taking up the slack. There was a hollow *thump* as the weapon fired. The grenade spun through the air for a hundred yards, struck the window frame and detonated in a puff of white smoke. A hundred harmless-looking 'fingers' were flung out by the blast, each one a tiny fragment of white phosphorus. Each blazed with an incredible heat, and each would burn to the bone if it fell onto human skin.

Moments later there was an unearthly screaming from the inside the building. 'How's that, man?' Boerke yelled out. 'Let the fuckers fry.'

Before Berger could answer there was a muzzle flash from an adjacent window. The driver's glass of the rear Toyota shattered, and Moynihan felt a searing pain as a razor-sharp shard of shrapnel tore into his right eye.

He grabbed a rag from the vehicle's dash and stuffed it into his eye socket, to try to staunch the flow of blood. 'Feck it!' he yelled. 'Will one of you feckin' gobshites get a bead on that sniper!'

'Okay, you thick-skulled Afrikaner scumbag, cover

150

me!' Berger yelled. 'Time to smoke the bastards out.'

'Wait for one more grenade, man,' Boerke yelled back.

He loaded up another white-phosphorus round, levelled his weapon and fired. The instant he did so the big American scooped up his weapon and sprinted across the open space towards the ruined building. An enemy gunman broke cover and opened fire, spraying rounds at the big American's heels. He did so for just long enough for Boerke to get a fix on him, and the Afrikaner launched a grenade almost down the man's throat. The round exploded, showering the enemy gunman with white-hot balls of searing pain. Screaming in agony he fell from the window and landed on the pavement with a dull thump.

Berger arrived at the base of the building, his heart pounding fit to burst. The fallen enemy fighter was writhing on the ground in front of him, his skin a mass of tortured burning. The big American levelled his weapon, his finger on the trigger. But then he thought of Jock McKierran pumping his blood out into the Beirut dust, and he changed his mind. He'd let the militiaman suffer. His horrible screaming would ring in the ears of his fellow fighters, and they would either flee in abject terror or fly into a blazing rage. Either way they'd be more likely to break cover, in which case either he or Boerke could kill them.

Berger vaulted over the enemy figure and disappeared inside the building. He began his urban manhunt with the big machine gun held level at his hip, inching into the shadows.

Back at the checkpoint Kilbride ripped a sleeve off his medical tunic and thrust a balled-up wad of dirty cotton into Jock McKierran's mouth.

151

He stared into the big Scotsman's face. 'Jock – bite on this. It's going to hurt like fuck, but I've got to do it . . .'

Kilbride forced his left hand into McKierran's groin wound, opening up the ragged vent that had been torn in the flesh. As he did so, he inserted his other hand and reached upwards, feeling for the severed end of the artery. For a second or so he groped around in the warm, sticky mess. Then he felt the ragged end of a rubbery tube shape, and clamped his fingers around it. He held his breath and grabbed it tighter, pulling downwards as he did so. As he tugged with all his force, the artery reacted by trying to retract still further into the pelvic cradle. The big Scotsman ground his teeth into the wad of cloth, as slowly, painfully slowly, the artery began to emerge from the bloody wound.

'Smithy! Paddy! Bronco! Someone get over here!' Kilbride yelled. 'I need help! NOW!'

Boerke barely flinched. He was one hundred per cent concentrated on the far building, waiting for the chance to strike, as the big American went about his business of flushing out the enemy. Smithy heard Kilbride's call, but the burly Sergeant was trying to staunch the flow of blood from his own wound and knew he could be of little help. No point in bleeding to death, he told himself, for then he'd be no use to anyone. In the rear vehicle Moynihan looked up through his one good eye. Feck it, he told himself. McKierran's a feckin' Scotsman, so worth the saving. It would've been different if it was that English gobshite Smithy.

Using the cover of the vehicles, Moynihan scuttled forwards to Kilbride's position. As he caught sight of the two men he felt physically sick. Both were plastered in blood, and for a split second Moynihan wondered which of them was the worse injured. Moynihan and

152

Kilbride set to work, one man holding the artery while the other tied a cotton tourniquet around its bloodied end. Just as they finished doing so there was a savage burst of gunfire from the direction of the ruined shopfront. From the sound of the weapon Kilbride knew that it was Berger's machine gun. There was an answering burst from an AK47, and then another, longer burst from the big GPMG that sustained itself for several seconds.

Bill Berger was on the ground floor of the enemy building, pumping rounds up through the wooden ceiling where the surviving enemy gunmen were hiding. As he ceased firing a bloodied corpse tumbled down the nearby stairwell. It hit the ground with a barely audible sigh, as the lungs of the dead man emptied of their last breath.

Berger sank back into the shadows and loaded a new ammo belt. As he did so he kept his eyes on the stairwell, just in case anyone was still alive up there and capable of fighting. With a new belt of rounds in the weapon he stepped around the enemy corpse and began to climb the stairs. Five minutes later he knew that the building was clear. There were two dead bodies inside, and one dying man outside on the pavement.

Berger grabbed his walkie-talkie. 'Building clear. Let's get outta here.'

As he exited the doorway he heard a horrible gurgling noise to his left. He turned and levelled his weapon at the enemy figure on the pavement. Somehow, the burning man was still breathing, but his face was one of total agony and the eyes were begging for death. Berger fired a short burst into him, giving the man the peace of the grave.

At the front of the convoy Kilbride and Moynihan

were struggling to load Jock McKierran into the Toyota. As they did so, Kilbride forced himself to think. With half his eyeball hanging out of its socket Moynihan was useless for driving, so the two of them could tend to McKierran on the road out of there. Berger would have to take the rear vehicle, as Smithy too was out of action, and Boerke could take the truck. Which meant that he would need Emile to drive the lead Toyota and find them a route out of there.

Kilbride searched around for their Lebanese fixer, but he was nowhere to be seen. He hurried along the convoy, and as he did so he heard a faint sobbing coming from beneath the truck. He bent down and caught sight of Emile, curled into a foetal position and with his head cradled in his hands.

Kilbride reached in, grabbed Emile by the collar and dragged him to his feet. With barely a moment's hesitation he punched him once, hard, in the face. Emile flinched and stumbled backwards, recovered, and put his hand to his mouth: it came away covered in blood. He stared at it for a second, uncomprehendingly, and then a wave of anger swept over him. He lashed out, but Kilbride sidestepped the blow and grabbed Emile by his arms.

'Get a fucking grip!' he yelled. 'You hear me, Emile? No more hiding under the fucking truck and sobbing for your mother. We've got three injured, McKierran's fucking dying and I need you to drive. So get in that fucking vehicle and fucking drive! DRIVE!'

'Where to . . .?' Emile asked, falteringly. 'Which route . . .?'

'Just get us back to the safe house, Emile. We're through the fucking checkpoint so there's got to be a way. Just drive!'

154

An hour later the battered convoy rolled up at the metal gates of the safe house. Emile had been forced to take the long way around Beirut. And despite their best efforts to help him, McKierran had lost one hell of a lot of blood en route. As the vehicles pulled into the safety of the compound, Kilbride knew that it was touch and go as to whether the big Scot would make it. They'd have to lie up at the safe house all day long and make their getaway at nightfall – which meant they had several hours in which to try to save him.

It wasn't Abdul Sali's favourite way to spend a Sunday afternoon, at a drinks party at the villa of the manager of the Imperial Bank of Beirut. Still, it would have been rude not to go, and the background rumble of the renewed fighting seemed to add a certain frisson to the gathering – a group of stalwarts continuing to party as the ship went down.

Abdul Sali had a decidedly odd relationship with the English. On the one hand he admired their sang-froid – their ability to keep the bank running smoothly and the lawn perfectly mown and the party invites going out, in spite of the war. On the other hand they were infidels, Crusaders, and close friends of the cursed Israelis. In a way he would have wished them all dead, if they weren't such excellent bankers and guardians of the people's money.

He grabbed some smoked salmon from the finger buffet and vacillated over a glass of wine. Again, he was typically torn. On the one hand Islam forbade the drinking of alcohol. On the other, it seemed rude towards his English hosts to refuse. He decided to take a glass to sip from politely, ensuring that little of the evil brew would pass his lips. He looked around for someone interesting to talk to. As he did so, he noticed Timothy Cuthbert, the manager of the Imperial Bank and the host, approaching him.

'My dear Abdul Sali – wonderful to see you.' Cuthbert grabbed his hand and shook it, taking several seconds to let go. 'So good of you to come. Got to keep the home fires burning, you know.'

Before Abdul Sali could think of a suitable reply there was an interruption. A message boy had arrived. He gave a tug on Cuthbert's sleeve and whispered something in his ear.

'Private matter, old boy,' Cuthbert remarked, tapping the side of his nose. 'Back in a jiffy.'

Relieved of Cuthbert's company, Abdul Sali busied himself with a beautiful young Arab lady who worked at one of the Kuwaiti banks. Within a few minutes the two were deep in conversation. Suddenly there was a sharp rapping from behind them. Abdul Sali turned to see Cuthbert banging the flat of his hand on one of the trestle tables. It was laden with sandwiches and jugs of iced fruit juice, which sloshed about and spilled a little of their contents. The noise of chatter in the garden died away.

As Timothy Cuthbert turned to speak to his garden-party guests, Abdul Sali felt his heart miss a beat: the British banker's face had gone a deathly white. In the last five minutes he seemed to have aged as many years.

'Erm . . . Thank you all for coming,' Cuthbert announced quietly. 'Most kind . . . Got to keep a stiff upper lip, what with the war and all . . .' His voice trailed off into inaudibility. His gaze came to rest on Abdul Sali and he winced visibly. 'No easy way to say this, so here goes . . . There has been an incident at the bank. Imperial Bank, that is. Several of you esteemed

156

customers . . . An incident that is most grave and troublesome.'

'What sort of incident?' Abdul Sali blurted out.

'What sort of incident?' Cuthbert repeated. 'Well, you could say a disastrous one, Abdul Sali, distinctly disastrous. The bank lies in ruins, apparently. Looks like the rest of the Green Line now . . . Several dead militia at the scene . . . Could be militia looting, no one seems to know. But the bank's in absolute ruins.'

'But what about the *vault*?' Abdul Sali snapped.

Cuthbert took a gulp of his wine. 'The vault? The vault's history, Abdul Sali. Big gaping hole where one wall used to be. Big mess where the safes used to be. Big void where the money used to be. It's gone, Abdul Sali. Gone. Empty. Cleaned out. Whisked off into chaotic, murderous Beirut, never to be seen again, no doubt.' He shook his head. 'I can't believe it. They can't have got into the vault. Yet it's empty . . .'

Before Cuthbert had finished speaking Abdul Sali dumped his wine glass and bolted for his car.

'Take me to Bank Street!' he barked at his driver. 'Rue Riad al-Sohl. I don't care if it's in the Green Line, just get me there.'

As his silver Mercedes roared out of the villa gates Abdul Sali was already trying to plan his next move. If the bank truly was in ruins and the vault empty, where could he run to in all the world to escape the wrath of the Sheikh?

Kilbride and his men had lain low all that Sunday and tended to their wounded. Smithy and Moynihan's injuries were not life-threatening, but McKierran's condition had worsened. Partly due to the morphine they had given him and partly due to the loss of blood,

157

the big Scot was semi-delirious. During one of McKierran's more lucid moments, Kilbride had asked him if he wanted an emergency medical evacuation. It would mean breaking radio silence, and it would more than likely blow the whole operation wide open. But Jock McKierran remained adamant: he wasn't about to jeopardise their mission.

As darkness descended on the warring city Kilbride and his men changed into their black fatigues and loaded up the RIBs with the last five tons of the gold. Earlier they had divvied up Emile's share of the loot, which was remaining with him at the safe house.

Kilbride got the three RIBs roped together in line astern, with fifteen feet between each craft. That way, Boerke and Berger could take the lead boat, with one man steering and one using the night-vision unit as they coasted down the Beirut River. Smithy and Moynihan, the two walking wounded, would man the central RIB, and Kilbride would ride in the rear craft, along with Jock McKierran.

At 10 p.m. the boats were ready for departure. Kilbride, Boerke and Berger stood in the darkness on the grassy river bank and said a final, exhausted farewell to Emile. But as they turned towards the boats there was a rustle in the darkness and a ragged figure emerged from the gloom. The four men froze as the person stumbled across the ground in front of them down towards the river. He reached the old jetty and made a beeline for the makeshift bed – an old door propped up between an upturned fridge and a desk.

When he was no more than fifteen paces away the man glanced up, straight at Kilbride and his men. He stood stock-still for a second, his mouth hanging open in shock. Then he turned and fled. Kilbride levelled his

M16 at the fleeing figure, but decided against shooting. He lowered his weapon, gesturing for the others to do likewise. There had been enough killing already, and if the mystery man disappeared his friends might come looking for him.

As the figure was swallowed up by the night, a terrified voice rang out. '*Al Israelis! Al Israelis! Al Israelis!*'

Kilbride grinned wearily to himself. Whoever the mystery figure was, he had obviously mistaken Kilbride and his men for an Israeli raiding party. Which was fine, as far as Kilbride was concerned. Let the man go ahead and talk, if anyone would listen to him. Doubtless he would provide a wild report about a massive force of Israeli commandos invading Beirut from the river. It was a fine source of disinformation if ever there was one.

The journey down the Beirut River went without mishap, and by 10.30 p.m. the three craft began powering away from the cursed city. As the boats hit the open ocean Kilbride felt as though he was waking from a deep trance. For forty-eight hours greed had possessed him and his men, and they had been gripped by gold fever. *Gold fever.* That had been their mission password, and for three days they had all been totally consumed by it. But now the fever had left him. Kilbride felt exhausted. Drained. A husk. And big Jock McKierran was lying at his feet in the bottom of the boat, close to breathing his last.

Kilbride made a promise to himself there and then. Whatever else happened on this mission, if McKierran didn't make it, his family would be getting Kilbride's share of the money. There was no way Kilbride could keep it for himself. It would be small compensation for a much-loved father, brother and son, but at least it would be something.

Two hours later they reached Ramkine Island. Ward and Johno were sinking yet more of the gold to the bottom of the cave. Nightly was at the surface, loading up the gold bars to lower them to the depths. Kilbride and his team made Smithy and Moynihan comfortable, and set up a new intravenous drip for McKierran. Then they began unloading the last of the loot. When that was done Kilbride broke out the back-up radio set, powered it up and sent off a tersely worded message.

'Kilo One, Base. At FMB. Two walking wounded, one unconscious. Request immediate exfil. Urgent. Out.'

He waited several minutes before he heard the faint beep-beep-beep of the reply. It gave the nearest possible exfil time as being 9 p.m. the following evening, and provided the coordinates to rendezvous with the submarine.

The message ended with the following words: 'JJ to LK. Cat is out of bag. T-bollock knows target was hit. Prepare cover story. Base to Kilo One, out.'

'JJ' were the initials of the squadron sergeant major, Jimmy Jones, and 'LK' were Kilbride's initials. 'T-bollock' didn't require much figuring out. The SSM was giving Kilbride the nod that they were in the shit big time with Major Thistlethwaite.

Kilbride was hardly surprised. As soon as they'd taken their first casualty Kilbride had known that they would need a cover story. With McKierran now at death's door there would be serious questions asked. And in all likelihood there would be an after-action inquiry. Kilbride could think of only one cover story that just might work, and that was to tell the truth, or

160

at least ninety per cent of the truth as he saw it, backed up with some gold.

He called the men together for one last briefing and explained what he had in mind. There were no objections to his proposal from any of those present, Nightly included. Most of the men couldn't have cared less. They were sick to death of the bloody gold.

The old man sat in the shadows of his office and contemplated a dark, dark moment in the history of the struggle. He was calm. There had been others. Few as dark as this, but there *had* been others. Each time the cause had survived and they had lived to fight another day. They would survive this one, too. He stroked his beard contemplatively. Who could have done this, he wondered? Who could possibly have believed that they would get away with it? That the wrath of his people, his fearless Mujahedin, would never be unleashed upon them?

There was a gentle knock at the door. A few seconds passed and then the door opened a crack. The bearded face of a younger man peered around it, hesitantly. With difficulty the old man pulled his focus back to the present and ushered the figure into the room. The younger man seated himself before him, and waited for the tea ritual to begin. Without even bothering with it the old man began to speak. It was a sign of the urgency of the moment that the tea ritual had been dispensed with. Such a thing had never happened before.

'What news, Ahmed?' the old man asked of his lieutenant.

'Sheikh . . .' the younger man began, spreading his hands before him. 'As yet, we have nothing. There is not a whisper on the streets as to who is responsible for this

161

monstrous crime. But we will find them. Given time we will find them. And then vengeance shall be ours . . .'

The Sheikh held up a hand to silence the younger man. 'No talk of vengeance . . . Waste none of your energy on thoughts of vengeance. Focus every essence of your being on finding them. That is your sole and only task. *Find them*. And find the people's money. Once you have done that, *then* we will talk of a vengeance that will be Allah's own . . .'

'As you say, Sheikh. Your words, as always, are deeply wise.'

The Sheikh nodded, and began to pour some tea.

'Sheikh . . .' the younger man said, hesitantly. 'There is one thing. A fool of a Syrian labourer who sleeps down by the river. He swears blind that he saw a force of Israeli commandos . . .'

The Sheikh looked up sharply, his hooded eyes looking like those of a hawk. 'When was this?'

'In the early hours of Sunday morning. It would fit with the timing of the raid. But Israeli commandos raiding the Imperial Bank of Beirut? It makes no sense . . .'

'It would make *every* sense,' the Sheikh snapped. 'But how would they have known our money was there? It is almost inconceivable . . . *Abdul Sali al-Misri!* Abdul Sali al-Misri, our *trusted* banker who appears to have disappeared into thin air. What of him? Has that dog come to heel yet? Has that mongrel cur been tracked to his lair?'

'We have searched his residence and his country retreat. There is no sign of him at either. He is running. But we will run faster and further and we will find him.'

'It is good.'

'You think he bears some responsibility, Sheikh? That he might have been . . . somehow . . . involved?

Surely he is no friend of the Israelis?'

'Who knows? Money makes strange bedfellows . . .
We need to find him. I have some questions to put to
him. Many, many questions.'

Major Thistlethwaite leaned back in his chair as he eyed
Kilbride. The Lieutenant stood there before him,
dishevelled, unshaven and unwashed, the scent of war
still strong upon him. His eyes were red and puffy with
sleeplessness, his shoulders slumped with exhaustion.
The Major had him exactly where he wanted him and
was determined to show no mercy.

'Let's get this absolutely straight,' the Major said,
glancing across at Sergeant Major Jones and grinning
smugly. 'You have one member of your troop at death's
door and two badly wounded; you've fired off enough
ordnance to fight a small war; you have eight-point-
seven-five tons of gold in your possession, which was
until recently the property of the Imperial Bank of
Beirut. And this is all a result of a failure in radio
communications – is that it?'

'Yep,' said Kilbride.

'So, just what on earth possessed you to go in and
clean out the Imperial Bank of Beirut's vault? My
original orders were crystal clear: HMG were after
some terrorist papers, not the whole bloody gold
reserves of the bank! In addition to which, you were
ordered to withdraw. *To withdraw.* How do you
explain that little lot, Kilbride?'

'I can't.'

'Let's recap, shall we? No one ordered you to assault
the bank – in fact, you were ordered to withdraw. But
attack it you did, regardless of your orders. No one
ordered you to raid the bank vault, but raid it you did.

163

No one ordered you to steal fifty million dollars' worth of gold bullion, but you proceeded to do so anyway. And in the process you have ended up with one man practically dead and two others seriously injured. It's the sort of stuff that nightmares are made of. You're finished, wouldn't you say so, Kilbride?'

'Probably.'

'I would just volunteer one thing in Kilbride's favour,' Sergeant Major Jones interjected. The Major had placed him at the end of his desk and to one side so that he could witness Kilbride's full humiliation.

'Would you, indeed, Sergeant Major? Extraordinary. I'm listening. In fact, I'm all ears. I can't imagine what in the world you could possibly find to say in Kilbride's *favour*, but do go on.'

'Well, it may be hard to understand why the silly sod did what he did, but it wasn't for his own benefit, was it? I mean, he got the terrorist documents and the gold's been delivered to Cyprus – all fifty million dollars of it. So it's not as if they thieved it for themselves, or anything.'

'Kilbride, do you think you deserve credit for what the Sergeant Major has just pointed out? Or do you think it just makes you appear doubly stupid? Doubly incompetent? Your actions doubly illogical? Or is the only possible conclusion to be reached that you are clinically insane?'

'I don't give a shit,' said Kilbride. 'I'm dog-tired. I've got two men badly wounded, another one fighting for his life. I need to get a wash, a sleep and to be with my men. I don't give a shit, Major. End of story.'

Kilbride turned to leave.

'If you walk out of that door, Kilbride, I will be recommending you for a court martial.' Kilbride kept walking. 'And not just you, Kilbride. Think about it: you walk out that door and it's nine dishonourable discharges. That's one for you, and one for each of your men. I'll even argue the same for the dead man, McKierran, as by all reports he stands little chance of making it. That's all of you Kilbride. *All your merry men.*'

Kilbride spun around to face the Major. 'Bastard! This has got fuck all to do with my men . . . *I* may have disobeyed orders but *they* did not. They were under my command for every minute of this mission. Whatever we did out there, I ordered my men to do it. So don't try and fuck with them too.'

'So you *admit* you disobeyed orders?' said the Major, with a triumphant sneer. 'He admits it! Incredible – he actually admits it! Odd, that – because I have been repeatedly told that your radio unit was inoperable, so it was nothing more than a communications break-down. But no, the truth is finally out: you deliberately disobeyed orders, didn't you, Kilbride?'

Kilbride was tired of all this, tired of the Major and all his shit. It was time to tell it like it was. 'Correct – there never was a radio malfunction. I bent the lug pins in the battery housing. Get it checked out. It's completely fine. I told my men the radio had gone down and ordered them to hit the bank. They acted on my orders because I am their troop leader and it's what they're trained to do. So to clarify matters, for the record, with the Sergeant Major as my witness – *I alone disobeyed orders*. You can do your fucking worst with me, Marcus, but not with my men.'

'As a confession of guilt, that's a pretty superlative one, Kilbride. I'll start preparing your court-martial papers right away, shall I? But before I do, any chance you might enlighten me as to the *motive* behind your freelance bank robbery? I'm just curious. It would make the case against you one hundred per cent perfect, not just ninety-nine per cent perfect, as it is now. Bank robbers don't normally hand over the loot at the end of the job, do they? Or am I missing something?'

'You ever wanted to prove someone wrong?' said Kilbride, quietly. 'You know, prove them wrong whatever the cost? Someone who's got their head so far up their own backside they have to clean their teeth through their arsehole? You said the plan for the raid would never work, Marcus. Piece of *shit*, you called it. I proved you wrong. Simple as that, really.'

The Major turned back to his desk and began writing. 'Get out, Kilbride,' he snapped. 'You're finished. I would imagine a place will be found for you on the first flight back to Britain. Best you go and say your goodbyes . . . Oh, and one more thing,' he added, without bothering to look up. 'Before you leave, I'm going to have the Sergeant Major search your gear, and that of your men – just in case you forgot to hand over *all* the loot. I don't actually believe you're smart enough to have hidden any, but just in case.'

Kilbride's face remained a blank, inscrutable mask. 'Do I have your word that you'll leave my men out of this? They were under orders. Their actions should attract no blame.'

'Listen, Kilbride, if I can find a way to send the whole bloody lot of you down, I will. You and your little fan club, your troop – you're all alike. Birds of a feather . . . No discipline . . . You're the problem, the whole bloody lot of you. And this will be a finer unit when the madmen like you are gone. Get out, Kilbride. Leave. You're history.'

166

Kilbride glanced across at Sergeant Major Jones, and with a flick of his eyes he indicated the door. The burly Sergeant Major inclined his head imperceptibly, and slipped quietly from the room. Kilbride stood his ground and waited for the Major to notice the ice-cold predatory essence that had crept into the room. The Major glanced up from his desk. Kilbride stared at him, a current of brute, animal aggression lying just below the surface of the coal-black pools of his eyes. The Major twitched. He tried to hold Kilbride's gaze, then lost his nerve. For a second he searched for Sergeant Major Jones, his head darting about nervously.

Kilbride stepped closer to the desk and leaned forward until he was eyeball to eyeball with the Major. 'It's no use, Marcus, you're on your own,' he announced, quietly, his voice laden with menace. The Major recoiled from Kilbride's breath, just inches from his face. 'You're a lucky man, Marcus – I'm willing to do a deal with you. You leave my men out of this and I'll take your court martial, Major. I'll never darken your door again.'

Kilbride paused. 'But you go after my men, and I promise you you'll never be shot of me. Not even when I'm on the outside. This will never be finished – *not until I say it's over*. In some dark alley, down some deserted country lane, at home with your family snugly asleep upstairs – I'll find you, Marcus, I'll find you. When you're least expecting it, I'll find you. Wherever you are, I'll find you. I'll track you down and I'll root you out and I'll exact my revenge . . .'

The Major stared up at Kilbride. His jaw hung slack and his face had gone a sickly shade of pale.

'You fuck with my men, Marcus, and I promise you I'll pursue you to the grave. And when I find you, you'll

167

wish you were already dead. Don't ever forget, Marcus: I've made you a promise. A solemn promise. And I never break my fucking promises . . .'

With that Kilbride spun on his heel and strode away. As he headed off to check on his wounded men he was nursing a cold, murderous rage. He entered the ops tent and spotted a familiar figure hunched over a chessboard. It was Knotts-Lane. Kilbride ignored him and headed for the rear. Ernie Jones, the radio operator, was in the midst of transcribing a message.

'Any news, mate?' Kilbride asked. 'Smithy and Moynihan? Jock McKierran?'

'Not much. There's this just come in.' He handed Kilbride the scribbled message. 'Says Smithy and Moynihan are on a flight out of here, back home by midday today – their condition's stable. As for McKierran – he's too bad to be flown anywhere, so he's staying at the hospital . . .'

Kilbride glanced over the message. 'Thanks, mate. Keep me posted, will you?'

Kilbride turned to leave. As he did so he noticed Knotts-Lane staring over at him. The man's eyes were a deep reptilian green as they tracked him across the tent, and Kilbride noticed an air of smug satisfaction about him. It made his blood boil.

'You seem happy,' Kilbride announced, as he went to pass. 'Just beat yourself at chess again? Or are you celebrating the improvement to your face from that pig-ugly scar?'

'Guess you'll be sad to be leaving us,' Knotts-Lane remarked, ignoring Kilbride's jibe. He had a barely perceptible sneer on his face. 'Well – we'll all be sad to be losing you, too.'

Kilbride paused. 'I didn't know I was leaving.'

'Word is you are. No big surprise, really, not after your little Beirut caper. Pulling a stunt like that can end a man's career. Must be the influence of that dumb American rubbing off on you . . .'

'A stunt like what – radio failure? I didn't know having radio failure was such a fucking crime.'

'Radio failure? Come on – you'll have to do better than that. Like I said, I know you, Kilbride. You've been up to something.'

'So tell me what you know.'

'I know *I*'d like to know where you stashed the gold.'

'Actually, I was planning on stuffing it up your arse. Might stop you from talking out of it the whole fucking time.'

Twenty-four hours later Kilbride was strapped into a seat in a C130 Hercules transport aircraft. As the plane climbed away from Cyprus, he stared out across the glittering waters of the Mediterranean. Somewhere out there lay Ramkine Island – and one hundred million dollars in gold bullion hidden beneath the waves. Seven days earlier he had made a pact with his men to rob the Imperial Bank of Beirut. One of them, McKierran, was still at death's door. Kilbride had visited him in the army medical unit, but the big Scot had still been unconscious. And two of them, Smithy and Moynihan, might well be invalided out of the services. Kilbride knew that the responsibility was chiefly his. It was a heavy burden to bear.

If this mission and his pending court martial were ever going to make any sense to him, Kilbride would have to return to fetch that gold. For only by doing so could he possibly make amends.

PART TWO

CHAPTER EIGHT

Present Day: Kigamboni Beach, Tanzania, East Africa

Kilbride curled his toes in the hot tropical sand, settled further into his deck chair, reached across for a chilled beer from the picnic table and glanced across at Berger. The big Yank was standing in the shade of the lush forest that backed onto the beach. He was doing his best to chat up Kilbride's maid, who was preparing a lunch of fresh-caught fish. Typical: Berger never had been able to keep his hands off the ladies.

Kilbride drained his beer and gave Berger a shout. Twenty minutes later the two men were ploughing through the brilliant blue of the sea on their fibreglass long boards, scanning the gently undulating horizon for the next big swell. There was always a lull like this, and then the strongest waves tended to come in sets of four. The trick was to wait for the right moment to catch the big one.

Behind the blinding white sands of the Tanzanian coastline lay a green swathe of jungle, rolling onwards towards a distant range of hills. The squat silvery trunks of baobab trees dotted the forest, broad of beam and implacable. For Kilbride, the baobab had come to symbolise Africa, and Africa had come to mean home. There was a sense of space and freedom here that Europe had long ago lost. It was awesomely beautiful country – apart from the sharks that lurked in the waters. But they came with the territory.

Kilbride and Berger were in their fifties now, and they both needed something to keep the juices flowing. Surfing was the thing, and the sharks just gave an added touch of adrenalin-boosting risk. Neither Berger nor Kilbride had ever completely lost their fitness from the years spent in The Regiment (and, in Berger's case, Delta Force). They could just about hold their own with some of the younger surfers.

The American spotted a big swell. 'What d'you reckon, buddy?'

Kilbride glanced at the blinding blue horizon, shading his eyes. 'The second one? Yeah, let's do it.'

As the big wave approached, both men turned and began paddling furiously towards the beach. For a second Kilbride heard the roar of the water over his shoulder, and then he felt the powerful thrust of it lifting the tail of his board. He paddled faster, trying to catch the wave and become part of it as it raced in towards the thin sliver of silver that marked the distant shoreline. His board accelerated and in one swift movement he sprang into a standing position, his legs bent at the knees.

Moments later Kilbride executed a quick roller turn, swivelling his shoulders to face the wave and riding up the front of the wall of water. He reached the foaming white of the wave crest and went to flip the board around. But he was no longer as flexible as he had once been. As he shifted his weight to his front Kilbride lost his footing, and in an instant he had wiped out. The wave swallowed him, sucking him under and trapping him in its roaring, throaty depths.

Kilbride felt its raw power bending him over and arching his back, the individual vertebrae popping as it did so. It was a horrible feeling. He held his breath and tried to relax. Twenty seconds later the wave spat him out of its rear side. Kilbride took a massive gulp of air and floundered around for the smooth fibreglass of his board, heaving his body onto it again. He lay there, gasping for breath and scanning the horizon for the next wave. The last thing he wanted was to be hit again and go under for a second time.

He glanced towards the beach, but Bill Berger was nowhere to be seen. He must have caught the wave well and surfed in towards the shallows. Kilbride did a quick mental inventory of his body to check if there was any damage. Fifteen years in the SAS had left its mark on him, but there were no new or unusual pains and he seemed to be okay. He rested his head on his forearms, breathed deeply, and stared out to sea.

Kilbride's mind wandered to thoughts of the Lebanon. Bill Berger reckoned the time was right to go and fetch their gold, and Kilbride was tempted to agree with him. At the time of the bank raid Kilbride had thought the Lebanese civil war might last a couple more years at most. But it had dragged on for a decade, the killings and counter-killings sparing no one. Dozens of ceasefires had come and gone, and each time the hatred had proved incurable. Christians, Muslims, Palestinians, Lebanese – all of them had innocent blood on their hands. It had looked as if nothing could bring about an end to the killing.

But then a force of fifty thousand Syrian troops had invaded the Lebanon, and under Syria's iron fist the fighting finally stopped. But a new form of terror took its place, with Syrian-sponsored assassinations and killings becoming the norm. With Syria's blessing, and backed by Iranian money and arms, thousands of Palestinian refugees formed armed militias to wage war on Israel on the Lebanon's southern border. Israel countered by invading and occupying the south of the country.

The militias took their fight to the world stage: the Lebanon became the number one sponsor of global terrorism. Armed factions hijacked aircraft, blew up embassies and kidnapped like there was no tomorrow. By the early 1990s Hezbollah alone was said to have thirty thousand men under arms. These armed groups worked in close cooperation with the Syrian secret police as a shadow – and shadowy – paramilitary force. And for twenty years the Lebanon had remained a closed – and terrorised – nation.

Kilbride had returned to the Lebanon twice to try and assess the chances of retrieving their gold. The first time had been in 1987, a year after the end of the civil war. He had travelled alone, posing as a journalist. But at every turn he had been followed and harassed by the notorious Syrian secret police, complete with their 1970s-style leather jackets and huge mirror-shades. It had quickly become clear to him that there was little hope of returning with his men to salvage their 17.5 tons of hidden treasure.

Ten years later he was back again, flying into Beirut in the company of Bill Berger. This time the Syrian secret police had intercepted him upon arrival at the airport. One look at his and Bill Berger's passports – a

176

Brit and an American who together had stamps covering most of the world's war zones – and hours of questioning followed. Eventually, the Syrians had convinced themselves that Berger and Kilbride were Israeli spies, and they were frogmarched onto a return flight home.

But now all that had changed. Under the threat of international sanctions Syria had been forced to withdraw. In the power vacuum that followed, Hezbollah and Israel had gone to war. But faced with a barrage of international outrage both sides had rapidly tired of the fighting, and peace had been restored. Kilbride could hardly believe it, but Beirut city was being rebuilt as a thriving business and social centre, and the economy was on the up. Most importantly of all, foreign tourists were returning to the Lebanon in their droves.

European and American visitors were rediscovering the fabulous sun and sea of the Lebanon's Mediterranean coastline, and this provided the perfect cover for Kilbride and his team to return and recover their loot. In between partying, sunning themselves and doing a touch of scuba diving they could sneak off to the Palm Islands and quietly salvage their 17.5 tons of gold. Or at least, that was what Bill Berger had argued over a couple of beers the previous evening.

Kilbride could find few reasons not to go along with this, apart from the obvious one: of his original team Kilbride himself now had the most to lose. A decade ago there had been a private diamond security operation in West Africa, and Kilbride had got lucky. He had saved his client's life. In return, the grateful diamond dealer had ensured that Kilbride walked away a relatively rich man. It was nothing compared to the sort of treasure hidden in that cave in the Lebanon. But it was enough to have bought him a slice of idyllic Tanzanian beach, to have built him his dream home, and to have set up his dive-tour business.

Kilbride glanced across the water at the big wooden dhow, moored at the jetty off the beach. She was a graceful Al Sambuq vessel, of Arabian design and build, and she was part of what the diamond money had paid for. Originally, she had been built as a cargo vessel and a pearl diver, but now she was used exclusively for carrying dive tourists. The 2D logo – the Diving Dhow – was plastered across her bow, in yard-high lettering, alongside her name, the *Marie-Claire*. He wondered how the first Marie-Claire, his wife, would react if he told her he was going back to the Lebanon.

He pushed that thought to the back of his mind as a breaker rolled in towards him. Deciding to let it pass, he turned to face the wave, rose up on one knee, pushed the nose of his board underwater, and then dropped down flat as the wave hit. Man and board sliced through the base of the wave, coming to the surface on the other side. Kilbride was about to congratulate himself on a classic surfer's duck dive when he felt a painful twinge in his lower back. It was in exactly the same spot as an old war wound from his final days in the SAS.

After the Lebanon bank raid Kilbride had been placed on a court martial, at the insistence of Major Thistlethwaite. But Kilbride's overall boss at The Regiment had done little to hide his opposition to this. Citing reasons of 'operational secrecy' he had kept getting Kilbride's hearing date pushed backwards, keeping Kilbride deployed on classified operations overseas. In 1981 he had been sent to Afghanistan, as part of a small clandestine force training the Mujahedin to fight the Soviet Red Army. But three months into the mission he'd taken a fall down a cliff and smashed several vertebrae in his lower back.

With the court martial still hanging over him, Kilbride had taken this as his cue to get out of The Regiment. In the spring of 1983 he had cut his losses and resigned – but not before Major Thistlethwaite had got his comeuppance. Three years previously the SAS had been involved in its most high-profile mission ever – the breaking of the Iranian Embassy siege, in London. Millions of viewers had watched the assault live on TV. In an instant the SAS had become a household name and The Regiment's most persistent critics had been silenced. And Major Thistlethwaite had been quietly transferred into a different line of business.

Kilbride had gone on to work in the private military sector. He'd spent the next ten years doing security jobs for oil companies and mining operations in remote corners of Africa. There had been one or two small wars, but nothing to write home about. And like several other ex-SAS men Kilbride had agreed to be kept 'on call' by Her Majesty's Government, just in case his specialist services were ever required. In due course he'd taken on half a dozen jobs, all of which were ultra-secret deniable operations – highly paid, but with a high degree of risk involved.

After each of those clandestine ops, Kilbride had found himself returning to work in Africa. Over time, he started to feel more and more at home there. It was a raw, untamed continent, with wide-open spaces and a lawlessness and freedom that suited his maverick ways. In Africa, Kilbride could be a free spirit with few ties. And whilst there had been many women over the years, there were none who had managed to pin him down.

A fling in his early thirties with Sarah, an English girl, had resulted in a son, Mick. But the relationship hadn't lasted, and they'd gone their separate ways. Kilbride remained close to Mick, who was a chip off the old block. He'd been chuffed as nuts when Mick followed his dad into UK special forces – joining the Special Boat Service. Mick had spent a year on exchange with the SEALs – the US military's equivalent of the SBS. He'd loved every minute of it, especially the American girls' fondness for his 'cute English accent'.

But when Kilbride was in his late forties he'd fallen for Marie-Claire, a Tanzanian air hostess. He'd met her on a British Airways flight from London to Dar-es-Salaam, Tanzania's former capital city. She was the most beautiful, gentle woman he'd ever dated, and he figured that if she'd have him, then it was time to hang up the gloves. Over several months he'd persuaded her to stop working the long-haul flights – BA, thrice weekly to London. As her parents were keen to see them married, Kilbride had obliged. They'd built their dream home on the paradise beach plot and had set up the diving business.

Two sons had followed, and together with their dog Sally that made up Kilbride's happy family. A daughter would be good, he figured, but there was time enough for that. His big son, Mick, had just left the military and gone into private security work – which left him plenty of time to drop by The Homestead each Christmas to share some beers and some war stories with his dad. All in all it was a good life and Kilbride was happy with it – that was until Bill Berger had started banging on about the Lebanon gold again.

Bill Berger was typical of the breed, Kilbride reflected. After a career in Delta Force distinguished far more by heroic actions than by advancement in rank, Bill Berger had joined Kilbride on the private-security circuit. A wild adventurer at heart, he'd made and lost a bundle of money and had burned his way through two marriages. It was the nature of the work that there were a lot of foreign locations and a lot of foreign women. Each time Bill Berger's wife of the moment had found out what he'd been up to she'd taken him for all he was worth.

From what Kilbride knew of the other lads from the original Beirut bank job, few of them were faring a great deal better. Only Boerke seemed to be doing all right: he'd returned to South Africa and was running a bar that doubled as a brothel.

Kilbride flicked his gaze towards the horizon. The tide was turning, and with it the swell had died. He glanced towards the beach. Bill Berger was standing in the shallows, waving him in. Kilbride kicked out for the shore. Nixon, his Tanzanian cook, would have lunch ready by now – hopefully some fresh-caught red snapper, grilled over an open fire on the beach. Life was good, Kilbride reflected. But he could feel a change coming, feel the irresistible draw of that gold bullion hidden in that cave in the Lebanon.

If anything, the years had been kind to him. His hair was a little whiter, his beard longer and more tangled, his eyes sunken and shadowed by dark, craggy brows. But the sparse frame of the old man belied his general good health. A life of abstinence and devotion to the struggle and the one true God had seen him reach a grand age. The weather was a few degrees colder here in the Syrian mountains, less gentle on his old bones. And there were few of the domestic comforts of Beirut to ease his passage to the other side. But he didn't seem to

181

be suffering. He had recently been given a full medical by a Syrian doctor: his cholesterol was low, his blood pressure normal and his heart remained strong.

Paradise still seemed as if it might be a long way off, the old man reflected wryly. Which was a good thing, because he still had a great deal to do in this world. To lead such a glorious resurgence, to walk in the footsteps of the Old Man of the Mountains, the legendary leader of the original Assassins – this was a truly honourable calling. Some of the younger recruits had even started calling him by the same name – 'the Old Man of the Mountains'. This was something he did not encourage. He was the spiritual figurehead of the Black Assassins, and that alone was enough. He didn't require a grand title.

Theirs was a mission that would rock the infidel West like never before, the old man reflected. It would prove once and for all that Islam was the one true faith and that its warriors were on the march. Should they succeed – and he could foresee no reason why they would not – doubtless his reward would be great in Paradise, whenever he might reach it.

There was a gentle knock at the door. The old man looked up through his tired eyes. Little light filtered into the underground bunker where he kept his office and spartan quarters. They were ill-lit by one bare bulb hanging from the ceiling and a couple of spluttering oil lanterns. No matter. The old man had cataracts, and his eyesight was fading, so the lack of light troubled him little. Most importantly, his mind remained sharp, his concentration focused, his intentions crystal clear and unshakeable.

'Come in,' he commanded softly.

The door opened and a figure entered the room. He

182

had a craggy face and close-cropped, sandy hair. His eyes were a piercing cat-like emerald green, and they shone with an unusual level of fervour. The visitor took a seat as indicated by the old man, and sat cross-legged before him on a rug on the floor. They shook hands, both touching their palm to their chest in a gesture of peace. The visitor looked his age, his features folded and lined with the years, the track of an old scar disfiguring his right cheek. But like the hide of a rhino his was a tough skin, and his expression was now strengthened by a burning religious zeal.

The Searcher prided himself on having lost little of his prowess over the years. What he now lacked in physical strength he more than made up for in experience, plus the cunning and guile of the veteran warrior. The old man gestured with his eyes to the burns on The Searcher's forearms and hands, where he had shielded his face from the Viper Strike's terrible blast. Several weeks ago the bandages had come off, and the wounds appeared to be healing well. This was more than could be said for several dozen of the other brothers, who had been torn to pieces by the Americans' cowardly air strike. No matter, the old man reflected, the number of recruits to the cause was limitless, or so it seemed.

'You are healing well?' the old man asked.

A faint smile curled The Searcher's lips. 'Your Holiness, for an old warrior I seem to recover quickly.' For a foreigner, he spoke almost faultless Arabic.

'It is good,' the old man murmured. 'It is the faith that keeps you strong, my brother, healing the body of a true believer.'

The old man indicated the tea things with a gentle sweep of his hand. He served – the age-old ritual unchanged, the brass pot lifted high to pour a stream of foaming liquid into each glass. He pushed a bowl of sugar towards his visitor. He never had quite worked out whether this foreign warrior, this convert to the One True Faith, did or did not take sugar. Sometimes he seemed to have six lumps; at other times he abstained completely. He was hard to fathom as a man generally, a true enigma. He was the old enemy, yet here he was in their midst behaving as one of the truest believers. Why was it that the converts always seemed to be the most zealous? the old man reflected. Their adherence to the faith seemed more absolute, somehow, their hatred of the infidels more all-consuming.

The old man raised a glass to his lips. 'Doubtless it is important business that brings you to speak with me, Muhammad Mohajir.'

Muhammad Mohajir – Muhammad the Searcher – was the visitor's chosen Islamic name. The old man knew that he had also called himself The Searcher in his previous life. He hoped that now he had found the one true faith he had truly stopped searching.

'It must be exceedingly important business,' the old man continued. 'For what else would make you break off training the brothers? What else would make you halt the preparations for their sacred mission? And all to come to speak to an old man like me?'

'Sheikh, Your Holiness, there is something I heard within the camp that both worries and excites me. In the sickbay I overheard some brothers talking. If I may . . .'

'Please, speak freely.'

The Searcher's eyes were burning with excitement. 'Sheikh, I heard that you are searching for some gold that went missing during the Beirut civil war. And whilst this may not be the Holy Mission that you have allocated to me . . .'

'Go on, Brother Mohajir.'

'I'm grateful, Sheikh. I think I know who stole your gold, and I may even have an idea where it is. I believe it remains hidden in the Lebanon somewhere . . .'

The old man looked up sharply. 'How so, Brother Mohajir? How is it possible? How could you know?'

The Searcher stared at the floor. 'Sheikh, before discovering the one true faith, before making the acquaintance of Your Holiness, I served for another cause. This you know. I was lost for many years . . . During that previous life, I served with the British SAS – the forces of the infidels. In January 1979 there was an operation in Beirut against the Imperial Bank of Beirut. The raid was carried out by a group of nine men who blasted their way into the vault. One man almost died and two were badly injured—'

'It cannot be,' the Sheikh cut in, barely able to hide his astonishment. 'British soldiers robbed the bank? But how? And why? And how did they . . .'

The old man's words trailed off. He had just been struck by the enormity of what his visitor was saying – that was if it was true. Of all the different groups that he had suspected over the years – the Christian Militia, the Israelis, the Italian Mafia even – this possibility had never crossed his mind. Part of him doubted the visitor's story, but what on earth would possess him to lie? If he trusted this brother to train the elite of the Black Assassins for the most important mission in the history of Islam, why should he doubt him now? The old man gestured for The Searcher to continue.

'Sheikh, these nine men brought back fifty million dollars in gold bullion to our base. But at the time I suspected there was more. Now I am convinced of it, and that the portion of gold they hid was yours, Your

Holiness – or at least the gold of the people, of the struggle. It sounds incredible, Sheikh, and I can see that you are shaken by it . . .'

'If you tell me it is so, I think I must believe you, Brother Mohajir . . .'

'It is difficult to understand the mindset of these people, but they are driven by the basest desires. Money, women, life's ephemeral luxuries – all things that are transient, that pass. They care little for the eternal in life – for belief, for faith, for finding the one true path.'

The old man nodded. 'I can conceive that it might be thus with these infidels. Continue.'

'Sheikh, I now believe that they hid this gold somewhere between Beirut city and their Cyprus base – which has to mean somewhere in the Lebanon. And I believe it is still there, Sheikh.'

The old man held up his hand, to silence The Searcher. 'Please tell me all that you know. But please, no conjecture. We are in no hurry – so start from the very beginning. Give me only the facts to which you yourself can testify before Allah. Let us build up the fullest picture based upon facts only. Then we can move into the realms of conjecture.' He began pouring some more tea. 'How did you first hear of this, brother? And who was in charge of the operation?'

An hour later The Searcher had finished telling the Sheikh all that he knew about the Beirut bank job. The old man reached behind him, opened a wooden chest and pulled out a scrap of paper. He held it out to his visitor.

'Brother Mohajir, perhaps this will make some sense to you? I have had this for many years, and always it has remained a mystery to me. That is, perhaps, until today . . .'

The Searcher glanced at the paper. It was a hand-scrawled list of names. 'Mr Boss. Mr Busman. Mr Bronchos. Mr Smithilee. Mr Nightilee . . .'

'I was given this by one of the bank security guards,' the old man added. 'Before he escaped he overheard some of their names . . . But I have never heard of names such as these. The last two sound almost . . . Indian?'

The Searcher shook his head in amazement. 'It is a list of names.' He glanced up from the paper and smiled. 'Your Holiness, these are the men who carried out the raid, only these are their *nicknames*. And they're so badly spelled you'd never guess . . . If you have another sheet of paper, Sheikh, I think I can remember all of their real names. Plus there was a Lebanese fixer with them, one Emile Abdeen.'

The old man reached behind him in the shadows. 'And there was this,' he announced. He turned around and held out a faded-looking Rubik's Cube. 'It was found in the bank vault itself.' The old man spread his hands in a gesture of bewilderment. 'Tell me, does it also mean something?'

The Searcher shook his head in amazement. 'The South African . . . Boerke. He left his calling card behind . . . If you have that sheet of paper, Sheikh, I'll give you all their names.'

Kilbride's beachside home had been designed by an old school friend, a high-flying architect who lived in London. He had started by mapping out all twelve acres of the site, including every tree of any consequence. During construction the house and three guest cottages were skilfully woven into the forest. From the simple

187

wood-and-glass windows and whitewashed walls of the main residence, a series of raised wooden walkways radiated out to the guest cottages and down to the nearby beach and pier. The bulbous baobab trees, with their twisting, stubby limbs, thrust their bulk over and above the property, half obscuring it from view. And as dusk fell the noise of insects was quite deafening, as the darkness of the forest enveloped all.

Kilbride had called the place 'The Homestead'. It was the first time since his teens that he had lived in his own home, as opposed to a military base or camp, or a rented hotel room. Power was provided by solar panels, so there was never a shortage of hot water or electricity. From the military point of view, of course, The Homestead was a complete disaster. Had it been designed with defence in mind, a 500-yard swathe of vegetation would have been cleared on all sides, to offer good fields of fire. As it was, any attacker could get to within mere feet of the place without being seen. But Kilbride hadn't built it with such in mind: he hoped that he'd more or less left those days behind him.

The tourists loved The Homestead as a departure point for dhow trips, diving on the reefs or dolphin watching. There was a campsite at one end of the beach where most chose to stay, and a five-star hotel a little further down the coastline. Whilst the sun would beat down all day long from a burning African sky, The Homestead remained bathed in the cool shadows of the forest. It was the perfect place for the visitors to have a relaxing sundowner at the end of a day at sea. All night long the gentle rhythm of the ocean would soothe the sleep of those staying at The Homestead. And as dawn broke over the still sea Kilbride often fancied he could hear a leaf falling in the silent forest.

Invariably the first awake, Kilbride would leave a sleeping Marie-Claire and pad barefoot down the walkway towards the beach. On his way, he would pop his head around the door of his two sons' room. If the elder, David, was awake, he would sling him over his shoulder and carry him down to the beach. Once released, David would scurry across the sand, chasing crabs down their holes. If David was asleep, Kilbride would fetch Sally, his German shepherd, and go for a long jog on the pristine night-cool sands. Sally was an ex-SAS war dog, and fiercely loyal to Kilbride. They retired their military dogs early from The Regiment, for obvious reasons, so she was still relatively young and fit.

When Bill Berger had invited himself to stay, Kilbride had told him that he was welcome on two conditions. One, he wasn't to discuss the Lebanon mission in front of Marie-Claire. Kilbride didn't want to worry her unnecessarily. Two, he had to keep his fucking hands off Kilbride's maid. Tashana was a beautiful young girl from the local Chagga tribe, and rumour had it she was about to be married. Her fiancé was said to be a young Chagga fisherman with muscles like iron, and Kilbride didn't want the big American causing any trouble.

Originally, Kilbride had objected to having any domestic staff at all. He had always led a fiercely independent existence and he saw no reason why his family life should be any different. But then his wife had explained things. In the nearby villages Kilbride would be seen as a man of immense wealth and standing. He would be expected to provide some local employment. Not to do so would be seen as deeply insulting, and would alienate the local community.

So now they had Tashana, the maid; Nixon, the cook; and a group of six young men who crewed the dhow. Although Kilbride paid them well by local standards, his monthly wage bill was far from crippling. It was the down season right now in Tanzania, the midst of the January rains, so his ship's crew were laid off until the summer. Nixon, their giant of a chef, was a permanent fixture at The Homestead. He'd been with Kilbride for a decade or so, and Kilbride trusted him about as much as he had ever trusted any man, including his mates in The Regiment.

The evening after their surfing adventures Kilbride and Berger headed down to The Slipway, a swanky new development on the southern side of Dar-es-Salaam. The Slipway Bar was a short drive from The Homestead, and was one of Kilbride's favourite watering holes. It had a relaxed low-key atmosphere and a shaded terrace built out over the sea. Kilbride and Berger each ordered a Kilimanjaro beer and settled down to enjoy the warm African evening. At a table three away from them sat a group of local girls dressed in tight jeans and figure-hugging T-shirts. As they chatted and laughed and flashed their smiles, Bill Berger could hardly keep his eyes off them.

The beers arrived, ice-cold and beaded with drops of moisture. Kilbride took a thirsty pull on his. 'That's goooood . . .' He tried to catch Bill Berger's eye. 'I've been thinking over what you said last night, mate. Maybe you're right – maybe it is the right time to go—'

'Say, buddy, where do all these women *come from*?' the big American interrupted. 'I mean, is it *always* like this? Everywhere I fuckin' go they're bursting out of their hot pants, tight little arses like you never seen before . . . I mean, if you'd goddamn *told* me it was like this I might never have married that Jewish-American bitch and got in the mess I am now . . .'

Kilbride leaned across the table and swiped his friend's bottle. 'Hey!' Berger objected. 'Gimme back my beer . . .'

'Keep your eyes off the women and your mind on the job in hand,' Kilbride told him, with a steely grin. 'There'll be plenty of time for that later, when the rest of the troops arrive.'

Kilbride handed Berger his beer. The big American took a defiant swig. 'Ain't never no harm in looking. Anyway, what d'you mean, "the rest of the troops"?'

'Don't know if you noticed, mate, but when you were drinking beer and flirting with my maid I was off working. I sent a quick email to the boys, suggesting a meeting at my place. It's January and pissing with rain in England or Ireland or wherever, and I got an overwhelming response.' Kilbride raised his beer. 'It looks like were going to have company.'

The two men drank a toast. 'Nice work, buddy. So who's coming?'

'I got four confirmed – Smithy, Moynihan, Ward and Johno. Boerke's got a clunky internet connection down in the South African veld somewhere, but he'll confirm. Nightly's trying to get clearance from the wife. Only Jock McKierran I've not heard back from. But that's not unusual. Months go by and I don't hear much from the man . . .'

'How's he doin'? I ain't seen nor heard much of him since Beirut . . .'

Kilbride glanced at Berger, a troubled look on his tanned features. 'He's confined to his wheelchair, isn't he, and that isn't going to change. When he was hit, I thought it was just the artery was gone. But the bullet

191

must've ricocheted off his pelvic bone and lodged in his lower back. They got it out, but the damage was already done. He's got the use of his hands, and he's got feeling from the pelvis up – but below that it's pretty much dead ground.'

'That's pretty shitty . . . Pretty goddamn shitty all round.'

The two men drank in silence for a while, staring out across the ocean. The bar's terrace faced due east, and people gravitated to it in the early evening. Tonight's sunset was proving dramatic as ever, a big golden orb sinking behind them, casting its dying rays over a blood-red African sea.

'There might be some hope,' Kilbride remarked, turning back to the table. 'Dunno if you've heard, but there's this new stem-cell process being pioneered in the Czech Republic. They can rebuild nerve cells, even . . . So they might be able to do something about Jock's back. Trouble is, it's still experimental. Can't get it on the public health service or anything. So it'll cost an arm and a leg to pay for privately. Which brings us back to the Lebanon . . .'

Berger nodded. 'Don't it just . . .'

Kilbride leaned closer across the table. 'I did some preliminary research this afternoon. Hard to believe it, but the Lebanon is *crawling* with tourists again.' He grabbed a napkin and began sketching out a rough map. 'The Palm Islands lie off Tripoli, remember, around here. We need to spend several days moored in this vicinity without arousing suspicion. The country doesn't have a *big* dive scene yet, but there is one, and Tripoli's pretty much at the centre of it, which is good for us.'

'What d'you have in mind, buddy?'

Kilbride drained his beer and ordered two more. 'Let's say the nine of us – well, eight, 'cause McKierran's hardly going – let's say we head in there on a dive cruise. We take the dhow and sail up to the Lebanon posing as a bunch of sad old wrinklies diving . . .'

'Speak for yourself. I'm in the first flush of youth.'

Kilbride rolled his eyes. 'Whatever.' He flipped the napkin over and did a quick second diagram. 'We head up the coast, through the Suez Canal and we're practically in Lebanese waters. The dhow's perfect, 'cause she's ocean-going and big enough to take the cargo. There's seventeen-point-five tons, remember? Tell you the truth, it's one of the main reasons I got her. You don't need that sort of cargo capacity for running dive tours.'

Berger scrutinised the sketch map of the route. 'Okay so far. In fact, I like it. It's simple and neat with not a lot to go wrong. Only problem might be pirates off Somalia, so we'll need some shooters to deal with them. What's there that's legit to dive on in the vicinity of them islands?'

Kilbride picked at the label of his beer bottle. 'Ah, well, now for the bad news . . . You're not going to believe this, mate, but the Palm Islands have been declared a *Nature Reserve*. It seems like they're a breeding ground for migratory birds, or something. The whole bloody area, the sea included, has been put off limits. In fact, the only way you're allowed in there is with a permit from the NPAL.'

'NPAL?'

'National Parks Authority of Lebanon.'

Berger shook his head in disbelief. 'You're shittin' me. Tell me you're shittin' me. *Fuckin' NPAL. Migratory birds . . .*'

193

Kilbride grinned. 'It gets worse. The Lebanon Government plans to develop the islands under some United Nations wetlands treaty. They've got plans for picnic areas, raised walkways, overnight camping facilities, video tours, a visitor centre, interactive learning resources and robotic guides.'

'Fuck me backwards and sideways, buddy . . . You tellin' me we hid our seventeen and a half tons of gold in the middle of a fuckin' *theme park*?'

'It hasn't happened yet, but a year or less from now, yeah, that's about the long and short of it . . . Now for the good news.'

'You mean to say there *is* some? I was just about to order me twelve more beers and go say hello to the girls.'

'There is, mate. She's the HMS *Victoria*, and back in the good old days of Empire she was the flagship of the British fleet. She was one of the first iron warships ever built, but there was a bit of a fuck-up and she sank. She went down like a brick and over half the crew were lost, including the Admiral-in-Chief. She had an enormous iron ram for a bow and the screws were still turning as she went under. She hit the seabed nose first and going like a bat out of hell and she stuck fast. Her stern sits in some seventy metres of water, her bows far deeper . . .'

'Great, buddy, thanks for the maritime history lesson. What the hell's it got to do with us?'

Kilbride smiled. 'When HMS *Victoria* sank the Admiral was attempting to drop anchor off Tripoli harbour – *just north of Ramkine Island*. People have been looking for the shipwreck ever since. It's just been found. The site's been declared a maritime military grave and access is restricted. But if you do your sums, mate, our great-grandfathers could have served on that ship. There's one Lebanese–British dive group who've been licensed to take dives down on her. I've already had an email back from them saying they'd be delighted to host us. Like I said, she lies in over seventy metres of water, so you need some serious kit to dive her, which is a great cover for all the gear we'll be needing.'

'Divin' the ship gets us close enough to sneak off and salvage the gold?'

Kilbride nodded. 'We anchor up somewhere between the wreck site and the boundary of the Palm Island National Park. During the day we dive the wreck. At night we check out the cave. Over several nights we raise the gold and ferry it across to the dhow. Then we up anchor and sail away. I've been racking my brains for any problems, but I can't seem to find any.'

Nick Coles hardly felt as if fate was smiling on him during the last days of his service with MI6. It was early on a Monday morning and he had just received irrefutable proof that The Searcher had survived the Viper Strike attack. Nick stared at the image lying on his desk, into the eyes of the man he had so nearly managed to kill. The photograph had been taken with a long lens several weeks after the attack. It showed that The Searcher had been badly burned on his hands and arms, but also that he was still very much alive. Nick had already shared the news with his bosses at MI6. But he still had to tell General Peters, in SOCOM, that Sea Strike One had failed to kill its target. And he wasn't looking forward to doing so.

Nick picked up the printout of the intelligence report that accompanied the photo. The first pages dealt entirely with The Searcher's seeming indestructibility, and Nick had had quite enough of that. He flicked through and his eyes were drawn to the heading 'Terrorist Funding'. The document outlined a report that the Black Assassins were supposedly hunting for some five hundred million dollars' worth of gold bullion. The bullion originated from a Beirut bank vault that had been looted at the height of the civil war. Nick was hardly surprised that they needed the money. Sending out lone assassins and their support teams to simultaneously hit seven of the world's foremost leaders was going to prove costly. But five hundred million bucks should just about do it.

Nick read on. The Black Assassins had recently had a significant breakthrough in their search for the gold. Infuriatingly, that breakthrough was attributed to his nemesis, The Searcher. Apparently, The Searcher had provided the Black Assassins with vital new information about the original bank robbery and who had been responsible. So now the bastard wasn't only training them, Nick fumed, he was sorting out their funding, as well. *If only Sea Strike One had got him.*

Over the years Nick had got to know The Searcher well. The man was a loner and a chameleon, one who could quickly win the respect of others by immersing himself in their culture and their religion. In the dirty war against the Soviets, in Afghanistan, The Searcher had distinguished himself by becoming more of a Mujahedin than the Mujahedin. He had been sent in to train the 'Muj' how to use British Blowpipe surface-to-air missiles. But he'd ended up joining them on active combat operations and shooting down several Soviet helicopters packed with young conscripts. At the time there were cries that The Searcher had 'gone native'. As a result he had been booted out of The Regiment.

The Searcher had reacted with a deep bitterness and anger. As far as he was concerned he'd wholeheartedly embraced his Afghan mission and his actions had gone well beyond the call of duty. And all he had got in return was rejection and punishment. But Nick had still felt that The Searcher was the sort they could use in The Project, as the British Government's top-secret black operations unit was called. Islamic radicals were being viewed as the new threat to the West, and anyone who could effectively infiltrate their ranks was extremely useful. Nick had invited The Searcher to become one of his 'retreads', as the ex-special forces operators working for The Project were called.

The Searcher had accepted, and Nick had proceeded to use him for dozens of jobs in far-flung corners of the Islamic world. But over the years he had witnessed his man going increasingly off the rails. The Searcher believed that his country had abandoned and betrayed him. The longer he was immersed in the Islamic world, the more the Muslims became his people, Islam his system of belief. Nick should have reined in The Searcher years ago, while he'd still had the chance. But the man had proven too useful on too many occasions. Before he knew it, Nick had created a monster . . .

As he finished reading the briefing paper something clicked in the far recesses of Nick's brain. He'd heard about this Beirut bank robbery somewhere before, but from an entirely different source. In a flash it came to him: *Kilbride*. Nick punched a key on the computer terminal in front of him and double-clicked on a file named: 'Retreads'. A list of some three hundred surnames appeared, arranged alphabetically. He searched under 'K' and pulled up Kilbride's file. Then he clicked on another file in 'K', under The Searcher's real name – that of Knotts-Lane. For several seconds he scrutinised the two men's military records: sure enough, both of them had been deployed to Cyprus at the time when Kilbride had pulled off his Beirut bank job.

Nick shook his head and chuckled. He didn't believe in coincidences. In 1979 Kilbride had pulled off his multi-million bank job. Word would have gone round their Cyprus base like wildfire. Fast-forward two decades from there, and Knotts-Lane had taken up the terrorist's mantle of murder and hatred. And then he had heard about the same Beirut bank raid, but this time from an entirely different source – his spiritual figurehead, the Old Man of the Mountains. Only the actual quantity of gold stolen was three times the amount that Kilbride had delivered to Cyprus. It wouldn't have taken a genius to work out what had happened to the missing millions.

Nick pushed back his chair, folded his hands over his stomach and contemplated what he'd just discovered. Presumably the bulk of Kilbride's gold was still hidden in the Lebanon somewhere, and The Searcher's information had taken the Black Assassins that much closer to finding it. In which case, Kilbride would be best served by going back to retrieve it before the enemy got their hands on it. Certainly, if Nick shared this new intelligence with Kilbride he would be forced to do so, or face losing the gold.

Nick smiled to himself. A plan had started forming in his mind. It was hazy at first and opaque, but it gained form and substance with every passing second. *The enemy of my enemy is my friend,* Nick told himself. Maybe there was a way to turn all this to their collective advantage: his own, The Project's, MI6's, and even Kilbride's. Maybe there was a way to use this to hit the Black Assassins a killer blow – one that would finish The Old Man, The Searcher and all their would-be murderous accomplices once and for all.

Nick picked up the phone. One of the peculiarities of being a Project man was that he was based at the Chelsea Barracks, rather than across the water at MI6's puke-green glass-and-metal headquarters. Nick preferred the serried ranks of grey and faded red brick of the Barracks, any day. As a Project man he served as an uncomfortable liaison between the Retreads and their intelligence and political taskmasters. It wasn't an easy job, marrying up the two sides. But he only had a year to go before retirement. And if he could wrap up all this Black Assassins business, there just might be an MBE at the end of it all.

As he waited for an answer on the secure line to his MI6 liaison, Nick checked the documents on his computer screen. Who had been Kilbride's commanding officer at the time of the bank robbery? he wondered. Nick scanned the relevant file: 'Q Squadron's CO has been found unsuited to special-forces soldiering, and moved sideways to the Secret Intelligence Service'. Well, that was a start. In 1982 Kilbride's CO had been shunted across to MI6. He had probably retired several years ago, Nick reasoned, but maybe they could pull him back in again for just the one job. After all, the Major – now Colonel – was sure to know Kilbride and his men reasonably well.

Nick cut the connection, redialled and placed a call to the MI6 switchboard. It was highly unlikely, but worth checking out all the same.

'Nick Coles here, over at Chelsea Barracks,' he

announced. 'Just checking – d'you have a Colonel Marcus Thistlethwaite with you? If so, I'd like to have a quick word with him . . .'

CHAPTER NINE

After their Sunday-evening beers Kilbride and Berger spent the following morning putting some flesh on the plans for the gold-retrieval mission. Out the back of The Homestead there was a small, well-equipped annexe, and it was from here that Kilbride conducted his business. Each man sat before one of Kilbride's flat-screen Apple computer terminals. One was networked with a broadband wireless internet connection, the other was off-line and reserved for the type of work that Kilbride preferred to keep away from prying eyes.

There was a deal of work to be done before the meeting with the rest of the lads, scheduled for the following weekend. Kilbride settled down to research the names and ancestry of those lost on HMS *Victoria*, the iron battleship now lying on the seabed off Ramkine Island. If he and his men were to pose as the descendants of deceased crewmen, they'd better get the names straight.

An hour into the task Kilbride's concentration was broken by a phone ringing and he reached instinctively for his mobile. But then he recognised the ring tone for what it was: it was his Thuraya satphone. He rarely received calls on this system, which was restricted to one use only: voice communications with his controller at The Project.

Kilbride grabbed the bulky receiver. 'Yes.'

'Kilbride? It's Nick.'

'Is it? I was expecting Big Ears or Noddy.' Kilbride didn't exactly dislike Nick Coles, but he couldn't say he trusted him, either. He tolerated the man for the lucrative work he sometimes pushed his way. 'It's a dedicated line, Nick. Of course it's you. Bit early for you suit-and-tie boys to be up and working, isn't it?'

'It is, but something's come up, something pretty damn serious. I'm not calling you with the offer of a mission. This is something completely out of the normal ballpark. In fact, I'd like to come out on the next available flight and talk it through with you, face to face, if that's all right.'

'Give me an idea, Nick. A sense of what we're talking about.'

'We're talking about the Lebanon, Kilbride. A lot of . . . missing gold. And someone who knows about it, someone who really shouldn't. This information is hot, Kilbride, and you and I need to meet. These people are dangerous. Very.'

At the mention of the words 'Lebanon' and 'missing gold' Kilbride had sat bolt upright. The fact that Nick Coles had come to learn of their hoard of gold bullion was very worrying; that unknown others also knew about it was a potential disaster.

'Do you have an interest in this, Nick? I mean does MI6? HMG? The Project?'

'We may have. These people are dangerous enough to

have appeared on our radar screens, let me put it that way.'

'We do need to talk,' Kilbride confirmed. 'When and where?'

'I've just been checking flights. I can get an overnight to Dar-es-Salaam, arriving early tomorrow morning.'

'Fine. I'll book you a room at the Sea Breeze Hotel. It's quiet, discreet and reliable, plus you'll enjoy the view. They'll send a driver to meet you at the airport. Call me when you get there.'

Kilbride cut the connection and replaced the Thuraya's handset. He was silent for a few seconds, as he tried to imagine how news of the gold could possibly have leaked. Maybe one of the lads had got talking during a drunken evening down the pub. But that didn't explain how news could have reached *the wrong side*. Kilbride suddenly thought of Emile. Maybe their Lebanese fixer had thrown a lot of money around after the war. Maybe the wrong people had picked up on that, and Emile had talked. Kilbride made a mental note that they should try to track him down. Emile knew enough, so maybe he was their weak link.

Kilbride turned away from the computer to see Bill Berger watching him. The big American raised one eyebrow. 'Problems, buddy?'

'Problems? Yeah, you could say that . . . Put it this way, you'd best put all our plans on hold. I've got an unexpected meeting to attend . . .'

The following morning Kilbride left The Homestead early. He'd spent a restless night and yet he remained baffled by the whole thing. On arrival at the Sea Breeze Hotel Kilbride ordered a full cooked breakfast and a pot of tea, to be served on the hotel's terrace. The view over

203

the sea was breathtaking, and this early in the morning he had the place almost to himself.

An hour later the nondescript figure of Nick Coles made his way across the terrace to greet him. He had flown club class and had managed to grab six hours' sleep on the plane. His grey suit was a little crumpled, but after a quick freshen-up in his hotel room he wasn't feeling too bad. The last time he and Kilbride had seen each other had been six years ago, in London. So while Nick tucked into a breakfast the two of them caught up on old news.

Nick finished eating and placed his knife and fork carefully on his plate. He eyed Kilbride. 'More tea?'

'Yeah, tea is good. Look, thanks for coming, Nick. I'm sure you have your own agenda, but thanks, anyway. Why don't you tell me what you know?'

Nick leaned his elbows on the table, linked his fingers together and rested his chin on them. As he began speaking his stare was locked on a point at the centre of the table and his voice was barely audible.

'We have a source in Syria, or rather MI6 does. For three years that source has been keeping watch on a new terrorist group. They call themselves "The Black Assassins". You've probably never heard of them. Few people have . . . But if they get their way all that will change. They're planning the world's worst-ever terrorism spectacular. They model themselves on the original Assassins, from Crusader times. The originals you have heard of, I think?'

'Pretty mean bunch of operators, by all reports,' Kilbride confirmed. 'Sort of the Muslim equivalent of your Knights Templar. They had a cult of getting stoned on hashish before operations, or so the rumour goes. I tried to get something similar adopted by The

Regiment, but the top brass were having none of it . . .'

'Something like that, yes.' Nick smiled. In a way he liked Kilbride, and he appreciated his offbeat sense of humour. 'The spiritual leader of this new group models himself on the original Grand Assassin – the Old Man of the Mountains. They plan to simultaneously assassinate seven of the world's top leaders, very publicly, on live TV if they can manage it. The leaders of America, Britain, Germany, Australia, Russia, China and Saudi Arabia have been singled out. They're training for this right now in a remote camp in the Syrian mountains. We think that they are two or three months away from being ready to strike, maybe less . . .'

'Seven leaders in one go – that's a pretty tall order. Why China and Saudi Arabia? And why no Israel?'

'Well, we suspect Israel has been omitted because their security is too damned hot to be easily breached. As for Saudi Arabia, they seem to think the Saudi Royal Family aren't doing a particularly good job of ruling the Saudi Kingdom. Guardians of Islam's most holy shrines and all that . . .'

'And China?' Kilbride prompted.

'Well, apparently, whilst we "infidels" simply believe in the wrong god – i.e. not theirs – the Chinese are *far worse*, because they are completely god*less*. And as far as these lunatics are concerned, having no god at all is worse than having chosen the wrong one.'

Kilbride shook his head. 'Unreal. Completely fucking unreal . . . But what's all this got to do with the Lebanon?'

'Everything. I'm going to present you with a scenario . . . Let's cast our minds back to January 1979. You led your troop on a mission to rob the Imperial Bank of Beirut. You returned to your Cyprus base with fifty

205

million dollars in bullion. Those are the known facts. But let's say you stole rather more than that amount, and let's say the majority of the gold remains hidden somewhere. Now, imagine if that gold was originally the property of the Old Man, or at least of his people. Fast-forward to the present day and let's say he's never stopped looking for it. Let's say he's got hold of a list of names that includes most, if not all, of your men . . .'

Nick scrutinised Kilbride's face for a second but his expression gave nothing away. 'I'll continue . . . Imagine the cost of trying to assassinate the world's seven foremost leaders. Finding that one hundred million dollars in bullion – which has to be worth four or five times that amount now – would have to be a priority, don't you think? That's what you're up against, Kilbride.'

Kilbride took a gulp of his tea and eyed the Project man. 'Only if your story's true, Nick. As far as I recall, the fifty million bucks I returned to Cyprus was all there ever was.'

'What are you afraid of, Kilbride? We can't work together on this if you won't trust me.'

'You could be trying to set me up, Nick, haul my arse and those of my men up in front of some court somewhere. You know the sort of thing.'

'It's not what I do, Kilbride. Law enforcement isn't my thing. I'm The Project, remember. We do black ops. We've worked together enough for you to trust me on this one.'

'Okay, let me present you with a little scenario of my own,' Kilbride countered. 'Let's say the British and American governments are shitting bricks over these Black Assassins. Let's say you're waiting and watching and trying to track the individual Assassins as and when they move. Trouble is, there's dozens and dozens of them – so how to keep track of them all? Better to strike first and wipe them out while they're all in one place. If you deal with the training camp then you've dealt with the problem, haven't you, Nick?'

Nick nodded. 'We were thinking something along those lines, yes.'

'And that's where we come in, isn't it, Nick? Because if what you're saying is true we have a very good reason to hit the Assassins. In which case, you can sit back and let us do the job for you.'

Nick smiled. 'We believe it makes complete sense – for us and for you. They have your real names. They have their people everywhere. We know they're watching the airports. I don't believe you'd be able to so much as breathe in the Lebanon without them having eyes on you. So you can't go in to get your gold without being prepared to take these people on. If you did it would be a suicide mission, and we like to think that those are the tactics of the enemy, not us.'

'I suppose we could cut a deal with the Old Man of the Mountains. You know, fifty-fifty – they keep half and we keep half. What d'you reckon, Nick?'

'I don't think he's the deal-doing kind.'

'No, neither do I, somehow . . .' Kilbride glanced out to sea. 'If we agree to "take these people on", what can you offer us, Nick?'

'We can offer you complete intelligence back-up, so you will know everything we know, as soon as we know it. We can offer complete surveillance cover when you go in, both in terms of satellite coverage and communications monitoring. If the enemy are talking, you'll know about it. Ditto if they're on the move. We can offer you any weaponry you might wish for, delivered clandestinely to any location you want in the Lebanon.

In short, you should think of this as a Project mission, only you're a little more . . . freelance than usual.'

Kilbride threw out a question, the one that had been eating at him all night long. 'How did the Old Man get our names, Nick?'

Nick paused for a second as he considered how to answer. 'Well, we don't actually know. We believe it was from one of the guards at the bank. There's also a Lebanese fixer the SAS were using . . .'

'Emile.'

'Yes, Emile. They know about Emile. We think they haven't got to him yet. We're trying to find him first.'

'Where is he?'

'London somewhere. But it doesn't make a lot of difference. He's no safer there. These bastards have their people everywhere.'

Nick's last words had been spoken with real vehemence, which surprised Kilbride. Whatever else Kilbride might think of Nick Coles, he knew that he was a consummate professional.

'You don't like these people, do you, Nick? I mean, you *really* don't like them. It sounds like this has become unusually *personal* for you. Has it, Nick? Why?'

Before leaving London Nick's bosses had warned him that on no account should The Searcher's role be revealed to Kilbride. Having an ex-SAS man in bed with the Black Assassins could muddy the waters, London had argued. Nick had disagreed. It meant that there was a weak point in his story, and Kilbride was already probing.

'I'm a year away from retirement, Kilbride. These people are my problem, and a blot on my copybook. So yes, it has become a little . . . personal.'

'Not convincing, Nick. That makes it *inconvenient*. It doesn't make it *personal*.'

Nick shrugged. 'Sorry, that's all I have for you.'

Kilbride knew that Nick Coles was holding back on him. It certainly wouldn't be the first time with these people. He would just have to keep digging.

'How do they think they're going to hit these seven world leaders, Nick? They've got the best security money can buy, twenty-four/seven. That's not going to be an easy target.'

'To a certain extent they're modelling themselves on the original Assassins. The originals trained for years, studied their targets for months on end, and then struck singly or in small groups. They were quite prepared to die, and in most cases knew that their mission was bound to end in their death. Add in some modern technology and explosives, and that's what you're up against. Plus they've developed one or two ideas all of their own. Take their "baby bombs" – I mean "baby" as in soiled nappies, rather than small. Hold up a live baby for the President to get a cutesy photo opportunity, only strapped around its middle is its own tiny explosives belt . . .'

Kilbride shuddered. 'So what d'you expect a bunch of old geezers like us to do about it? How are the nine of us – eight, with Jock in a wheelchair – going to stop the Black Assassins?'

Nick smiled, weakly. 'Ah, now that's where we were rather expecting you to come up with something . . .'

'Great. So, if we can't find a way of hitting them then the deal is off?'

'Well, there has to be a quid pro quo, doesn't there? I mean, we can't go backing you to go and recover your gold and that's it, it's purely a private job. There has to be a greater good, a spin-off.'

'Why us? Why don't you send in the boys to raid their Syrian camp? I'm sure they're still pretty hot. Or put in a couple of Predator UAVs and bomb the fuck out of them from the air.'

'Well, we did send in a UAV, actually.'

'You did?'

'Yes. The strike failed. The Black Assassins have some Iranian-made surface-to-air missiles. They tried to shoot down the UAV, and we can't risk the same happening again. And if we send in ground forces just imagine the risk. You remember Eagle Claw, the US hostage-rescue mission? The Iranians ended up parading captured US aircraft on live TV. Imagine if the same were to happen here, and we don't even have the excuse of a few hostages . . . It would inflame the Islamic world. In short, it's just not doable.'

'Why don't I just wait it out, Nick? Sooner or later you're going to have to do something – hit the Black Assassins, before they hit you. We can just wait for that to happen, then toddle off and get our gold.'

'I don't think you have the time. I'm being honest with you, Kilbride – I think the enemy are that close to finding it. *That close.* Trust me on this one.'

'Somehow, I still don't think you're telling me everything, Nick.'

'I'm telling you all that I can, Kilbride. Come up with a plan to hit them. There has to be a way. You and your men were true mavericks in your day. You'll think of something . . .'

'Okay, let's say we go for this. At the end of the day we get to keep what's ours, right? There's not going to be any fucking around, is there?'

'The gold is yours to keep, Kilbride. We would like to have our expenses covered at The Project, of course, as we'll be helping to bankroll your mission. As you know we have to be more or less self-financing these days. Might I suggest our expenses plus a one hundred per cent uplift upon successful retrieval of the loot. How does that sound?'

Kilbride snorted. 'Cheapskates . . . Fine, as long as we cap The Project's expenses at a million dollars. With your uplift that's two million repayable by us.'

'Absolutely. Absolutely.' Nick smiled. 'So, I take it we have a deal.'

Something had woken him. Emile wasn't quite certain what, but recently there had been a tom-cat prowling around at night, trying to get in through the living-room cat flap. Emile worked as a lecturer in a local college and he had been up late, preparing some lessons. He had chosen to sleep on the sofa so as not to disturb his wife and kids. Perhaps it was that cat again. Emile went to check.

Theirs was a small split-level flat in the Streatham Hill district of London, hardly the most salubrious of neighbourhoods. Ever since the Lebanon bank job Emile had chosen to play it softly-softly. He'd spent his money sparingly, and kept the bulk of his gold hidden where no one would ever find it. From what he had heard, some very dangerous people had had money stolen in the Beirut civil war, and they were still very much seeking its return.

As Emile went to check the cat flap, he felt a faint breeze on his face. That was odd – the door into the rear garden seemed to be ajar. He was sure he'd closed it. As he went to shut it, a faint shiver ran up his spine. A black shadow detached itself from the curtains, and before Emile could turn around the intruder had looped a garrotte around his neck.

Emile went down on his knees with a boot in the back, the life-breath being choked out of him. A second black-clad figure appeared. He stood over Emile as he writhed in panic, his hands clawing uselessly at his throat. The first Assassin tightened his grip on the garrotte. Emile tried to beg for mercy, his eyes bulging and the words strangled in his throat. He knew instinctively who these people were. For the last thirty years he had lived in dread of this moment. Finally, they had found him. *They had come.* Those from whom he had taken the gold had come to retrieve what was theirs.

The second figure signalled to the first to loosen his hold. He squatted down in front of Emile. His face was shrouded in a black scarf, only his eyes showing.

'Listen to me, Emile, you traitorous pig,' the man's voice hissed in Arabic. 'We will rape your wife and torture your children, very slowly in front of your eyes . . . We will gag them, so that no one will hear them scream, but we will leave their eyes free . . . They will watch you watching us do this to them, and you will witness their agony and terror. They will see that you do nothing to help, Emile, and they will despise you for it for ever . . . And then we will kill them all. Do you understand, Emile?'

Emile nodded, his eyes wide with fear.

'So, Emile, if you don't want this to happen you must tell me everything you know. *Everything.* The raid on the Imperial Bank . . . If you tell us everything, we will let your family live. And we just might let you live, Emile. But first you must tell us everything.'

Emile nodded. He felt the garrotte loosen and he

gasped for breath. Once he'd recovered a little he began to talk. He told of the original SAS mission and the discovery of three times the expected amount of gold bullion, and the decision to steal the lot. He told of ferrying the gold across Beirut in the Red Cross convoy. And he told about the safe house and the boats that disappeared down the Beirut River into the night.

Where had the gold been hidden? the Black Assassin asked Emile. Where had it been hidden? Emile told him that he didn't know. He didn't even know that it had been hidden. Perhaps Kilbride's men had ferried it out to a waiting British warship? Again and again Emile's interrogator asked the same question. Tearfully, Emile begged him to believe him when he said that he didn't know. And he begged him not to harm his family.

Finally, the interrogator went as if to waken Emile's wife and children. Emile cracked. He blurted out a name – Enfeh – a coastal village in the north of Lebanon. They had hidden the gold at Enfeh, Emile said. They had hidden the gold in the ruins of a coastal chapel, the Church of Our Lady of the Wind, in among the derelict tombstones. It was the first thing that had come into his head and it was a complete lie, of course. But at least it might buy him some time.

The interrogator smiled. 'We will search the infidel church at Enfeh . . . Pray that we find the gold, Emile. Pray to Almighty Allah that we do so – for your sake and that of your loved ones. If not, we'll be back, Emile. Don't try running. We'll know where to find you.'

With that there was a final tug on the garrotte and then Emile was allowed to fall free of its terrible embrace. The two black figures flitted out the back door, and within seconds they were lost in the shadows of the garden.

Their scarves removed from their faces, the two Black Assassins made their way to the top of Emile's street. As they went to get into their car a female voice called out to them from a side alley.

'You gentlemen after some business?'

They glanced in the speaker's direction. Two women in long plastic boots and skirts that ended at thigh level leaned against a street lamp. One was a black girl with peroxide-blonde hair, the other an older-looking redhead. The black girl lifted her skirt to reveal a pair of tiny pants.

'You filthy infidel whores,' the interrogator, Sajid, spat at them in Arabic. 'You dirty, corrupt temptresses. Come the day that the black flag of Islam flies over this morally bankrupt country, we shall clean the streets of you scum . . .'

'You couldn't fucking afford us!' the redhead jeered as their car drew away from the kerb.

Sajid ignored the remark and pulled a mobile phone from his pocket. It was time to report in to the Old Man of the Mountains. He had asked to be updated as soon as they had found Emile. He would be pleased, very pleased, to learn of the Enfeh discovery.

Back in his apartment Emile lay on the floor, his trousers soaking wet where he had pissed himself in terror. The family cat came from somewhere and nuzzled into his face, but Emile was sobbing into the carpet and was unreachable. His mind was already going into shock over what had just happened to him, trying to deny the terrible threat now facing his family.

Following his meeting with Nick Coles Kilbride had talked things over at length with Bill Berger. In one fell swoop their mission had gone from being something of a jolly in the Lebanon to a full-on showdown with one of the world's most daunting terrorist outfits. It was some change. But Bill Berger seemed to take it all in his stride. In fact, Kilbride had a sneaking suspicion that his big American buddy relished the prospect of some action again.

Kilbride put a call through to Nick Coles telling him that they were signing up to his proposition, pending the agreement of the rest of Kilbride's men. For now, neither he nor Bill Berger had the slightest idea how they were going to hit the Black Assassins, but at least they could spend the next few days working on their options. The other members of Kilbride's team weren't due to arrive for another four days, by which time Kilbride hoped to have the bare bones of a working plan in place. The two men divided their tasks: Kilbride would research the original Assassins, Bill Berger their modern namesakes.

Kilbride was an avid reader of the ancient Chinese warrior-philosopher Sun Tzu. In his book *The Art of War* Sun Tzu identified the first priority before going into any battle: 'Know your enemy'. Kilbride wrote 'KNOW YOUR ENEMY' in black marker pen on a sheet of A4 paper and tacked it up above his computer. That was going to be the driving thrust of his next few days' research. Bill Berger topped that by scribbling 'BLOW YOUR ENEMY' on a separate piece of paper, and tacking that up over his own screen.

On the evening of day three of their research, Kilbride and Berger got together for a heads-up on the patio out the back of the office. Tashana, the maid, brought out a tray of beers. Before leaving, she flashed Bill Berger a wide smile when she thought no one was looking.

He flipped the top off the first bottle. 'Y'know what,

buddy? You seen how Tashana's lookin'? She's gone all doe-eyed. Y'know why? It's 'cause I've had my goddamn head stuck in your computer these last few days, rather than stuck up her skirts.'

'Is that right? I thought you'd promised to keep your hands off her, and keep your mind on the job in hand.'

Berger flashed his gap-toothed smile. 'I can't help how the lady's feeling . . . I'm tellin' you, buddy, she's got the hots for me. And what am I doin' about it? Sweet fuck all, that's what . . .'

'Listen, mate, you're no good to any woman if you're dirt poor or dead. So tell me what you found out.'

'All right. Well, the Black Assassins – estimated numbers three to four hundred strong. Their Syrian base is a goddamn mountain fortress and we don't even wanna go there. Add into the picture their buddies in Hezbollah and all that lot, and this is what you've got: thousands of young men ready to die for a cause; a string of kidnappings, car bombings, suicide attacks and aircraft hijackings; enough weaponry to start a small war and the ability to operate just about any-where in the world. So, we ain't gonna outfight them on the ground, that's for sure.'

Berger took a pull on his beer. 'No surprises there. It's this next bit that bugs the shit out of me. These people have run some seriously sophisticated ops, with some truly off-the-wall kinda ideas. And you know what struck me most? They're the kinda ideas that you and I might've dreamed up, were we on the side of the bad guys . . .'

'Like what?'

Berger picked up a sheet of paper and began reading. 'October 1985, a four-man terrorist team used rigid inflatable boats to hijack the *Achille Lauro*, a cruise ship, and executed an American passenger. *Bastards*. November 1987, two hang-gliders were used to fly from Lebanon into Israel. Six Israeli soldiers were killed and eight wounded. August 1988, first of several sorties using hot-air balloons. I mean, who'd have thought it – goddamn *hang-gliders and hot-air balloons*. September 1990 . . . The list goes on and on . . . And get this, buddy: they've even started flying missions using Iranian-made Ababil UAVs . . .'

'They've got their own *UAVs*?'

'Sure they have. This is no tinpot outfit, buddy. So what I concluded from all this is that they've got someone pretty darn hot who's training 'em . . . Now, if we ain't gonna outfight 'em then we gotta outsmart 'em, and the trouble is they're smart. You gotta admit they've got a certain sophistication, a certain style. Like old slant-eyes Sun Tzu there said, get to know your enemy. I just dunno what you do when you find out they're a bunch of suicidal fanatics with brains to boot . . .' Berger shrugged. 'So what did you come up with?'

'Terror,' Kilbride said. 'The original Assassins' strength was rooted in their power to create raw fear. They were founded by Hassan-i-Sabbah, in 1090, the original Old Man of the Mountains. He recruited young men to go out and kill without regard for their life. The most popular version of the legend has it that they were stoned up to the eyeballs on hash. Hassan made it clear that this was their religious duty, and the promised reward was Paradise. Loads of women, wine, good nosh – you know the story. So far it sounds pretty familiar, doesn't it?'

Bill Berger grunted an acknowledgement. He never had been much of a one for fairy tales.

'But then it starts getting weird. The Assassins nearly

always worked alone, spent months getting to know the victim's daily routine, and then killed them in public with a dagger. So far, so normal. But get this: they nearly always killed them *in a mosque and during Friday prayers.*'

Bill Berger frowned. 'What the hell?'

'I know. I mean all this talk of a sacred Islamic hit squad, and yet they chose to kill *on a Friday* and *in the mosque* . . . It doesn't make any sense. Now, there is another version of the legend. In that one their name derives from the Arabic word *Assasseen*, meaning "The Guardians". The Guardians of the Secrets were a secret society, a bit like the Knights Templar. There was little that was strictly *Islamic* about them – they were taught the hidden powers of the ancients. They rarely targeted Christians and were hated by the Islamic world. At one stage they even tried to ally themselves with the Crusaders. It's this second version of the story that I go for.'

Bill Berger scratched his head irritably. 'Okay, buddy, I'm enlightened. Fascinatin' stuff. But where's it all goin'?'

'Patience . . . The Assassins' invincibility was based upon terror. You come and try and get us and we'll assassinate you, that was the basic threat. But the Assassins *were* defeated, and you know who did for them? The Mongol hordes. The Assassins became too full of themselves, sort of swallowed the myth of their own invincibility. Then the Mongols came along and saw through all their bullshit. They besieged their mountains fortresses, and killed every living thing: men, women, children – even the cats and dogs were put to the sword.'

Bill Berger rolled his eyes. 'This *is* goin' somewhere,

218

ain't it, buddy? I mean, the boys're turning up tomorrow and we gotta have something for them.'

'People think of the Mongols as an unruly, savage rabble,' Kilbride continued. 'Far from it. In truth they were elite warriors centuries ahead of their time. They had the best training, iron discipline, top-notch reconnaissance and intelligence gathering, and great mobility and comms. They used trickery and cunning in combat, like attacking from behind enemy lines. In short, the Mongols were a lot like us, mate.'

'So, buddy? So where's all this takin' us? What's the secret to blowin' the Black Assholes to hell?'

Kilbride stared at Berger for a second, then cracked up laughing. 'I've no idea, mate. I just thought I'd make you sit through all that history shit 'cause I know how much you hate it. I'm not sure it teaches us a fucking thing . . .'

Bill Berger narrowed his eyes. 'Son of a bitch, Kilbride . . .' Then he, too, burst into laughter.

But beneath the humour Kilbride was seriously worried. He'd spent three days wrestling with the problem and was no nearer to working out how the eight of them were supposed to wipe out the Black Assassins. At present he had no alternative but to lay the issue before the lads when they arrived the following morning, and see if they could come up with something.

Sometime in the early hours of the morning Kilbride found himself torn out of a deep sleep. A voice was clamouring inside his head: he'd had an idea, a flash of subconscious inspiration, and that was what had woken him. As he scrabbled around for a pen and paper he tried to remember what it might have been. And then he had it. A Trojan horse. *A Trojan horse.* Somewhere in

the landscape of his slumber he had hatched a plan . . .
He scribbled down some barely legible notes, then sank
back down onto the pillows: he would sketch it all out
in greater detail over an early breakfast.

At 7 a.m. Bill Berger set off with Nixon to collect the
lads from the airport. Everyone from the original Beirut
job was expected, barring Nightly. He'd sent Kilbride
his apologies via email: his wife was expecting their
third child and having kids was an expensive business.
He couldn't afford to come. Kilbride had offered to pay
for his flight, but Nightly had insisted that whatever the
men decided he would go along with. He for one was on
for the mission. Kilbride detected that the troublesome
soldier from his 1979 troop had mellowed over the
years. There was a humility about the man that he
hadn't expected.

At 11 a.m. Kilbride's Mercedes jeep was back at The
Homestead. The lads piled out and greeted him with a
chorus of: 'Hello, you old fucker.' Since leaving the SAS
Kilbride had run into nearly all of them on the circuit,
as the private-security business was called. Iraq,
Afghanistan, Liberia, Iran, the Congo – they'd ended up
in all the usual places. The only exception was Jock
McKierran. Kilbride was thrilled that the big Scotsman
had made it, and he knew that he had Smithy to thank
for that. Smithy had driven up to Scotland, picked up
McKierran, and stuck by his side all the way to Dar-es-
Salaam.

Once the men had dumped their kitbags, they
gathered at the front of The Homestead for a welcome
beer. Smithy gazed at the white sands and blue waters
of the tropical ocean, just at the end of the garden.

'Bloody nice place you got here, mate,' he remarked

to Kilbride. Tashana, the maid, appeared with a trayful of beers. Smithy gave a low whistle. 'Bloody lovely crumpet, 'n' all.'

Kilbride grinned. 'Piss off, mate – she's already accounted for.'

'Yeah,' Bill Berger added. 'She's promised to marry a Yankee . . .'

'In your dreams,' Smithy countered. Just then another woman emerged carrying a plate of snacks. She had the face and figure of Halle Berry in *Die Another Day*. She made her way across to them. 'Jesus,' Smithy hissed, 'she's even more gorgeous. Where d'you find—'

'Let me introduce *my wife*,' Kilbride cut in. 'Marie-Claire, this idiot's my old mate Smithy. And meet the rest of the boys . . .'

Marie-Claire took Smithy's hand as he stared in embarrassment at the sand. 'Don't worry,' she smiled. 'Two kids and yet I'm still *more gorgeous* than Tashana? You've just made my day.'

'How did a nice girl like you end up with a doddery old fucker like Kilbride?' Smithy asked, trying his best to recover his cool.

Marie-Claire ruffled Kilbride's hair. 'Of all the marriage proposals, his was the only one that came with a bunch of idiot mates. How could I resist?'

The rest of the men had a good laugh at Smithy's expense. It seemed as if Kilbride's wife had more than got his measure. After they'd necked the beers, Kilbride took his men into the office. Nixon had prepared a tray heaped with sandwiches, plus several pots of tea.

'Know your enemy. Blow your enemy!' Smithy snorted, as he read aloud the signs hanging above the computers. 'No bloody guessing who came up with the second. Who invited the bloody Yank along? Why can't this just be an English job, for Queen and Country . . .'

''Cause you'd fuck it up, that's why,' Bill Berger cut in.

'Sure, you're forgetting the Irish too,' Moynihan added. 'For you'll be needing the luck of a Paddy on this one . . .'

'And the balls of a South African, man,' Boerke added.

'Plus I'm half Welsh,' Ward piped up.

'And I'm a Cornishman,' Johno added.

'And Nightly's from Mars,' Boerke remarked.

'Aye, and don't forget the Scots,' McKierran growled. 'We even bring our own wee chairs with us these days.'

There was a ripple of laughter at McKierran's joke: it was good to know that the big Scot wasn't touchy about his wheelchair-confined status.

'Right, enough arsing around,' Kilbride announced. 'This is the proposed schedule. Today's Friday and most of you are flying out on Monday morning. I want to use today and tomorrow for mission planning. Saturday night we hit the town. There's a place called Q-Bar, and trust me, you'll like it. Sunday is a day of rest. Believe me, after Q-Bar you'll be needing it . . .'

There was a raucous chorus of shouting and chants of 'Q-Bar! Q-Bar! Q-Bar!'

When the noise had died down a little, Ward glanced up at Kilbride. 'So the Lebanon mission's on, is it, boss?'

The room went very quiet. All eyes were on Kilbride. 'There's a few things still to sort. But yeah, I reckon it just might be, mate.'

222

CHAPTER TEN

Kilbride spent the next two hours running over developments since the original 1979 bank job, in particular the designation of the Palm Islands as a protected nature reserve. Then he outlined his and Bill Berger's plan to return to the Lebanon posing as a team diving the wreck of HMS *Victoria*. He outlined all the advantages, including the wreck's proximity to Ramkine Island and their hidden gold, before moving on to the problems.

He filled the men in on his links to The Project – an organisation that most of them already knew existed – and recounted his recent meeting with Nick Coles. It was clear that there could be no gold-retrieval mission without dealing with the Black Assassins. Then he laid out the offer that Nick Coles had made to them: weapons, comms, intel and surveillance back-up, in return for the elimination of the enemy.

They broke for a late lunch. There was a sombre atmosphere in Kilbride's office as the men sat around, munching through a giant pile of Nixon's sandwiches.

They'd come here expecting a simple operation in which little could go wrong. Instead they now knew that they were pitted against the enemy from hell.

Once the men had eaten Kilbride threw the discussion open. 'If anyone has any idea how we go about hitting these bastards, then let's hear it. Anything, however wacky, 'cause we're up against it.'

There were several seconds of silence before Bill Berger spoke up. 'I've an idea, buddy . . . Last night I kinda maybe hit on something. Seems to me we might be lookin' at this all wrong. We're presuming the Black Assholes are gonna be onto us as soon as we hit Lebanon. But what about a one hundred per cent covert operation? How about we head in from the sea, hit the cave unseen and retrieve the gold unseen? A totally covert job and no one knows we've even been there. The Black Assholes, The Project – they can all go screw themselves.'

'Nice idea,' said Kilbride. 'There's one problem. You've got seventeen and a half tons of gold. There's no covert craft that could get in and out of the cave with even a fraction of that sort of cargo. Plus you need the dhow, or something similar, for your onward journey. That's always going to be highly visible.'

'I've got an idea, boss,' Smithy volunteered. 'Probably totally bloody stupid, but you did ask. You smelt the gold into earth-moving equipment – you know, like JCB buckets, or something. You paint it up to look the part, then you ship it out of the Lebanon like it's bog-standard earth-moving kit.'

Boerke snorted. 'Where does all this take place, man? In the cave?'

Smithy glared at him. 'No. But there's got to be metal workshops all over the bloody Lebanon.'

224

'There are,' Kilbride confirmed. 'But it doesn't help. To get the gold to the smelter you still have to retrieve it from the cave, and that's where they'll see us and hit us.'

'Plus you think people won't talk?' Boerke added. 'You have seventeen and a half tons of gold being turned into digger blades in a backstreet Beirut smelting works, and no one's going to blab? Get real, man.'

'All right, so you park a trawler next to the bloody cave, fill the nets with gold, haul them up and it sails out of there,' Smithy retorted. 'What's so bloody stupid about that?'

'It's highly visible,' Kilbride cut in, before the South African could slap Smithy down again. 'Plus the Palm Islands are a National Park, remember? There's no fishing, no diving, no anything allowed, unless you have a permit.'

Smithy scowled. 'So where the fuck does that leave us?'

'Och, there's always a way,' McKierran growled. 'Just we need to be canny about it . . . Take a look at me, lad. Knackered from the waist down, so I use my arms to get around.'

'Jock's right – we've learned something already,' Moynihan added. 'We know we can't do this secretly. And if we can't, then we'll be needing some luck and some trickery . . .'

'Trickery,' Smithy muttered. 'Always was your bloody speciality.'

Moynihan ignored the dig. 'What we need to be doing is somehow fooling the enemy into *letting* us remove that gold . . . I can't think of a way myself, but that's what we need to be looking at. End of feckin' story.'

225

Kilbride allowed the discussion to run and run. The general conclusion seemed to be that they needed a ruse – a trick to sneak the gold out from under the enemy's nose. The only trouble was, no one could think of one. Finally, Kilbride decided to try out his own plan on the men. If none of them had yet thought of it, maybe the enemy wouldn't, either.

'Any of you know about the sacking of Troy? After years besieging the city of Troy, the Greeks reckoned it was time to give up. But before leaving they built a massive wooden horse and left it outside the gates. The Trojans opened the gates and wheeled the horse inside, thinking it was a gift from a defeated enemy. They hit the wine and started to party hard. But the belly of the beast was hollow, and it was stuffed full of Greek troops. Halfway through the Trojans' piss-up the Greeks burst out of the horse and trashed the place. That's what we need – our own Trojan Horse. We need a decoy shipment of gold.'

Kilbride glanced around the room. 'Imagine you make up seventeen and a half tons of fool's gold. It looks like gold, it feels like gold, only it isn't gold. Imagine if that shipment of false gold is quietly hidden somewhere in the Lebanon. Then we turn up, very publicly, and head off to "retrieve" it. The enemy see us and they follow us. They watch us unearthing our hidden loot, or so they think. They attack. We fight back. But eventually, we're beaten. The enemy seize the "gold". They celebrate. They go crazy. They drop their guard.'

Kilbride paused to catch his breath. All eyes were on him now. Boerke shifted, impatiently. 'Go on, man.'

'Okay, now imagine that we've done the deal with The Project. We've got total intel and comms back-up.

226

We know the enemy's every move and we know when they're about to attack. We plan our defence accordingly, so we can put up a realistic fight but still get out alive. Now, imagine that we've split forces. Think of it as an A Team and a B Team. The A Team are dealing with the decoy gold. The B Team have got the dhow anchored off the Palm Islands, and they're happily diving on the wreck of HMS *Victoria*. As soon as they get the call that the enemy have taken the bait, they launch the gold-retrieval mission. They operate at night, using RIBs to remove the gold and bring it back to the dhow. By the time the Black Arseholes have realised they've been had, all of us – *and the gold* – will be long gone.'

Kilbride could feel the excitement in the air now. The men knew that this version of the mission just might be doable.

'Okay,' he continued. 'The dhow is crewed by those who are least physically capable of the decoy mission. No disrespect – but that's Smithy, Moynihan and McKierran . . .'

At the mention of his name McKierran looked up sharply. 'Ye mean to say I'm fookin' *in*?' he asked. 'I'd always imagined you bastards would be leaving me behind . . .'

Kilbride grinned. 'You're on the dhow, Jock, and you'll be mighty useful. We need every one of us for this mission, and maybe a couple more, too . . .'

Jock McKierran grinned. 'Och, why not just call our end of things Operation Three Cripples?' He glanced at Smithy and Moynihan. 'I mean, we've Popeye Moynihan there with his gammy eye, Hopalong Smithy and myself, Wheely Jock McKierran . . .'

Kilbride laughed. 'Okay, Operation Three Cripples it

227

is. That leaves us lot – Berger, Boerke, Ward, Johno, Nightly and myself – on Operation Trojan Horse. Everyone all right with that?'

Kilbride glanced around the room to see if there were any objections, but the men just nodded their approval.

'Right, I reckon that at three the B Team is undermanned, and you need two extra blokes. So, I'm proposing we bring in two young lads – fit sorts who can handle salvaging seventeen and a half tons of gold. I have two blokes in mind. They're both in their late twenties, both ex-special forces and, most importantly, I trust them.'

'Why?' Boerke demanded. 'What makes you trust them?'

'One of them's my son. My son from a previous woman. Mick Kilbride's his name. He's ex-SBS. His closest buddy, Brad, is an ex-US Navy SEAL. They'd join the dhow crew and dive on the gold, whilst Moynihan and Smithy operate the RIBs. And McKierran, you'd man the mother ship at all times. You'd use RIBs with those hybrid diesel–electric engines. By day when you're diving the wreck you use them on diesel mode, which charges the batteries. At night when you're salvaging the gold you run them on silent electric mode.'

Kilbride had sketched out most of the plan over breakfast, and was making up the rest of it as he went along.

'The dhow's a big old girl,' Kilbride added, 'and I reckon you'll be able to strap the RIBs onto the deck and sail with them from here. You'll need weapons, 'cause there's pirates around the Somali coast, but I reckon we can organise you something locally . . .'

Kilbride ran through some of the other mission

details. By now it was approaching midnight and despite the buzz of excitement in the room the strain of travel and jet lag was starting to get to the men. Kilbride had one last issue to raise before they headed off to get some sleep.

'There's one problem. I want everyone to think about this between now and tomorrow. Operation Trojan Horse only works if we have The Project's backing. And that, as you know, is a two-way deal. At present Trojan Horse may fool the enemy, but it doesn't *destroy* them. The Project will only back us if we can find a way to blow the Black Assassins to hell. For ever and for good. And that's what we need to crack.'

The men wandered off to their rooms, leaving Kilbride and Bill Berger alone on the office patio.

'That was a darn good show in there, buddy,' Bill Berger remarked. 'Awesome plan. But where the hell did it come from? Last night we didn't have a clue: this morning, you got it ninety per cent sorted.'

'Tell you the truth, I was awake half the night, and that was when the idea hit me. But don't rely on me doing the same tonight. I've been racking my brains, but I haven't a clue how we hit these bastards . . .'

Bill Berger shook his head. 'Me neither, buddy, me neither.'

The following day was spent brainstorming the issue, but by the time Kilbride and his team were ready to hit the Q-Bar, they were no nearer to finding a solution. The few ideas thrown up had been just as quickly shot down in flames.

The Q-Bar was an hour's drive away in downtown Dar-es-Salaam. As usual it was heaving, and Kilbride took a table against the wall facing the dance floor and bar. Kilbride ordered drinks and several large jugs of lager arrived, along with eight glasses. A band was playing in a space next to their table, pumping out good 1970s dance numbers and some disco beat. The noise made conversation all but impossible, which meant more time to concentrate on the beer and the girls. The place was heaving with honeys, and not a few were casting lingering glances in their direction.

Bill Berger was the first to his feet. Before he could even make the dance floor he was grabbed by a tall smoky-skinned beauty. The rest of the lads let forth a wild cheer as the big American started bopping away to the beat. The girl certainly knew how to move, and before long he had his hands on her lithe hips and was giving her his best gap-toothed grin. Bill Berger had always been one for the ladies, and Kilbride presumed that all thoughts of Tashana the maid had been driven from his mind. Which was a relief, as the last thing he needed right now was trouble at The Homestead.

The beer flowed, the girls flashed their smiles, and Kilbride's men were captivated by it all. One by one they joined Bill Berger on the dance floor, until only Smithy, Boerke and Kilbride were left at the table. The rhythm pounded, the Q-Bar grew more and more crowded, and the room got hotter still. The dance floor became a sweatbox, where already-skimpy T-shirts clung tightly to glistening bodies. The girls reverse-danced into the men, shaking their hair in their faces and thrusting their tight butts up against them. Only Boerke remained unmoved by it all. He ran a similar bar down in the Cape. As for Kilbride, he was a regular here, so the girls knew him and pretty much left him alone.

Suddenly a cute little lady appeared at Smithy's side,

230

and in one slick move she slid herself onto him. 'Not dancing?' she asked over her shoulder. She wriggled further onto his lap. Then, in his ear: 'If *I* dance with you, would *that* change things?'

'Too bloody right it would,' Smithy enthused. 'Where you lead and all that . . . I'd follow your arse bloody anywhere . . .'

Soon the bulky Sergeant was jerking about to the rhythm, along with the rest of the men and their girls. Kilbride and Boerke exchanged glances. It was good to see the men enjoying themselves. They had the mission of a lifetime ahead of them, and they were no longer in the flush of youth. Best to enjoy life now while they still could, for some of them would doubtless not be making it back from this one alive.

An hour or so after Bill Berger disappeared, he was back at the table. He poured himself a beer and took a greedy pull. 'You know what, buddy?' he remarked to Kilbride. 'Lovely girls, 'n' all, but I ain't interested in none of them. Tashana's the one for me.'

Kilbride laughed. 'Piss off, mate. Since when did you get serious about any woman?'

Berger eyed Kilbride. 'Listen, buddy, I seen what you got goin' here and I'm impressed. A good, honest woman; a place to live like fuckin' paradise; a couple of great kids. You're in a country where no woman's ever gonna sue your ass off, 'cause that just don't happen here. They appreciate a man, that's what I seen, and I mean *really appreciate*. I'd like a slice of that myself, buddy. That being the case, Tashana's gotta be the one . . .'

'They're not all night fighters in here, mate,' Kilbride interjected. 'There's a lot of girls come here that are students and stuff, just looking for a man.'

231

'Yeah, maybe—'

Bill Berger's reply was cut short by a drunken Smithy cannoning into their table. 'I've sussed it,' he blurted out. 'The Black Arseholes . . . We parachute a load of girls from the Q-Bar into the Black Arseholes' camp, along with a few crates of Kilimanjaro lager. That way they'll think they're in bloody Paradise already, so there's no need to go dying to get there. That should take the fight out of 'em. Whadyureckon?'

Kilbride grinned. 'I like it, mate. We'll put it to the vote tomorrow.'

'Only we're not parachuting my Janey in,' Smithy added, nodding at his sexy young thing. She was fetching more drinks from the bar. 'Once we've got the loot I'm gonna make an honest woman out of her. I promised her. I told 'er I'd buy a beach plot next to yours, mate, and settle down for a life of ease in the sun. And that fucking wife of mine – "*you'll never amount to nothing.*" That old dragon will never darken my door again.'

Kilbride slung an arm around Smithy's shoulders. 'You could do worse, mate. What does . . . Janey do? You know they're not all angels in here . . .'

'Nah, she's not like that. Seriously, mate. She's already said we ain't going to do anything tonight. She's a student, studying some 'ology or other. Can't remember which. She's like a proper girlfriend. I feel like I'm eighteen years old all over again . . .'

Smithy weaved off to rejoin his woman and Kilbride turned back to Bill Berger. 'You serious about this Tashana shit? I mean, you only just met her . . . The age difference . . .'

'What is it, thirty years? So what, buddy? What's it between you and your lady? It's got to be pushin' twenty with you guys.'

232

Kilbride remained silent, largely because it was. Somehow it didn't seem to matter so much in Africa. The girls just seemed to appreciate the more mature man, believing that he was more solid, less likely to stray, a stronger base upon which to build a home and a family.

'I've told her, buddy: once the mission's over and I'm back safe 'n' sound, the lady gets a big diamond . . .'

Kilbride grimaced. 'I've got a bad case of déjà moo.'

'You what?'

'The feeling I've heard this bullshit before.'

'Ha, ha. You can jerk my chain all you want, buddy, but I'm serious. She ain't gonna live in the States, but what the hell? I'd be more 'n' happy to move out here . . .'

'Fucking hell, at this rate I'm going to have the whole bloody lot of you living on my doorstep. And I came out here for the quiet life . . .'

At 5 a.m. Smithy stumbled out of the Q-Bar with Janey on his arm. The rest of the lads had already left, all apart from Moynihan. The Irishman had drunk himself into a stupor and they had found him asleep under a table. Smithy manhandled him into the back of a cab and together they set out for The Homestead. On arrival, he and Janey half carried the comatose Irishman to his room and dumped him in his bed. Then, somehow naturally, their feet led them down to the beach. They kicked off their shoes and for a while they strolled hand in hand in the breaking surf. The sea was warm between their bare toes and inviting . . .

When they were a good distance from The Homestead Janey turned and faced Smithy. She was going for a swim, she told him, with a provocative smile. Smithy tried to object – the undertow, the sharks . . . But she teased him gently, and let her dress drop to the sand. She stood for a second, proud in her skimpy silk bra and tiny panties, and then she was in the sea up to her thighs and splashing salt water at him. Smithy laughed, ran after her, chased her around in circles, splashed her back. And then he was stripping down to his boxers, joining her in the warm water.

She came to him then, dripping wet, her skin glistening, and wrapped her arms around his neck. He lifted her up and held her clasped to him, her tiny weight easy in his arms. As the sea washed over them her mouth found his ear, her tongue nibbling and flicking inside.

'You strong, powerful *man*,' Janey whispered. 'You big, beautiful *man*. I've changed my mind – I *want* you . . .'

Smithy carried his woman up to the beach. He laid his shirt down for her and then lowered her onto the sand. She slipped herself out of her wet things and lay there, naked before him. Smithy hardly dared look. She was so lithe and firm and so fucking beautiful. Her breasts were beaded with drops of sea water, glistening like dark pearls in the moonlight. Smithy lowered his head and feasted upon them. She knotted her fingers in his close-cropped hair and guided his head lower . . . This woman was so gorgeous he'd do anything for her . . .

They made love slowly at first, but with increasing desperation, as each strove to possess and consume the other. When they were finished they lay alongside each other, naked and sated, wrapped in each other's embrace, skin against skin and sweat and sea water intermingling.

'That was lovely,' she whispered in his ear. 'That was so wonderful . . .'

Smithy couldn't find the words to respond. Suddenly he was all choked up. He began to cry, silently at first. He tried his best to hide it, but the heaving of his chest gave him away. Janey just held him close and stroked his hair. When the tears had passed she asked him what was wrong. Smithy sat up and stared out to sea, his arms hugging his knees. He started telling her about thirty years of a failed marriage; about the last time anyone had ever held him, *really held him*, with affection and passion and desire.

'*You'll never amount to anything,*' his wife had always told him. '*You'll never amount to anything. You'll never amount to anything. You're a loser. A loser.*' Well, he and the lads were about to prove her very bloody wrong . . .

Smithy and Janey lay on the beach almost until sunup, wrapped in each other's arms and the warmth of the African night. They talked and they talked. Smithy told her his own fairly simple life story: a non-existent education; an early army career; his entry into the SAS; the Beirut injury and being invalided out of the military. His sense of loss at leaving and his alienation on the outside. The dog years of working in crap security jobs, made all the worse by a seriously dysfunctional marriage. A sense, somehow, that life was all for nothing.

For her part, Janey had also had a tough time of it. The stigma of a teenage pregnancy, followed by a forced marriage to a man who had never cared for her and used to beat her up in front of their infant son. After six years Janey had found the strength to leave him, and despite the shame she'd gone back to live with her parents. She was now trying to fund her way through college so that she could provide a life for herself and her child. But it was never easy. She was a mature student, being all of twenty-nine years old, and her parents had little money to help her. So sometimes she did what she had to do to pay the course fees . . . The rest was left unsaid.

Smithy smoothed her hair and breathed in its exotic musky perfume as he reflected on what she'd just told him. So sometimes she slept with people for money. What of it? It was no worse than what he'd done for the last thirty years – killing people for a living. Somehow it drew them closer together, this shared experience of life on the dark side. Smithy felt a real connection with this woman tonight, on this beach, a kind of closeness like he'd never felt before.

'No man should ever beat a woman . . .' Smithy murmured. He turned Janey's face towards him and gazed into her warm, gentle eyes. Pools of dark honey, that's what they reminded him of. 'Look, I've got one more job to do, Janey. I'm not going to kid you – it's dangerous. But once it's done we'll be sorted. I'll come back and I'll marry you, that's if you'll have me. I'll settle down, maybe buy a place on this beach. What d'you say? There's nothing for me in England, that's for sure. Just a dead marriage with no kids.'

'You spent thirty years and no children?' Janey asked in amazement. 'It's not possible. No African man would ever put up with—'

'Forget about all that,' Smithy interjected. 'Forget about her. I have. Let's think positive . . . I'm not in the spring of youth, but I'm still strong and healthy. We'll have a good life together. No worries about money.

236

And kids. Come on, Janey, you've got the one – how about some more, eh?'

Janey laughed. 'Maybe seven, one for each day of the week . . .'

It was Smithy's turn to laugh now. 'You're joking, aren't you?'

'No. African women like to have big men . . . and big families.'

'All right, it's a deal. I come back, we get married, and then we bang out six kids, quick as we can, like. What with the one you got already, that'll be the seven – just like the doctor ordered.'

Janey laughed, and kissed him on the cheek. Then she was serious for a moment. 'I've heard many promises, Smippy . . .' She still couldn't pronounce his name properly, which amused him. 'Don't make these ones empty . . .'

Smithy got onto one knee and took her hand in his. 'I'm a lion-hearted Englishman, Janey, and you are the woman of my dreams. When I make a promise, there's no going back. You ask Kilbride. There's a motto in the military where I come from: "Who dares, wins." I'm daring all on this next mission, Janey, and you are the prize I'm after winning – you and the six little ones that are going to follow . . .'

Sunday was a wash-out at The Homestead, with most of the lads failing to surface until mid-afternoon. After a few hours spent on the beach they gathered for a beer in the evening. Kilbride did a quick round-up of the operational plans, and laid out a provisional schedule leading up to the mission itself. As he did so Kilbride exuded a quiet calm, in spite of the issue of how to wipe out the Black Assassins remaining unresolved. Smithy and Boerke had volunteered to remain with Berger and Kilbride at The Homestead. Together, they were bound to hit on a solution – or so the men believed. For one of the first lessons they had all learned in The Regiment was that no enemy was ever invincible.

The Old Man's eyes flashed a dark anger. 'Why has it not been found? You tell me this Emile revealed all – yet still no gold!'

The young man in front of him held up his hands to try to calm the Sheikh. He had never before seen the Old Man so angry. Anger, passion, desire – these were not the emotions he had ever associated with the Old Man of the Mountains. His was a life of complete abstinence, of stillness and iron control, of absolute devotion to the one true God.

'Your Holiness, we did find Emile,' Sajid objected. 'I questioned him myself. He told us the gold was at Enfeh. We have checked. There is nothing there. He lied to us, Sheikh. He lied.'

'Then return to London and cut out his heart,' the Old Man snapped. 'But first, you cut out the hearts of his children. And you force him to eat them while the flesh is still warm. See if that might persuade the infidel dog to talk. Once you have done so, kill him and his wife.'

The Old Man waved Sajid away. He backed out of the room, his mind already focusing onto his new mission. He grinned, a wolfish grin. If he was to execute the whole family as ordered, he and Abdul might as well have some fun with the wife first . . .

'Wait!' a familiar voice commanded. The young man turned back to face his spiritual master. 'You appreciate the value of your holy mission, brother? Without this money, nothing can proceed. Islam waits with bated breath for this Great Day, the Day of the Seven Assassins. So do not fail us, Brother Sajid. Do not fail. On your head be it if you fail . . .'

When he turned away again the smile had been wiped off Sajid's face. He would torture this Lebanese dog Emile until he cried for mercy. He would write the greatness of God, of their cause, of their Brotherhood, in the infidel's blood on his walls. He would make the wife and children beg for death, for an end to their suffering. And when he and Abdul left their London flat, not one of their infidel hearts would still be beating . . .

Kilbride had broken down mission preparations into four areas, each to be dealt with by one man. Berger would draw up a shopping list of weaponry to be presented to Nick Coles. There were several new pieces of kit that he had been dying to try out, and he wanted them all for this mission. Boerke was dealing with logistics. He had to get the A Team and B Team into the Lebanon by sea and air bang on schedule, and organise the delivery of a serious amount of weaponry to each of them. Smithy had taken on the difficult task of figuring out how to make up 17.5 tons of decoy gold. He'd volunteered to do so largely because he knew some shady figures in the London underworld.

As for Kilbride, he was organising delivery of the decoy gold into the Lebanon, and finding a suitable place to hide it. Plus he was still wrestling with the thorny problem of how to wipe out the Black Assassins. *No enemy is ever invincible,* he kept telling himself. No enemy was ever invincible, as the Mongol hordes had proven against the original Assassins.

239

On the Tuesday after the lads had left, Smithy was working away at one of Kilbride's computer terminals. He was feeling happier than he had done for many years. He had a mission to prepare for, a future that just might be going somewhere and a beautiful young woman to share it with. He'd agreed to meet up with Janey on the Wednesday evening, after a heads-up with the others. But the longer Smithy looked into the making up of this shipment of fool's gold, the more it turned out to be a bloody nightmare.

Kilbride wanted a near-perfect decoy shipment that would stand the scrutiny of experts. Lead was the obvious starting point, Smithy reasoned, as it was a heavy metal that was easily smelted. Might lead replicas of the original gold bars, covered with gold paint, do the trick? But lead, he soon discovered, was less than *half* the weight of gold. If made the correct weight, a replica gold bar produced from lead would be fifty-four per cent too large. Anyone who knew their gold – and they had to assume that the Black Assassins did – would never be fooled. Other common metals – brass, copper, steel – were equally useless.

Finally, a friend in the London mafia gave Smithy a personal introduction to 'Goldenboy Gus', a maverick American who acted as a middleman for various interests in the precious-metals business. If it was borderline legal, and there was money to be made, Goldenboy Gus was the man. Over the phone Smithy told him his cover story – that he was producing props for a feature-film company, and needed to make up an entirely realistic shipment of gold bullion. Goldenboy Gus told Smithy that he didn't give a damn who or what he was making them for. There was nothing strictly illegal in producing a false shipment of gold bars, so Gus was happy to advise.

Gus went on to explain how to manufacture the perfect fake gold bars, ones that would be all but impossible to detect. He knew a factory in China that could manufacture them, no questions asked, and China was also the source of the metal used. However, there were two potential drawbacks: the first was cost. Gus did some quick calculations. The raw metal costs were twenty dollars per kilo. Seventeen and a half tons equalled 17,850 kilogrammes, which at twenty dollars per kilo made $357,000. With each bar weighing 12.5 kilos, there would be 1,428 bars. Allowing one hundred dollars per bar manufacturer's cost, that would add another $142,800 to the bill. So, the cost would be $499,800, plus Gus's five per cent facilitating fee. That made a final total of $524,790. It had to be some feature film with a budget to cover that little lot, Gus figured.

The second problem, Gus explained, was getting the right stamps on the bars. After a gold bar was cast, the manufacturer's logo and serial number were stamped onto it using a steel punch. Smithy's 'replica' bars should be no different. If Smithy could provide accurate images of the manufacturer's marks to the Chinese, then the whole job could be wrapped up at the factory. That last bit might be illegal, Gus added, so officially he could have nothing to do with that.

Gus advised Smithy to come back to him and place an order 'if the film's producers – ha! ha! – get the budget sorted.' Once Gus put their order through to the Chinese, they could knock out that sort of shipment over a long weekend. He would need fifty per cent of his facilitator's fee up front, Gus added, the rest on delivery.

By the time Smithy had signed off communications with Gus it was well into the early hours of Wednesday morning. Alone in the office, Smithy leaned back his chair and considered what he'd discovered. Five hundred thousand dollars seemed like one hell of a lot for a false shipment of gold. But that's what The Project was there for, Smithy reasoned, to help bankroll the mission.

It was odd, but the obscure metal that Goldenboy Gus had advised him to use sounded somehow familiar. Tungsten. *Tungsten*: where had he heard that name before? Smithy went into Kilbride's poky office kitchen to make himself a coffee. As he stirred in the milk he was hit by a blinding flash of inspiration. An image came into his mind – a memory from his early days in the military – of a tungsten projectile, a weapon they had used with awesome effect against an entrenched enemy position. Smithy felt a surge of excitement. If he was right he might just have cracked it. He might just have figured out how they were going to hit the enemy harder than ever they could have imagined.

With a pounding heart Smithy hurried back to his computer. He pulled up the Google search engine and punched in the words: 'Oerlikon 25mm gun projectile'. A picture of a sleek 25mm round appeared on screen, next to an image of an Oerlikon heavy machine gun. *I was right, I was fucking right*, Smithy thought. The tip of the 25mm round used in that gun was manufactured from tungsten, as were scores of other armour-piercing and bunker-busting bombs. Tungsten was immensely heavy and immensely hard, with a ridiculously high melting point. And its capacity for causing lethal destruction was almost unlimited . . .

After just a few hours' sleep Smithy was up early,

double-checking his research. He resisted the temptation to share it with the others, Kilbride included. This plan was his baby, his beautiful idea, and he couldn't wait to see their reaction when he presented it to them that evening.

At 7 p.m. the men gathered on the patio with a case of cold Kilimanjaro beers. Each briefed the others on what he'd achieved over the past three days. Bill Berger was particularly proud of his newest discovery on the weapons front. The US military had recently developed a Masterkey weapons system, consisting of the Diemaco variant of the M16 assault rifle with a Remington 870 Modular Combat Shotgun mounted under the barrel. The end result was a dual 5.56mm assault rifle with an underslung pump-action automatic shotgun. Half a dozen Masterkey systems were at the top of the shopping list to be presented to Nick Coles.

For his part, Boerke had hit upon an ingenious delivery system to get their weapons in country. The US military had just developed a new Unmanned Aerial Vehicle (UAV), code-named the CQ-10A Snow Goose, one designed purely for clandestine cargo deliveries. It consisted of a propeller-driven cargo unit slung beneath a paragliding-type chute. The Snow Goose would be released from a mother aircraft, navigate its way to the drop zone and deliver the weapons. Boerke wanted two Snow Goose drops scheduled: one to deliver a weapons package to the dhow crew at sea, the other to make a weapons drop to the A Team somewhere in the remote Lebanese mountains.

Kilbride spoke next, and outlined the means to deliver the decoy gold to the Lebanon. It would be packed into a standard shipping container at its place of origin, and shipped to the Lebanon as 'brewing equipment'. Kilbride had already gone about setting up a London-registered company, Lebanon Wineries Ltd, which would import the shipment into the Lebanon. Shipping containers were sealed and labelled at their port of export, and fewer than one in a hundred were searched upon arrival at the Port of Beirut.

A local truck driver would be hired to deliver the shipping container to its destination. Kilbride had located a farm with a couple of old barns at Wadi Jehannam, not far from the mountainous border with Syria. Lebanon Wineries was in the process of purchasing the farm, ostensibly to set up a new vineyard. Lebanon did produce some fine wines and it was a growth industry, so the cover was totally feasible. Upon arrival at the farm the shipping container would be unloaded into one of the barns, and the barn doors would be sealed shut. And there it would sit, until Kilbride and his men came to 'retrieve' it some several weeks later.

But try as he might, Kilbride had been unable to crack the enigma of how to destroy the Black Assassins. The answer had to lie in the decoy mission somehow, but he couldn't for the life of him work out what it was. It would come to him, Kilbride assured the others. He just needed more time, that was all.

Smithy was the last to deliver his update. He talked through his dealings with Goldenboy Gus, explaining how tungsten was the perfect metal for the decoy gold, as it had a density more or less exactly the same as gold. He explained how they could get the decoy shipment made up in China, no questions asked. As tungsten had such a high melting point, it wasn't possible to cast the fake bullion. Instead, you'd start with a rectangular slab of machined tungsten, and cast that into a bar mould by coating it in a thin layer of lead, which has the same softness and feel as gold. Finally, you'd electroplate the whole thing in real gold, and bingo – you'd have your perfect fake bullion.

'Now this 'ere's the really clever bit,' Smithy announced. He whipped out a large book and plonked it down on the table, underlining its title with his stubby index finger. '*The Industry Catalogue of Gold Bars Worldwide,*' he read, haltingly. 'Not the most sexy of covers, is it? But believe it or not, this book has a picture of every sort of gold bar that's ever been made. Awesome. It even gives you the exact sizes and stuff, and shows you the makers' stamps. It's like a DIY forgers' guide . . . It cost me five hundred dollars, plus the courier fee to get it here – so it's the most expensive book I ever purchased. Not that I've got a big library, mind, except for the porn. Still, I reckon it was more than bloody worth it, don't you?'

The men stared at the book in amazement as Smithy flicked through from one glossy picture to the next. He paused at a photo of a gold bar displaying a winged-staff logo, entwined with two cobras.

'See,' he announced. 'That's the one, ain't it? Awesome.'

Boerke nodded. 'The Schöne Edelmetaal London Good Delivery Bar. You can't mistake it.'

'Right, cost,' Smithy continued. 'To get seventeen and a half tons made up costs a cool half a million. Sounds a lot, don't it? But not when I tell you how we can use seventeen and a half tons of this stuff to blast the Black Arseholes into that Paradise they're all so bloody keen to reach . . .'

Kilbride glanced up from the book and stared at Smithy, his mouth agape. 'Hold on a minute. You mean to say you've bloody cracked it? Without breathing a bloody word to anyone, least of all me? I've been tearing my bloody hair out . . .'

Smithy held up a hand to silence him. 'If you'll just let me continue . . . Now, tungsten is so bloody hard and so dense that it's used to tip armour-piercing rounds and bunker-busting bombs. Put it together with some high explosives and it's nasty, lethal. Take a look at these.' Smithy handed around some printouts from the internet. 'See those Oerlikon twenty-five-millimetre rounds – they're tungsten-tipped. See those combat-shotgun pellets – they're solid tungsten. And those BLU-122 bunker-busting bombs – they're sheathed in the bloody stuff.'

'Okay, buddy, we're impressed,' Bill Berger growled. 'So what's the secret? We beat the Black Assholes over the head with the tungsten bars, is that it?'

Smithy grinned. 'Close. Think what the Black Arseholes are going to do with that shipping container, once they've "captured" it off of us lot. They're going to head for the hills as fast as they can. In fact, sure as arseholes is arseholes, they'll make for their camp in the Syrian mountains. When they get there, they'll have taken seventeen and a half tons of rock-solid, hard-as-fuck tungsten right into the very midst of their camp. And guess what happens next . . .'

Smithy paused for dramatic effect. No one uttered a word. He knew that his plan was brilliant, and their speechlessness confirmed it for him.

Smithy rubbed his hands together excitedly. 'Imagine we've packed the centre of that tungsten shipment with a bloody great charge of RDX high explosives. And imagine there's a tracking device and a remote-controlled detonator in there too. We'll have just

246

delivered the most awesome weapon ever into the heart of the enemy camp. When the tracking device tells us it's there and we hit the detonate, the RDX is going to blow fifteen hundred bars of tungsten into a hundred thousand shrapnel fragments. Boom! It's like a bloody great big nail-bomb. End of bloody story, as Moynihan would say.'

Smithy sat back and eyed the three of them. There was a stunned silence.

Boerke shook his head in amazement. 'Beautiful, man. Absolutely fucking beautiful.'

'I love you, Smithy, I love you,' Bill Berger muttered. 'You got the biggest bunker-buster the world has ever known, buddy, and the Black Assholes are gonna be history.'

'It's the ultimate Trojan Horse,' Kilbride announced in amazement. 'You bastard, Smithy. I've been killing myself and you bloody well knew the answer all along.'

More beers were cracked open and the men drank toast after toast to Smithy's 'bloody great big nail-bomb'. Once The Project heard about the Tungsten Bomb they would green-light the mission in a flash. They'd be fools not to. Smithy's plan was brilliant, and totally beautiful.

It was 2.30 a.m. by the time Smithy remembered his date. He had got so carried away that he'd totally forgotten Janey. With a flash of panic he punched her number into his mobile phone. It rang and rang, but there was no answer. He cursed himself for being so stupid. It was the one big downer of an otherwise perfect evening.

The men retired to bed knowing that the mission was now one hundred per cent doable. Kilbride paused in his living room and placed a CD on the stereo. As he sat back and enjoyed the music he cracked open a last cold beer and drank a final toast to Smithy's bloody great big nail-bomb.

CHAPTER ELEVEN

Before he was even fully awake Kilbride knew what had woken him. A low, throaty growl was coming from the direction of the bedroom window. It was barely audible and certainly not enough to rouse a man under normal circumstances: but this was far from normal and Kilbride knew it for what it was – an urgent warning. His dog Sally had been through the Defence Animal Training Centre in Leicestershire before spending the next four years on active duty with the SAS. Sally didn't growl at nothing. They had an intruder outside their window.

The hairs on the back of Kilbride's neck had gone up, and he could sense the imminent threat. He forced himself to remain where he was and breathed deeply as the adrenalin flooded into his veins. His instincts were screaming a warning at him that the unknown prowler was a danger to him and his family. He could feel his heart pounding, his blood throbbing in his temples. It was one thing to have spent thirty-odd years on the front lines of various wars: it was quite another to have his family menaced in this way.

Sally's growling changed imperceptibly, rising to a slightly higher pitch. She would know instinctively that her master was awake now, and she was signalling to him that the prowler was coming closer. Kilbride chanced a quick glance at the window. All he could see was Sally's squat, powerful form silhouetted against the faint glow of moonlight, her head and body immobile and one hundred per cent focused outside. The growl became a low snarl, and Kilbride guessed that the figure was at the half-open window now, peering in.

He felt his wife shifting beside him slightly. *Don't bloody wake up now, lover,* he willed her. *Stay sleeping. Stay still. Be cool. Whoever they are, wait for them to leave.*

Any man who tried to come through that window would be a fool, Kilbride told himself. Sally would go for the groin area, dragging her victim screaming to the floor in a rictus of agony and terror. And then she would hold him in the vice-like grip of her jaws until ordered to do otherwise. The thought comforted him somewhat. But then he remembered that his two sons were alone and unprotected in the bedroom next door. For an instant Kilbride almost lost it and bolted for their room. But he held himself in check. Sally was hugely protective over the kids, and she would immediately know if the enemy had refocused their attention onto their bedroom.

There was the sharp crack of a breaking twig, clearly audible through the open window, and Sally's snarl lessened. The intruder was withdrawing. It appeared to have been a surveillance mission only. Kilbride knew that Sally would be using her acute powers of hearing to track the intruder's progress. Her growl died to a faint, throaty murmur, which meant that the enemy had to be retreating further into the forest.

Kilbride gave it another minute, then rolled away from his bed. Keeping low in the room he grabbed a black T-shirt and a pair of olive combat trousers off the bedside chair. Then he reached under the bed frame and ripped aside a length of gaffer tape. The squat black form of a Remington 870 pump-action shotgun fell into his open hand. It had a short ten-inch barrel, an eight-round magazine and a pistol-grip butt, making it a compact and devastating weapon at close range. The shotgun had been Kilbride's weapon of choice in the Malayan rainforests, along with 'Bones', a black Labrador war dog. Over the months spent fighting in the jungle, Bones and he had become inseparable, even sleeping together in the same basher.

As Kilbride went to open the bedroom door he gave a faint, barely audible whistle. Sally broke off her lonely vigil by the window and was immediately at his heel. Kilbride slipped out the beachside entrance of the house. He paused for a second at the door of Berger's hut, and then thought better of it. He had always preferred to operate alone when on a manhunt with his war dog. It made the instinctive bond between man and beast more intense, rendered the chase and the final dance of combat more mutually binding. Kilbride skirted around the property and came to a stop at the open bedroom window.

He was now standing where the enemy had stood some ten minutes before. He crouched down and traced the outline of a footprint in the soft earth. From the curved ripple-like imprint he could tell that the intruder had been wearing jungle boots. It was no African villager, then – as if he'd needed any confirmation. He squatted on his haunches and waited, letting the silence of the night-dark forest sink into him. As he did so, his eyes adjusted to the gloom. Faint slivers of moonlight filtered down through the leaves, weaving a patchwork of silver on the forest floor.

He placed his arms around Sally's thick, muscular neck, and whispered reassurances in her ear. She knew she was on the hunt now, and it was a long time since she had last been so. Kilbride had had her for five wholly peaceful years, and he wondered if she might have got rusty. For an instant he wondered the same about himself, but quickly forced such thoughts to the back of his mind. He grabbed some of the damp earth and smeared it around the exposed skin of his face and neck until it took on a similar hue to the forest shadows. For a second or two he fingered the cold steel of the shotgun, then rose to his feet.

'Let's go,' he whispered.

Sally took the lead, her head bent low and shifting from side to side as she tracked the scent of the enemy. A short distance from The Homestead she stopped and gently pawed the earth. Kilbride bent to inspect her discovery and saw that two further sets of boot prints had joined the first. Two men had waited here while the third had gone ahead to peer through Kilbride's window. There were three enemy, at least, probably a fourth back at their base or vehicle.

With his fingers Kilbride traced two rectangular imprints where the men had rested their weapons, butt downwards, on the forest floor. As he did so his hand caught on something soft and man-made. He raised it to his face. It was a fragment of cellophane. They had unwrapped a set of batteries here, which meant that they might well be using night-vision goggles. Either way it had been a sloppy operation, at least by SAS standards. They had left all the signs for him to follow.

Kilbride now knew that he was up against three or more men armed with rifles, and possibly using night vision. Even with Sally to assist him, that was a considerable force to be up against. For a second he considered going back to fetch the others, but the lone hunter in him prevailed. He would track the intruders to their lair and *then* return to fetch his men. Kilbride rose to his feet, Sally rising with him. Silently as a pair of shadows, man and dog flitted through the baobab forest, climbing inland and upwards as they did so.

Five minutes later Kilbride knew where the enemy were holed up. Their path through the forest led to a nearby kopje, a tumbled outcrop of giant boulders the highest of which rose above the treetops. He had reckoned he'd find them here: it was the only place from where they could keep watch on The Homestead. But even from the top of the boulder pile they would see precious little, due to the density of the forest. The enemy had tried to obscure the last few yards of their route into the rocks by using a tree branch to brush away their footprints. But it was too little and too late: Kilbride had their location nailed. Whoever they were, he was astounded by their lack of jungle craft.

Sally led him to the very edge of the kopje. Here their path passed between two towering baobab trees. Kilbride was amazed to see that the enemy had marked their route with a blaze, a strip of white trunk glowing faintly in the moonlight. But as he went to step through the opening Sally froze, Kilbride freezing with her. His sixth sense was kicking in big time, warning him that one wrong step would finish him. During the years spent fighting in Malaya and Borneo Kilbride had learned to trust the instinctive animal powers of his sixth sense absolutely. It was a lesson he'd never forgotten. Sally dropped to her stomach, her muzzle on her paws. Kilbride dropped alongside her, the Remington held before him. He could read the dog's every move and this one signalled extreme danger.

Sally 'pointed' with her nose up ahead, and Kilbride tried to focus in among the rocky shadows, searching for the human form of an enemy. As he watched and listened, he noticed a thin streak of silver glistening in the moonlight. It was suspended at ankle height, just above the path, and was barely inches in front of them. In a flash Kilbride realised what Sally was trying to tell him. The danger wasn't up there in the kopje – it was two feet in front of her nose. A tripwire had been strung between the two baobab trunks, each end attached to a grenade. The tripwire was there to serve a double purpose: it would kill anyone approaching the kopje, and warn those hidden there of any such approach. Kilbride and his dog had been one step away from death. It seemed that he had underestimated the enemy.

Kilbride backtracked down the path, being careful to place his steps within the footprints of the enemy. In that way he covered his tracks, as they would find no prints in the morning other than their own. Having put some distance between himself and the kopje, he looped around to the far side and made a beeline for the dirt road. Here there was a well-used path, which the kids from the nearby village used to come and play on Kilbride's land. At the junction with the dirt road Kilbride found a pair of fresh tyre tracks, sharp in the night-dew dampness of the sand. These led him to the enemy's vehicle.

Half-hidden in the forest was a Toyota Corolla

saloon car, with a hire company's sticker on the driver's door. It was locked, but Kilbride soon got around that. Leaving Sally to guard his back, he rifled the glove compartment. There were three items of interest: one, a Koran; the second, an *SAS Jungle Survival Handbook* written by an ex-member of The Regiment; the third, the used stub of an airline ticket issued in Damascus. More parts of the puzzle fell into place: the enemy were clearly Muslim; they had been doing a crash course in jungle warfare; and they had started their journey in Syria.

For a second Kilbride considered disabling the car, but time was getting on and he had to get back to The Homestead. As he retraced his steps he reflected on what he'd discovered. The kopje was close to his home, barely three hundred yards away, which made it a risky hiding place. As you couldn't actually see his house from there, he could only conclude that the enemy had to be using some specialist eavesdropping gear and that three hundred yards was about the limit of its range. The kopje was a favourite playground for the village kids, so whoever the enemy were they had done little to check out the viability of their hideout. That was all the more reason to hit them soon and hit them hard. The last thing Kilbride wanted was some local kids surprising the gunmen in the morning – and getting themselves blown away as a result.

Back at The Homestead Kilbride headed straight for his office. He grabbed a black marker pen and a sheet of A4 paper. He scribbled in large letters: SOMEONE'S LISTENING. HEADS-UP ON THE BEACH IN FIVE. He made his way to Berger's cabin and let himself in quietly. But as Kilbride went to part Berger's mosquito net, he realised that the big American was far from alone. Curled up beside him was the lithe form of Tashana, the maid. Kilbride groaned inwardly. The crafty Yank bastard. Still, it was no time to deal with that now. He shook Berger awake and held up the sign.

Five minutes later Kilbride was joined on the beach by Berger, Smithy and Boerke. He had left Sally at The Homestead, very much on guard. The men walked in silence away from the house, until Kilbride was satisfied they were well out of range of any listening gear. They spoke in hushed tones, down where the inrush of the sea would better mask their voices. As quickly as he could Kilbride outlined the events of the last hour. Then he proposed his plan of attack. It was approaching 5 a.m. and he wanted to hit the enemy before dawn.

He would send Sally into the kopje first. In the close, dark confines of the rocks Sally's sudden assault would be terrifying. The shock alone would drive the enemy out, let alone the raw animal fear. Sally would account for one or two of them, and the rest would be up to Kilbride and his men. Kilbride scratched a quick diagram in the sand showing the positions of The Homestead, the kopje, the enemy vehicle and the dirt road. He figured that the enemy would flee in the direction of their car, and that was where Kilbride and his men would set their ambush.

'Any questions?' he asked.

'What about weapons?' said Smithy.

'We've got the one shotgun. Plus we've got Sally and the element of surprise.'

Smithy snorted. 'What, four wrinkly fifty-somethings with one shotgun and a dog against how many tooled-up terrorists . . .?'

'Four. Maximum five. You wouldn't get more than that in their vehicle.'

'Still, it'd be nice to have something to even up the odds a little . . .'

'How's about we dismantle their booby trap and reset it on their escape route?' Bill Berger suggested. 'Those two grenades – that'd fuck 'em up some.'

'We don't have time,' Kilbride countered. 'Dawn's, what, half an hour away. And anyway, it's too risky.'

'I've an idea, man,' said Boerke.

Kilbride glanced at him. 'Go on.'

'You have some traps hanging on your office wall. They look to me like mantraps, from the slaving days. Are they still working, man?'

Kilbride nodded. 'You know how to use them?'

Boerke smiled an evil reply.

'Right, this is what we do. Smithy, Berger, go and fetch three pickaxe handles from the boathouse. Boerke and I will get the mantraps. We set the traps first, then move back thirty yards or so. They flee from Sally, hit the traps, I mallet the rest with the Remington and then the three of you move in and club any of the fuckers left standing.'

'One more thing – you gotta stop their car,' Berger added. 'If they get past the geriatric brigade with their gardening implements, then that's their getaway vehicle. How about you get the big Mercedes jeep parked up on the dirt track, broadside on to the road. They make contact with that girl, they ain't gonna be none too happy about it.'

'There's only one fucker making unwelcome contact with a girl around here,' Kilbride retorted. Having discovered Bill Berger in bed with Tashana, he couldn't resist having the dig. 'But you're right, mate. I'll get Nixon to take the Merc G-wagon up there, quietly and slowly as he can . . .'

257

Some twenty minutes later and a low, ghostly form approached the location of the tripwire booby trap. Sally knew exactly where it was this time, and she carefully stepped over it. Kilbride followed her. They stopped near the entry point to the kopje. It was barely first light, but Sally could fight as well in the dark as at any other time.

Kilbride crouched down and ruffled the fur of her neck. 'Go get 'em, girl,' he mouthed in her ear. 'Go get 'em.' He pushed her gently forwards.

Sally knew that she was on her own now. She padded ahead to where the soft forest floor ended in a grey wall of boulders. A narrow twisting channel ran up into the centre of the kopje, which was just wide enough for a man – or a dog – to pass through. At the entrance to the passageway Sally stiffened. Her ultra-sensitive powers of smell could detect the individual chemicals that combine to make explosives, and she had been trained to recognise danger when she did so. The smell of the human enemy was also strong here, and to Sally the combination of the two meant that another booby trap had been set.

Sure enough, a thin three-foot-long tripwire was strung across from one boulder to the other, at just above ground level. Sally stepped over it and crept ahead into the black rocks. Her mind was focused on her hearing now, and she could already detect the noise of her prey up ahead. Two men were snoring. Another was talking. To one side of her she heard a snake's scaly uncoiling as it sensed a danger far greater than itself and slid into the rocks. And she could smell the faint drift of tobacco smoke on the damp forest air.

Sally reached the last corner of the passageway, where it opened out into a central clearing at the top of the kopje. The enemy were just feet away from her now. She dropped to a belly crawl, so that her body shape blended in better with the darkness, and inched her head around the rock wall. She could make out the forms of three men. One was smoking, one was talking, and the third was cleaning his weapon. Sally had learned to recognise the long silhouette of a gun and know that it spelled maximum danger. She sensed that there were two sleeping figures out of sight to her left, which was where the snoring was coming from.

A yard in front of her muzzle there was a further tripwire, although this one was attached to some empty tin cans as opposed to grenades. It was designed to provide a last warning rather than to kill – a grenade detonated in this enclosed space could finish off everyone, those who had set the booby trap included. Sally calculated the distance to the nearest figure. It was some ten feet, which was an easy leap for a dog her size. She tensed her muscles and gathered herself for an explosion of animal power and aggression. These were the men who had intruded on her territory and were threatening her survival and that of her human 'family'. She would gladly kill them all.

The first they knew of Sally's presence was a black wolf-like form flying through the air, teeth bared in a terrifying snarl. The nearest enemy figure went down under ninety pounds of pure muscle and canine fury, Sally's jaws tearing at his throat. The victim tried to scream, but her bite stifled his cries. For a split second the others were frozen in pure terror and disbelief. None of these men had been to Africa before, and it had crossed each of their minds already that evening that they were in the midst of the untamed bush. In the raw horror of the moment each man now feared the worst.

Hyenas? Leopards? Lions, even? It could be anything attacking them.

One of the figures opened fire, a long burst from his AK47 passing over the heads of the tangle of bodies that marked Sally's attack. Bullets slammed into the surrounding forest, the kopje ringing with the smack of lead into wood and the splitting of branches. Sally barely flinched. She had been trained to show zero fear towards the sounds of war: weapons firing, explosions, human screams. She wrenched her jaws away from her first victim and launched herself at the second. She sank her teeth into his weapon arm and he let out a horrible cry as her fangs pierced it to the bone. He tumbled over backwards, his AK47 clattering onto the bare rocks. The three remaining enemy fighters turned and fled in terror, their Arabic curses ringing out across the forest.

One hundred and fifty yards away, Kilbride and his men crouched in the dark undergrowth. Each handler was supposed to be taught never to identify too closely with his dog, in case he or she were killed. But it never worked that way. The bond between man and canine was unshakeable, and Kilbride felt sick with worry for Sally. He heard the thumping feet of the approaching enemy, fleeing in headlong panic along the path. He readied his Remington, setting it to gas as opposed to pump-action mode. Utilising its automatic feed the weapon could fire off its magazine of eight shotgun shells in one continuous burst, throwing out a wall of lead that would stop just about anything.

As the sound of the enemy drew closer there was a sharp metallic snap, followed by a terrifying, unearthly screaming. Boerke grinned. A mantrap had found a victim. Feet pounded onwards, and a figure rounded a bend in the path. Kilbride held his fire until the enemy fighter was almost upon him, hoping to catch them all in the one burst. He squeezed the trigger gently and the quiet of the forest erupted in a deafening explosion, fire spitting from the shotgun in a long, continuous tongue of flame. Three shotgun rounds blasted into the man's chest, lifting him up and throwing him backwards into the undergrowth. There was a short, piercing cry, and his bloodied torso hit the forest floor.

Kilbride kept his weapon in the aim and waited: he had five rounds left, and there were still an unknown number of enemy out there. Suddenly there was a burst of return gunfire. Bullets chewed into the canopy of vegetation, the noise of the weapon magnified in the confined space of the forest. Kilbride dived into some cover. From his prone position he nosed his weapon forward in the general direction of the enemy's muzzle flash. The main advantage of the shotgun was the wide arc of devastation that blasted forth from its barrel. Even if you couldn't locate the enemy exactly, the Remington still had an odds-on chance of hitting him.

Kilbride fired again, five shotgun rounds pumping into the darkness. This time he could almost hear the hollow *whack-thump* as the shot impacted with a human body, and sense its falling. There was a long, low agonised wail, followed by the frenzied jerking of branches, as an enemy figure tried to crawl away. Kilbride glanced over at Boerke and Smithy, and nodded in the wounded man's direction. In an instant the two of them had disappeared into the gloom, pickaxe handles held at the ready.

Kilbride and Berger waited, trying to sense the direction from which the next threat would come. Kilbride was out of ammunition now, so it was all down to hand-to-hand combat. That, and their cunning and guile. From the direction of the mantrap came a long, crazed burst of gunfire. Rounds went ripping through the branches above Kilbride as the enemy figure loosed off a whole magazine into the trees. The firing stopped and the forest went deathly quiet again. The smoke of battle hung in the air, and a sharp slick of cordite caught in Kilbride's throat. Berger signalled that he was going forward to deal with the mantrap victim. He melted into the forest. Kilbride gripped the barrel of his shotgun: if any of the fuckers came down that path he would club them to death with his weapon.

The big American crept up unnoticed on the fallen enemy figure. He had one leg caught at ankle level in the serrated jaws of the mantrap. His trousers were ripped and torn around the vicious metal teeth, revealing the pink-red of his shredded calf muscle. He had fought long and hard to free himself from the vice-like grip of the trap, but all he had succeeded in doing was driving the jagged iron deeper into his flesh.

The young fighter's fingers shook uncontrollably as he tried to slot the curved steel shape of a fresh magazine into his weapon. For a split second Berger sensed the man's all-consuming terror. Then he raised the pickaxe handle and brought it down hard on the back of his skull. There was a crunch of wood on bone, the victim's eyes rolled up into his head and he fell unconscious. As Berger straightened his shoulders, the forest fell silent. He sensed, instinctively, that the battle was finally over. But as for the war, the big American figured that it had only just begun.

The sun had barely risen by the time Kilbride and his men recovered the bodies and took them and the two survivors to The Homestead. He threw a rough bandage

262

around the mauled neck of Sally's second victim, the only one of the enemy who was still conscious. Smithy and Berger went off to search the kopje and discovered a satphone, several sets of night-vision goggles, a rifle microphone and some headphones. They also found a bag containing passports, airline tickets and several thousand dollars in cash.

From the tyre tracks alone, Kilbride knew that the enemy had arrived at the kopje late the previous night – so even with their listening gear they would have overheard precious little of any import. What worried Kilbride more was who had sent them and why, *and how they had managed to find him*. Outside of family and close friends, Kilbride didn't advertise his place of abode widely. Everything – the dive business, The Homestead – was registered under his wife's name. The enemy had to be linked to the Black Assassins, that much was clear: but it was chilling that they had tracked him down to his own home.

Kilbride took the one conscious prisoner across to the patio at the rear of his office. It was a little separated from the main house and about as private as he could make things. As far as he could tell, his wife and kids were still asleep and he didn't want to disturb them, or the staff, any more than he had to. He got the prisoner seated on the ground, his back against the office wall, his hands and feet tightly bound. Sally was shadowing her master's every move, and the prisoner was watching the big dog with a dark terror in his eyes.

Kilbride and his men started questioning the prisoner. At first he feigned no understanding of English, so Kilbride got Nixon to translate. The big, muscular Tanzanian spoke passable Arabic, which was a common enough language along the coastline. Who had sent him, how had he found The Homestead and what was his mission? Kilbride asked. But to each question the prisoner spat out the same bitterly defiant answer: he would not talk. They could kill him if they wished. He didn't fear death. He would be a martyr in a glorious cause. But he doubted if they had the will to kill him in cold blood, as they were Western infidel pigs . . .

Before that last phrase was finished Nixon belted the prisoner in the mouth. He growled a few words of warning at him. The prisoner spat out some blood and a chipped tooth, followed by a vitriolic burst of Arabic. Nixon reacted by punching him again, this time in the face and with all the force he could muster.

Kilbride placed a restraining arm on the big Tanzanian's shoulder. 'Don't kill him just yet . . . What's he saying, Nixon?'

'I told him to show you some respect, Mr Kilbride. He told me to go to hell. He said that I was a stinking black dog and a slave to the white man.'

Kilbride grinned. 'You should've punched him harder.' He stroked Sally's thick neck. 'Ask him the same questions again. Tell him if he won't talk I'll make him the dog's dinner.'

Nixon did as Kilbride had asked, but again the prisoner refused to talk. He refused to believe that Kilbride would set the dog on him in cold blood. And, in truth, Kilbride was loath to do so. Apart from the disturbance of the man's screaming, he didn't like the idea of using Sally in this way. She was trained to track and attack a dangerous enemy, not a defenceless prisoner whose arms and legs were bound.

'Kilbride, man, didn't they ever teach you how to torture someone?' Boerke announced. 'Let's stop buggering about. Nixon, go and fetch me a carving knife, a large one.'

Nixon glanced at Kilbride, who shook his head. Boerke and Kilbride locked stares – baleful ice-blue against smouldering coal-black. Neither man's gaze wavered.

'We need this fucker to talk, man. Let's cut him up a little . . .'

'This is my fucking home, Boerke. My wife and kids live here. And now you want to add this little fucker's dying to their day . . .'

For an instant Boerke stiffened. Then he dropped his eyes to the ground. 'I guess I misjudged things, man.'

Kilbride shrugged. 'Whatever. Forget it. We'll get this shit to talk. He's a scrawny little scrag-end of a man. Is this the best that Allah can throw at us?'

The prisoner lifted his head, eyes blazing. 'Burn in hell, godless pigs. I never talk!'

'Fuck me, so the little runt does speak some English!' Smithy exclaimed. 'The lying little bloody—'

'Hold on, man, I just thought of something,' Boerke interjected. 'Pigs . . . Nixon, you have some pigs in your garden, man. Go and fetch me one, the biggest you have, and some rope. And that sharp knife . . . Come on, man, I'll help you. Trust me, Kilbride, I know a way to make the little shit spill his guts with the least disturbance possible . . .'

Five minutes later Nixon and Boerke returned, dragging a large pig behind them. Although the animal had lived happily at The Homestead for many years, it knew instinctively that something very bad was about to happen to it, and it was struggling for all it was worth. Nixon hauled the pig over to a tree, slung the rope across one branch and heaved the animal into the

265

air by its back feet. Boerke removed his shirt, revealing a remarkably lean and muscled body for his age. He grabbed the carving knife and tested the blade with his thumb before turning to face the prisoner.

'You watching carefully, kafir?' he called out. The prisoner spat a gob of mixed blood and mucus in Boerke's direction. 'That's good, kafir, good. Now, what does it say in your holy book? "The animals that forage beneath the earth are not *Halal*, they are unclean."' Boerke turned to the pig. 'Well, this is what you'll be getting, kafir, if you don't start talking . . .'

Boerke sliced deep across the pig's throat and a bright red stream of blood pulsed out into one of the buckets. He held it close under the beast's head until it finally stopped kicking. Boerke turned away from the dead animal and strode across to the prisoner. He crouched down in front of him, his white torso smeared with flecks of gore.

'What time is it?' Boerke asked, talking more to himself than to anyone else. 'Half past twelve. It's pretty much lunchtime, kafir. And guess what you're going to be getting? Ask him the questions again, Nixon, one last time.'

Nixon repeated the questions, but still the prisoner refused to talk. Boerke got him lying on the ground on his back and attempted to force a metal funnel into his mouth, but the man kept his jaws firmly clamped shut. Boerke drew back his arm and punched him once, with lightning speed, in the mouth. There was a sharp crack as the prisoner's front teeth shattered. Before he could recover Boerke jammed the funnel inside, holding it there while Nixon poured the first of the warm pig's blood into it. Nixon hadn't appreciated the prisoner's 'stinking dog, black slave' comment, and as far as he

266

was concerned the man on the ground was getting exactly what he deserved.

Boerke grabbed the prisoner's nose with his one free hand, forcing him to breathe through his mouth or suffocate. As he tried to do so he found himself gagging on mouthfuls of pig's blood. The prisoner thrashed about and jackknifed his body before going into a violent vomiting fit. Boerke and Nixon backed off a little, realising that they would get no answers if they killed him. Once the prisoner's physical state got back to something approaching normal, Boerke grabbed him by the hair and showed him the bucket.

'Two-thirds full, or one-third empty, it doesn't make a lot of difference, man. You start talking or your next course is going to be more of the same.'

The prisoner responded with a stream of Arabic invective. Boerke glanced at Nixon. 'Guess those weren't the answers we were looking for, man?'

'He made remarks about you that I don't care to repeat, Mr Boerke. Then he said that he is vomiting out the pig's blood, so no harm comes to him in Islam.'

Boerke ran a bloodied hand through his blond hair. 'Stupid bloody kafir. Okay, this fucker's going to talk if it kills me.' He glanced at Kilbride. 'You sure you don't want to use the dog, man . . . ?'

Kilbride shook his head. 'Not unless I have to. The noise. Plus . . .'

'I can understand, man. It'll ruin a good animal.' Boerke smiled, a thin, predatory smile. He picked up his knife and rose to his feet. 'I have a better idea, man. A far better one.'

He strode across to the pig, and in one savage movement he slit it open from the underside of its chin down to its pelvis. He pushed a hand inside its stomach

267

cavity and started hauling out handfuls of intestines. By the time Boerke had finished gutting the animal, he was covered in gore and had two bucketfuls of mixed pig's blood and intestines.

Smithy glanced at Kilbride, a look of revulsion on his face. 'What's he doing now? I reckon he bloody enjoys this sort of thing . . .'

Boerke peered into one of the buckets. 'Stop being such a pussy, man . . . Okay, looks like it's about ready.' He picked up the buckets, a pail in either hand. 'Let's go and feed the kafir to the sharks.'

'Now you know,' Kilbride remarked to Smithy. 'And it's not such a bad idea.'

Before he had taken two steps Boerke stopped. 'Hold on, man, there's one thing I forgot. We have to wrap the parcel first, before we give it to the sharks.'

Boerke turned back to the pig carcass and began to skin it. The operation went smoothly in the lean South African's hands. Soon he and Nixon had the pigskin laid out flat on the ground, glistening in the midday sun. Nixon fetched a ship's needle and thread, and then they carried the prisoner over to the pigskin and laid him in the centre of it. As he writhed and twisted and fought to break free, Boerke started to sew the bound man into the fresh pig's hide.

For several minutes Boerke worked away with the needle and thread, all the while getting Nixon to explain to the prisoner exactly what they were going to do to him. First, the 'chum' – the mixed pig's blood and intestines – would be thrown off the end of Kilbride's pier. Sharks can smell blood from several miles off, Boerke explained. The more chum they threw in, the more it would whip the sharks into a frenzied bloodlust. By the time they threw the prisoner into the sea the bloodied pigskin would drive them to distraction, and in seconds he would be torn into shark-bite-sized pieces.

Boerke acted as if he knew his Islamic theology reasonably well. In fact he was largely bullshitting, but he figured that the prisoner had been brainwashed by his fanatical leader and knew little about the true tenets of Islam. Boerke reminded the prisoner that at the very point of his death all parts of a Muslim's body must be 'accounted for' or else he would be unable to enter the hereafter. If the prisoner didn't talk he would be torn apart by the sharks, so by anyone's reckoning there would never be any 'accounting'. And there would certainly be no chance of the prisoner being buried by sundown on the day of his death, which was another rule of strict Islamic law.

Boerke smiled an evil smile. 'You really want to go to Hell, is that it, kafir? Because when I feed you to the sharks, that's where you're headed. Paradise, those seventy-two virgins, all that good life you've been promised – all of that will be fucking history, my friend.'

For the first time since the questioning had begun there was real terror in the prisoner's eyes. He had no fear of death, but the very thought of eternal damnation was torture to him. Boerke completed his sewing job by fixing the pig's head on top of the prisoner's own, its snout dangling in his eyes. Then the four men carried their gruesome parcel down to the pier. Luckily, it was hidden from The Homestead by a thick clump of trees, which meant that their shark-feeding activities would be largely obscured from view.

Boerke got a plastic mug and threw the first of the chum into the water. As they waited for the sharks to appear, he thought up a further refinement to his plan.

Kilbride was amazed at how completely focused the South African's mind could be, especially when the object of that focus was how to cause maximum terror.

'Nixon, man, listen. You will love this one, I think. Go get the wheelbarrow and fetch this kafir's three dead friends. We'll feed them to the sharks first, just so he gets the general idea.'

Nixon gave a wide, flashing smile. 'Yah, Mr Boerke, I like it.'

As Nixon went to fetch the corpses, Boerke kept throwing in the chum. A cupful every other minute and soon there was an oily red slick stretching a good way into the sea. Nixon returned and dumped the three dead men on the pier. Boerke chucked a couple of cupfuls of chum over them and then turned back to scrutinise the sea, one hand shading his eyes.

'Here they come, man,' he announced.

A pointed dorsal fin approached the pier. It was quickly joined by a second, and within minutes there were several dozen sharks circling. Boerke took a big handful of guts and threw it into the midst of them. The water boiled and thrashed as the sharks fought each other for their share of the feast.

Boerke smiled. 'Looks about ready to me.'

He bent down to peer into the prisoner's face. 'Now remember, kafir, you're all trussed up in a pig's skin, which is hardly the best way to go and meet your maker.'

Without further comment Boerke and Nixon picked up the first corpse and threw it into the sea. It hit the water with a hollow slap, lay there for a second face downwards, and then the first shark hit it like a steam train. It struck from below, driving the corpse several feet out of the water before fish and human body tumbled back into the ocean. The sea became a savage, boiling maelstrom as several giant sharks fought and tussled over the carcass, jaws gaping and teeth flashing white and bloodied red. Without a word, Boerke and Nixon picked up the second and third corpses and hurled them in after the first.

Boerke bent down and dragged the prisoner's head up by his hair. 'You ready to talk, kafir? Or you want to follow your friends?'

There was no audible response, just a faint jerking of the head from side to side as if to say 'No'.

Boerke dipped his cup into the chum again and threw its contents in the prisoner's face. 'The stupid kafir's never going to talk. Best we get him over the side, don't you think, Kilbride, man?'

'Fine by me,' Kilbride replied, picking up on Boerke's cue. He got to his feet. 'Come on, Smithy. I've had enough of this shit. Feed him to the fucking sharks for all I care.'

Boerke and Nixon tied a loop of rope around the prisoner's ankles and shoved him off the pier. He dropped head first towards the water. The rope went taut as his shoulders hit, leaving just his head below the surface. A second later a sleek white shadow came powering up from the depths. Boerke and Nixon yanked on the rope with all their strength, just as a massive set of gaping jaws opened around the prisoner's head. His body shot upwards as the shark's jaws snapped shut, two jagged rows of teeth missing their prey by inches. The man on the rope was left dangling free, five feet above the sea and staring at the sharks below him, ready for his next submersion.

The prisoner's terrified cries were enough to stop Kilbride and Smithy in their tracks. In among his screams they reckoned they could hear a childlike sobbing, and a phrase being repeated over and over and over and over again.

'Man, that was close,' Boerke remarked. 'Might not be so lucky next time, kafir. Come on then, Nixon, lower away. There's plenty more where that came from.'

Nixon shook his head. 'He is saying he will talk, Mr Boerke. He is saying he will tell us everything.'

'Is he, Nixon, man?'

'Yes. And he is begging us not to feed him to the fish.'

'Best we haul him up, man. But if he's messing with us, he goes straight back in again. You tell him from me, Nixon – I am not taking any more shit from this one . . .'

Nixon translated Boerke's words, and the prisoner's choking reply. 'He pledges on the life of the Holy Prophet that he will talk, Mr Boerke.'

'It's the word of a kafir, man. What's that worth?'

Nixon glanced at Boerke. 'I think we can trust him, Mr Boerke. No Muslim pledges on the life of the Prophet lightly. To do so would be a disrespect and a sin . . .'

Boerke nodded. 'Okay, let's haul him in.'

Once back on the pier the prisoner lay in a heaving mess, his body curled up in the foetal position, his arms covering his head.

Boerke and Nixon waited for him to recover enough to talk. 'You know something about Islam, is it, man?' Boerke asked. 'What these kafirs believe in . . .'

Nixon nodded. 'My father was a Muslim, my mother a Christian. Such mixed marriages are not so rare here in Tanzania. We are a very tolerant people. So I am a Muslim by birth, Mr Boerke . . .'

'Shit, Nixon, man – I never knew . . .'

Nixon grinned. 'Ha! You are worried, Mr Boerke? Worried that I am a Muslim being made to torture a fellow Muslim? No need. This man is no Muslim and neither are his "Brothers". They are evil killers, Mr Boerke. They take a peaceful faith and they turn it into one of hatred and murder. I am a Muslim by birth, Mr Boerke. But if I had my way, we would take every one of these bad people and feed them to the sharks . . .'

Boerke held out a hand to Nixon. The lean Afrikaner and the big Tanzanian shook hands. 'I don't care what religion you have, Nixon, man. I'm glad to have you on our side.'

Kilbride, Smithy and Boerke gathered around the prisoner as Nixon went about asking him the same questions all over again. As the prisoner started talking, so Boerke kept chucking another cupful of chum over the edge of the pier, just to remind him that it was still feeding time down there. He and the Brothers had been sent by the Old Man of the Mountains, the prisoner confirmed. They had travelled from Syria to Tanzania to spy on Kilbride and the rest of his team. The Old Man had given him Kilbride's home address, but he didn't know how the Old Man had come by it. And their mission had been to gather as much information as possible on the Lebanon Operation.

What was the 'Lebanon Operation'? Kilbride asked. And who had funded and armed them? The Lebanon Operation was the Old Man's name for the original Beirut bank robbery. The Old Man was desperate to know where the gold was hidden, and Kilbride and his team were the key to finding out. As for their funding, it had come from the Old Man. And their weapons, those had been smuggled down from Somalia, cross-country, and passed to them locally.

There was a Lebanese man, one Emile Abdeen, whom the Brothers had tracked to London, the prisoner added. This Emile had fed them much information about the original bank raid, confirming that the gold was hidden in the Lebanon. Once the Old Man had his hands on the gold, then the Day of the Seven Assassins would proceed as planned. Once they had the money they required to fund the operation, they would strike. And that was all the prisoner knew. They could feed him to the sharks, but he had told them everything.

Boerke glanced at Kilbride, an evil smile on his face. 'He's told us all he knows. I believe him, man. So let's send him back to his people. Let's send the kafir home, man.'

Kilbride looked confused. 'What the hell for?'

Boerke nodded at the pathetic figure lying on the jetty before them. 'As a warning, man, a warning. To show them what we'll do if they try to send any more of their people after us.'

Kilbride waited for his Thuraya satphone to show three bars on its screen, indicating a three-satellite pick-up, and then punched in the number.

'Nick Coles,' a voice answered.

'They've tracked us down.'

'Kilbride? Who did?'

'The enemy, Nick. The fucking Black Assassins, or whatever name they call themselves. They were here, Nick, here on my doorstep. How the fuck did they find us, Nick?'

'Erm . . .'

'*How did they find us, Nick?*'

274

There was a second's silence. 'There's something we haven't told you . . .'

'You'd better be fucking careful, Nick. They came to my fucking *home*. I don't like being lied to . . .'

'No one's lied to you, Kilbride. It's just . . .'

'No more crap, Nick. I'm warning you . . .'

Nick Coles's mind was racing. He was fairly certain how the enemy had found Kilbride: The Searcher had led them to him. It wouldn't have been very difficult. He would have contacted some of his old colleagues from The Regiment, few of whom would have known about The Searcher's conversion to the terrorist cause, and they would have led him to Kilbride. But Nick's strict orders were to keep The Searcher out of the picture. And there was an alternative explanation.

'We've found Emile,' Nick announced. 'Unfortunately, he's dead. His body was discovered yesterday . . . Apparently, he'd been dead for some days.'

'Where? How?'

'Here in London. The police have logged it as a "random killing". We have a rather different theory. We don't think the words "Die, Infidel Pig" scrawled across the walls in the victim's blood supports the random-killing theory. Quite the opposite, in fact.'

'You think he talked? Why would they have killed him if he'd talked?'

'I don't know. But they killed his wife and children too. I went down to the murder scene. You've never seen such savagery . . .'

'The bastards . . . But it still wouldn't explain how they found us. Emile knew nothing. Well, nothing like that, anyway.'

'Maybe there were clues, things you've not yet thought of – things you might not remember, even. Who

275

knows what was said and done in the heat of battle, all those years ago?'

Kilbride considered this for a moment. 'We need to talk, Nick. If they found us here, they can come for us again. We need to accelerate the mission schedule.'

There was a slight pause. 'I'll check flights, Kilbride. But, tell me – you *have* thought of a way to hit the enemy, haven't you?'

'The plan from our end is perfect, Nick. It's a slice of genius . . .'

'In that case I'll catch the first available flight. Shall I book the same hotel?'

'Well, I would extend you an invitation here, Nick, only I'm not so sure you'd want to stay. See, we have this little problem with the Black Assassins. They keep wanting to drop by. Call me when you know your flight details.'

Nick Coles replaced the Thuraya handset and leaned back in his chair. A faint smile spread across his grey features. He was just digesting the contents of the phone call, and on balance he was feeling pretty good about it. The enemy had been to Kilbride's home, his sanctuary, his family's place of safety, and caused whatever mayhem he didn't like to imagine. Which meant that for Kilbride this had now become intensely personal. There was no way out for him now – unless he and his family started running, and ran for the rest of their lives. And Kilbride wasn't the running kind.

CHAPTER TWELVE

Kilbride was impatient for the meeting to begin. He'd run through the previous day's conversation in his mind several times, and something told him that Nick Coles was lying. There was no way in which Emile could have led the enemy to The Homestead. Operational security had been tight on the Beirut mission, and Emile would have known only their nicknames, at best. He certainly knew none of their personal details, and few of their operational ones.

Kilbride welcomed Nick Coles with a brusque handshake. There followed a quick exchange of pleasantries, and then it was down to business. As succinctly as he could, Kilbride laid before him the details of Operation Trojan Horse and the tungsten bomb.

'The beauty of it is that you'll be able to track the shipping container right to the very heart of the enemy camp,' said Kilbride. 'What we need is your agreement to hold off detonating the bomb for as long as possible. We'd like a minimum of twenty-four hours, so that we can load up the bullion and get the hell out of the Lebanon. I presume that's doable?'

Nick smiled. 'I can't see a problem, Kilbride . . . It's magnificent – the plan, I mean. A true stroke of genius. You know the *real* beauty of it? It's that the enemy embrace the engine of their own destruction. They have every reason to congregate around it in great numbers, and marvel at it . . . To celebrate. And even as they celebrate . . . *Kaboom*, as they say. In one fell swoop no more bloody Assassins. No, it's inspired, simply inspired.'

'We've got a factory in China lined up to make the tungsten-gold shipment. They can turn it around in a week, maybe less. We need someone to construct the RDX charge and place it within the shipping container, plus the detonator and tracking device . . .'

Nick waved a hand dismissively. 'We have people who can organise all that. I'll get someone onto it right away.'

'Why not use Moynihan, Nick? He's ex-Regiment and the best explosives man I know.'

'What an excellent idea. You speak to Moynihan and let me know.'

'The other advantage of the Irishman is that he won't charge. I'm trying to keep costs down, Nick. It's not cheap to make up that tungsten shipment. It's a half-million dollars . . .'

'Don't worry, Kilbride, we'll cover it. It's been rubber-stamped from on high. Don't worry, you just concentrate on planning the mission.'

'How're things looking on the Emile front?' Kilbride asked, abruptly changing the subject. 'Any developments?'

'No, and I'm not expecting any. I think we all know

who did it, and why. But we're allowing the police to run with their random-killing theory. It wouldn't do for the public to learn that a terrorist group has tortured and murdered a whole family in London. Might lead to just a hint of panic, don't you think?'

'One of your specialities, is it, Nick? Withholding information?'

Nick bridled. 'What the devil is that supposed to mean?'

'There's no guarantees, not even for us, are there, Nick? There's no guarantees you'll share everything you know with us, as soon as you know it.'

'Sorry? I don't know what you're driving at. Brilliant plan – Operation Trojan Horse. But now I'm afraid you've lost me . . .'

'Emile never led the enemy to us, Nick. It's just not possible. There's something else. Don't look away, Nick. It'll just confirm my worst suspicions . . .'

Nick glanced at Kilbride. 'Look, I've told you all that I *can* tell you.'

'You're holding out on us, Nick, and it had better not be mission-critical. If it is . . .'

Nick Coles rubbed his temples. The tension was getting to him. 'Look, I'll make you a deal, Kilbride. I think you know all you need to know. Nothing I could tell you would make one iota of difference to your mission. And I promise that if it ever gets to the stage where that changes, then I'll talk. Is that enough?'

Kilbride shrugged. 'I guess it'll have to be. There's one more thing, Nick. Operation Trojan Horse is predicated on the enemy knowing our every move. You say they have the airports watched and they'll be tracking us as soon as we arrive in country. Maybe. But we have to be certain, Nick. We have to be *certain* that they follow us, attack us, and make their getaway with the dummy gold. I presume you have avenues to let them know exactly when we're arriving?'

'Well, we're not exactly on speaking terms, but yes, we do have ... people. We have people on the ground in Syria who pass us information. They can certainly pass a little bit back the other way.'

'Make sure the enemy know just enough, Nick. They need to know enough to swallow the bait, but not to get us killed.'

'Of course.' Nick shifted uncomfortably in his seat. 'Erm, there is one other thing,' he ventured. 'My people have said that they'd like the gold delivered to a British base, after retrieval. They just want to ensure that The Project's investment in the mission is safeguarded. Cyprus is the nearest . . .'

Kilbride stared at Nick, incredulously. 'You mean you don't trust us to deliver up your two million?'

'Of course we trust you. But the high seas are a potentially hazardous place for any operation, and pirates operate off the African coast. No one wants the gold . . . disappearing before either The Project – or you, for that matter – can recoup their investment.'

'So what exactly are you suggesting?'

'I'm suggesting that we have a chopper on standby. When you're ready we do a pick-up and drop you on Cyprus. You'll leave us the two million, and you catch a flight onwards to wherever you wish. The chopper can fly below radar level, nap of the land and all that stuff, so it won't be detectable.'

Kilbride shrugged. 'I'll put it to the rest of the lads.'

'I'm told it's a deal breaker, Kilbride. If you won't agree then our role in all of this may be placed in jeopardy. I'm sure you understand . . .'

On the drive back to The Homestead two things crystallised in Kilbride's mind. The first was that his instinct was correct. Nick Coles knew more than he was saying and had been ordered not to reveal it to Kilbride. It irked him that this was so, but there was little that he could do about it. The second thing was that The Project had started playing games. The demand that Kilbride and his team should deliver the gold to Cyprus was complete bullshit, and Kilbride suspected a hidden agenda. There was only one way to deal with it. Ridiculous though it might seem, they now needed a second decoy shipment. They needed the first to fool the enemy, and the second to fool their own people – The Project, MI6 and HMG in turn.

That evening Nick Coles took dinner alone on the hotel terrace. The service and the food were excellent, and he looked forward to a long, leisurely meal of several courses, all washed down with a bottle of crisp French Chablis. As he tucked into a starter of braised king prawns served with a hot, spicy sauce, he ran over the details of Kilbride's plan one more time. He could just imagine the scene: the Black Assassins gathered excitedly around the shipping container, when suddenly their world would disintegrate around them . . .

He was pulled away from his thoughts by one of the hotel waiters. 'Excuse me, sir. Is everything to sir's liking?'

'Very fine,' Nick confirmed. 'Excellent, thank you.'

The waiter bent closer. 'Sir, there is a lady who would like to join your table. She is alone, you are alone, and she thought you might like some company . . .'

Nick looked where the waiter indicated, and his jaw

281

practically dropped to the table. Perched on a stool at the bar was one of the most beautiful and exotic female specimens he had ever seen. While she had the grace and the poise of an African woman, there was something of the Arab about her in the warm, coppery skin, the arched brows and the almost sharp line of her nose. *She wants to come and sit with me,* Nick found himself thinking, in amazement. As if to confirm that this was what she wanted the woman smiled, showing a flash of dazzling white teeth. She looked to be no more than in her early twenties. Christ, she wasn't just beautiful, she was *young*, Nick told himself.

'Sir, shall I say to the lady to join you?' the waiter prompted.

Nick tore his gaze away from her. 'Oh, by all means, yes, do.'

The waiter pulled up a chair and set a second place opposite Nick. He gave the woman a slight nod, held the chair for her and she sat down. She held out a hand to Nick and introduced herself as Sairah, a student at Dar-es-Salaam University. The waiter gave Sairah a menu and she ordered. There were a few seconds of awkward silence, and then Nick asked her what she was studying. Tourism Management, Sairah told him. The curriculum was a little boring, but at least it had good job prospects.

Nick did his best to break the ice by cracking a few jokes, and soon they were onto their second bottle of Chablis. He plucked up the courage to ask Sairah where she was from, exactly. She had remarkable looks, he explained, quite unlike any that he had seen before, and he liked to think of himself as fairly well travelled. She came from Somalia, Sairah said – so she had a mixture of Arab and African blood. By the end of the second bottle of wine, Nick had confessed that he found her quite extraordinarily beautiful, although he hoped she didn't mind him saying so . . .

They moved on to desserts. Nick ordered more drinks – a single malt for himself, a Baileys on ice for her. Sairah asked if she could try his sweet, a tiramisu. When he offered her his plate she demurred, and asked him to feed her instead. After a moment's hesitation, Nick leaned across the table and placed a spoonful of the rich dessert between her lips. He would never have been so brave to do so were it not for the wine. Dutch courage, and he was glad of it – especially when her pink tongue darted out and flicked away a speck of cream. Nick felt himself going weak at the knees.

Sairah read the agitation in his eyes, and threw her head back and laughed. Then she asked him for another spoonful. As he leaned across to feed her again, Nick tried to disguise the embarrassment that he was feeling by cracking a joke.

'Two cannibals are eating a clown: one says to the other, does this taste funny to you?'

Sairah smiled. 'Don't worry, Nick,' she murmured, in her rich, exotic accent. 'I know you're shy. I like it. Don't try to hide it – it's cute.'

Nick glanced across at the waiter, wondering what he must be thinking, but the man didn't seem to be paying them much attention. In fact, there were several other male diners who also had been joined by pretty young females, though none quite so stunning as Sairah. Nick guessed that the waiters had an informal deal going with the girls, to hook them up with lone male guests. And if he had landed Sairah as a result, then he was all for it.

When it came time for them to leave, no one seemed

the least bit surprised that Nick placed an arm around the sensuous curve of Sairah's back to steer her to the door. He had left a very large tip on the table, and he hoped that it would make up for any discomfort he might feel at breakfast the following morning. If nothing else it would buy the waiter's silence. As they passed through the lobby Nick felt as if he were in a wonderful dream. He gazed at their reflections in the elevator's mirror, as this exquisite woman pressed her body a little closer to him. It was a tantalising promise of things to come.

As soon as they entered Nick's bedroom, Sairah excused herself and went to the loo. Nick heard a flush and the running of water into a basin. She was obviously powdering her nose. For a second he wondered what state he'd left his bathroom in, and then he told himself to hell with it – he should relax. After all, he was drunk and about to get laid by the most beautiful woman that he had ever had the good fortune to coax back to his bedroom. Well, there hadn't actually been that much coaxing involved, Nick reflected, a little smugly.

He moved to the balcony and gazed out over the Indian Ocean. He couldn't remember the last time he had had sex with his wife. Apart from the children, who'd all left home, it was a stagnant, joyless marriage. He was pushing sixty and had to get his sexual thrills wherever he could – even if he had to pay. In fact, he rather *liked* the idea that he was paying for it. No money had been mentioned, of course, but Sairah had talked at length about how she struggled to pay her university fees. This was going to be a financial trans-action, he had no doubt about that. He was buying Sairah. Buying her sex. Handing over dollar bills to get access to her lithe young body.

284

For a second Nick wondered if he might have misjudged things, if maybe she had come to his room for a nightcap only and would be leaving with a chaste kiss. He took a pull on his whisky and lit up another cigarette. He only smoked when he drank, and only when he was away from the wife. It helped to calm his nerves, and right now the very thought that Sairah might actually walk away without having bedded him was causing him no small degree of concern. Over coffee she'd suggested staying the night. Surely that could mean only one thing?

There was the click of the bathroom door closing behind him and the pad of bare feet across the tiled floor. Nick didn't dare turn around. He took a long pull on his whisky and a draw on his cigarette, like a drowning man. Sairah joined him at the balcony, her bronze arms resting naked on the wooden railing. Nick stared out to sea, hardly daring to look at her.

Gently, playfully, she nudged him with her thigh, and somehow Nick knew that it too was naked. Finally, he glanced down at her, taking in the long golden legs, the tiny pair of polka-dot knickers, the wispy silk vest that barely covered her breasts. Nick felt a burning desire course through him, a bolt of sexual excitement such as he hadn't felt in years. Sairah glanced across at him, her deep, dark eyes willing him to lose himself in her – to let her take him places where his ageing body had all but forgotten that it could go.

'It's a nice view, isn't it?' Sairah remarked, her teeth smiling white in the darkness. She made no effort to indicate the sea. She left her mouth a little parted, and he could see the pink tip of her tongue. 'And tonight it's all for you . . .'

285

'Erm . . . delightful,' Nick managed to stutter. 'You really are a rare beauty.'

Sairah placed a finger over his thin lips. 'Ssshhh . . . No more talking . . .'

She led him by his hand into the bedroom. She took her time undressing him, each unfastening of a button on his shirt executed with a deft flick of her slender fingers. Every now and then she slipped a hand inside and raked his chest with her long, carefully manicured nails. They were painted a bright red, and for a second they reminded Nick of chilli peppers. No doubt about it: Sairah was going to be hot. She was working him up into a frenzy already, and she knew it.

Each time he tried to kiss her she pulled her head away. 'Not yet . . . wait,' she told him, teasingly. 'Wait until I'm ready . . .'

With his shirt off Nick tried for a second to pull his paunch in, the sort of thing he used to do on the beach when taking his summer holidays with the family. But then he thought better of it. Sairah wouldn't mind. She wasn't with him because he was a young Adonis. She was here for the money. So be it. He should stop pretending.

She pushed him, naked, onto the bed and knelt over him. In one swift movement she slipped her top up over her head and revealed herself to him – back arched, shoulders thrust back, surprisingly muscular and beautifully shadowed, breasts small and pert and ripe. Momentarily, Nick thought of the last time he had seen his wife Anna naked. He shuddered, and pushed the image to the back of his mind.

Sairah shook her hair free, and her braids fell down. They were like sweet rain after a cruel and parching drought, Nick told himself, a drought that had lasted longer than he cared to remember. *Let it rain, Sairah, you beautiful, gorgeous sex goddess, let it rain . . .*

Nick tried to sit up so he could kiss her breasts, but she forced him down again. 'Wait . . . Be patient . . . There's one more thing to come off . . .' She squatted beside him on the bed, and with a deft flick of her hand she slipped herself out of her knickers. He couldn't look. Not until he entered her heavenly body and possessed her did he feel he could do so.

Sairah leaned across to the bedside table and felt for her handbag. 'A girl should always come prepared . . . to meet a handsome Englishman,' she purred. She mouthed the word 'condom' at him, each syllable pursing her lips in a hugely provocative 'O'.

'Ah, yes . . . erm . . .' Nick was going to add that he had got some but they were in the bathroom. He carried them with him whenever he was on a foreign trip and away from the wife, although he couldn't remember the last time he'd had cause to use them.

'Relax . . .' Sairah urged as she pulled a silver packet out of her bag. She gave him a wicked smile. '*Now we're ready . . .*'

She bent over him with sensual, feline grace, clamping her lips on his, fiercely, aggressively, her tongue flicking hotly into his mouth. Nick kissed her greedily as he felt her hands unwrapping the silver package – his ticket to her inner paradise. He was losing himself in her, the exotic smell and feel and taste of her, the beautiful tautness of her lithe body, the smooth ebony smokiness of her skin. Her braids tumbled about him – like a curtain to hide their lovemaking, Nick thought. He felt a small prick on his left wrist, and there was a tiny flash of alarm in his head. But then Sairah bore down on him more heavily, straddling him more forcefully.

'Sorry, did I pinch you?' she whispered in his ear. She nibbled his ear lobe. 'I get a bit carried away when I'm excited . . . I might even bite you, too, if you refuse to be a good boy . . .'

Sairah forced her tongue deeper into his mouth, until she was eating him alive. She moved her mouth down to his throat, biting at his Adam's apple, pecking at his shoulder bones. Nick felt her pelvis thrusting down onto his stomach, the warm roughness of her pubic hair stroking his skin. He reached down to caress her and move her more centrally over him. But as he did so, Nick felt his arms go weak and his hands drop impotently to his sides. And all of a sudden Nick Coles's world went totally black.

The Searcher picked his way across the camp towards the quarters of the Old Man of the Mountains. He was curious. He'd been woken from his sleep and called to attend an urgent meeting. He nodded at the two sentries. Security was tight in the camp now, especially after the Americans' air raid. He caught sight of two other figures heading in the same direction as him. They were Brothers Sajid and Abdul, recently returned from operations in London. He paused to greet them, and together the three men made their way into the Old Man's underground bunker.

The Old Man greeted them in the usual way and began calling for tea. But somehow he seemed unusually agitated and unsettled, and The Searcher wondered what might lie behind this disquiet.

The Old Man glanced at The Searcher, fierce eyes staring out from under hooded brows. 'Brother Muhammad Mohajir, I am about to give you a new and most sacred mission,' he announced. 'The training for

288

the Day of the Seven Assassins is almost complete, I believe? You have done well. Very well. You will now take command of the mission to find the missing gold. I sense we are close, Brother, very close. There have been some significant developments . . . but also some *unholy disasters.*'

The Searcher felt Sajid and Abdul shift uncomfortably beside him. He sensed that their recent London mission might not have gone as planned.

The Old Man turned to them, and his face darkened. 'So, you found Emile and you killed him . . . Well done, Brothers. But you were not sent on this mission out of a need for *revenge.* You were sent to extract information. *Information.* Information that would lead us to the gold. Yet you returned with nothing. I do not care how much this infidel dog and his family suffered. All I care for is the Holy Mission – and that you have failed to advance at all. Answer me this: how could you take on this holy duty and *fail?*'

'We could not extract information that didn't exist, Your Holiness,' Sajid protested. 'How could we—'

'Silence, Brother Sajid!' the Old Man roared. 'You sought only to kill, not to further your holy duty. As for the rest of your mission – the search at Enfeh turns up nothing. *Nothing.* And now we have the five Brothers captured or killed in Africa. Tell me, Brother Sajid, what sort of planning went into their mission? Not even one day did they survive before the enemy found them. We had this gift from Brother Mohajir, this priceless gift . . . He revealed to us where the enemy are living, and yet you failed so spectacularly . . .'

'Have they talked?' Sajid blurted out. 'Did the infidels force the Brothers to talk?'

'I doubt it very much,' the Old Man replied. 'I doubt

it because Muhammad Mohajir trained them, and gave them the skills and the courage not to. And I gave them the spiritual strength to resist all. But as for you, Brothers, a catalogue of unholy disasters assail you. And yet you try to make excuses for why you have failed! Do you not know you should be begging for the Great One's mercy and forgiveness!'

The Old Man snatched up a cane that lay by his side and in a sudden movement he struck Sajid a savage blow across the face. For someone so ancient and wizened there was considerable force behind the blow. He dealt several further strikes against the faces of the two men, before his anger was sated.

'You will understand why the command of this mission passes to Brother Mohajir.' The Old Man smiled in The Searcher's direction. 'There is one very positive development.' He dragged a mobile phone from inside his robes and pulled up a picture on the screen. He passed it to The Searcher. 'Ignore the girl. It is the man we are interested in. He is an agent of the British Government and he is working closely with the team who originally stole the gold. The pictures were taken last night. There are several in a similar vein. The man is married. I presume he will not want his wife to see such things. And thus I presume that he can be persuaded to betray his fellow countrymen and tell us all that he knows.'

The Searcher smiled. 'I take it that you'd like me to have words with him, Your Holiness? Perhaps it is just by coincidence, but I think I know this man. His name is Nick Coles . . .'

Nick awoke with a splitting headache and a mouth that tasted like the bottom of a rabbit cage. He reached

290

across the king-size bed for Sairah, but she was nowhere to be found. He opened one eye and listened for the sound of the shower. But it was quiet in his room, and there was no sign of her clothes. Nick swilled some water from a glass. He couldn't believe how bad he was feeling.

He flailed around for his watch on the bedside table. It was 11 a.m. Maybe she was at college, at one of those boring Tourism Management lectures she'd talked about. That was probably it. But today – today was a Saturday. Did they have college lectures on a Saturday here? Nick comforted himself with the thought that she'd taken his mobile number. She'd promised to spend the weekend with him. No doubt she'd call.

He tried to remember the sex to cheer himself up, but oddly he couldn't. All the more reason to get Sairah over again tonight, for a more sober and concentrated session. He wondered if she might have called already, or sent him a text while he was asleep. He felt about for his mobile and checked the screen: 'You have unread messages.' He clicked on the first one excitedly, noticing that it had a picture icon attached to it. Maybe Sairah had sent him a picture of herself, to tide him over to the evening.

The message opened. There was no text, only a grainy photo of a naked and comatose-looking Nick Coles, with an equally naked Sairah beside him. She had sent him a photo, but it wasn't quite the sort that he had been expecting. With a sinking feeling he flicked through the others. They showed himself and Sairah in a series of ever more explicit poses, and each one was hugely compromising. He opened the last message with a shaking hand. It showed a naked Sairah kneeling over his prostrate form, holding up a sign scrawled in black marker pen: HI ANNA – WISH YOU WERE HERE.

My God! How the hell did she know his wife's name? As far as he could remember from the fuzz of the previous evening he hadn't even told her that he was married. But there had been those two bottles of Chablis, and several glasses of whisky. As well as wiping out his memory, the drink must have considerably loosened his tongue.

There was a text message accompanying the last picture. 'Ring this number. Don't delay. It could be very dangerous for you.'

Nick felt a sudden surge of anger. This was blackmail, pure and simple. Well, what if it was? What of it? What was a young Somali girl living in Tanzania ever going to do with some dirty pictures of Nick Coles? She had no idea who he was, so she could hardly sell them to the press. She couldn't contact his family, friends or employers because she didn't have a clue who they were. In fact, the more he reflected upon it the more impotent her threat became. 'It could be very dangerous for you.' Who was she kidding?

Nick shuffled across to the mini-bar and felt around for some bottled water. God, he felt bad. He ripped off the plastic cover and unscrewed the top, necking back the contents in one go. He knew what to do in response to her text message. It was one of his favourite courses of action: he would do absolutely bloody nothing.

Nick made his way gingerly to the hotel pool. He reckoned Sairah must have drugged him so that she could get those photos. He probably couldn't remember fucking her because he hadn't done so, he reflected ruefully. She'd dosed him up before any of that could really get started. Well, if she did have the audacity to call him he would give her a piece of his mind. He'd also have words with the hotel staff, that damned waiter in particular.

Nick plunged into the emerald water of the pool, held his breath and swam a length without surfacing. He came up gasping for air and breathing heavily. He swam hard for several minutes, and then decided to take a rest under one of the sun awnings. He felt a little better already. Maybe he could get one of the staff to bring him some fresh fruit juice and an enormous pot of coffee, to help sort out his head.

As he slumped onto the plastic recliner he heard the ring tone of his mobile. He picked it up and glanced at the caller ID. It showed a private number. It was probably *her*.

'Yes,' he snapped.

'You didn't call. I told you to call.'

Nick sat up, immediately alert. This wasn't Sairah. The voice was male, and British-sounding, although the accent had just the slightest hint of an Arabic lilt to it.

'Who is this . . . ?' he began.

'Listen, Nick Coles of MI6 and The Project – I do the talking, okay?'

Nick was speechless. Whoever this was they knew a damn sight more about him than he would have wished.

'That's better. It's been a long time, Nick. Still, I'm surprised you can't place the voice. We all loved the photos, by the way. Not exactly over-endowed in the manhood department, are we, Nick? If that's the best an agent of the British Government can come up with, what have we possibly got to fear? I don't think your wife Anna will be too impressed, either. But it won't be the size of your manhood she'll be worried about, will it, Nick? "Hi Anna – wish you were here." I loved that one . . . Nick, are you there? Say something. It's your turn to speak now.'

It had been a long time – eight years or more – since Nick had last heard that voice, but he recognised it all right. It still possessed the same arrogance, the same perpetually mocking tone. It was his nemesis: Knotts-Lane, The Searcher, *Muhammad Mohajir*, the protégé of the Old Man of the Mountains, and the trainer of the Black Assassins. For the umpteenth time Nick cursed the fact that the Sea Strike had failed to kill him.

'Knotts-Lane.' Nick spoke quietly into the phone. 'Knotty, to your friends. Or Muhammad Mohajir, as I hear it is now . . . How are the burns, by the way? I trust they're healing well?'

'You know, Nick, that was a cheap trick and so typical of you cowardly infidels. You ran to your Yankee masters, just like you always do . . . Just one brave suicide bomber, Nick, that's all you would have needed. We have hundreds, ready and willing to die for the cause. But you, you're all so fearful of death, aren't you, Nick? It's pathetic, really. Oh, and the burns are healing fine – my faith keeps me strong.'

'I'm so glad. What is it you want? I presume you *do* want something.'

'Oh indeed, yes. You see, His Holiness had some gold and it was stolen from him and now he wants it back. You can understand that, can't you? Here's the deal, Nick. You tell us what your friend Kilbride is planning, and the pictures will never see the light of day. You tell us everything, and the pics disappear. Otherwise, I'll be emailing them to your good lady wife. Oh, sorry, I forgot. She doesn't use email, does she? Well, maybe I'll just have to deliver them in person . . .'

'Fine, you can show my fucking wife,' Nick snapped. 'I don't give a damn. The marriage is dead and buried, anyway.'

'And how about your children, Nick? Maybe they'd like to see the pictures too? There's Lucinda, Clarissa and James, I believe? I can give you their university details if you'd like them. Lucinda is at Bristol studying law, Clarissa is at Bournemouth art school . . .'

Nick ran a hand exhaustedly across his face. 'You fucking bastard . . .'

'Nick, Nick, don't be like that. His Holiness is only asking for the return of what is rightfully his . . . I think you're probably not feeling very well this morning, Nick. You drank a little too much, and then I fear Sairah might have drugged you. So here's what I'm going to do. You have twenty-four hours to make your decision. I want to hear from you by Sunday evening, latest. A word of advice in the meantime, Nick: don't forget to call, and stay away from the girls.'

The line went quiet and Nick presumed that Knotts-Lane had called off. It had been an echoing connection with a slight time lag, as if his tormentor was speaking on a satphone. But then his voice came on again.

'Oh, one more thing, Nick. I almost forgot. The stakes are a little higher than your family being upset over a few dirty photos. If you refuse to play ball, we'll kill you, Nick, and maybe all your family too. If you doubt me just look at what happened to Emile. You underestimated us once. You thought a little unmanned aircraft could deal with us. Don't ever do so again. Islam is on the march, Nick. You're the old order. The future is ours. We're unstoppable.'

There was a click and this time the phone line really had gone dead.

Nick stared at his mobile in disbelief. Suddenly a weekend with the woman of his dreams in a sun-washed Dar-es-Salaam hotel had turned into his worst-ever nightmare. He'd fallen for the oldest trick in the book: the honey trap. How could he have been so stupid? How could he have let it happen?

Nick would probably never know for sure, but he could put together a credible scenario. The enemy were still watching Kilbride, and they had picked up on his and Nick's meeting, so revealing where he was staying. And Sairah? She was probably exactly who she'd said she was. For a few hundred dollars she would have pulled the little photo job, no questions asked. Why shouldn't she? It was easy money.

Even as he pondered on these dark thoughts, a spark of hope ignited in Nick's mind. Surely there had to be a way to turn this around, or at least engineer a vast improvement on the present situation. It would mean confessing to his superiors that he'd been the subject of a classic entrapment. But he wouldn't be the first to have been ensnared in that way, and if they saw the photos of Sairah they'd probably understand.

If Operation Trojan Horse was to work, they needed a way to alert The Searcher to Kilbride's arrival in the Lebanon. When Kilbride had outlined his plan the previous evening, Nick had presumed that they would simply leak this information to the enemy. But surely there was now an even better way? Now they had a direct line to The Searcher himself. The Searcher believed he was blackmailing Nick and thus forcing him to talk, which provided the perfect cover. The Searcher would suspect nothing.

Nick waved one of the waiters over and ordered a cafetière of maximum-strength coffee. He still felt pretty rough, but at least his mental state was improving. The Searcher's arrogance was beyond belief, as was his conviction of his own invincibility. And maybe that was his big weakness, his fatal flaw. As Nick poured himself a cup of hot black coffee, he was reminded for a second of Sairah. It had been a roller-coaster twenty-four hours, that much was certain. And if he really did have to be put through all this, the one thing he regretted most was that he never had fucked her.

Back in his room Nick placed a call to Kilbride. 'They're closing in,' he announced.

'What d'you mean?'

'They just paid me a visit at the hotel. Or at least one of their . . . associates did.'

'Fuck.'

'Exactly. They're watching, Kilbride. Be careful. I'm all right and I'm catching my flight back to London tomorrow as planned. I'll keep my head down in the meantime. But the quicker we can do this, get it all wrapped up, the better.'

'Understood. We're ready to move. Just as soon as that decoy gold is in position, we're ready.'

'I'm going to work on the China end of things now, Kilbride, from the hotel. It might mean disturbing a few people's weekends, but what of it? Mine's hardly been a pleasant and relaxing one, and it's far from over. Let's start building our tungsten bomb.'

That afternoon, Kilbride briefed Berger, Smithy and Boerke on the new developments. With five of the enemy having turned up at The Homestead, the savage murder of Emile and his family, and now Nick's unwelcome hotel visitor, it was clear that they had to get moving. Kilbride outlined an accelerated schedule that would get all elements of the plan in place within two weeks, at which time they would activate Operation Trojan Horse. Last but not least, Kilbride told the three of them about The Project's new demand that they should deliver the gold to Cyprus. It met with an angry response from his men.

'Deliver the gold to Cyprus?' Smithy snorted. 'I don't trust them one bloody inch.'

Boerke scowled. 'It's clear, man, that they are trying to fuck with us.'

Bill Berger slammed a fist onto the table. 'So let's fuck with them back! We just ignore 'em, load up the dhow with the loot and we're outta there. Or am I missing something?'

'We do that and they'll be onto us,' said Kilbride. 'They'll get a warship steaming after us, and in no time we'll be heading for Cyprus under escort. No, we've got to play ball with them, or at least *make it appear as if we are* . . . Let's say the dhow ships out from here with three ten-point-five-metre RIBs on board. And let's say that upon arrival in the Lebanon the RIBs are packed with seventeen and a half tons of gold – or at least something that we could pass off as being the gold. That's just under six tons per RIB, plus the boats – so maybe twenty tons in all. Is there any chopper in the world that can carry that sort of payload?'

'We make the best goddamn choppers in the world, and nothin' we have can handle that,' Bill Berger volunteered. 'I mean, the CH53 Super Stallion's the biggest we got. And what can she manage, fifteen tons maybe, and even then she's maxed out.'

Smithy snorted. 'Typical bloody Yank . . . The world's biggest chopper is the Mi-26 HALO, and she's made by the Mil company, in Russia. So she's essentially a *Soviet* aircraft. She can carry twenty tons, no problem.'

'Tell me more,' said Kilbride.

'Right: the Mi-26 HALO's loaded from the rear, up a ramp, just like a Hercules. You can drive a truck right into her – that's what she's designed for. She's forty metres long, and with the tail ramp lowered she'd take the three RIBs all right . . . She's got no armaments as standard, but you can always bolt a couple of chain guns onto the side doors. What more d'you need to know?'

'How do we get hold of one?' Kilbride asked.

'Easy. There's several firms that lease them out of Russia. They'll even fly one out in stripped-down form on a bloody great big Antonov AN24, and rebuild her on delivery. You pay half the hire costs up front and they can have it to you within forty-eight hours.'

'Just out of interest, mate, how d'you know all this?'

'I worked as security in the oil industry, out in Nigeria. They used the Mi-26 all the time. She's a big old bird but she flies bloody beautifully – that's if you have a crew who know how to handle her.'

'Right – I want one leased for the duration of this mission,' said Kilbride. 'We need it boxed up and delivered to the British military base, Cyprus. I want it sat there for several days looking big and ugly and very capable of lifting seventeen and a half tons of gold. Find out the cost, and I'll get it cleared with The Project. Last but not least, d'you know a good crew we can use?'

Smithy rubbed his hands together excitedly. 'I know just the man. He's ex-New Zealand Air Force, special-forces squadron. He's got more hours on Russian choppers than anyone I know. Plus he's half Maori and

299

hung like one, with the balls to boot. I take it he'll be needing them?'

Kilbride nodded. 'Get the HALO, get the crew, and I'll explain what I have in mind. Right, anyone got any plans for tonight?'

Berger and Boerke shook their heads.

'I might be hitting the town,' Smithy announced, a little self-consciously. 'There's something I've got to get sorted . . .'

Kilbride eyed the burly sergeant. 'There is? Like what?'

'It's Janey,' Smithy muttered. 'I ain't seen nor heard nothin' of her ever since I stood her up, Wednesday night. That's three days back . . . She won't take my calls. I know where she'll be tonight, though. One of her friends told me. I'm going down there to find—'

'Not alone you're not,' Kilbride interjected. 'I'm sending Nixon with you. He'll be happy to look after you, just as long as you buy him all the beer he can drink.'

'I don't need looking after. I just need to see her and sort this out.'

'All loved-up and full of heartache – of course you need looking after. Nixon's going with you, and that's that . . .'

An hour later and Smithy and Nixon were loitering at the bottom of a flight of stone steps that led up to the Terrace restaurant. The Terrace was one of Dar-es-Salaam's more exclusive dining venues, with a panoramic view over the city's Mzizima Bay. Nixon had already carried out a covert recce of the dining area and confirmed that Janey was up there, having dinner with a seriously overweight Indian businessman. Smithy could hear the gentle notes of piped music drifting down from the dining area and could just imagine a fat, sweaty Indian with his greasy fingers grasping Janey's own slender hand.

'What now, Nixon?' he hissed. 'Can't stand here like a couple of spare pricks all night long.'

'Why not go to the Q-Bar?' Nixon replied, with a broad grin. 'Bound to be plenty of other girls—'

'I don't want *other girls*,' Smithy cut in. 'I want bloody Janey. And that greasy Indian fucker better watch it, or I'll skewer him on a spit and roast him over a fire . . .'

Nixon rolled his eyes. 'Hold on, Mr Smithy, let me think for a second . . . I think I recognise that Indian man. Mr Rajit Tengupta – he runs a chain of car importers. They bring in cheap vehicles from Dubai. More importantly, he is married.' Nixon winked at Smithy and squared his shoulders. 'Leave this to me . . . You have a pen and paper? Write Janey a message. Tell her you're waiting for her here . . .'

Nixon folded Smithy's note in his pocket, straightened his shirt and strode up the stone steps. He had a quiet word with the head waiter, and was ushered over to Mr Tengupta's table. Making his apologies, Nixon asked for a quiet word. With bad grace Mr Tengupta agreed. He levered his considerable bulk out of the chair and stepped to one side. Nixon leaned over the balcony with his back to the dining area. Down below him he could see Smithy stiffen as he caught sight of the pair of them.

'Quickly now, I am in the middle of my eating,' Mr Tengupta panted. 'What is all this disturbing me for?'

Nixon lowered his voice. 'Trust me, I am your Good Samaritan, Mr Tengupta. I am trying to do you a service

301

. . . Do I have your word that everything we discuss will be kept confidential?'

Mr Tengupta wiped a handkerchief across his brow. 'Of course, of course.'

'I am a private detective,' Nixon announced. 'Your wife, Mrs Tengupta, hired me to keep watch on you. She suspects . . . indiscreet behaviour on your part. Now I, like you, am a red-blooded male, and the attraction of a young lady never fades, does it, Mr Tengupta?'

'Are you trying the blackmailing?' Mr Tengupta gasped. 'Because if you jolly well are . . . An innocent meal with a young woman . . .'

'If you will just listen, Mr Tengupta. Your wife is on her way right now, to this very restaurant. I had to report that you were here. At the same time I wish you no harm because no man likes to be caught by his wife . . .'

'My God, my wife, here . . .' Mr Tengupta gasped. 'She is the most imposing woman . . . Most imposing . . . She will cause such commotions. What am I to do? How can I stop her?'

'You can't stop her, Mr Tengupta. As you say – a most imposing woman . . . Your only option is to leave, right now – there's no time to lose. You give me the money to cover the bill. I'll explain everything to your . . . dining companion. Get out, Mr Tengupta, get out while you still can . . .'

'Thank you, my friend, thank you.' Mr Tengupta handed Nixon a bundle of money. 'Here, this should cover it. And here is my card. Call me in the week. I should like to be hearing more about my wife's interest in my privates.'

Without a backward glance Mr Tengupta turned and waddled from the restaurant. As the panicked and overweight Indian reached the bottom of the steps, Smithy stuck out a foot and tripped him.

'Sorry, mate, I didn't see you,' he quipped as he helped the struggling Indian to his feet. 'You're not hurt or anything, are you . . . ?'

Nixon strolled across to the dining table. Janey looked at him enquiringly. 'Your dining companion was called away on urgent family business,' Nixon announced quietly. 'He left me the money to settle the bill. In the meantime, read this.' He passed her Smithy's note.

'I know you, don't I?' Janey said, as she took the folded paper. 'You're Kilbride's man.' She glanced at the note. 'Is this from . . . ?'

'Just read it,' Nixon replied. 'And let me tell you – you don't know a good man when you see one. Now, I am going settle the bill.'

Janey unfolded the piece of paper in her lap. I'M SORRY, she read. I didn't mean to stand u up. I meant every word I said on the beech. All of it. I'm waiting at the botom of the steps for u. Smippy xxx

A half-hour later Smithy and Janey were walking across the white sands of Coco Beach, itself a short taxi ride from the Terrace restaurant.

'You ruined my evening,' said Janey accusingly. 'You told Rajit a pack of lies. How dare you? You're incredible . . .'

'*Rajit*? You mean lard arse?' Smithy countered. 'What sort of evening were you going to have with . . . Rajit, anyway? I mean, d'you actually . . .'

Janey rounded on him, her eyes blazing. 'Go on. Say it. Do I actually *sleep with him*? Not very often, no. He's too old and too fat and he usually eats too much. And he gets bad indigestion. But sometimes . . .'

'The bloke's a bloody human hot-air balloon . . .'

'You think it matters!? He helps pay my university fees. He *looks after me*. That's more than I can say for—'

'For me? What did I bloody do? All I did was forget that we were meeting . . . One evening! I was busy, something came up with the lads. It happens. But I've been phoning you every hour for three days since. Don't that say something?'

Janey shrugged. 'I stopped believing in you . . . I've heard it all before, Smippy. Promises, promises, people promising the world. Each time I believe it, and when it all proves to be lies another little part of me dies. But I believed you. I believed everything you said. And it hurt too much to think you'd lied . . .'

Tears welled up in Janey's eyes. 'I just want a home, a family and an education. And a good man. Is that too much to ask? You stood me up. I was heartbroken. I called Rajit . . .'

Smithy drew her to him, and she buried her face in his shoulder. 'Nah, it's not so bad . . .' He stroked her hair, breathing in the warm, spicy smell of her. 'And it don't matter. Not now. Not now I've got you here, in my arms . . . All thanks to Nixon. He's an operator, ain't he? Old Rajit's terrified of his wife, mind. You see the way he left the restaurant? White as a sheet and moving pretty fast for a fat one. Or at least he was until he tripped over my ankle . . .'

Janey laughed. Then sobbed some more. Then laughed again. 'I like a man who makes me laugh . . .'

'And cry? You like a man who makes you sob your bloody heart out, too?'

Janey shook her head, and wiped her eyes. 'No.'

'Right then, let's start over as we mean to carry on.

I'll make you laugh till you're fit to drop, as long as you stop dating fat blokes. I'll give you that home you want. I dunno how you'll manage seven kids and a university career all at the same time, mind. Something'll have to give . . .'

The two strolled on across the sands of Coco Beach as Smithy mapped out a golden future. Nixon followed at a discreet distance. He glanced at his watch. If Smithy would only get a move on they could all catch a last few beers at the Q-Bar.

Moynihan pulled a stub of pencil from behind his ear and checked his sums one last time. The Irishman knew he would get no second chance with building this bomb: he had to get it exactly right first time. It was a trade-off between maximum explosive force and the space that that amount of explosives occupied. What Moynihan hadn't quite appreciated was the density of the gold, the incredibly small volume of 17.5 tons of the stuff.

RDX explosive has a density of 1.8 grammes per cubic centimetre, so 2,000 kilogrammes would have a volume of 1.1 cubic metres. Incredibly, 17.5 tons of gold – some 18,000 kilogrammes – would take up a *smaller* volume, some 0.95 cubic metres. So when making up the explosive charge he'd have to be careful to ensure that it could be hidden by the fake gold bars. If any of the RDX was visible, even a cursory inspection by the terrorists would give the game away.

Moynihan pulled his duvet jacket closer and glanced across at the shipping container. The deserted warehouse that Nick Coles had found was draughty, and he'd had no idea that China could be so cold. If he did use 2,000kg of RDX he'd need to cover five faces of a 1.1-metre cube with the tungsten bars. The sixth face would be formed by the steel floor of the shipping container. So the thickness of the metal 'jacket' would be twenty centimetres, or two tungsten bars. The overall size of the 'gold' pile would then be twice what it should be, but he very much doubted if the terrorists would notice. It would still appear an impossibly small cargo, for 17.5 tons of material.

Perhaps he'd go for a compromise, Moynihan reflected. He recalculated the size of the charge required to turn the 17.5 tons of tungsten into one giant shrapnel bomb. With an explosive velocity of 8,750 metres per second, 1,000 kilogrammes of RDX was about the minimum he could get away with.

RDX was hardly the most modern of explosives, Moynihan reflected, but it was still one of the best around. No one really knew where the name RDX had come from, but Research Department (Composition) X was most likely. RDX was developed during the Second World War, when experimental British explosives were each given a Research Department Number, for example RD11. But the story Moynihan had heard was that the Research Department developing RDX had blown itself to pieces, and so it became known as Research Department X – RDX. Hopefully, the explosive charge that he was now building would have a similar effect on the Black Assassins.

CHAPTER THIRTEEN

The week had passed in a blur of phone calls and planning as the day of the dhow's departure approached. Kilbride woke early on the Friday morning but decided to have a bit of a lie-in. He snuggled up to Marie-Claire, her back to his stomach and his breath in her thick dark hair. This was his wife's favourite position: wrapped in his strong arms she felt secure and contented, as if nothing could ever come between them or cause them harm.

There was a sharp knock on the front door, repeated a little louder when no one answered. Kilbride cursed, went to get up and then heard Nixon dealing with it.

He caught a few fragments of a conversation: 'FedEx . . . Parcel for Mr Kilbride . . . Needs signing for . . .'

He gave up trying to sleep and went to check. Nixon handed over a brown parcel wrapped in standard FedEx plastic packaging.

'Feel the weight of it, Mr Kilbride. You would never believe something that size could weigh so much.'

Kilbride looked Nixon in the eye and grinned. 'I hear you sorted out Smithy's little problem last night . . .'

'Yah! I hear reports that Mr Rajit Tengupta is being unusually attentive to his wife, of late . . .'

'Nothing wrong with that,' Marie-Claire remarked as she wandered in from the bedroom. She had a gown wrapped around her and was stifling a yawn. 'We all like a bit of attention . . . What's in the parcel?'

Kilbride knew when he had been caught, so there was no point in not showing her. He took the parcel over to the kitchen table, ripped off the FedEx packaging and tore open the tape. He unhooked the cardboard flaps, scrabbled about in the packaging and pulled out a slim metal bar. It was twenty-six centimetres long by eight wide, and as he lifted it out of the packaging Kilbride felt an overwhelming sense of awe . . .

He ran his fingers across the cold surface, tracing the form of the winged staff stamped into the metal, the two cobras entwined around it. Across one end of the bar was the serial number COBRA 405, plus the words 'FINENESS 9968'. It was a perfect copy.

'Unbelievable . . .' Kilbride muttered to himself. He held the bar up to the light and it shone with the unmistakable sheen of gold. 'Unbelievable . . .'

He searched through the box, and found the shipping invoice. 'ITEM: 400-oz. Sintered 99.9% Tungsten Bar. Lead and 24 Carat Gold-plated.'

The bar had been couriered to him from China, just so that he could check its authenticity. No doubt about it, it would take a real expert's expert to tell this from the real thing. He felt Marie-Claire's presence at his shoulder. 'Here,' he announced, as he handed her the bar without warning.

'Ouch!' Marie-Claire remarked in amazement, as the

bar went falling through her fingers. Kilbride caught it just before it hit the floor.

'What is it? Did I damage it? I didn't damage it . . .' Marie-Claire asked, anxiously. 'It is *so* heavy . . .'

'It's fine,' Kilbride replied with a chuckle. The courier must have woken their oldest son, who came wandering into the kitchen. Kilbride placed the bar on a low wooden bench. 'Let's try David on it. David, come here. What's this, eh?'

His three-year-old boy went to grab the bar, but it slipped through his grasp. He laughed and glanced at his father, clearly appreciating the game. He went to grab it again, this time knowing to hold it more tightly. Slowly, he raised one end of it with both hands.

'He did it! He did it!' Kilbride cried out.

Marie-Claire gave a round of applause. 'So what is it?' she asked. 'It's somehow beautiful . . .' Kilbride could detect a hint of worry in her voice, and he had a good idea what was coming.

'It's a bar of tungsten. Weighs almost exactly the same as gold. And it's plated in twenty-four-carat gold, hence the colour. Amazing, isn't it . . . ?'

'You're going, aren't you?' Marie-Claire demanded as she gazed into his eyes. 'You're going back to the Lebanon . . .'

'Lover, before we married I told you that there would be times when I disappeared on work,' Kilbride replied evenly. 'I said there might be times when I wouldn't tell you what I was doing . . . that it'd be safer for you not to know. This is one of them.'

Marie-Claire sighed. 'I didn't sign a contract.'

'But you knew that's how it was going to be.'

'Tell me something. We're here in this beautiful home on this beautiful beach with this beautiful family.' She took his hand and placed it on her stomach. They'd just recently found out that she was pregnant again, and this time Kilbride was hoping for a girl. 'A family that's growing . . . We don't have money problems. So try to help me understand; why are you going?'

Kilbride glanced down at their eldest son. He knew that if he was ever parted from his children he would die inside. His son gazed back at him, his normally smiling eyes now etched with worry. David was old enough to understand that his dad was going away somewhere, and that his mum didn't want him to go.

'Not now,' Kilbride responded. 'I'll tell you later – this evening, okay?'

'No, it's not okay,' Marie-Claire replied, softly. 'There'll always be a "later" and one day you'll just be gone. I've already had the house turned into a war zone . . . It's destroying our life, our happiness. *I need to know*. I'll deal with the kids, and then you're going to tell me, all right?'

Kilbride nodded. She was right. The danger was all around them now. She did deserve to know. Marie-Claire gathered David into her arms and carried him off into the TV room, singing gently as she went.

'Postman Pat, Postman Pat,
Postman Pat and his black-and-white cat . . .'

A minute later she was back. She made some coffee and set it down on the kitchen table. 'Talk to me,' she commanded. 'I'm not going to try and stop you. I just want to know. We're in danger here, aren't we?'

Kilbride rubbed a hand exhaustedly across his face and began telling Marie-Claire all that he was up to. An hour later and he had failed to convince his wife of the need to vacate The Homestead for the few days that he would be away in the Lebanon. It was their home, she'd told him, and no one was forcing her to leave.

Kilbride smiled. 'I thought you'd say that . . . That's what I love about you. You're not afraid. I'll make the necessary security arrangements. You'll be safe here, I promise . . .'

Kilbride carried the gold-plated tungsten bar out to his office and presented it to Boerke, Berger and Smithy. To them it appeared to be a perfect copy of a Schöne Edelmetaal London Good Delivery Bar, as the 400-ounce (12.5kg) bars were called. Kilbride left them admiring the fake gold bullion and went to have a word with Nixon. He found him down by the jetty, sorting through some junk in the boathouse.

'Nixon, I need your help. You know any local furniture makers around here?'

'My cousin runs a furniture factory, Mr Kilbride. Why?'

Kilbride handed him a piece of paper, with a design for a crate sketched on it. 'I need a hundred and twenty wooden boxes making up, each pretty much identical and with those dimensions. And I need it doing in forty-eight hours' time.'

'Ah, this should be no problem, Mr Kilbride.'

Kilbride handed him another sheet of paper, a photocopy of the winged-staff stamp. 'Each box has got to be stamped with those markings. You think your people could do that?'

'Yah, this is the easy bit,' Nixon rumbled. 'There are men who make their living in the market carving stamps for people. Leave it to me.'

'Thanks, Nixon. One more thing: I need you to call in the dhow crew. All six of them. Tell them I'll pay

311

them double time, as I know it's early and not the season yet. I want them to fill each of those boxes with sand and load them into the dhow's hold.'

Nixon raised one eyebrow. 'Sand? A hundred and twenty boxes full of sand? They may ask some questions, Mr Kilbride.'

Kilbride shrugged. 'Then triple their wages, and tell them I've got a big sandcastle I need building somewhere. And Nixon, this is sensitive, but I know I can entrust it to you . . . You remember those people who came to attack us?'

Nixon smiled, showing a wide set of perfect teeth. 'Ah – you mean the ones we fed to the sharks?'

'You got it. Well, there's always a chance that they or their friends might return. I don't think they will, but . . . You know I've got to go away for a few days? In your own quiet way I want you and the dhow crew to act as security for The Homestead. I'll be leaving you with the Remington, and I want you to go buy six hunting shotguns in the local market. Arm the crew. If the enemy returns, I want them to be met by a wall of lead.'

Nixon placed an arm around Kilbride's shoulders. 'Don't worry, my friend, I would never let any harm come to your family. We will throw a ring of African steel around The Homestead.'

'Nixon, tell the crew I'll quadruple their wages. And tell them at the end of all this they get to keep their shotguns, as well . . .'

Nixon smiled. 'If those people are stupid enough to come again, we shall give them a *traditional African welcome*. I hear the sharks are especially hungry at this time of year . . .'

'You asked me to call you once I knew something.' Nick

Coles was speaking into a telephone handset from the bowels of the MI6 building. He was surrounded by several colleagues, a team that had been cobbled together to man Operation Trojan Horse from the London end. 'I have the mission details.'

'That's good, Nick, very good,' The Searcher's voice purred on the other end of the line. 'Once we have what we want, those pictures will be destroyed, Nick. You have my word on that. But no games. If I get a sense that you're messing with us the gloves are off, Nick.'

'All right, all right!' Nick snapped, feigning anger. 'I've heard enough of your threats. Kilbride and his team are leaving one week from now, flying BA from London to Beirut, arriving two-thirty p.m. They've hired a couple of four-wheel drives and will be heading up into the mountains. You can't miss them. They'll lead you to the gold.'

'Where is it, Nick? The gold . . . We would prefer to get there first, if we may. I'm sure you understand.'

'You think they'd be stupid enough to tell me? I don't know where it is. Just follow them.'

'It sounds too easy, Nick. Tell me more. How many of them are there? Will they be armed? What security measures are they taking? Do they have back-up?'

'Look, Knotty, let's not over-dramatise things. They're six middle-aged men, none of whom have seen combat in years. As far as I know they're on their own and unarmed. I would have thought that you and the Brothers would be more than a match for them.'

'What do they know, Nick? About us, our interest?'

'They know you sent some people to spy on them in Tanzania. But they were caught, so they think you're still in the dark. As indeed you would be, were it not for this phone call . . .'

313

'Thanks, Nick. But no games, eh? You hear any more, you call me. Any changes of plan. Anything that might upset our day.'

Nick replaced the receiver. His anger hadn't been entirely acted. His hatred for that man knew no bounds.

The leader of the London end of operations placed a hand on Nick's shoulder. 'You think he swallowed it, do you, Nick?'

'I think he's so full of his own shit he'd believe he was God if enough people told him. The arrogance of the man.'

Nick's controller smiled. 'Islamic converts . . . He *is* a little full of himself, isn't he? I'm so glad they pulled me out of retirement for "just the one last job". I get a strong sense that this one is going to be most exceptionally satisfying . . .'

It was the Sunday evening and the dhow would be departing at midnight. She was fully fuelled up and there was plenty of fresh water and food in the galley. The three RIBs were strapped onto a massive wooden scaffold erected to the aft of the main mast. The diving gear was stowed in the ship's hold, along with a generator and compressor for refilling air bottles. Nixon had got the hundred and twenty wooden crates filled with sand and stowed in the ship's hold, just as Kilbride had ordered. And an arms drop by a Snow Goose UAV was scheduled for 4 a.m., just off the Tanzanian coast.

Moynihan and McKierran boarded the boat and prepared to cast off, but there was still no sign of Smithy. Kilbride wasn't unduly worried. He reckoned a woman was involved and there were some last-minute goodbyes being said down on the beach sands.

Kilbride waited by the pier, with Sally at his side. Over the past few days the big Alsatian had really taken to Smithy, which was fortunate. Kilbride had decided that Sally would be joining the B Team and sailing with Smithy, Moynihan and McKierran to the Lebanon.

Just after midnight Kilbride caught sight of a burly figure hurrying down the beach towards him. By the time he reached the pier Smithy was out of breath and sweating heavily.

He grabbed his backpack and shouldered it. 'Bloody glad we're not walking there, that's for sure,' he panted. 'Talk about bloody unfit.'

Kilbride grinned. 'With all the shagging you've been doing I'm surprised you've got the energy to lift your pack. I trust your woman's suitably heartbroken . . . Good luck, mate – we'll be seeing you in the Lebanon.'

Smithy grabbed Kilbride and gave him a bear hug. 'Listen, just in case I don't make it back—'

'Bollocks, mate, you're indestructible,' Kilbride cut him off. He nodded at the boat. 'Here, take Sally's lead, 'cause she's going with you. You'll be missing your woman so much I figure you need the company. Plus she's the best security money can buy.'

'Bloody awesome . . .' Smithy ruffled Sally's shaggy mane. 'Right, I'll be seeing you, boss. Come on, Sally, look lively. Let's go waste these bastards.'

The dhow cast off and chugged throatily into the dark night. Boerke, Berger and Kilbride stood on the pier and watched her leave. There was no cheering and no major send-off. Just a few muttered prayers and a quiet goodbye, as each man wondered which of the others he might never see alive again.

*

Kilbride had his back to the wall and a beer in his hand as he scanned the crowd in the Q-Bar. He was four days away from departure and this was going to be his last meeting. It was about time, too: he was sick to death with all the planning and just wanted to get on with the mission. He'd chosen the Q-Bar as the venue because it was noisy and crowded. If anyone was watching they'd have trouble catching any of Kilbride's conversation. He'd kept an eye on his rear-view mirror on the drive in, and he reckoned he hadn't been followed. But you could never be certain.

Burt Joubert, his South African bush-pilot friend, made his way across the bar towards him. He stuck out a hand to greet Kilbride. 'How is it, man?'

Kilbride grinned. 'It's good. Fancy a beer?'

'I'm off the beer, man. A fruit juice maybe.'

Kilbride ordered the drinks and the two men spent a few minutes catching up on old news. They'd met in the Congo several years back and had gone on to work together in various war zones. Burt had a small farm up-country, with a dirt airstrip from where he ran his air-charter business. He owned a couple of Buffalo transport aircraft, which were exceptional workhorses, and until recently he had been doing very well. Then a rival air-charter company had spread some seriously nasty rumours about Burt's professionalism and the business had dried up. Kilbride had heard that Burt was in real financial trouble.

'I need a job doing, mate,' Kilbride yelled above the noise of the bar. 'I can't afford to pay up front, but if we pull it off you'll never have to work again.'

'Sounds interesting, man. I presume it's highly dangerous.'

'Pretty much,' Kilbride confirmed. 'Remember when

316

we flew that mission over Sierra Leone, and you dropped a loop of gasoline into the jungle? Chucked in a couple of grenades at the end of the loop, and the whole lot went up. Fried a load of those rebel bastards, the ones who were chopping off little kiddies' hands?'

Burt grinned. 'It wasn't gasoline, man. It was a variant on that Vietnam-era foo gas. You mix styrofoam in with the diesel – makes a DIY napalm. Forms a sticky gel – vastly more unpleasant for the enemy.'

'Right. Well, I need you to fly in a tanker-load of that stuff to Beirut. You'll have to sit on the runway for forty-eight hours, on call. If you leave at the end without deploying the foo gas, there's a million and a half in it for you. If I do call you in you'll need to dump it on the bad guys and fry the fuckers. And that's a five-million job.'

'Dollars?' Burt queried.

'Dollars.'

'Sounds good to me, man.' Burt took a sip of his fruit juice. His competitors had been spreading bullshit rumours that he was flying his planes pissed on vodka the whole time. He'd stopped drinking completely, as a way to counter the gossip. 'Mind telling me something of your mission? I mean, it's not a coup or anything, man? I'm not likely to get my crew arrested and the Buffalo impounded when it all goes tits-up?'

'Here's the short version. There's a load of loot hidden somewhere in the Lebanon. Me and a bunch of my ex-SAS mates are going to fetch it. Unfortunately, a bunch of mad Islamic terrorists know about it, and they'll be following us. If we can't shake them off we may need to call in the air force. That's where you come in.'

'What sort of terrain am I likely to be operating

over?' Burt asked. 'There's no jungle out there, man. Just a lot of mountains and a lot of coastline and not a lot in between.'

'I'm not sure. Coastal is most likely. Would that stuff work if you dumped it over the sea?'

'Foo gas? Of course, man. It would sit like a slick on the ocean's surface. Only thing that might spoil it is real rough weather, sort of breaks it up . . . But it has to be real rough, man. Otherwise, you put a match to it and . . . boom.'

'Boom.' Kilbride raised his beer glass. 'I'll drink to that.'

Burt raised his fresh pineapple juice. 'I'll need to book a crew and get some airport clearances. When do you need me ready by, man?'

'Two days from now. Once you've got your crew together pay a visit to The Homestead and I'll brief you on your area of operations.'

Smithy stared out over the dark waters. The throb of the diesel engine and the rocking of the boat lulled him, tempting him to sleep. But they were just off Somalia, and pirates were known to stalk these waters. He pinched himself awake. All three of them were on deck and trying to stay alert, although Sally would no doubt be the first to sense any trouble. In his lap Smithy cradled the cold steel of a Diemaco assault rifle with an underslung M203 grenade launcher. The airdrop of arms by the Snow Goose had gone like clockwork. If any pirates did care to bother them, they'd be getting a nasty surprise.

Moynihan had let McKierran take the wheel for the last few hours. The big Scot was proving remarkably handy to have around, in spite of the wheelchair.

318

Smithy glanced at the Irishman. 'What're you thinking, Paddy? You're quiet . . .'

'Sure, I'm thinking about children, so I am.'

'You don't have none, do you?'

'I don't, and there's no home without them.'

'Bloody hell, that's a bit morbid to be thinking just prior to going in . . . You all right?'

'Ah, sure I am. It's just, I think I met someone . . .'

'Awesome. You're thinking of settling down? So am I, mate.'

'Sure, that's the idea – if she'll have me.'

'She'd be a fool not to, wouldn't she?'

'She's a fair bit younger than me. Sure, I'm no great catch as things presently stand. Tell you the truth, now, that's why I'm here.'

'What, you think you'll catch your woman with the gold?'

'Sure, with a bit of luck I'll be going home to Ireland a very wealthy man . . . It might make a shade of difference to how she views things, end of story.'

Smithy stared out to sea. Maybe there was some truth in what Moynihan had said. How much was Janey's love for him driven by money? Fuck it, maybe it was and maybe it wasn't. But at least she'd never done him down, never said that he'd *never amount to anything*.

And there was another thing, too. He'd kept it quiet from the rest of the lads, but Janey had been to the doctor and she was pregnant. She was going to have his kid. A Smithy Junior. Well, that was enough for him. It was more than his wife had ever done for him in thirty years of marriage. End of story, as the Irishman would say.

Kilbride called the men of the A Team together for a final

pre-mission briefing. Two days earlier, Ward, Johno and Nightly had flown out to join Boerke, Berger and Kilbride at The Homestead. All six men would be leaving for the airport at 5.30 a.m. the following morning. They would be travelling in civilian clothing and carrying nothing on them that was the remotest bit military. If anyone asked, they were six blokes going on a jaunt in the sunny Lebanon.

Kilbride pointed at a map of the Lebanon that he had taped to the office wall. 'Right, we arrive in Beirut at 2.30 p.m. The airport's on the south of the city, here. We've then got a drive north to this point, here. We overnight at the Hotel Chbat, in Bcharre town, which is just a few klicks short of our destination, the farm at Wadi Jehannam. Bcharre is an ancient Christian stronghold, so our going there will make perfect sense to the enemy – who will be following us.'

'Why not head straight for the farm?' Ward asked. 'Why the stopover?'

'We need to take a weapons delivery, and the Yanks have agreed to do a weapons drop into the hills around Bcharre.'

'What if the airdrop fails to materialise?' Nightly asked. 'If there's storms over the mountains or something?'

'Good question. If that happens, we wait. Once the weather clears we reschedule the delivery. We are not going in unarmed. To do so would be—'

'Suicide?' Nightly queried.

'Right: suicide. In Bcharre there'll also be a tractor unit for an articulated truck waiting for us. I've arranged to have it delivered to the hotel by a local heavy plant-hire company, from where Boerke takes over. He claims to have some experience driving trucks.

Let's hope he didn't gain it all driving on South African roads, 'cause they're bloody lethal.'

Boerke smiled. 'If you can drive in Africa, you can drive anywhere, man.'

Kilbride turned to a second map. 'This is a close-up of Wadi Jehannam. We chose it as the hiding place for some very good reasons. First, it's one of the remotest parts of the country. There's a few semi-nomadic Bedouin around and that's it, which means few prying eyes. Second, there's lots of derelict land, so it's quite feasible for us to have hidden the gold there for all these years. Third, it offers the enemy the perfect terrain in which to ambush us.'

'Gee, well, that's a relief,' Bill Berger snorted. 'Got any targets we can pin on our goddamn backs while we're at it?'

'I still don't like it, man, setting ourselves up for an ambush,' Boerke added.

Kilbride shrugged. 'None of us do. But that's the key to Operation Trojan Horse. There's only one place where it makes sense to ambush us. Once we leave the farm our route takes us along this dirt track, which passes through a narrow, twisting defile – here. We'll be forced to slow to a crawl to negotiate it, and they'll have perfect cover. That's where they'll hit us. It's perfect for them for another reason, too. A side road branches off here towards a border crossing into Syria. That's the route they'll use to take the decoy gold back to their camp.'

'Why don't they hit us at the farm?' Ward asked. 'Why wait until we're on the move?'

'Because they'll want to be certain that it's the hiding place of the gold. Upon arrival at the farm, we use the tractor unit to tow the trailer and shipping container

321

out of the barn. Soon as the enemy see us doing that, they'll assume it's the target. And once they see us heading back the way we've come, they'll be a hundred per cent certain. They need to hit us very hard and get in and out quickly, and the gorge is the ideal place for them to do so.'

'Sounds lovely,' Nightly quipped. 'Like a bullet in the head.'

Kilbride grinned. 'Yeah. But remember, they don't hold all the cards. We'll have full satellite and comms coverage at all times. We'll know exactly where they are, exactly what they're saying to each other, and exactly what they're planning. We'll have a Psion laptop with us and we can download satellite images via the Thuraya satphone. Any pics we want we can have them: their convoy on the move, their ambush positions, their commander having a dump behind a rock, even.'

There was a ripple of laughter, which quickly died away.

'What then?' Ward asked. 'Once we've been successfully ambushed, that is . . .'

'All being well we head for Tripoli, which is about forty klicks away. We use the local dive tour to ferry us out to the dhow. We'll just be some more of their dive buddies joining the dive on HMS *Victoria*. Then we load up the last of the gold and the dhow sets sail. Once she's under way the six of us transfer into the RIBs and make for our ocean rendezvous with the Mi-26 HALO. Then it's just a short flight to Cyprus, where we unload our cargo and convince The Project they've got what they're looking for . . .'

CHAPTER FOURTEEN

BA Flight 516 touched down on the hot Beirut tarmac five minutes ahead of schedule. Kilbride and his men had been flying for sixteen hours, Dar-es-Salaam to London, and then London to Beirut. On the first leg Kilbride had managed to grab some sleep. On the second he had run over all the developments of the last few days, just to make sure that he had missed nothing. There had been a spot of trouble with the dhow off Somalia, but once a mad, wheelchair-bound Jock McKierran had pumped half a dozen shotgun rounds into the pirates' boat, they had rapidly made themselves scarce.

Two days ago the dhow had dropped anchor off the Palm Islands, and Kilbride's son Mick and his buddy Brad had joined the ship. Smithy, Moynihan, Mick and Brad had then started diving the wreck of the huge iron battleship HMS *Victoria*. According to Smithy's last report phoned in on the Thuraya, it was all going like clockwork.

Half an hour after touching down at Beirut airport Kilbride and his men were spewed out into a chaotic arrivals hall. Kilbride searched the crowd for a man with a card bearing his name. He found him and was led to a couple of waiting Mitsubishi Shogun four-wheel drives. The men loaded their bags on board and set off on the drive into northern Lebanon. As Kilbride pulled out onto the airport slip road, he sensed a vehicle close behind him. He checked his rear-view mirror. Two cars back was a Toyota pick-up, another one close behind it. Those were the vehicles to keep an eye on.

Three hours later they reached Bcharre town. The Hotel Chbat perched in splendid isolation on the side of the rugged Qadisha Valley. It had two self-contained dormitories, and Kilbride had block-booked one of them. It would make the perfect place to assemble his private army. A gleaming white Ford tractor unit was in the hotel parking lot and the keys and hire documents for the truck were waiting at reception. Kilbride handed both to Boerke, who immediately went to give the vehicle the once-over.

At midnight Kilbride and his team prepared to set out for the arms drop. They wore dark clothing and blacked up their faces with a burned cork – no one had wanted to risk bringing any camouflage cream through the airport. Before setting out, Kilbride put a call through on the Thuraya to Nick Coles.

'Nick? It's Kilbride. Any developments?'

'Nothing pressing,' Nick replied. 'You've had a tail since the airport, but I'm sure you're aware of that. They've also got a tracking device on your lead vehicle.' Nick chuckled. 'Funny, they've been tailing you so closely that I can only conclude they don't trust the technology that much.'

'Where are they staying, Nick? Tonight. You have a fix on them?'

'We do. Opposite side of the valley. There's a dump of a place called the Makhlouf Resthouse. We tracked their vehicles to it . . .'

'Any chance they've got eyes on us now?'

'Unlikely. You've picked a classic spot, actually. Perched on the side of the valley with few sites overlooking it. They'd have problems getting close . . .'

'Any changes on the airdrop?'

'None. Same coordinates. Same time tonight.'

'Thanks, Nick. We'll speak tomorrow.'

Kilbride cut the line. It was 1.30 a.m. and time to head into the hills. An hour later he and his men were crouching in a patch of craggy forest, high above the Qadisha Valley. They craned their heads skywards, waiting for the UAV to appear. Suddenly, Kilbride detected a flash of green silk high above him. There was a faint rush of wind, and the squat form of the Snow Goose UAV glided out of the darkness. It crashed against a stunted tree, righted itself and thumped into the rocky earth on its two stubby skis.

For several minutes Kilbride and his team remained where they were, observing the drop zone. If anyone else had seen the UAV arrive, they would be sure to show themselves. When he was certain that they were alone, Kilbride had his men gather around it. The aircraft stood shoulder high, with a stubby nose cone housing a propeller and drive unit. But the bulk of the fuselage was taken up by six cargo housings, three to either side. One by one the covers were removed and the weapons crates unloaded. Before leaving, Kilbride bundled up the parachute and stuffed it into one of the empty cargo housings.

Each man shouldered a crate and began the trek back to the hotel. The weapons were heavy and

325

unwieldy, but at least it was all downhill. Wherever possible the Snow Goose UAV had been built from combustible components. At 5 a.m. sharp it was programmed to self-destruct. Separate incendiary charges in the nose cone and tail would blow, incinerating the aircraft. By sunrise, all that would remain on that mountainside would be a twisted heap of smoke-blackened metal.

Once back inside their room Kilbride and his men started disassembling the crates and reassembling the weapons. Kilbride and Ward had opted for the Masterkey weapons system – the Diemaco assault rifle with the underslung Remington MCS shotgun. Boerke, Nightly and Johno had gone for the Diemaco with an underslung M203 40mm grenade launcher. Berger had opted for the belt-fed FN Minimi Squad Assault Weapon, a light machine gun and the most concentrated piece of firepower the team now possessed. And each man had a SIG-Sauer pistol as his personal reserve weapon.

Packed into one crate were six 66mm LAW disposable rocket launchers. Several boxes of 5.56mm ammunition made up the bulk of the remainder of the kit, plus a dozen No.80 white-phosphorus grenades. Finally there was a cardboard crate sporting a skull and crossbones, and with the letters POISON stamped across it. This contained half a dozen canisters of Agent BZ-16, a state-of-the-art nerve gas that Berger had ordered. It would render any victim unconscious for twelve hours, without actually killing them. And its main advantage was that it was totally untraceable in the human system.

By 4.30 a.m. the weapons were checked, loaded and packed into the vehicles, at which time Kilbride told the men to try to get some rest. They had a long day ahead of them.

Smithy peered into the ghostly grey-green depths of the pool as he waited for Mick Kilbride to give a tug on the rope – the signal that he should start hauling. They had a fixed line going down to the seabed: the two divers loaded up the bullion at depth, whereupon Smithy and Moynihan hauled it to the surface. They had been here for five hours now, and the young Kilbride and his buddy Brad had stirred the water into a thick pea soup. Visibility was down to a couple of yards, but it hadn't seemed to faze them, and Smithy thanked his lucky stars that they had the two young lads doing the toughest of the work.

Smithy took a look around him at the cave. It was exactly as he remembered it, and being back here again was a mighty strange feeling. He glanced across at Moynihan. The Irishman was taking the last of the gold bars and stowing them in the bottom of the RIB. The big 10.5-metre craft had a set of three powerful diesel-electric engines at the rear, and she had a serious cargo-carrying capacity. Without completely overloading her, the RIB could carry some six thousand kilogrammes of cargo and still be able to squeeze her way out of the cave.

To one side of the RIB lay a pile of wooden crates, those that Smithy, Moynihan, Mick and Brad had ferried across from the dhow earlier that evening. Smithy's torchlight glinted on the stamps depicting a winged staff entwined with two cobras that adorned each of the boxes. He grinned to himself in the half-light. On each journey they would bring forty wooden crates from the hold of the dhow and dump them here in the cave. They would return with 470-odd gold bars and stow them in the ship's hold. It was exhausting work, but one journey per night over three nights and they should have the operation finished. And all of it would have taken place under cover of darkness.

Burt lined up the Buffalo with the runway and began his final descent. A flash of dawn light illuminated the mountains to the east, and he figured that he had to be the first aircraft into Beirut that morning. He glanced across at his co-pilot, a black Kenyan named Peter. Beirut would be the furthest afield that Peter had ever flown, and his first time outside Africa. Behind him sat Volker, a taciturn white Zimbabwean navigator-cum-engineer. And in the jump seat to the rear was Shortie, the aircraft's loadmaster and a fellow South African.

'I hear Beirut's a party city these days,' Peter remarked, speaking into the radio mike attached to his headphones. 'Pity we won't get the chance to visit . . . All those foxy Arabian girls . . .'

Burt nodded, and turned back to the runway. A few seconds later there was a faint screech from the front tyre and the aircraft bounced a little, settled and trundled down the tarmac. The Buffalo had an unrivalled short-take-off-and-landing (STOL) capability, being designed for operations on remote bush airstrips. The aircraft was also capable of flying at extraordinarily slow speeds, down to eighty knots or less. Landing at Beirut airport was a breeze for her.

Burt taxied over to the arrivals bay and shut down the engines. Leaving his crew to look after themselves, he wandered across to the pilots' reception area. He was dressed in a crisp white pilot's uniform, with a peaked pilot's cap and gold flashes on his shoulders and sleeves. Burt delivered his story to the airport authorities – that he was delivering some equipment from a South African vineyard to a new Lebanese concern up-country. He presented his flight manifest for inspection: it showed one Toyota 'spraying tanker', and a four-metre RIB that would be returning with the aircraft.

Burt cracked a joke that the RIB was their life-raft in case they ditched at sea. Then he explained that he'd have to sit on the apron for a while because his customer had still to give him the coordinates for his onward journey. No one seemed particularly interested in Burt's flight or its cargo. A Lebanese Customs official strolled over and peered into the aircraft's hold. He spotted a bottle of Jack Daniels whiskey, which Burt had deliberately left visible. After a few brief words, the bottle of whiskey changed hands and there were smiles and handshakes all round. Burt and his crew were free to use the pilots' canteen and freshen-up facilities, and to remain on the apron for as long as they needed.

Once back in the Buffalo's cockpit Burt pulled out the Thuraya satphone that Kilbride had given him. He flipped up the tubular black aerial, punched in Kilbride's number, and listened for a ring tone. He checked his watch: 6.45 a.m. He grinned to himself as he imagined Kilbride thrashing around in his sleep as he tried to find the phone.

'Kilbride,' came a groggy-sounding voice.

'Sorry, man, did I wake you? Just a quick call to say the Soup Dragon has landed. We're on call, man. I'll only hear from you if you need us, isn't it?'

'Correct. Nice to have you with us, Soup Dragon. Sit tight.'

*

By 9 a.m. Kilbride had the convoy back on the road. On the outskirts of Bcharre they picked up their tail again, although now the enemy vehicles seemed happy to hang back and rely on the tracking device. Kilbride took the route north-east, the peaks before him fresh with a sprinkling of snow. Over the next hour the road grew more narrow, eventually becoming a dirt track winding its way into the mountains. Finally, the convoy swung into a steep-sided gorge and the vehicles slowed to a crawl. Within minutes the towering rock walls had blocked out the sunlight, throwing the vehicles into a cold and shadowy gloom.

Kilbride eyed the dark terrain closing in on them. 'Ambush alley, mate. This is where they'll hit us.'

Bill Berger peered around him, an uncomfortable expression on his rugged features. 'The Valley of Death, buddy . . . Better pray it's only them that's gonna be doing the dying . . .'

Kilbride glanced at him, scrutinising his features. It wasn't like his big American buddy ever to show signs of fear or concern. They pressed onward in a tense silence. Finally the far end of the gorge spewed them out onto a flat, desolate plain.

'Wadi Jehannam,' Kilbride announced. He checked his map. 'See that group of stone buildings? That's the farm.'

'I been in some godforsaken dumps before, but this place gives me the creeps . . . You wanna set up a vineyard here, you're on your own, buddy.'

Kilbride checked his rear-view mirror. The big Ford truck was close behind him with Boerke at the wheel, the second jeep close behind that. He gunned his engine and forty minutes later pulled his vehicle into a flat earthen courtyard. On one side was a walled olive grove, on another a large stone-sided barn, whilst a flat-roofed farmhouse made up the third side of the courtyard. The men dismounted and gathered around Kilbride's vehicle. Apart from the wind whistling through the trees, the plain was eerily silent.

'Right, unload any gear you need into the farmhouse,' said Kilbride. 'Keep your weapons hidden in the vehicles but handy. As you're doing so think arcs of fire and all-around defence, just in case they do try to hit us here. Heads-up in the olive grove in five.'

Kilbride headed for the farmhouse and pulled out the satphone. He dialled Nick's number.

'What do you see, Nick?' he asked.

'Just as you anticipated, they've pulled up in the gorge. I would imagine they have eyes on the farm from where they are. We've also got a further movement of vehicles coming down from the Syrian border. Looks like reinforcements.'

'That second force – how many vehicles? How many people?'

'Three more pick-ups. Doing a rough head-count I'd say six in each. That's eighteen altogether, plus the six already with you.'

'Twenty-four, or four-to-one in their favour. How d'you fancy our chances, Nick?'

'Erm . . . I wouldn't like to say.'

'Nick, I'm going to show them the truck. *The prize.* I expect them to react by setting an ambush in that gorge. As soon as you see – or hear – anything, let me know.'

Kilbride cut the phone. He gathered the men around him in the cover of the olive grove.

'Okay, seems like they've sent for reinforcements,' he announced. 'So we have twenty-four enemy in half a dozen vehicles. I've just had confirmation that they're holed up in the gorge we passed through—'

'You mean Death Wish Valley?' Boerke interjected. There was a ripple of nervous laughter. 'I'll tell you this for free, man, it's none of us will be dying in there.'

Kilbride stared at Boerke for a second. It was odd the effect that driving through the ambush site had had on his men. All this talk about death . . . Was it a kind of bravado, or were Berger and Boerke really spooked by it somehow?

Kilbride tried to shake off the creepy feeling that had settled over him. 'The shipping container's parked up in the barn,' he continued. 'It's hidden behind a false wall of logs. Rip that down and tow it out – use the Ford tractor unit. Remember, this is all about letting the enemy see the prize. There's only one way out of here, which is back the way we've come. So they know we have to pass back through that . . . valley sometime soon.'

'We got us a great defensive position here,' Berger remarked, as he eyed the surrounding terrain. 'Clear arcs of fire as far as the eye can see. And look at the walls – solid boulders. We could hold the fuckers off for days, buddy. It sure beats heading into that valley . . .'

'That's exactly why they'll never hit us here,' Kilbride countered. 'Once we know their intentions, then we'll make our move. But if they set an ambush in that gorge, that's where we'll be heading . . . In the meantime, keep a lookout. And see if you can't act *excited*. It's a truck full of gold, remember, a fortune beyond your wildest dreams . . .'

The men spent the next hour making a big show of opening the barn's wooden gates and retrieving the shipping container. Boerke jumped into the cab of the

332

gleaming white Ford, revved her up in a cloud of diesel smoke and inched the trailer out of the barn. The blue container was covered in dust and debris from breaking down the wooden wall. It really did look as if it could have been sitting there for two decades or more.

With the prize now in full view, the men settled down in the olive grove for a lunch of tinned food. One or two jokes were cracked, but they fell pretty flat. The atmosphere was tense and jumpy. During several decades of special-forces soldiering none of these men had ever set themselves up as bait before. They were trained to go on the offensive, to spearhead operations, and being this exposed just didn't feel right somehow. As for deliberately driving into an enemy ambush, that was causing the men some serious problems.

At 4.30 p.m. the Thuraya rang. Kilbride grabbed it. 'What's the score, Nick?'

'Just as you predicted: an ambush has been set in the gorge. It's easiest for me to send you the pictures, if you have the Psion working. I think they'll tell you everything you need to know.'

'Give me a few minutes, then send the pics across to us. Anything else?'

'One thing. We intercepted a mobile phone call from the commander of the ambush party, to the Old Man himself. He sounded rather excited. It seems he thinks that truck you've just been moving is carrying their missing gold.'

'They swallowed the bait.'

'It would appear so.'

'Thanks, Nick. Keep me posted.'

Kilbride fired up the Psion and downloaded the satellite photos. What he saw was a classic ambush, and he was more than a little impressed by the speed and professionalism with which it had been set.

'Who are these people?' Kilbride murmured as he stared at the screen. 'That's the sort of ambush *we* would have gone for . . .'

He called Berger and Boerke over to take a look. 'What d'you make of that?'

Berger studied the images for several seconds. 'That, buddy, is a killer ambush.' He jabbed a finger at the computer screen. 'Oil drums, split in two down the middle. They've laid them flat, what, thirty feet apart, the open side facing the road. You can bet your bottom dollar they're full of gasoline. There's ten half-drums, five on each side. That's a kill zone of some one hundred and fifty feet. See them dots set back a little? They'll be the Claymores. We hit the kill zone and they trigger the Claymores, the fuel drums blow and the whole gorge becomes a blazin' inferno. We drive into that valley and no one's coming out alive. Bushman?'

Boerke gave a faint inclination of his head. 'We get hit by that ambush and we're dead – simple as that, man.'

Kilbride stared at the computer screen, a dark frown creasing his forehead. 'Who the fuck are these people?'

'Does it matter, man?' said Boerke. 'I know all I need to know, which is that they are the enemy. They kill us or we kill them, that's all there is to it.'

Kilbride glanced at Boerke. 'You're forgetting one thing: the enemy have to walk away from this one alive, and with the prize.'

Boerke gestured at the satellite images of the gorge. 'Listen, man, I have a bad feeling about that place. Always have done, ever since we drove through it. And I never ignore my instinct. If we drive into that valley we will all die in there, man.' He flicked his gaze towards

334

Bill Berger. 'I think our American friend feels the same way.'

Bill Berger nodded. 'Ain't no other way to describe it, but it feels kinda evil in there.'

'So what d'you suggest?' Kilbride demanded.

'Simple, man – we don't drive into the valley . . . You said you wanted to make a show of fighting, but let them seize the truck. Well, how about we take the fight *to them*. Let's say we stage a vehicle breakdown, just this side of the gorge. Then we hit them by surprise, tonight, and turn their ambush against them. Think about it, man. We could fry a significant number of the fuckers in that gorge . . . The survivors will be forced to come after us: we flee and abandon the truck. I think it would work, man.'

'Hell, anything beats drivin' into fuckin' Death Wish Valley,' Bill Berger added.

Kilbride stared into the computer screen. He'd been so focused on steeling himself to lead his men into that ambush that he'd never even considered the alternatives. Suddenly, he knew with a burning conviction that Berger and Boerke were right. The valley was a death trap. And the only option open to them was the one that Boerke had outlined.

'It's a good plan you got there,' he announced, with a relieved smile. 'Let's do it. Thank fuck I've got the two of you with me . . .'

Bill Berger checked his watch. 'What are we, two hours from sundown? All it takes is a couple of guys to sneak in there tonight, trigger the ambush and get the hell out again.'

Boerke glanced across at Berger with his cold blue eyes. 'Wrong, man. All is takes is *one* man. I work best alone.'

An hour later and the three vehicles pulled away from the farm. A mile short of the gorge Boerke began flashing the lights of the truck. The convoy rolled to a halt. Boerke got down from the cab and levered open the engine cover. He leaned inside, played around with a few spanners and came up cursing. The truck had blown a fuse, he announced. He needed daylight to fix it. They would have to camp where they were until morning.

Forty-five minutes later a lone figure slipped away into the shadows of the night. With the natural sense of a born hunter, Boerke skirted a patch of scrub that lay to the south and climbed into the rocky folds of the gorge. He had a black woollen hat covering his white-blond hair and a thick smearing of cam cream on his face. His eyes adjusted quickly to the darkness and he travelled light and fast. He had a commando knife on his webbing belt and a SIG-Sauer pistol in a chest holster. On his back he carried a daypack with a bottle of water, an infrared strobe light, a set of passive night-vision goggles (PNGs) and several white-phos grenades.

Boerke picked his way up to the edge of the gorge, then headed west keeping just below the ridgeline. He counted his paces as he walked, keeping a rough track of the distance travelled, and halted when he figured that he was too close to the enemy to remain standing. He dropped to a crawl and covered a further two hundred yards. Then he removed his backpack, squatted down and pulled out his passive night-vision goggles. He scanned the slope below him, the eerie green glow of the night vision picking out the ambush positions. The enemy had set all eight of their sentries on this side of the gorge, giving them a clear field of fire into the killing zone.

Boerke checked for the enemy vehicles and found them, bunched up at the far end of the valley, along with the rest of the enemy's men. He selected his route down the hillside and slipped away. He made for a gully that cut down the slope and slunk into its shadows on his belly, doing a leopard crawl. Five minutes later he stopped again. For several minutes he waited and listened, immobile in the rocky darkness. It was a wild and brutal landscape and Boerke felt completely at home here. He held his mouth open to act as a sound trap and to boost his hearing. He detected an enemy sentry, not thirty yards ahead and to his right. Then he spotted the silhouette of a second, further up the valley, plus two more down below him.

He removed three grenades from his backpack and laid them on the rocky ground. He took the first, slipped the pin free and placed the sliver of metal softly on the earth. He brought his arm back and hurled the grenade up and outwards towards his right, the clip flying free as he did so. Without waiting to see where it landed he grabbed the second grenade and did a repeat performance, hurling this one in front of him and to the opposite side of the road. The first grenade landed with a clearly audible thud, by which time Boerke had a third arcing its way through the air towards the enemy positions.

There was a muffled cry of alarm as the sentry reacted to the vaguely metallic thump of the grenade landing – and then it exploded. There was a sharp crack, and a shower of blinding white balls of light shot into the air. A split second later the burning phosphorus hit the first oil drum, and the gasoline went up in a massive *whump!* In quick succession the second and third grenades exploded – and suddenly the Valley of Death had become a fearsome inferno.

Boerke dropped low and scurried for the shadows of the gully. Behind him a Claymore fired, cooked off by the flaming gasoline. There were muted screams as the ball-bearings tore the enemy sentries apart. Screams followed screams as more gasoline ignited and the valley bottom became a boiling sea of flame. Boerke paid no attention and made for the ridgeline. But suddenly there came the staccato bark of a weapon firing. Boerke halted for a second, worrying that he'd been spotted. But it was impossible, he told himself. His attack had been too savage and too quick. He pressed ahead but was forced to dive for cover as bullets started kicking up the dust all around him. As he hit the deck he felt an odd kick to his left thigh. Boerke rolled behind a rock and went to crawl away, but his left leg refused to respond.

Below him were more enemy cries, followed by probing bursts of gunfire, and Boerke knew for sure now that he'd been spotted. He put his hand down to inspect the damage. As he brought it up to his face it glowed red and angry in the fiery light. It was slick with blood. Suddenly, a third Claymore fired off and the gunfire coming in Boerke's direction ceased, to be replaced by a horrible screaming. Boerke prayed that the enemy soldier would die quickly, asking God to gift him that one enemy life, so preventing him from revealing Boerke's position to his fellow fighters. He was not a strictly religious man, but he had been born and brought up a Christian, and he still prayed in times of dire need.

Boerke could feel a stump of bone sticking through

his blood-soaked trousers, just above the knee. The bullet must have shattered his femur, and only a severed artery would produce that amount of bleeding. He reached down and grabbed his commando knife. With his other hand he tore the khaki scarf from around his neck. Gritting his teeth he sat up and tied the scarf around his thigh, with the knot hard on the damaged artery. He thrust his knife beneath the knot and twisted it several times, each turn tightening the tourniquet. When the blood stopped spurting he shoved the blade through the thick material of his combats, so holding it fast.

From his left chest pocket Boerke pulled out a syringe of morphine. He broke the protective cover off the needle, punched it into his arm and drove the shot home. He had six phials of morphine with him. It should be enough to get him back to Kilbride. Using his arms and his one good leg he began to haul himself back up the gully, dragging his injured limb behind him. He counted to one hundred, forcing himself to keep going, and then collapsed for a minute's rest. He leaned against a boulder, his injured leg stretched out before him. His face was bathed in sweat and burning from the heat thrown up by the fire below. Three more times he went back to his task, dragging himself higher and higher up the gorge, but the ridgeline still seemed impossibly distant. Waves of exhaustion and pain ripped through him.

Boerke reached for another syringe of morphine, punching it into his arm. Sweet release flooded through his body, filling him with a floating, unearthly calm. That Boerke had made it this far and was still conscious was little short of a miracle. He knew he needed to drink to replace lost fluids, but the very thought sickened him. As he scrabbled in his daypack for his water bottle, his hand felt the hard shape of the infrared strobe. He pulled it out and stared at it for a second, his dulled senses trying to comprehend what it was. Then he flipped up the power button and clipped it to the rear of his backpack. He couldn't explain why he had done so, but that was what the years of training had ground into him. He turned onto his stomach and began to inch his way upwards once again.

Down on the barren plain of Wadi Jehannam Kilbride felt a growing sense of unease. The whole of the sky above the gorge was lit up an angry red, the heavens like an upturned umbrella of burnished copper. Boerke's one-man counter-ambush had clearly been spectacularly successful, but they had expected him back some time ago. Kilbride had his men drawn up in all-round defensive positions, as they waited for the enemy to counter-attack, as he knew they would. But there was still no sign of the tough South African. Suddenly, Kilbride heard the ringing of the Thuraya. He grabbed it and hit the answer button.

'What?' he demanded.

'Spectacular light show, Kilbride. Congratulations. I take it you decided to strike first. Something decidedly odd, though. We've picked up an infrared signal on strobe, moving slowly up the valley. Very slow. Keeps stopping. I'm not there on the ground, of course, but I'd say you may have a man wounded . . .'

'Well done, Nick. What's the GPS coordinates?'

'Erm, one minute . . . GPS coordinates are 34.27.18 / 36.06.41. Moving steadily south up the valley side. Anything more we can do to help?'

Kilbride snorted. 'Call in a search-and-rescue

340

chopper? Just keep your eye on it. If there's any change, let me know.'

Kilbride cut the line. He grabbed his map from his trouser pocket and called Bill Berger over. He spread it out across the vehicle bonnet and traced the GPS coordinates.

'Boerke's been hit,' Kilbride announced. 'There's an IR on strobe, moving slowly away from the ambush site, up the side of the valley towards the ridgeline. It's got to be him.' Kilbride glanced at Berger. 'I'm going to bring him in.'

Berger shook his head. 'No way, buddy. This ain't about heroics or any of that shit, it's just about what's practical. You're in command and you gotta stay here with the men.' Berger glanced at his watch. 'I got twenty-one thirty-three by my piece. If I'm not back within the hour, you get in the jeeps and you get the fuck outta here. Okay?'

Kilbride saw the sense of what Berger was saying. It was no time to argue. Berger picked up his Minimi, turned and loped off into the shadows. The big American jogged across the valley floor, making a beeline for the ridge. If he could get to Boerke quickly enough, maybe they'd be okay. As he pushed ahead the surrounding terrain was lit up by the valley inferno, the glare being thrown back from the night sky in weird, dancing shadows. A boulder reared up before him, jet black, harsh and threatening, and then it was thrown into sudden stark relief as an explosion ripped through the gorge.

Berger reached the ridgeline a sweating, panting wreck. He forced himself to keep moving, staying down off the high ground for fear of being silhouetted. Once the valley bottom was directly below him he

341

stopped and took cover behind a boulder. He pulled out his GPS and checked his position with Boerke's last known coordinates. By rights the South African should be one hundred feet below him. Berger got to his feet in a crouching run and began to shuffle his way down the valley side. Loose stones kicked out at his passing, tumbling downhill, and Berger cursed at the noise he was making.

Boerke heard the approaching figure before he saw him. He drew his SIG-Sauer pistol and flicked the safety off. His senses were dazed but he took aim as best he could. When Bill Berger appeared around a group of rocks above him Boerke's stoned mind equated the big American with an enemy soldier. The squat form of the ammo box on his Minimi machine gun had mutated into the curved magazine of an enemy AK47, Berger's movements being those of a prowling enemy fighter. Boerke squeezed the pistol's trigger, three times in quick succession. The rounds skitted off the rock to Berger's left side, missing him by inches.

The big American rolled to the right, landed with a thump and raised the Minimi to fire. Instead, he found himself face to face with the wounded South African. Boerke swung his pistol around, preparing to fire again, but Berger was too quick for him: he lashed out with his weapon, bringing the muzzle down hard and smashing the South African's hand to the ground.

Berger pounced on Boerke, pining him to the deck by his throat and kicking the pistol away from him. 'Cut the crap, you dumb Afrikaner scumbag!'

Boerke stared back at him, his pupils dilated with the morphine. For a second he looked completely blank, but then a flash of recognition came into his eyes.

'Try anything else that fuckin' stupid and I'm fuckin'

342

leaving you,' Bill Berger hissed. 'You got it?'

Boerke nodded a vague understanding. 'I'm with you, man,' he mouthed, but the words were slurred and barely comprehensible.

Berger dropped the Minimi to his side and felt along the South African's injured leg. There was the sharp end of lacerated bone sticking through the trousers and the tight constriction of the tourniquet above it. Berger fished in his pocket for some morphine and waved it in front of Boerke's face. *You want some more of this?* The South African nodded, his eyes glazed with exhaustion and pain. Berger punched the syringe into him. Then he grabbed the handle of Boerke's commando knife, pulled the blade out of his trousers and loosened off the tourniquet. For a few seconds he let the artery bleed. If the tourniquet remained too tight for too long, Boerke's leg would be finished in any case.

'You ready?' he whispered, bending low over Boerke's face. 'I'm gonna have to carry you. It's gonna hurt.'

Boerke nodded. But as the big American went to lift him he heard a faint movement from behind. Berger turned slowly and spotted an enemy fighter some fifty yards below him, silhouetted by the fire on the valley floor. Two more figures were to his right, moving slowly up the hillside towards their position. He and Boerke were in the shadows of the gully, and Berger reckoned they hadn't been spotted yet. But it was only a matter of seconds before they would be seen.

He groped in the darkness for the Minimi. He touched the cold metal of the weapon and hoisted it off the ground, but as he did so he dislodged a rock. Below him the enemy figures froze. With an AK47 levelled at the hip the nearest fighter turned in Bill Berger's direction. Slowly the big American brought the Minimi to bear at the shoulder, knowing that any sudden movement would be spotted. He sighted his weapon and squeezed the trigger.

The Minimi barked, a streak of flame sparking in the darkness, and Berger heard rounds punching into soft flesh. As the first man went down he adjusted his aim. The second enemy figure dived for cover and Berger followed him down with a stream of lead. He saw the body jink as a round hit, heard the enemy cry out in agony. Without pausing Berger poured a long burst of fire after the third figure, turning the slope below him into a killing ground. When he'd shot off what he reckoned was half the 200-round ammo belt he ceased firing. He grabbed Boerke by the crotch and one arm, hauled him up onto his shoulder in a fireman's lift, reached for the Minimi and ran.

Fifty yards further up the hill he dumped the South African behind a boulder and sank to his knees. Above the noise of his pounding heart Bill Berger could still hear the unearthly screaming of the enemy wounded. He hoped that that would hold them up a little. He pulled out three high-explosive grenades from his chest pouch and laid them in front of him. He grabbed one of Boerke's water bottles, took a long pull himself, and then tried to force some liquid between the wounded man's lips. Boerke was losing consciousness, his eyes glazing and his lids drooping. Berger checked his watch: 10.29 p.m. It was four minutes short of the one-hour deadline that he'd given Kilbride. There was no way he could make it back in time. He just had to hope that Kilbride would hang on.

Berger pulled the pin on the first grenade and lobbed it as high and as far as he could. He'd been a prize baseball pitcher at high school, and his throwing arm had lost little of its strength. The other two grenades followed in quick succession, and under the cover of the explosions Berger was up and running again. He made an oblique line for the ridge, aiming to take the shortest route back to Kilbride. As he did so he heard the distant roar of engines starting up below and behind him. The enemy vehicles were on the move.

Back on the plain of Wadi Jehannam, Kilbride had pulled the two Mitsubishi jeeps in close to the Ford truck. With the three vehicles and his men clustered together like this, the enemy would have a hard time getting a clean shot at a target. He was hoping to buy himself some time, gambling that the enemy wouldn't risk harming the truck and its precious cargo.

Kilbride and Nightly took cover behind the engine compartment of the right-hand jeep while Ward and Johno got into a similar position to the left. The engine was about the only part of a civilian vehicle that offered any real protection from enemy fire. Kilbride was worried sick about Berger and Boerke: the one-hour deadline had already passed, and still there was no sign of them. But there was no way he was leaving without them: all the gold in the world wouldn't buy friends like those.

For the umpteenth time he scrutinised the entrance to the gorge with his night-vision goggles. As he did so, he spotted the first of the enemy vehicles nosing its way out of the valley and onto the flat of the plain. Five other vehicles followed, none of them showing any lights, and in line astern they started to crawl forwards. Kilbride reached behind him and grabbed an LAW 66mm rocket launcher. He flipped it out into extended-fire mode, steadying his aim on the bonnet of the vehicle. He signalled to Nightly to do the same with a second LAW.

Kilbride held his fire as the convoy advanced. The enemy commander had his vehicles spaced well apart. Maybe he feared a second ambush, this one set by Kilbride and his men. Well, there *was* an ambush of sorts – but it wasn't quite what the enemy would be expecting. The accurate range of the LAW was three hundred yards max, but Kilbride was going to try deploying it at over twice that range. Over the years he had worked out that the LAW could be fired in one of two ways: it was designed to be used with a flat trajectory aimed directly at the target; but it could also be fired into the air for a longer elliptical delivery. There was a simple rule of thumb: for every extra hundred yards in range he should aim two fingers' width above the target.

When the enemy convoy was still some eight hundred yards away Kilbride pulled the trigger. A split second later Nightly's rocket followed. There was a double flash of flame that lit up Kilbride's position in a stark glare as the two missiles streaked unseen through the air. The first struck in a shower of sparks just in front of the lead enemy vehicle, and exploded on the far side of the road. An instant later Nightly's missile hit, the 66mm projectile tearing into the centre of the enemy convoy. A pick-up disappeared in a sheet of flame, the soldiers in the vehicle's rear being thrown into the air by the blast.

Kilbride glanced at Nightly. 'Nice shooting, mate.'

Nightly shrugged. 'I just got lucky, boss. Don't expect a repeat performance.'

There was an answering death rattle of gunfire, but Kilbride and his men were well beyond the range of the enemy's AK47s. The firing ceased. Kilbride wondered what the enemy commander would do next. There were a few seconds of eerie silence and then a single shot rang out. A windscreen shattered, showering Kilbride with glass. Further rounds followed on single shot, punching their way through the thin metal skin of the jeeps. Kilbride noticed that with each impact there was a puff of white smoke at exactly the spot where the bullet had hit.

The enemy commander had a sniper on his team. For a second Kilbride wondered what weapon he was using: it had to have a range of a thousand yards or so, so it was probably a Soviet Dragunov or similar sniping rifle. It also had to have a night scope, for Kilbride's vehicles were totally dark and there was no other way the enemy could have located them. And he was using phosphorus-tipped bullets, which accounted for the puff of smoke each time he scored a hit. From those alone the sniper could judge his range and adjust his aim onto target.

First a fearsome ambush had been set, now there was an expert sniper: again Kilbride wondered who on earth he was up against on the other side. He ordered his men to respond as best they could. With two LAWs already expended, Kilbride knew that they had to conserve their stocks of the one-use rockets. He and his men began returning fire with their Diemaco assault rifles on single-shot. The enemy were two hundred yards beyond its optimum range, but even at this distance it still made a passable sniping rifle.

As Kilbride's team and the enemy sniper traded shots, he tried to put himself in the opposition commander's shoes. Even if he had mortars or other heavy weapons, there was no way he could risk using them. To do so would endanger the truck and its precious cargo. He would have to get his men closer to Kilbride's position, where they could put down accurate small-arms fire. In which case, he would have to send out his men on foot in a flanking manoeuvre. Kilbride popped his head up over the bonnet and swept the enemy position with his night-vision goggles. As he did so a round slammed into the far side of the engine compartment. Sure enough, the enemy commander had done just as he had anticipated: figures were moving forward on either side of the road.

Kilbride warned his men of the new threat, and they started to snipe at the advancing fighters. Kilbride squeezed off a round and saw one of them go down. Whether he was hit or simply taking cover Kilbride couldn't be certain. Either way, he was painfully aware that they couldn't hold them off for ever, and that there was still no sign of Berger or Boerke. Over the deafening crack of their own gunfire, Kilbride sensed a noise in the background. He tried to refocus his hearing, and as he did so he realised it was the fierce ringing of the Thuraya. He grabbed it, punched the answer key and clamped it to his ear.

'Kilbride!'

'Thank Christ for that.' It was Nick's voice and he sounded flustered. 'I've been ringing and ringing . . . Listen, that IR strobe – it's moving out of the gorge and down towards your position. Moving at quite a pace, too. I'd say it's a man running . . .'

'Which direction?'

Nick gave him the bearing and Kilbride cut the connection. With his night-vision goggles he swept the valley floor towards the south-west of their position. Almost immediately, he picked up on the hunched figure of Berger with the injured South African slung

348

across his shoulders. They were moving at a fast pace towards them. He swept the night-vision goggles across to check on the enemy, and in a flash he realised that Berger's line of march would take him right into the path of the advancing foot soldiers. Berger clearly hadn't noticed the men on foot – and Kilbride had to find a way to warn him.

He grabbed a LAW, signalling for Nightly to do likewise. Hurriedly, he explained his plan. The two men steadied the LAWs on the bonnet of the vehicle. If they overshot there was always the danger that they would hit Berger and Boerke. Kilbride fired first, his rocket skitting across the dirt road and exploding just short of the advancing enemy soldiers. Nightly fired next: there was a second's delay, then his rocket struck bang in the midst of the lead enemy fighters. There was an intense flash of flame as bodies were ripped apart by the blast.

Kilbride glanced at Nightly and raised one eyebrow. 'Fucking nice shooting! Mate, you've got nerves of steel . . .'

Nightly grinned, and turned back to his assault rifle. Kilbride grabbed his night-vision and searched for Berger and Boerke. He picked up on them again, this time looping out around the enemy position to come in from the flank. Kilbride warned Nightly to be ready to bug out as soon as the big American reached them. Then he crawled across to Ward and Johno to tell them the same.

Five minutes later and Kilbride heard a strained shout coming from the shadows to their front. 'Cover me – I'm comin' in!'

The four men switched their weapons to automatic mode and began pumping rounds into the advancing enemy soldiers who broke ranks and dived for cover. As they did so the ghostly figure of Berger came pounding onto the road, the limp form of Boerke dangling from his shoulders. With a superhuman effort he surged ahead towards Kilbride's position. An enemy soldier spotted him and yelled to alert his comrades. Bullets slammed into the road, kicking up the dust at Berger's feet. For a split second Kilbride was certain that they'd got him, but it was Berger diving for the cover of the nearest vehicle. The big American hit the dirt with a hollow thump as he used his body to break Boerke's fall.

'Hit the detonator!' Kilbride yelled.

Ward punched the firing device and a hundred yards ahead there was a blinding flash of flame. A charge of RDX exploded, setting off a pile of booby-trapped grenades and ammo. The crack of the exploding rounds gave the impression that a major counter-attack was under way. As a thick cloud of smoke drifted across the road, Kilbride and Nightly dragged Boerke into the nearest jeep, while Johno, Ward and Berger piled into the rear. Kilbride lobbed a last white-phosphorus grenade in through the window of the second four-wheel drive, gunned his engine and accelerated away. As he skirted the truck there was the crack of the grenade exploding, and the abandoned hire vehicle burst into flames.

The Searcher stood in the rear of his pick-up, his gaze fixed on the battle scene up ahead. One enemy vehicle was a flaming wreck, and the other seemed to have disappeared. He sent his men in on foot, ordering them to check for enemy booby traps. Slowly, they filtered in among what remained of Kilbride's position and declared the all-clear. The Searcher stared at the truck, sitting there before him on the road. *The prize.* The prize was within his grasp.

Yet he remained wary. Kilbride and his men had fought well, but how they had managed to discover the ambush in the gorge escaped him. Whoever had triggered it had been a brave and resourceful soldier, and it never ceased to amaze him how men without belief, those who had failed to find the One True God, could still demonstrate such courage. There were mysteries that even he, a Brother and a true Holy Warrior, would never fathom.

The Searcher had lost eight Brothers in the gorge, maybe a dozen overall. But Kilbride must have suffered serious casualties himself, for what else would have made him abandon the gold? He had reports of two of Kilbride's men hit in the gorge. Blood had been found, plus an abandoned pistol. If both of them were lost then Kilbride would be down to four men – a third of his force wiped out. Then there was the burned-out jeep. Had Kilbride lost another two there? Perhaps there were only two left alive, which would explain why he was running.

The Searcher pulled the convoy to a halt a hundred yards short of the enemy position. He felt a kick of adrenalin as he eyed the truck, the shipping container perched on its rear. But there was little time to glory in the moment. It was 11 p.m. and he needed to get back over the border into Syria before daybreak. He ordered his men to check the tractor unit. The engine cover was still open and it seemed as if it had had mechanical problems.

The Searcher went to inspect the rear of the truck. The shipping container was secured by a thick padlock and chain. He had little doubt what it was carrying, but he still needed to be certain.

351

'Brother Sajid, shoot the lock off,' The Searcher commanded of his lieutenant.

Sajid raised his weapon and fired a long burst at the padlock. The shattered metal fell away. The Searcher vaulted up onto the flat bed of the trailer, and with Sajid's help he threw open the steel doors of the shipping container. He shone his torch beam into the dark interior. All his wariness evaporated in an instant. There, glowing in the shaft of light, was the golden hoard. He had succeeded. He had won the prize.

For a second The Searcher considered sending a couple of vehicles after Kilbride. He would dearly love to kill him – or, better still, capture him alive. He would carry him back to their camp in chains. He would force him to watch the Seven Assassins departing for their Holy Mission, knowing that it was his failure that had gifted them the means to carry out their attack. But the Old Man's orders had been clear and wise. He was to let the enemy go and concentrate on bringing the gold safely back to their camp. Vengeance would be left to God, just as the Old Man had promised him it would be.

There was the coughing of an engine and then the throaty roar of the truck revving. The Searcher smiled to himself. They were mobile. He ordered his men to form up in convoy, two pick-ups leading the truck and two behind it. They moved out and headed back into the fire-ravaged gorge, passing the burned-out wrecks of two of their vehicles. No matter, The Searcher told himself. Their arrival in the camp was just hours away, and with it their moment of glory. He would present the prize, at which stage he, Brother Mohajir, would have surely become the most trusted lieutenant of the Old Man of the Mountains.

As dawn broke over the plain of Wadi Jehannam, Kilbride nosed his vehicle into a deserted patch of woodland. Although still driveable the jeep was badly shot up and had clearly been in a firefight. Ward had got a drip into Boerke, but he was still in a bad way. And Nightly had taken a bullet in the arm, although luckily it was only a flesh wound. The men needed to eat and rest and gather their strength for the next stage of the mission. The jeep needed checking over to make sure that it would make the drive to Tripoli. And they needed to tend to their wounded.

Having parked up in some cover, Kilbride put a call through to Smithy. All was going well on the dhow, Smithy reported, and in forty-eight hours they would be ready to depart. Kilbride told him to bring one of the RIBs and meet them at a deserted end of Tripoli's Al Mina port area at midnight. He planned to make the drive to Tripoli after sundown, when the damage to their vehicle was less likely to attract attention. They had full trauma kits and a sickbay aboard the dhow, and Boerke would stand as good a chance there as he would in any Lebanese hospital.

Right now the order of the day was rest, recuperation and cleaning of weapons and kit. Kilbride set a rotating watch, just in case they were disturbed, and sent Berger off for a long sleep in the vehicle. The big American was dead on his feet, which was hardly surprising. After that solo rescue mission it would take him a lifetime to recover.

Or maybe it wouldn't, Kilbride reflected wryly. Maybe all it would take would be a couple of intimate massages from Tashana. Her arse was cute enough to persuade any man to make a miraculous recovery.

The Brothers gathered around the truck in a seething throng. Word had swept through the camp like wildfire that The Searcher and his men had returned. Every one of the Black Assassins wanted to share in the moment, the glory of the knowledge that the Holy Mission for which they had all been preparing would soon be launched upon an unsuspecting infidel world. The Searcher stood in front of the truck as he waited for the Old Man himself to appear. The sun was barely over the mountaintops, and it promised to be a glorious day.

Finally, the Old Man emerged from his bunker and picked his way down the hillside, using his stick to help steady himself. He raised his head, and his gaze met that of The Searcher. He signalled for him to reveal all.

'Brothers Sajid, Abdul – show them the prize,' The Searcher commanded.

The two Brothers went to open the container. There was a dull metallic *clunk* and the door started to swing wide. A reverential hush fell on the crowd as the rear of the shipping container revealed itself to them. Inside the ribbed metal walls there was a pile of shining golden bars. The Searcher stepped inside, bent and picked up one of the bars, its weight smooth and cold in his grasp. He turned and held it up for all to see. Below and before him the throng of assembled brothers broke into wild, frenzied cheering, brandishing their weapons in the salute of the Holy Warrior.

The Searcher stepped down from the container and made his way across to the Old Man. The crowd parted ahead of him. He stood with his head bowed, holding out the golden bar.

'Here, Your Holiness,' he announced softly. 'God

354

willing, this is the key that will unlock your dreams.'

The Old Man took the golden bar in his talon-like grip. He gazed on it in rapture for a second, then turned to address the crowd.

'Brothers, today is a truly glorious day. With this' – he held the golden bar aloft – 'with this we can achieve our dreams! With this, we can deliver on our Holy Promise to the One True God! With this, God willing, the Seven Assassins are assured of a great and glorious victory. With this, we shall shake the Infidel world to its very core. Let the Christian dogs and the unbelievers shiver and cower in terror when the wrath of the Seven Assassins falls upon them.'

A wild cheer went up from the crowd. The Searcher stood at the Old Man's side and basked in the reflected glory. The Old Man had already declared the day a rare Holy Day, and the Brothers would have a day of rest and feasting. Seven goats – symbolically, one for each of the Seven Assassins – would be roasted over an open fire. There would be the singing of Islamic poetry, and the scholars among them would recite *Hadiths* from the Koran. It was a day to enjoy, a day to celebrate, a day for The Searcher to feel that he was truly *chosen*.

He strode across to the shipping container and went to close the door. As he did so, something caught his eye. He had always been fastidious and mess offended him. During the firefight with Kilbride's men a stray round must have pierced the shipping container. It had damaged one of the golden bars. The Searcher picked it up. The bullet had struck at an oblique angle, tearing a shallow groove across the pure golden surface of the bar.

He ran his hand across the rough silver sharpness of the broken metal. Suddenly it struck him as odd that the bar should show silver where it had been damaged. Surely it should show gold? For a second he felt a cold panic gripping his heart. But no, he reasoned, it had to be the lead of the bullet that had bled the shining ribbon of silver across the bar, not the other way around – for the alternative was unthinkable. But what if it wasn't the bullet that had left its mark on the bar? What if it had simply revealed what the inside of the bar was made from?

The Searcher stared at the damaged bar – and the longer he did so the more a dark doubt seeped into him, like poison. He stuffed it into one of the deep pockets of his robe and ordered the shipping container closed. Then he called together the Brothers from the previous night's mission and ordered them to accompany him to the camp's armoury. After all the fighting they had to rearm themselves, he explained, before they could relax and enjoy the day's celebrations. After all, a Black Assassin had always to be combat-ready . . .

They drove in convoy to the far end of the camp. Here there was a sunken firing range and an underground armoury. The Searcher was confident that Abu Jihad, the armourer, would be at work, as always. He wore jam-jar glasses and had the skin of a worm, as he never saw the light of day. Brother Jihad never seemed to rest from his bomb-making activities as he sought to better refine the weaponry that the Brothers had at their disposal. And he certainly knew how to build his bombs.

The Searcher had the Brothers park their vehicles in the armoury's bunker-like compound, and Abu Jihad began to issue them with a resupply of ammunition. Once the process was complete, The Searcher dismissed the other Brothers and told them to wait for him outside. Alone with Abu Jihad at last, The Searcher turned to speak to him about what was on his mind. Brother Jihad had been a scientist of some standing in his past life, before he had given up everything to dedicate himself to the cause of the Black Assassins.

'I'm curious – how does one test for gold, Brother Jihad?' he asked.

Brother Jihad snorted. 'This gold shipment – the whole camp has gone mad with gold fever. Well, they can keep it, if you ask me. What is it? A yellow metal. What's to be so excited about?'

'Of course . . . But do you know how to test for gold, Brother?' The Searcher persisted.

'It's simple, isn't it? You weigh it. There's very little in this world that weighs as heavy as gold. If you're still in doubt then you drill into it, and test the filings with nitric acid. If that doesn't do it for you, you have to use an X-ray fluorescence spectrometer.'

'Can you do anything like that here, Brother?'

Abu Jihad glanced up through his thick glasses. 'You have something you need testing, Brother? Where is it?'

The Searcher produced the damaged bar from under his robes. He showed it to Brother Jihad, tracing the line of the bullet mark with his fingers. 'This is what worries me,' he announced. 'Is that the silver of the lead from the bullet or . . .?'

'Or the inside of the "gold" bar, you mean?' Abu Jihad took the bar and weighed it in his hands. 'Feels about the right weight.' He grabbed a set of scales and placed the bar on them. 'I normally use these for weighing the explosives, so I get exactly the right amount for each belt.' He scribbled down a number. 'Right, the weight in grammes divided by the volume of the bar in cubic centimetres should equal nineteen-point-three if it *is* gold . . .' He punched some numbers into his calculator. 'Hmm . . . nineteen-point-one. Within the margin of error.'

Brother Jihad reached over and grabbed a drill. 'I guess I'd better do the acid test.'

He placed the golden bar on the bench, pulled the drill's trigger and pressed the bit into the soft metal. For a microsecond it turned out an exquisite fluff of golden filings, but then they changed to a bright silver as the drill cut into the lead. A few seconds after that the note of the drill changed as it hit the tungsten core and struggled to cut deeper. A puff of smoke rose from the drill, and the acrid smell of burning metal filled Brother Jihad's workshop.

'There's your answer,' Abu Jihad remarked, failing to notice that The Searcher had gone white as a sheet. 'Gold plate, then it looks like a three-mil layer of lead, with a very hard metal core. I wonder what metal it is? Fascinating . . . Maybe tungsten?'

Abu Jihad glanced up, but The Searcher was nowhere to be seen. He had already bolted from the room.

CHAPTER FIFTEEN

Nick Coles ran a tired hand across his face. It had been a long day and a long night, and it was far from over yet. He'd been on the go for forty-eight hours, and all that was keeping him awake was caffeine and adrenalin. Still, just a little longer and Kilbride's twenty-four-hour window would have expired, and they could blow the tungsten bomb. As far as Nick was concerned the time couldn't pass too quickly. The whole of the Black Assassins, some three hundred fighters or more, were gathered around the shipping container. Even the Old Man himself was there. A carnival atmosphere had taken over their camp. It was the perfect time to hit the button and detonate the bomb.

Nick heard a squelch of static in his earphones, which meant that a signal was coming in from GCHQ, the British Government's electronic-intercept centre. His computer screen told him that it was a phone intercept, and from the code name he knew it was The Searcher making the call. A disembodied voice started talking in his headphones, providing a simultaneous translation of the Arabic phone call.

The Searcher spoke first. 'Your Holiness – pull everyone back from the container!'

The Old Man answered. 'What? Brother Mohajir? Speak up!'

'Get everyone back. Save yourselves. It's a trap!'

'A trap? How is it possible . . . ?'

'Move, Your Holiness! Get the Brothers moving. Now! Move! Into the bunkers!'

Nick felt his blood run cold. Somehow, The Searcher was on to them. He snapped off his headphones and turned to his boss.

'Sir, they know it's a trap. We have to hit them now, sir. Now!'

'You certain, Nick?'

'Absolutely. Now, sir.'

'Then do it, Nick. Blow it sky-high.'

'Sir.'

Nick turned back to his computer and started punching in a sequence of numbers and letters – the code word to trigger the charge of RDX explosives at the heart of the tungsten bomb.

The Old Man stumbled to his feet. In his right hand the mobile phone was still connected, and The Searcher's voice was screaming at him to pull the Brothers back from the shipping container. One of the Brothers was on his feet, rocking gently backwards and forwards, halfway through a Koran recital, his eyes closed and his voice pitch-perfect in its sonorous incantation. The Brothers were transported by the Koran chanting to another, faraway place, where birds sang and the rivers ran clear and the girls—

'Everyone back,' the Old Man cried, his words

choking on the harsh dry fear in his mouth. 'Everyone back!'

He tried to shout louder, stabbing a gnarled finger towards the shipping container, but the words died in his throat. He lashed out with his cane against those at his feet, flailing about like a madman. For a second the Brothers stared at him in total confusion – and then they were struck by a sudden realisation of what the Old Man was trying to tell them.

He was mouthing a single phrase over and over and over again: 'It's a bomb! A bomb! A bomb!'

A wave of hysteria rippled outwards from the Old Man: Brother stumbled over Brother as the Black Assassins' Holy Day transformed into a moment of panic and fear. At exactly that instant a tiny radio receiver at the heart of the shipping container bleeped once, as Nick Coles's coded message was received and understood. A split second later a small detonator charge ignited, and a microsecond after that one thousand kilos of RDX exploded with a force like that of a small atomic bomb.

The steel walls of the shipping container vaporised instantly as a hundred thousand shards of jagged metal death blasted forth, pulverising the tractor unit of the truck and igniting its fuel tank in a giant ball of flame. The fearsome metal vortex pulsed outwards from the epicentre of the blast with an unsurpassed lethality, scything down all in its path. An instant later the assembled mass of the Black Assassins had ceased to exist, their bodies struck down and shredded as an awesome wave of devastation swept over them.

Because of its immense density and hardness, the tungsten fragments had absorbed virtually the full energy of the explosion. The wave of death rippled onwards across the valley floor, tearing into the Assassins' vehicle compound and shredding the Toyota pick-ups as if they were paper. Burning-hot shards of tungsten lacerated the fuel tanks, and in seconds the compound became a sea of boiling flame. The main oil-storage tank was hit, shards of metal slicing through it like a thousand hot knives through butter. A massive belch of oily smoke shot skywards as the ten-thousand-litre fuel tank burst asunder, a tidal wave of fire engulfing the adjacent communications centre and the office block.

The wall of metal death pulsed onwards and outwards, obliterating the camp of the Black Assassins . . . before finally expending the last of its awesome power on the distant valley walls.

Nick Coles punched some keys on his computer terminal and pulled up a satellite photo. It had been taken just seconds after the detonation, and the image took his very breath away. He stared into his screen at a terrible scene of utter devastation. Not a single thing remained alive down there. The valley of the Black Assassins had taken on the hue of a scorched and blasted wasteland. Nick cast his mind back to the carnival that had been under way just minutes earlier.

'Absolutely incredible,' he murmured. 'Absolutely incredible . . . Sir.' He gestured towards his computer screen. 'This just in, sir. Taken seconds after the blast.'

'Christ . . . That's extraordinary. Not a soul left standing, eh?'

'Absolutely incredible,' Nick repeated, unable to tear his stare away from the image on the screen.

'I think "awesome" is the word they use these days, Nick. In any case, I think we can safely say we've done for them, don't you? Get a copy of this to the Americans – General Peters at SOCOM, in particular. I think they owe us some heartfelt congratulations.'

'I suspect there may have been one or two survivors, sir,' Nick ventured.

'You do? Who?'

'That phone intercept . . . It was The Searcher, sir. I think he may have been absent from the area when the blast took place, along with a handful of his men. I'm just trying to acquire some imagery to confirm it.'

'Damn! Still, two hundred and eighty out of three hundred isn't so bad, is it, Nick? We got most of them, the Old Man included. I'd say the Black Assassins are finished. Get the imagery to the Americans. It's still very much our day . . .'

At the far end of the valley the blast wave had felt like an express train running right over them. Luckily, the ranges and the armoury were below ground level. Even so, several stray shards of tungsten had struck the vehicles, and Sajid had taken a flesh wound. Otherwise, The Searcher and his men had escaped more or less unharmed. But he could only imagine what horrors had befallen the mass of Brothers gathered around that shipping container. And as for the Old Man himself . . . His face set like cold stone, The Searcher ordered his two dozen fighters back to the main camp.

Upon arrival they were met by a scene of indescribable horror. Where the truck and the shipping container had once stood there was now just a vast crater. The ground had been scoured clear of all vegetation – not a tree or a blade of grass left standing. And as for the Brothers, not a living soul was to be found. A discarded boot here, a blasted, buckled weapon there; a chunk of barely recognisable human flesh . . . Their sacred camp, the Holy Mission, the Cause – all of it had been obliterated for ever.

The Searcher sank to his knees in the centre of the devastation. His fingers closed around a blackened, broken cane. It was the Old Man's walking stick. *The Old Man had perished here.* Somewhere among these pulverised human remains there lay the heart of His Holiness – cold, lifeless and dead. Yet The Searcher couldn't even find the pieces of his body to give him a proper burial. He bowed his head to the bloodied earth and wept as he had never wept before.

How could he have done this? The Searcher asked himself. *He was responsible.* He had captured the container of fool's gold; he had brought it into the heart of their stronghold; he had called the Old Man to celebrate; he had gathered the Brothers . . . He had fallen for the enemy's evil trick. In short, he had killed them. He had killed them all. He had brought a terrible death to the Black Assassins, and an end to all their worldly dreams.

The Searcher felt a hand on his shoulder. He turned to see Sajid and Abdul. 'The Brothers are wondering . . . what should we do?' Sajid whispered.

Their faces were stained with tears, their eyes hollow and empty. The sight goaded The Searcher into some form of action.

'There is only one thing left, Brothers,' he replied, through gritted teeth. 'We must find those responsible for this terrible crime, this sin beyond all sin. And we must make them pay for it with their pain and their blood.'

'But how, Brother Mohajir?' Sajid asked. 'We are finished . . .'

'We are still breathing God's air, and whilst we still

have breath we can fight. First, contact all our brothers in the Lebanon. Tell them to surround the airport. Give a full description of the vehicle being used by these murderous infidel dogs. And mobilise our friends to comb the country for anything suspicious, anything that might lead us to these infidel whores . . . *Anything at all, Brother*. I feel it in my heart that they are still in the country, and that we shall be avenged before God with their blood.'

The Searcher strode across to his vehicle and pulled out a small black briefcase. He unclipped the lid and flipped it open so as to form a small satellite dish. At least he still had his satphone. It would take him a while to acquire the three satellites that he needed for a firm enough signal. And he needed to charge up the satphone's battery, which meant he would have to run his vehicle for a while. But he would be patient. All things were possible with time.

And now he had all the time in the world.

It was the ringing of the Thuraya that had woken him. Kilbride groped for it sleepily and held the handset to his ear.

'Yeah, what is it?'

'We hit the detonate button, Kilbride.' It was Nick Coles's voice, and he was sounding exhausted. 'We had to. Sorry. But they'd rumbled our game. I promised to let you know if we did, hence the call. Ten minutes ago – and total devastation. If you've got the Psion handy I'll send you some pictures.'

'No need, Nick. Were there any survivors?'

'A handful. We're just getting some images through. Maybe two dozen, out of three hundred. I'd say they're finished, wouldn't you?'

'That's still enough to come after us, Nick. Keep an eye on them, will you? If they move, I want to know about it, okay?'

Kilbride glanced at his watch. It was 1.45 p.m. He'd been asleep for six hours or so, lying in the shade of their battle-worn jeep. He felt remarkably refreshed. They would need to get on the move soon. The drive out of Wadi Jehannam would take a good three hours, probably more with an injured man in the vehicle's rear. The road was rough, and they would need to take it slow. And then it was another three hours to the Tripoli docks.

Kilbride grabbed an opened tin of rice pudding and spooned some into his mouth. It was good energy food and fine eaten cold.

Nick Coles was feeling mightily pleased with himself. It was mission accomplished, or pretty much so, and he was driving home for the first good night's sleep in three days. He was looking forward to the weekend. His daughter was coming to visit with her long-standing boyfriend. There were rumours of an engagement, and although Nick didn't think the man was quite good enough for her – an *archaeology* student, of all things – the prospect of grandchildren pleased him no end. It would be something to sweeten his retirement, and Lord knew he needed it with that dragon of a wife with whom to contend.

He took the turn-off from the M3 to the A303 and began the long drive into the Wiltshire countryside. He had moved out of London five years ago, first to rented accommodation and then to the converted farmhouse. On one level they hadn't been able to afford it, but there was a little family money, and his government pension

366

wouldn't see him too badly off. In any case it was his dream retirement home, and after thirty-nine years of serving his country Nick Coles reckoned he'd earned it. Most importantly, there was the annexe – a place where he could hide from the wife and find a little peace in the world.

There was a soft trilling from his mobile. Perhaps it was his daughter phoning about the weekend. Nick punched the answer key on his hands-free and spoke into the speaker.

'Nick here.'

Silence for a second, unnerving in an odd sort of way.

'Erm, Nick Coles. Who is it?'

'You're dead, Nick.'

'Who is this?' he blustered, although he'd recognised the voice instantly.

'You're dead.' A cold statement of fact. The voice of The Searcher. Flat. Dead. Lifeless. Chilling. 'Maybe not this week. Not this month. Not this year, even. But every day you'll be glancing over your shoulder, Nick, running from shadows. I want you to know and to feel every day what it's like to face your death . . .'

'You didn't appreciate our little present, then?' Nick tried to put steel into his voice, but a cold chill had gripped him.

'You killed him. The Sheikh. His Holiness. Snuffed out his life . . . I've nothing left to live for. You killed the dream. All that's left is to kill you, Nick. Your death is what's keeping me going. You're a dead man, as sure as there is only one true God. Better get used to it.'

'And Kilbride? He sold you the lie, didn't he, Knotty? And like a fool—'

'Dead, too, as soon as we find him. And we will. You

367

killed the figurehead, Nick, but we have thousands of supporters. You can't conceive how much they hate you, and those like you. With their help we'll find him. And then I'm coming for you.'

'Promises, Knotty, promises. I've yet to see much delivery.'

'You could take a gun, go into your neat Wiltshire garden, sit in the greenhouse and blow your brains out. That's an option. Or there's always the coward's way out – in the garage with a hosepipe from the exhaust through the car window. It'd be a far nicer way to go – better than waiting for me to come and find you. But I want the joy of killing you all to myself. So hang on, Nick. *Hang on.*'

'Oh, I intend to,' Nick snapped. 'And into a grand old age.'

'Remember how we tortured the infidels in Afghanistan, Nick? We stripped them naked, sliced open their stomachs and pegged out their intestines in the Afghan sun. We gave them just enough water to keep them alive as the insects and the rodents came to feast. Just imagine it, Nick. You could hear their screams from miles around. I used to love that sound . . . *I* thought up that torture, Nick. It was *my* invention. And I've thought up something even better for you.'

'You bastard.'

'One of these days, Nick, I'll be seeing you. Sweet dreams.'

The line went dead. Nick Coles drove home in a cold silence. His mind was working overtime. His tyres crunched on the gravel drive as he pulled up at the brick-built farmhouse. He took his briefcase and went directly to the annexe that looked out over the back garden. He'd made his decision: Kilbride had to know.

368

Bugger orders to the contrary and bugger the consequences – *Kilbride had to know*. It had become a life-or-death matter now.

He punched the speed-dial number on the Thuraya that connected him to Kilbride. A voice answered.

'Kilbride, the Brothers who survived the strike, they're after you,' Nick blurted out. 'They're after revenge. They've got people out searching all across the Lebanon, got eyes looking for you everywhere. They're going to try to hit you, Kilbride.'

'Calm down, Nick, calm down.' Kilbride wasn't entirely surprised that the enemy were after them. What he needed now was Nick Coles to give him some details. 'Who's behind all this? The Old Man's dead, right? So who's coming after us?'

'There's something we didn't tell you, Kilbride . . . There's a Muslim convert in that camp. He's a Brit, and he's ex-SAS. One of your own. He's survived. He's coming after you.'

'Who is it? Give me a name, Nick.'

'Knotts-Lane. The Searcher. Or Muhammad Mohajir, as he is now.'

'Fuck me, that's all we need . . . How long have you known, Nick?'

'Ever since the beginning. I'm sorry, Kilbride. Orders. Told not to let on . . .'

'So why tell me now, Nick?'

'Erm . . . it's suddenly become very personal.'

'He's after you, isn't he, Nick? You set him up, so you have to die. Better hope we get to him first . . . Does he know where we are, Nick? Has he any idea what we're up to?'

'Not that I'm aware of. But anything's possible. Lebanon's crawling with his people . . .'

'I wish you'd told me earlier, Nick. Anything else you've held back from me?'

'No. That's it.'

'Thanks, Nick. Keep me posted. You see or hear anything, let me be the *first* to know this time.'

As Nick placed the Thuraya on his writing desk his hand was visibly shaking.

Smithy readied the RIB for the midnight pick-up. It was frustrating to break off their work like this, but he was looking forward to seeing Kilbride and the others. And, in any case, with Mick and Brad beavering away in the depths of the cave the gold recovery was going like clockwork. He and Moynihan would be in and out of Tripoli in an hour, and then he would return to the cave, load the boat with the gold and ferry it back to the dhow. One more journey on the following evening and they would be fully loaded. Smithy could hardly wait.

At five minutes to midnight the black RIB nosed silently into Tripoli's Al Mina port area. Smithy had already spotted the squat form of Kilbride's jeep on the quayside. He cut the engines and they drifted forward. Moynihan grabbed a wooden stanchion, pulled them in to the pier and tied them off. As he did so a face appeared above them. It was Kilbride. The two men manhandled Boerke down the ladder to the waiting boat. The others followed, bringing the last of the ammo and supplies with them.

Kilbride returned to the jeep, grabbed a last empty ammo crate off the back seat, flicked the keys out of the ignition and pressed the remote to lock the vehicle. As he did so the Mitsubishi's lights flashed three times and the alarm bleeped. Kilbride dropped to the ground, cursing his stupidity, and peered into the night. There were few signs of life in this deserted section of the port, but he had to be certain that no one was watching. Satisfied that they were unobserved, he hurried over to the waiting RIB.

Behind him on the dock a lone figure stirred. Rashid was a Syrian fisherman who had come to the Lebanon the year before to find work. He crewed a local fishing dhow, and earned a few extra Lebanese pounds by doubling as the ship's nightwatchman. The sound of the Mitsubishi bleeping had woken him, and then he had sensed the faint whisper of the RIB leaving the pier. As it had pulled out to sea he'd spotted its sleek form, black against the moonlit waters. Rashid counted seven figures in the boat, some of whom were clearly armed: seven unknown men heading off to an unknown destination.

When the RIB had gone a good distance Rashid crept across the dock to the jeep. He traced the bullet holes torn in one side of the vehicle. He checked the number plate and noticed the car-hire sticker: it was a Beirut hire vehicle. Here was an enigma: a bullet-riddled Beirut jeep and seven mysterious gunmen. Rashid checked his imitation gold Rolex watch, his pride and joy: it was half past midnight. Four and a half hours until *Fajr*, the first prayers of the morning.

He would report his finding to the local imam, a fellow Syrian who ministered to a largely Syrian congregation. Rashid felt certain that the imam would know what to do.

By 4 a.m. Kilbride had got things on the dhow shipshape. Boerke was in the sickbay, plugged into an intravenous drip which was feeding a strong dose of antibiotics directly into his bloodstream. The tough South African was still unconscious but he was responding well, and his temperature had already started to come down. Smithy, Moynihan, Brad and Mick had returned from the cave and stowed the penultimate shipment of gold in the dhow's cavernous hold. Kilbride had greeted his son Mick with a gruff bear hug. It had been over a year since he'd last seen him, when Mick had spent Christmas with them at The Homestead.

Kilbride gathered the men on deck for a quick heads-up. Smithy reckoned they'd have the last of the gold loaded by 10.30 p.m. the following evening. At which time they'd be ready to depart. Between then and now they'd lie low and keep watch. Just in case The Searcher and his cronies did manage by some miracle to track them down, Kilbride's plan was to hold them off for long enough for the dhow to set sail. Then they would head for international waters – with or without the last few tons of gold.

'One more thing,' Kilbride added, before allowing the men to get some sleep. 'I need one of those wooden decoy crates loaded with real bullion. We kick that off the chopper and show The Project some gold as soon as we reach Cyprus: that should prevent them from asking too many questions about the others . . . And I'm suggesting a slight change of plan. Mick, Brad – how do you fancy riding a slow boat back to Tanzania? I'd be happier with the added security, especially bearing in mind what the dhow's carrying.'

'Well, she ain't no cruise liner,' quipped Brad. 'But after three days of solid diving, I sure could use the rest.'

'Me too,' Mick added. 'Nowt like a leisurely cruise with a bit of shark fishing thrown in, is there?'

'Right, Moynihan, you've got two new crew members,' Kilbride continued. 'And I'd like two in return. One, Sally, 'cause I can't bear to be parted from her for the couple of weeks that the dhow'll take to get home. Two, Smithy, 'cause the man's like a young teenager in love, and he tells me he can't bear to be parted from his woman . . .'

Kilbride's last words were lost in a muted chorus of wolf whistles and catcalls. Smithy hung his head in embarrassment. It was true. He had asked the boss if he could catch a ride home on the chopper with the A Team. And all because his woman was waiting for him.

The imam of the Al Hamman Mosque was unsure if Rashid's 'news' warranted much attention. What had he seen? One shot-up vehicle and seven men leaving the docks in a boat. Tripoli had a thriving smuggling scene, so it could easily have been arms dealers, which didn't concern the imam much. Or it could have been drug smugglers, which concerned him greatly. Drugs were a curse and a scourge of the people, and they were forbidden under Islam. But even if it was drugs, there was precious little he could do about it. The drug smugglers were well-armed and ruthless operators.

It was 6.15 a.m. and the imam was starving. He dismissed Rashid and went to eat. As he washed his hands, the imam heard a ringing. He dried his hands on his robe and grabbed his mobile phone.

'Yes?'

'Imam Salah ad-Din? It's Sajid. Sajid from the camp of the Black Assassins . . . There is most terrible news. Many of the Brothers are dead . . . The Old Man himself, even . . . We are searching for the killers, and we believe that they are still in the Lebanon. A handful of foreigners, infidel dogs, driving a Japanese four-wheel drive. It has faced us in battle, so it will show the scars of fighting. Keep your eyes open and your ears to the ground, Imam Salah ad-Din, just in case you should learn of anything . . .'

'Wait!' the imam commanded, before Sajid could ring off. 'A fisherman was just here, two minutes ago, telling me this very story . . . By the grace of God, they are here, their vehicle parked at the dockside. I thought the fisherman had been dreaming, but . . .'

'Brother Mohajir!' Sajid yelled, once he'd finished speaking with the imam. 'We've found them! Tripoli . . . The port . . . A fisherman saw it all . . .'

'Calm yourself, Brother,' The Searcher commanded as he strode across to Sajid's vehicle. 'This is glorious news. But tell me from the start all that you have heard.'

'There is an imam in Tripoli, a Syrian and a good friend of the cause. I just spoke with him. Last night, at midnight, a car pulled up at the docks. Seven men got into a boat and it slid into the ocean. A fisherman was woken and he became suspicious. He checked the vehicle. It is peppered with bullet holes. It is their jeep, Brother. Brother Mohajir, we have them.'

The Searcher checked his watch: 6.30 a.m. 'How long for us to get to Tripoli, Brother Sajid?'

'Ten, maybe twelve hours.'

'Right, get back to the imam. Tell him to send some Brothers to discover where that boat has taken them. Tell him to be careful and not to raise the alarm. We'll be there before nightfall, by which time we need boats ready and as many of the Brothers as he can safely gather together, well armed and ready for glorious battle.'

The Searcher turned back to his vehicle and grabbed a map from the glove compartment. He spread it on the

374

bonnet and traced the route to Tripoli. Pray God they would get there in time. He glanced around the shattered wasteland of the camp. The Brothers, the Old Man – they would be avenged. He was certain of it now. He glanced back at the map. What could Kilbride be doing in Tripoli? Why hadn't he pulled out as soon as the trap had been sprung? Suddenly it hit him. *The gold.* The gold. Kilbride was going to retrieve the gold.

The Searcher cast his mind back to January 1979 and the original bank raid. After hitting the vault Kilbride and his team had left Beirut by sea, in several RIBs – that much he remembered. So maybe the gold had never been hidden in the Lebanon proper, as he had always imagined. Maybe it had been hidden *at sea.* If so, Kilbride and his men had . . . Suddenly, The Searcher was struck by an image so real that it was as though he was back there in that Cyprus camp, speaking with Kilbride in the SAS ops tent.

'*A word of advice . . . hide the gold at sea.*' That's what he'd told Kilbride, yet for all these years it had escaped his mind. '*No one will ever think of looking for it there. Gold is almost a hundred per cent indestructible – and it never corrodes in sea water. Never – not in a million years.*'

The Searcher pawed the map, searching for the most likely hiding place. The coastline was heavily populated, from Byblos right up to Tripoli itself, so not a lot of opportunity there. Where could they possibly have hidden so many tons of gold? He grabbed a Lebanon road atlas from the jeep. It was a far bigger scale than the map he had just been using. As he flicked through to the page that covered Tripoli, his gaze came to rest on a group of islands, just off Tripoli itself. The Palm Islands.

They were too insignificant to be marked on the larger map. There were no roads shown and no towns or villages, so presumably no people. Just three chunks of rock, sitting in splendid isolation in the sea. As he gazed at the map he was struck by a burning conviction. Suddenly he knew. *He knew. The Palm Islands.* Somewhere among those rocky outcrops and shallow waters Kilbride and his men were in the process of salvaging 17.5 tons of gold. It was the perfect place to have hidden their loot over all these years.

If only he could get to them, The Searcher reasoned, then all might not be lost. With the gold behind him, he could resurrect the dream of the Old Man of the Mountains. He could form a new band of Brothers – the New Assassins – and they could take up the Holy Mission once more . . . He himself could lead them, he could be their figurehead. They could build a new camp, further and deeper into the mountains. He could resurrect the Day of the Seven Assassins – and he could finish the job that the Old Man had begun.

'Sure, you best make yourself comfortable,' Moynihan announced. 'Anything you need? We're about to get under way.'

'No, man, I'm fine. It's just . . .' Boerke winced with the effort of sitting up. He had been conscious for the best part of the day, but was still drifting in and out of a high fever. He listened intently for a second, and then his arm shot out and grabbed Moynihan in a vice-like grip. 'Listen, man. *Listen.* Can you hear it?'

Moynihan struggled to free himself. 'Sure, hear what, you crazy feckin' gobshite? All I can hear is the sea and the birds, and I've been listening to that for what seems like a feckin' lifetime . . .'

'Shut up, man. Listen. You ever heard sea birds making a racket like that before? Listen, man, really *listen*.'

For a few seconds Moynihan strained his ears. He fancied he could hear an unusual sense of alarm in the birds' distant crying.

'Something's disturbing them, man,' Boerke continued. 'There's no predators on those islands. You've got to get a warning to Kilbride. *Now, man.* Tell him he's got company.'

Kilbride, Berger and Nightly crouched at the cave entrance, keeping watch on the waters outside. In the rear the wooden crates were being loaded aboard two of the RIBs. There was a faint, barely audible purr from the direction of the open ocean, and the sleek black form of the third RIB hove into view. Smithy cut the engines, hoisted them aboard and the long black craft slid silently into the cave. Kilbride glanced at Berger, and grinned. It was midnight, all the gold had been loaded aboard the dhow and they were bang on schedule. He could hardly believe that they were this close to pulling it off.

Kilbride jumped. The quiet of the night was broken by a ring tone, sounding loud and brash in the cool stillness of the sea cave. He made a grab for the Thuraya, and punched the answer button.

'What is it, Nick?'

'It's not Nick, it's Moynihan. Listen, from where we're sitting we can hear the sea birds going spare, down around Palm Island itself. I'm not sure myself, but Boerke's convinced it's the enemy, and that they're heading your way.'

'Shit . . . Right, make yourself scarce, Paddy. Head

for the open sea as quick as she'll go. Good luck. And tell Boerke, thanks for the warning.'

Kilbride cut the connection. He glanced at Berger and Nightly. 'We may have company. I'm going up top to check. Nightly, stay here and keep your eyes peeled. Bronco, let's go.'

Kilbride and Berger scuttled up to the top of the cliff and gazed back across the islands towards Tripoli. Up above Palm Island Kilbride could see a flock of sea birds silhouetted against the distant glow of the city lights. They were wheeling and cawing in the night sky and dive-bombing the cliffs below.

Kilbride glanced at Berger. 'Looks like Boerke's right. How the fuck did they find us?'

Berger shrugged. 'No idea, buddy. It'd be nice to know how many there are.'

Kilbride pulled out his Thuraya. 'What we need is some eyes in the sky.' He punched speed-dial button three, and a second later he heard a ring tone.

Burt Joubert was awake almost instantaneously and he punched the answer button. 'Soup Dragon.'

'It's Kilbride. We need you here yesterday. The Palm Islands. The place is crawling with the enemy. What's your time to target?'

'Ten minutes. Fifteen max.'

'Once you're overhead call me, okay?'

'Roger. Soup Dragon out.'

Burt reached up, punched a few buttons on the aircraft's console and fired up his engines. The noise woke his crew.

'We're in business,' he announced. 'Volker, get me to the Palm Islands, quick as you can, man.'

As it was the middle of the night Burt planned to take off with no clearance and showing no lights. He powered

378

down his radio so that none of the Lebanese authorities could give him any grief – not that he reckoned they would be awake at this hour. Once over the Lebanese coastline he would drop down to sea level, so for the most part he would be lost in the 'sea chatter' and invisible to any radar. No one would be coming after him, of that he was certain. Even if they did, where he was going they sure as hell wouldn't be able to follow.

The Searcher gripped the side of the speedboat to steady himself and eyed the dark humps of the low-lying islands to the south. He could sense that he was right. He knew Kilbride was in there somewhere, barely a thousand yards away across the open sea. They were closing in, and soon he would be face to face with a man for whom his enmity knew no bounds. He barked out an order to Sajid, directing him to the seaward side of the last island. He had already sent in a bunch of locals – Hezbollah activists and other self-styled Mujahedin – to flush Kilbride and his men out of their lair.

If Kilbride tried to escape by sea The Searcher would be ready to intercept him. If not, the local fighters would harry Kilbride until The Searcher and his fellow Assassins closed in for the final kill. They had fifty-odd Brothers swarming over the islands, and he had twenty Black Assassins with him in the speedboat, so seventy fighters in all. Plus the imam was rustling up further reinforcements back in Tripoli town. Either way, Kilbride was finished.

When the local Brothers had heard the news of the death of the Old Man of the Mountains, their grief and rage had known no bounds. Several had volunteered on the spot to martyr themselves and had equipped themselves to do so. It was wondrous to see true bravery, The Searcher reflected, the valour of the martyr for which the infidels had no equal. When faced with men such as these, how could Kilbride and his ilk possibly hope to prevail?

Leaving Mick, Brad, Smithy and Ward to load the last of the wooden crates, Kilbride took the rest of his men – Berger, Nightly and Johno – and set up fire positions at the mouth of the cave. It was a good vantage point from which to spot the enemy.

Most of the crates were loaded and in theory they could abandon the cave right now and make their getaway. The trouble was, Kilbride had no idea what enemy force they were up against and where they were positioned. For all he knew they might exit the cave and run right into an ambush at sea. It was better to wait for his eyes-in-the-sky to report in.

And the longer Kilbride stayed where he was and drew the enemy to him, the less chance that they might go searching further afield and stumble across the dhow. At all costs that had to be avoided. Once again, Kilbride and his men were acting as the bait. Only this time there was no prize to lure the enemy away from them. This time *they* were the prize, of that Kilbride felt certain.

Sally heard the aircraft before any of them. She pricked up her ears and that in turn alerted Kilbride. He turned to search the sky above and saw a faint shadow fleeting across the heavens. The Buffalo made one pass, high above the islands, and then Kilbride heard a ringing on the Thuraya.

'What d'you see?'

'We're using night-vision gear up here and it's quite a sight. The place is crawling, man. I'd say fifty, maybe more. They've just landed on the far side of your island.'

'Okay, wait until they're right on top of us, then let them have the foo gas. We'll be in the cave, so don't worry about us. Okay?'

'Roger. There's a couple of boats also, man, off to the north-east, but closing fast . . .'

'Do what you can, Soup Dragon. Good hunting.'

'I'll call you when I'm fifteen seconds to point impact. You hear the Thuraya – that's your warning, man. Take good cover, 'cause this island's going to fry . . .'

Kilbride and Nightly positioned themselves on one side of the rocky entranceway, Berger and Johno on the other. They waited in tense silence for the enemy to come. Kilbride had Sally behind him in some cover. She would remain there, immobile, until he ordered her to do otherwise.

Kilbride levelled his weapon at the cave entrance. He was feeling mighty good about the pump-action shotgun he had slung beneath his assault rifle. It was the perfect killing machine for this type of environment. Nightly and Ward had grenade launchers, and Berger held the Minimi machine gun at the ready. Kilbride was confident that they could hold the cave entrance for at least as long as it took the Soup Dragon to strike.

Sally stiffened and growled. A shower of rocks scattered into the sea at the cave entrance. The enemy were coming. A larger rock dropped and hit the water. A split second later there was a massive explosion that roared and echoed around the enclosed space. The 'rock' had been a grenade – but luckily the water had absorbed the brunt of the blast. A shadowy figure rounded the cave entrance, the water up to his chest as he forced his way inside. Kilbride's shotgun roared, throwing the enemy fighter back out of the opening and into the open sea. A second and a third figure tried to push their way inside, but the shotgun roared again and again, blasting a swathe of lead through the air.

There was silence for a few seconds and then a hand clutching an AK47 emerged around the edge of the rock wall. The gun belched fire, spewing a long burst of rounds at Kilbride and his men. Kilbride forced his body back against the wall and fired, pumping lead in the general direction of the hidden enemy. There was an agonised scream as shot tore into the soldier's exposed hand, and his gun tumbled into the water. A second and third enemy fighter tried the same trick – hand around the wall and weapon spraying off on automatic – but Kilbride's shotgun blasted each one of them in turn.

There was a moment's pause in the assault, the smog of cordite drifting with a faint breeze into the rear of the cave. Kilbride reloaded his weapon, punching eight new shells into the shotgun. A corpse washed at Kilbride's feet, carried into the cave by the swell. Kilbride glanced down at it. It was the body of a young soldier, but the features were pulverised into an unrecognisable mess. The dead man's tunic hung open, and Kilbride caught sight of a string of explosives strapped around the man's middle. The enemy were wearing suicide belts.

There was a noise from above like a man running and a figure dropped into the space of the cave entrance. Suddenly there was a blinding flash, and the figure disintegrated in mid-air. The cave walls channelled the blast from his suicide belt inwards, blowing Kilbride off his feet and flinging him against the cold rock. He recovered his footing just in time to see Bill Berger spraying the cave entrance with a long burst from his Minimi. Dark, screaming shapes crowded into the cavernous space, weapons spitting fire. Kilbride swung the shotgun around, flicked it to auto mode and fired from the hip. The Remington roared, pumping out eight rounds in less than three seconds, blasting the enemy soldiers off their feet and hurling them against the walls. Berger's Minimi barked and barked again, as wounded enemy fighters tried to swim away from the kill zone. Finally, the machine gun too fell silent.

The big American dropped back into the shadows of the cave wall, his weapon held at the ready. Kilbride went to reload. He noticed another body in the water at his feet. Suddenly, he realised with a shock that it was Nightly . . . He reached down and grabbed his comatose form, hauling him up and onto the ledge. As he turned him over he saw sightless eyes staring up from beneath a shattered forehead. What looked like a fragment of shrapnel had hit him straight between the eyes. Kilbride groped for a pulse, but even as he did so he knew that it was hopeless. He laid Nightly down on the ledge and gently closed his eyes.

Kilbride leaned back into the shadows, and alarm bells started ringing inside his head. He looked around himself, trying to work out the source of the danger. His ears were still deafened by the gunfire, and it took several seconds to register that the Thuraya was ringing. The Soup Dragon had to be in the last few seconds of her attack run. Kilbride screamed out a warning to his men to take cover, grabbed Sally and dived into a crevice in the rock wall. There was the roar of the aircraft overhead, and the sudden crack of AK47 fire as the enemy loosed off wild rounds at the shadowy form of the Buffalo.

As he approached the cliff face Burt pulled hard on the yoke and put the Buffalo into a steep climb. At the same time he gave a thumbs-up to Shortie to lower the aircraft's rear ramp. As the Buffalo roared across the enemy positions at 270 miles per hour it was already clawing steeply into the air. The ramp yawned open and Shortie released the chain that held the tanker in place. Gravity pulled the heavily laden truck earthwards, and it accelerated down the last few yards of the Buffalo's hold.

Before it jerked out onto the open ramp Volker chucked a grenade in through the tanker's open window. Suddenly the truck was falling free of the aircraft and plummeting downwards like a stone. It struck the cliff top rear-end first, the steel plates of the tanker rupturing and a fountain of foo gas spurting into the air. A split second later the grenade exploded, and Ramkine Island was engulfed in a sheet of boiling flame.

Terrified figures leaped from the cliff face into the ocean in a desperate effort to douse themselves. But the tidal wave of orange flame roared after them, until the sea itself became a sheet of blazing fire. The wave of burning foo gas sucked the oxygen from the cave entrance, hungry flames licking inside its walls. As the very air crackled and burned, Kilbride and his men pressed themselves back into the furthest shadows, shielding their faces from the searing heat of the inferno outside.

Once the flames had subsided a little, Kilbride readied himself to get the hell out of there. They would use the cover of the foo-gas strike to bust their way out of the cave. Kilbride gave the order to move out, and with Berger's help he grabbed Nightly's body and loaded it into one of the RIBs. Last of all, Kilbride coaxed Sally into the lead craft. Cautiously, they headed towards the cave entrance, using their oars to fend off the cave walls. As they drew closer Kilbride could sense the salty taste of the open sea, coupled with the reek of the burning foo gas.

Suddenly, a voice rang out, echoing through the cave. 'KILBRIDE! I know you're in there, Kilbride!'

Kilbride brought his RIB to a stop. He pulled Sally to her feet and manhandled her into a shadowy crevice in the cave wall. He put a hand to his lips to quieten her and signalled for her to wait.

'KILBRIDE! You remember me? You recognise the voice? It's hopeless, Kilbride. I know you're in there. Answer me. We may be able to do a deal.'

Kilbride signalled the boats further back into the cave. 'Knotty! How you doing?' he yelled out. 'It's been a long time.'

CHAPTER SIXTEEN

'Kilbride!' The Searcher's voice ran out again. 'I knew you wouldn't have forgotten your old friend. It's Muhammad Mohajir now, Kilbride, just so you know.'

'Muhammad Mohajir? Bit of a mouthful, Knotty. Anyhow, how're you doing?'

'How am I doing? Not so well, Kilbride. Lost a lot of the Brothers yesterday. And His Holiness . . . You never got to meet His Holiness, did you, Kilbride? Pity. You would have grown to like him. He would have shown you the way to the light. Now he's gone, Kilbride, and I hear that you're responsible . . .'

'I've got a great alibi, Knotty. I was here unearthing several tons of gold.'

'Is that right, Kilbride? The gold, you say. I figured as much . . .'

'Five hundred million in gold bullion, Knotty. Think about it. It's a lot of loot.'

Kilbride turned to his men and signalled for them to follow his lead. He grabbed one of the dive masks and an air bottle. He slipped the harness over his shoulders, leaving the mouthpiece hanging free so that he could talk. And then he pulled a canister of Agent BZ16 nerve gas out of his jacket pocket.

'You're up against the best, Kilbride,' The Searcher yelled. 'I trained them. And unlike us, they're young and fit. Give up, Kilbride. Surrender, and I'll guarantee you safe passage out of here. We'll settle for the gold. You get away with your lives. How about it, Kilbride?'

'What guarantees do we have, Knotty?' Kilbride yelled back at him.

'My guarantee as an honourable Muslim. My guarantee as an Assassin, a disciple of the Old Man of the Mountains and a brother to Saladin. You remember Saladin, Kilbride? We used to talk about him, back in Afghanistan, when you and I were on the same side. Saladin's word was his bond, Kilbride. And now you have *my* word.'

'What about your "Brothers"? Who guarantees them?'

'They take orders from me, Kilbride. I'm their trainer, their military leader. My word rules them. Throw down your weapons and come out, one by one. You'll lose the gold, but you'll get to live. Life, even for an infidel, is sweet, eh?'

'I want to see your face, Knotty. I want to look into your eyes. That's the only way I'll know you're telling the truth . . . Otherwise, there's no deal. We're old men, Knotty, and we don't have one hell of a lot to lose.'

The Searcher glanced at Sajid and the other Brothers gathered at the cave entrance, and mouthed a few words at them in Arabic.

'Keep your weapons down, Kilbride,' he called out. 'I'm going to show myself. I see a weapon raised, the deal's off, and we'll blast you out of that cave. It'll be your watery grave.'

'I hear you, Knotty.'

'Right – I'm coming into the entrance now.'

The Searcher stepped into the black opening of the cave. He had an AK47 held at the hip, with a torch attached. He shone it into the depths of the cave. 'How many of you are there, Kilbride? I count only five. Where's the rest of your troop?'

'Injured, invalided out – you know how it is. That's all of us, bar the one dead and a couple of wounded. Pretty fearless of you to come in here alone like this . . .'

'It's the deal you asked for, Kilbride. In any case, since finding the one true faith I haven't known much fear.'

'Paradise awaits, eh, Knotty?'

'You can mock, Kilbride. But you're an intelligent man – I'd have expected more of you. Knowledge of the One True God has given life meaning, conquered my fear.' He pulled aside his robe to reveal an explosive belt strapped around his torso. 'See? No fear. No fear of death. No fear at all . . .'

'Is that right? So how's the fear of dogs, Knotty? Remember the one that ripped your face open in the Panama jungle? You hated them back then . . .'

The Searcher glanced around himself nervously, shining his torch into the shadows. 'In Syria we eat dogs,' he snapped. 'Let's get on with it. I want you to show me the gold. Then I want you to walk towards me, in single file, and no weapons – you first, Kilbride.'

'I still need to look into your eyes, Knotty. It's the only way we can do this – the only way that I'll trust you. Take a few steps my way, Knotty, just so I can see you and be sure.'

'This is bullshit, Kilbride,' The Searcher yelled

angrily. 'I can just step back out of here and we'll torch this place – and you'll all fry. So stop fucking with me.'

'The threats don't work, Knotty. You need us – or rather, you need those boats loaded with the gold. Sooner or later the Lebanese authorities are going to put the navy or air force out here to find out what the hell's been going on. If you mallet this place, trust me, the boats are going down. The gold's at the bottom of the sea again, and you'll never get to it before the big guns arrive. Like I said, you need us, Knotty – which means we do this my way or not at all.'

'All right – I'll take six paces into the cave, Kilbride. But I've ordered my men to waste this place if you try any shit.'

With a few shouted words in Arabic to his men outside, The Searcher took six careful steps into the cave.

'This far and no further, Kilbride,' he announced. 'Now, let's get on with it – show me the gold.'

'Ready, lads?' Kilbride muttered. 'One last thing, Knotty,' he yelled. 'Before we let you see the loot, there's someone I think you should meet. SALLY – KILL!'

A giant wolf-like shadow leaped out of the darkened flank of the cave entrance, launched herself in the air with a savage snarl and sank her teeth into The Searcher's gun arm. As he toppled backwards Knotty let out a blood-curdling cry.

'I've never forgotten your fear of dogs!' Kilbride yelled as The Searcher hit the water, the big attack dog on top of him. 'Meet Sally, mate, and piss yourself with fear.'

The Searcher surfaced and let out a choking, gasping scream. Sally's teeth closed to the bone as she tried to drag him towards the inner end of the cave. The Searcher reached with his one free arm and punched the detonator button on his explosive belt. There was a faint *phut* beneath the water but nothing more: the suicide belt was soaked in sea water and had short-circuited.

Kilbride dropped off the cave ledge, hit the water and came back to the surface. He reached up with his right arm, hurled a gas canister towards the entrance of the cave then dived towards the cave depths. It spun end over end through the air and landed with a metallic clank against the far wall, hissing out a cloud of gas as it did so. The rest of his men followed his lead. As Sally dragged at The Searcher's lacerated flesh he began screaming in Arabic for his Brothers to attack. Black figures piled into the cave entrance, their weapons levelled and searching for the kill, but the cave appeared empty.

From below the surface of the water Kilbride watched the progress of the enemy fighters, their torch beams probing the shadows. A weapon fired, bullets fizzing into the sea, but Kilbride and his men were already well beyond their range. Suddenly, Kilbride saw a torch beam waver, and then a dark silhouette stumbled forwards and fell. Another Brother lost his footing and slumped into the water, his weapon drifting downwards towards Kilbride and his men in a slow, lazy corkscrew. And then another and another of the enemy figures went tumbling to the ground as they were hit by the cloud of nerve gas.

Kilbride gave it ten minutes, then signalled for his men to surface. As they did so, his first concern was for Sally. He spotted the attack dog slumped in the shallows at the rear of the cave, her comatose jaws still locked around a human form. Kilbride rushed across to her and dragged her out of the reach of the sea. He stooped until his cheek was next to Sally's and detected the faint warmth of her breath against his skin. She was still breathing. He lifted her up and carried her towards one of the waiting boats. The lads started the engines and manoeuvred the RIBs so that they faced the sea. They dragged Sally aboard and laid her down across the wooden crates in the bottom of the lead craft.

Kilbride and his team were still breathing from their diving tanks since the cave was thick with the gas. Just as he was about to give the signal to depart, Kilbride glanced back at the comatose form of The Searcher. Fuck it, he decided, they'd take the bastard with them. It would be one more prize for The Project, one more thing to distract them from the gold . . . Kilbride grabbed Berger and Ward and together they dragged The Searcher's body into the boat, laying him down alongside Sally. If the bastard came to he'd have the fright of his life when he found the massive dog at his side.

A quick burst of power sent the lead RIB gliding forward and Ward lifted the engines free of the water. It bumped over the shallows at the mouth of the cave and glided out into the open ocean. Kilbride signalled to go to full throttle, and the boat powered away from the dark cliffs. By the time the three RIBs hit the open sea in line astern, each boat was up on the plane and knifing through the waves.

Kilbride pulled out the Thuraya from where he'd stowed it on the RIB. He punched speed-dial button four, the number for the pilot of the Mi-26 HALO who was waiting for them on Cyprus. A flood of relief washed over him as he heard the laconic tones of the New Zealander answering.

'Fat Lady here. Where d'you need me, mate?'

'We need you at the LZ in fifty, repeat five-zero minutes,' Kilbride yelled. He could hardly make himself heard, what with the wind rushing past his face from the boat's slipstream. 'Can you make that? Our situation is hot, repeat hot, and we may have hostile company.'

'Not a problem, mate. See you at the LZ in fifty. Stand by.'

Kilbride had arranged the landing zone (LZ) some thirty kilometres out from the Lebanese coast, well into international waters. He closed his eyes and thought momentarily of sleep. His mind drifted to Marie-Claire and his kids, and he thanked God that he was still alive.

And then he thought of Nightly. The man had changed so much from his younger days. He'd turned into a humble and likeable soldier, with a killer aim on the LAW. But just as Kilbride and the rest of his men had been getting to know him again his life had been snuffed out in an instant. Nightly's death had cast a shadow over the mission. And back in England there was a wife who was now a widow and two kids – soon to be three – with no father any more.

The ringing of the Thuraya brought Kilbride crashing back to the present. Shit. If it was the chopper pilot cancelling the pick-up they were in serious trouble.

'Kilbride.'

'Soup Dragon here.' It was the voice of Burt, the pilot of the Buffalo. 'I'm afraid you've got company, man. There's a big Sun Seeker speedboat bearing down on you fast. Packed full of the nasty little bastards, it is . . .'

'If we go to diesel power can we outrun them?'

'You can, but only as far as the LZ, man. Then they'll

catch you. They might even get the chopper. No, man. There's only one thing for it. *I'll* have to deal with them.'

'But you're out of foo gas . . .'

'*Foo gas*, maybe . . . Watch the horizon to your backs, man. There's going to be a light show.'

Before departing from Africa Burt had deliberately fuelled the Buffalo with petrol, as distinct from avgas, the less flammable aviation fuel. It was one of the beauties of the aircraft's rugged turboprop engines that they could run on just about any flammable liquid. Burt banked the Buffalo around and brought her in low in line astern behind the enemy speedboat. When he was still some three hundred yards short of the sleek, powerful craft he began dumping his fuel. He overtook her and flew on ahead, a veil of gasoline trailing behind the aircraft and drifting into the sea.

Some five hundred yards in front of the boat Burt banked the Buffalo around in a sharp turn. Volker leaned out the side window and fired off a distress flare towards the sea. Before it even hit the water there was a giant flash and the petrol ignited. Fire ripped out from the ignition point, crackling and burning up the waves. The captain of the Sun Seeker saw the wall of boiling flame bearing down on him, and brought the speedboat around in a tight turn until it was heading back the way it had come. He pushed the throttle to the max and the craft leaped forward as he tried to outrun the flames. But the fire was quicker.

It flashed across the sea, caught up with the boat, flickered alongside and overtook her, and suddenly the craft was entombed in a wall of flame. For several seconds she thundered forwards, but this only served to whip the surface of the ocean into a crackling, burning frenzy. Figures dived from the boat to try to escape the flames, but the surface above remained a sea of angry fire. Suddenly, there was a hollow thump from the Sun Seeker as one of its internal fuel tanks exploded in a gout of flame. For a split second the inboard engines screamed wildly and the boat ploughed onwards, and then she broke into several pieces that tumbled in fiery abandon across the waves.

Burt glanced at Peter, his co-pilot. 'That's the end of that, man. It's also the end of the Buffalo . . .' He tapped the fuel gauge in the console above his head. The arrow was stuck on empty. 'We're out of fuel, man. Prepare to ditch at sea. It's a pity to lose the old girl, but . . .'

Burt turned to the rear of the aircraft. 'Volker, get the RIB ready.' He held out the Thuraya. 'And take this, man.' He grinned. 'You never know, we may still need it to call for a lifeboat or something.'

He put the Buffalo into a long, low dive. As he approached the surface of the sea, he brought the plane's air speed down to just above a stall. At seventy knots he settled her as gently as he could towards the waves. In the rear of the aircraft, Shortie and Volker already had the side door open. There was a splash and a bounce and the upturned nose of the aircraft struck a wave. Burt cut the engines on the high-set wings and the aircraft proceeded to do a perfect belly landing.

Before she had even come to a stop, Peter had the emergency hatch open at the top of the cockpit. As the Buffalo settled, all four men baled out. Volker and Shortie brought the RIB around from the plane's rear and hauled the pilot and co-pilot aboard. As they rowed away from the sinking aircraft, Burt turned to watch the raised tail fin disappear below the waves.

*

Kilbride watched the horizon as the flames died down to the east of them. Even from this distance they had spotted the Sun Seeker blowing herself apart. It was good to think that the last of the enemy might finally have been dealt with. It was ten kilometres, if that, to the LZ now and the three RIBs were flying along at thirty-five knots. The slipstream from the raised prow buffeted Kilbride around the ears and made it all but impossible to talk. He contented himself with searching the dark skies ahead for the squat form of the chopper.

Fifteen minutes later and the helicopter came homing in on them, the ghostly white form descending from the dark night sky. The pilot brought her down in a perfect hover, inching the giant aircraft ever lower towards the surface of the sea. The huge eight-bladed rotor kicked up a storm of spray as the wheels made contact with the waves. Still the pilot inched lower, until the open ramp of the chopper was resting on the ocean swell. Turbines screamed as the pilot held her steady, and the sea spray ripped about the faces of Kilbride and his men.

Kilbride gave the signal and the RIBs turned in line, his boat bringing up the rear. The big diesel outboards on the first RIB gave a throaty roar. She accelerated, making straight for the chopper's yawning hold, the body of the boat lifting clear of the water as the speed of the RIB took her up on the plane. There was a sharp crack, the RIB reared up, bounced over the chopper's ramp and crashed into the floodlit interior. One down, two to go, Kilbride told himself.

The second RIB powered forward, took the ramp at a fearsome pace, cannoned off one side of the chopper's gaping hold and skidded into the interior. There was a short delay as the flight crew used an internal winch to haul the second RIB alongside the first at the front of the hold. Then the loadmaster gave Kilbride a thumbs-up from the open ramp. Ward brought the bow around to face the helicopter and pushed the throttle lever fully forward. Kilbride felt himself thrust back in his seat as the engines roared behind him and the RIB powered ahead. Just seconds before the point of impact Ward cut the engines, tilting them out of the sea and forward into the boat.

For an instant the giant chopper reared above them. Then there was a sharp smack and the RIB bucked and slammed down with a sickening lurch, skidding into the hold. The boat slewed sideways, rode up onto the two RIB craft in front of it, twisted around and finally came to a shuddering halt. *They were in.* Quickly, they lashed the RIB to a steel eyelet set in the chopper's floor. Then Kilbride gave a thumbs-up to the Mi-26's loadmaster. The turbines revved to a fever pitch as the massive helicopter prepared to lift herself – and the twenty tons of extra cargo.

Inch by inch the giant aircraft rose, the swell sucking at her fuselage as she did so. Kilbride glanced out the open ramp of the chopper to see the sea whipped into a frenzied spray. For what seemed like an age the engines screamed at maximum revs, but the chopper just seemed to hold fast. She hung there, eight massive rotors thudding through the air above and the swell crashing mightily against the fuselage below. Kilbride locked stares with Berger as they gripped the side of the RIB craft. Then the giant chopper seemed to shiver once along the whole length of her airframe – and she shook herself free.

Suddenly they were airborne and powering upwards. Kilbride punched the air as a mighty cheer went up from the men. He ruffled the fur on Sally's neck, and as he did so he felt a twitch from her. She was coming around from the gas, which struck him as being odd, as the gas was supposed to knock out the victim for twelve hours or more. For a second Kilbride wondered if dogs were somehow less vulnerable to the gas than humans. Then he remembered that Sally had been at the rear of the cave, so she might not have breathed in a full dose.

He glanced across at The Searcher, just to check that he was still out cold. As he did so, he thought he saw an eyelid flickering. Kilbride looked down, his eye catching a faint movement. One of The Searcher's hands was twitching, fumbling instinctively around his waist. In an instant Kilbride realised that his fingers were groping for his explosives belt.

'NO!' Kilbride yelled. He dived forwards and as he did so there was an ear-splitting blast.

At the back of The Searcher's suicide belt one of the explosive cells had dried out enough to work. Abu Jihad, the Black Assassins' armourer, had been very thorough when building those belts, and he had included a back-up detonator circuit. In a stupor of half-consciousness The Searcher had hit his reserve detonate button, and the one good cell had exploded. It punched a hole in the floor of the RIB and threw The Searcher's body upwards, catapulting him into Kilbride.

The two men fell as one towards the chopper's open ramp. They landed hard, rolled once and tumbled into the ocean darkness outside . . .

Above the puttering of their outboard motor Burt heard a ringing of the Thuraya satphone. It struck him as being an odd noise, this far out on a deserted sea.

'Soup Dragon.'

'This is Fat Lady, mate. How're you doing? We got

us a problem. The boss took a tumble in the sea, mate. I can't risk putting her down again, 'cause we barely made it out the first time. Plus I'm real low on fuel. Reckon you could take a look, mate?'

'Shit, man, I had to ditch the Buffalo in the drink. We're in a four-metre RIB . . . Still, I reckon we could putter on over there. Might take us a while, but we've got bugger-all else to do.'

'I'd appreciate it, mate. The lads are going pretty wild in the back here. I tried telling 'em we can't do it, but I've got me a bloody mutiny on board . . .'

'What are the coordinates we're looking at, man? It's the LZ where he took the tumble, is it?'

'Pretty much, yeah, mate. Right, let me know when you find anything, eh?'

The Mi-26 hit the tarmac with a sickening lurch. The pilot had nursed the aircraft over the last few miles, coaxing her in to Cyprus with the tanks on empty. It was a miracle she had made it: they had been sipping on air for the last mile or so. As far as the pilot was concerned, they'd had no choice but to leave Kilbride behind. Had they gone around and searched for him the chopper would have run out of fuel and ditched at sea, and they would all most likely have been dead by now. But the men had taken a lot of convincing to turn west and head for Cyprus.

In the rear of the chopper's giant hold the atmosphere was as dark as the grave. The exhausted men slumped against the side of the RIB craft, their heads hung low, their shoulders hunched in pain and loss. In the final analysis, the pilot had been proven right, of course. But that didn't help much: they had still abandoned Kilbride in his hour of need.

As the chopper settled on the runway, Berger hauled himself to his feet and threw back the aircraft's side door. The first thing he saw was a bank of floodlights, and the figure of Nick Coles striding across the tarmac towards him. At his side was a tall, stooped figure, who seemed somehow familiar. As the rotors slowed to a thwooping stop, Nick Coles thrust out a hand to the big American. Berger stared at it with dead eyes, and failed to respond.

'You bloody did it!' Nick enthused, thrusting his hand forward again. 'Congratulations! Where's the man of the moment? Where's Kilbride?'

Berger glanced up, his face like stone. 'We lost him.'

'What? Kilbride . . . Where?'

Berger waved his arm, indicating the sea that stretched behind them towards the Lebanon. 'He didn't make it.'

The big American soldier stooped to lift a wooden box that they had readied by the door. It had a golden winged-staff stamp on its side. With Smithy's help he heaved it up over the sill of the chopper's entry hatch and dropped it onto the tarmac. It landed with a loud smack.

'What's this?' Nick asked.

'It's your fuckin' share of the gold, buddy!' Berger growled. 'Remember, you cut a deal with Kilbride? Go on, take a look. That's your share of the loot. That's dead man's gold.'

Nick stooped to inspect the crate. As he did so the tall besuited figure drew closer and stared over his shoulder with eager eyes. Nick levered off the lid and threw it aside. Inside were a dozen gleaming gold bars, cushioned in their packaging.

'Two million dollars' worth,' Berger announced, his

eyes like murder. 'That's what you asked for. That's what Kilbride died for. You demanded we bring it to Cyprus and we lost him on the way. So take it. I guess you think you fuckin' earned it.'

Nick glanced up at the chopper and tried to think of something to say, but he was lost for words. It was the taller, older man who spoke instead.

'And The Searcher? What news of *him*?'

The voice grated on Bill Berger's nerves. There was something familiar about it, and about the cut of the man's features. It came to the big American in a flash. The years hadn't changed the man much. It was Marcus Thistlethwaite, the OC of Q Squadron from all those years ago . . .

'Gone,' Berger grunted. 'Fell from the chopper with Kilbride.'

'Well, good riddance, I say . . .'

Suddenly, Berger had snatched up his Minimi and levelled the barrel at the older man's head, at point-blank range. 'Good fuckin' riddance to who, buddy?' he snarled, his finger white on the trigger. 'Best you think about it long and hard before you fuckin' answer me . . .'

Colonel Marcus Thistlethwaite stared back at the gun barrel unflinchingly, his old grey eyes showing little concern for the threat. Behind him, several soldiers moved forward, their weapons held at the ready.

'I don't think we need any of this,' he announced stiffly. 'You've rid the world of a menace. Good on you, I say. I'm sorry you've lost your man. But he didn't die in vain: the world is a far better place today because you dealt with the Black Assassins.'

Bill Berger didn't say a word. But he lowered the gun slowly.

'Unfortunately, it has cost us a little more than the agreed two million to run this operation,' Colonel Thistlethwaite continued. 'Especially as we have a bill from your fellow countrymen for one Sea Strike UAV. Costly toys, it seems. Unload the remainder of these boxes,' the Colonel snapped the order at the soldiers behind him. 'The gold remains here, I'm afraid, until we've made a full accounting of the mission costs. I'm sure you understand. Then we will pay you what is rightfully yours.'

Nick Coles was staring at the Colonel, shock written across his features. 'But, sir! That wasn't the deal . . .'

'Change of orders, Nick. Sorry, didn't I tell you? Only just heard myself, actually. Comes from the very top. We've got to make a full accounting of the mission costs, before . . . Anyhow, let's get the crates unloaded, quick as we can.'

The Colonel turned on his heel and a phalanx of heavily armed soldiers closed around him.

Bill Berger stared after him. 'You can run, Major, but you'll never fuckin' hide,' he growled. 'Not while I'm still breathing.'

The Colonel turned back to face the aircraft. 'As it happens, Captain, I don't like my orders any more than you do. Personally, I think you've more than earned your reward. But unlike your ilk, I generally tend to believe that orders are orders and should be obeyed. It's not in my nature to do otherwise.' He paused for a second, then pulled himself upright to offer Berger a stiff salute. 'I salute you, Captain, on a mission well accomplished.'

Colonel Thistlethwaite headed across the apron, a hunched, lonely figure, until he was lost from view. The wooden crates were heavy, and it took two soldiers to lift each of them out of the chopper's hold. There was a sullen silence in the dimly lit rear of the Mi-26 as Berger, Smithy, Ward and Johno watched and waited. The loss of Kilbride – and Nightly – had thrown a dark cloud over the mission, and none of them really gave a damn any more if the ruse worked or not. If a soldier dropped a crate and it spilled sand all across the tarmac, then Berger would just tell Nick Coles and the rest to go to hell.

'Erm . . . I'll get the chopper refuelled, shall I?' Nick asked quietly. Berger stared at him, wordlessly, his eyes a blank void. 'Look, I'm sorry. I genuinely knew nothing about all this. If I had done—'

'If you had done, what?' Berger grated. 'You'd have kept it a fuckin' secret, just like you fuckin' did about Knotts-Lane? I've had enough of your favours to last a fuckin' lifetime, buddy. If you'd told us about that traitorous bastard, Kilbride might still be with us . . .'

Nick stared in silence at the tarmac for a second. He knew that there was some truth to the big American's words.

'Look, I'm truly sorry,' he stammered. 'I really am. But right now we don't know what a hornets' nest you may have stirred up behind you. We don't want anyone – the Lebanese, the Syrians, or, God forbid, the Israelis – tracing the chopper back to Cyprus. So, once we're done unloading it's best we get you out of here. I'll bat for your team over the gold, you have my word. I'll fight your corner . . . Now, I'll get the ground crew refuelling you, shall I? Where do you want to go?'

'Get us clearance to fly to Tanzania,' Berger growled. 'Get us clearance to land at Kilbride's place. And do us one favour, even if you are a lyin', cheatin', double-crossing bastard. Phone Kilbride's wife and give her our time of arrival. And tell her that her man didn't make it home . . . I can't face getting there to break the news . . .'

'Of course. I'll make the necessary arrangements. And I'll say what needs to be said. I'm sorry.' Nick turned to leave – and then he halted. He turned back to the chopper and signalled to a couple of the soldiers to help him. Together, they bent and picked up the one opened crate of gold.

Nick and the soldiers hoisted it up to Bill Berger and Smithy. 'Here, take this. It's not much, but at least it's something. I'll get a rocket for allowing you to take even this . . . Kilbride's gone and two million dollars is something, at least . . . They'll have my guts for garters, but I just feel this is something I have to do. I've never met them, but give it to his family, will you . . . ?'

As the vast bulk of the Mi-26 powered across the ocean towards the beach, Marie-Claire set the stereo playing. It was Kilbride's favourite track of all time, Bob Dylan's 'Ring Them Bells'. She'd put the speakers down on the beach and she and Nixon had prepared a welcome-home buffet for everyone, complete with several bottles of chilled champagne and crates and crates of Kilimanjaro beer.

Marie-Claire stood with a child held in either arm, gazing out to sea at the aircraft that was bringing her man home. She smiled at Tashana, who stood on her right, next to Nixon. On her left was Janey, a new addition to the tribe. All three women were facing the rising sun that backlit the giant chopper a fiery bronze, waiting for their men to dismount onto the golden sands.

As the Mi-26 approached it reduced its speed,

preparing to land. Marie-Claire held her two boys tight to stop them rushing forward to greet the giant aircraft. The sand was wet from the receding tide, and they were standing well back to avoid the down draught of the massive rotor blades.

'*Ring them bells for the chosen few*' – the music played on. Kilbride believed that he was one of the 'chosen few', that his years in the SAS were a matchless gift in life. But it was the last words of the song that really did it for Kilbride – '*breaking down the distances between right and wrong.*' He'd always told Marie-Claire that the older he got, the more he saw the world in shades of grey. The most important thing was to live and let live.

The huge helicopter settled onto the sand, sunlight glinting on its riveted bodywork. Scorch marks peppered the thin skin of the craft, and for a second Marie-Claire's heart missed a beat. Surely her man couldn't be hurt? Wounded? Someone would have told her. That British man who had called to tell her about the chopper's arrival – he would have let her know.

The side door opened and Sally jumped down. She sniffed the sand, realised that she was home, and bounded up the beach towards them. She flew into the family's arms, almost knocking Marie-Claire over, and then the big dog began to lick the faces of the two small boys.

Marie-Claire glanced back at the chopper, her face aglow, half expecting Kilbride to follow next, the leader first down from the aircraft. Instead, the gaunt figure of the big American soldier descended onto the sand. Tashana let out a little cry, and rushed forward to meet him. At the bottom of the steps Bill Berger stood stock-still, his face streaked with blood and grime and his arms hanging impotently at his sides. Tashana flung herself at him. The big man did not respond.

Ward stepped down from the aircraft. He joined Bill Berger, his head hung low, his shoulders bowed with grief and exhaustion. As soon as they'd spotted the welcome-home party the men had known that no one had told Marie-Claire. Nick Coles had taken the course of the true coward and had chosen to say nothing. She didn't know that her man was missing in action, presumed lost – and which of them now had the courage to tell her?

Marie-Claire searched their faces, looking for a hint of welcome, a sign that they were all safe and that the war was over and that no one was ever having to go back there again. 'Where's Kilbride?' she murmured, as the first cold fingers of panic gripped her heart. 'Where's Kilbride?'

Johno stepped down from the chopper, eyes red with exhaustion, hair matted with filth and grime. 'Where's Daddy?' Marie-Claire heard her eldest, David, murmur. She looked down into his face, trying to hide her fear. 'He's coming. He's coming,' she tried to comfort him. 'You'll see.'

She stared back at the chopper, willing her man to descend. Maybe it was a tradition, she told herself, that troops returning from combat always let the commander dismount last. She tried to comfort herself with that thought, but her mind was screaming: *Where's Kilbride?*

This was the moment for him to step down, she told herself, for the song was almost over. She stared at the chopper's side door, willing him to appear, but the bulky form of Smithy emerged instead. Janey let out a yell, and sprinted for the helicopter. She threw herself at

405

the burly sergeant, but he barely registered her presence. He was staring over at Marie-Claire, his eyes empty pits of pain.

She stared back at him, desperately, willing him to say something, to explain what was going on. He shook his head, imperceptibly at first, as the tears started pouring down his grimy face. To Smithy's left, Berger felt his chin quivering and a tear rolled down the chiselled, granite features of the man who had been forced to take over Kilbride's command.

With a last few piano chords the song finished, the final notes drifting out across the dawn sands. The chopper's rotors slowed to a dead stop. A silence followed, as deep and as empty as the grave.

Suddenly, Marie-Claire rushed forward. 'WHERE'S KILBRIDE!' She dodged the soldiers and threw herself at the door of the chopper, but the vast, cavernous cathedral of the hold was empty. She turned and screamed at the line of men, at Smithy, Berger, Ward and Johno: 'WHERE'S MY HUSBAND? WHERE'S KILBRIDE? Where's Kilbride?' she sobbed as she collapsed into the sand. 'Where's Luke . . . Oh my God, no . . . Oh my God, no . . . Oh my God, no . . .'

Bill Berger turned away from his woman, Tashana's side. Feeling as if he were in a dream the big American stumbled across the sand and sank to his knees. He took Marie-Claire's shoulders in his massive hands and tried to lift her up, to turn her away from the aircraft, but she tore herself away from him. 'No. No. No. No. No . . .' She clawed at the sand beneath the chopper, hoping beyond hope that the giant machine might still deliver the man she loved.

Berger broke now. His features crumpled, the tears streaming freely down. There was no dishonour in a man crying. The only dishonour lay in their leaving Kilbride behind. He buried his face in his friend's wife's hair, rocking her from side to side.

'We had to leave him,' he sobbed. 'We had to leave him . . .'

Finally, Marie-Claire allowed the big American soldier to lift her up, a hunched, fragile, heaving figure. His arms around her shoulders, Berger turned her away from the chopper, and set her face towards the beach. There was a terrible finality in him doing so, and she knew that all was lost.

Burt was the first to spot it. They'd been searching the landing zone for hours now, and part of him refused to believe it. But there it was again, an arm raised and waving from the sea. He altered course and brought the RIB in towards the figure. As they nosed in closer Burt and Volker leaned over the side and hauled the survivor on board.

Burt slapped the figure on the back. 'Always said you were like a bit of old boot-leather, man. Bloody indestructible.'

Kilbride lay in the bottom of the boat and grinned up at him, exhaustedly. He tried to speak but his voice came out as a dry croak. Burt handed him a bottle of water, and Kilbride necked it greedily.

'Thanks,' he managed to choke out.

'Right, time to head for home,' Burt announced. 'Anyone got any ideas as to our route? We could try for Israel, Cyprus or back to the Lebanon. It's about the same distance either way. Best not head back to the Lebanon, eh? I reckon Cyprus is pretty dodgy too. Looks like we'll have to try for Israel, man. Volker, set a course for the nearest Israeli landfall. And Shortie, break out that medical kit and take a look at Kilbride.'

Burt grabbed the Thuraya from his belt. 'There's still some juice in the satphone, so I guess we can get a call through to the Israeli coastguard or something . . . But first I got to make another call . . .'

Burt punched a number into the Thuraya's keypad, then handed the phone to Kilbride. 'Best you let your family know we found you safe and well, isn't it, man?'

Two hundred and forty nautical miles to the south of them, the dhow chugged resolutely onwards. On the foredeck McKierran sunned himself in his wheelchair, and Boerke sat alongside him with a heavily strapped and bandaged leg. To the aft, Moynihan was at the wheel, his gaze set south and his mind dreaming of a woman back home in Ireland. And at the stern, Mick Kilbride and his buddy Brad were happily fishing for sharks – though they had yet to catch a single one. The dhow had observed complete communications silence ever since slipping anchor and steaming away from Tripoli. She had done so just in case anyone was trying to track, follow and find her.

She would remain like that until she reached Kigamboni, and had delivered her golden cargo home.

END NOTE

Readers may wonder how much of this story is true. The simple answer is that I don't know. I have been told about the original bank raid in great detail, but for obvious reasons, all of that information is unattributable and remains unverifiable. I have also been told that the gold was hidden and that at some later date a gold-retrieval mission was necessary. Whether this story remains purely an SAS urban myth with no truth to it whatsoever, or something more, I am unable to say for certain. Whichever is the case it makes for a fine story.

I'll leave the reader with one extra thought. In the course of writing this book I asked myself if there had ever been any other cases of special forces opportunistic robbery. In 1959, the SAS were deployed on anti-insurgent operations in Oman, the Gulf. A Squadron of elite soldiers had scaled Oman's Jebel Akhdar, the Green Mountain, the highest peak in the region. At the summit they discovered a cave guarded by enemy fighters. After firing rockets and hurling hand grenades the SAS men stormed the cave. Inside they discovered a stash of large wooden chests. Fully expecting them to contain ammo, they levered open the chests only to discover glittery heaps of Maria Theresa silver dollars.

Each wooden chest was piled high with the treasure, and the cave contained riches beyond the wildest dreams of the SAS men. They threw down their packs, emptied out the contents and stuffed them full of the Maria Theresa dollars. The men were laughing and joking and already planning their long retirements on the French Riviera. However, over the next two days they were mortared and machine-gunned by the enemy, and gradually treasure was dumped in an effort to lighten their loads and escape with their lives. This act of opportunistic SAS lighthandedness is reported in SAS-veteran Ken Connor's superlative book, *Ghost Force – the Secret History of the SAS*. The story is credited to the eyewitness account of an SAS sergeant who was present in the Jebel Akhdar at the time.

Since the Jebel Akhdar mission, I have heard of one or two other, equally-inventive freelance special forces operations – in the Balkans, Afghanistan and, most recently, Iraq.

For those readers whose interest in Submarine launched UAV's and UAV's in general has been piqued by this book, a good starting place to research them is www.globalsecurity.org. For those readers whose interest in gold, tungsten (wolfram) and metallurgy in general has been piqued by this book, take a look at Theo Gray's website, periodictabletable.com. For those readers who may actually wish to buy their own gold plated tungsten bar or cylinder (highly recommended by the author), go to Max Whitby's website, rgbco.com. And for those readers wishing to make up their own shipment of false gold, drop me an email via my website, and I'll put you in touch with the real 'Goldenboy Guss'.

www.damienlewis.com

Operation Certain Death

Damien Lewis

This book chronicles the story of the single most daring Special Forces operation since World War Two – Operation Barras; the attempted rescue by the SAS of the British Forces who were being held captive by the guerrilla gang the West Side Boys in the Sierra Leone jungle. The West Side Boys were a strange-looking bunch, wearing pink shades, shower caps, fluorescent wigs and voodoo charms they believed made them invulnerable to bullets – an impression re-enforced by ganja, heroine, crack cocaine and gallons of sweet palm wine. In 1999 a 12 man patrol of Royal Irish Rangers, who were training government troops in Sierra Leone, were captured and held hostage by the West Side Boys. They were held prisoner in a fortified jungle hideaway, with severed heads decorating the palisades and defended by some 400 heavily armed soldiers. Operation Barras, the mission to rescue them was a combined force of 100 Paras, 12 members of the Special Boat Squadron, helicopters from the Navy and RAF and, spearheading the operation, 40-strong D squadron of the SAS. Against amazing odds the hostages were rescued – over 150 of the enemy were killed. *Operation Certain Death* is a story of all out war. No hostages taken. Blood-letting on a vast scale inflicted on a very blood-thirsty enemy.

'What a story! As good as any thriller I have ever read. This is the lowdow' Frederick Forsyth

'Grotesque, glorious and utterly gripping' *Bolton Evening News*

arrow books

Bloody Heroes

Damien Lewis

The most explosive true war story of the 21st Century

It is the winter of 2001. A terror ship is bound for Britain carrying a horrifying weapon. The British military sends a crack unit of SAS and SBS to assault the vessel before she reaches London. So begins a true story of explosive action as this band of elite warriors pursues the merchants of death from the high seas . . . to the harsh wildlands of Afghanistan. The hunt culminates in the single greatest battle of the Afghan war, the brutal and bloody siege of an ancient mud-walled fortress crammed full of hundreds of Al Qaeda and Taliban. The story follows our handful of crack fighters as they battle against impossible odds and bitter betrayal to rescue fellow soldiers trapped by a murderous, fanatical enemy. Over eight days of vicious and medieval bloodshed some 500 enemy would be killed, but at the cost of dozens of British, American and allied casualties.

'The most dramatic story of a secret wartime mission you will ever read' *News of the World*

'A must read for all Damien Lewis fans' *Compass*

'The author has been given unprecedented access' *Zoo*

'Gripping' *Eye Spy*

arrow books

Highway to Hell

John Geddes

Present-day Iraq is a crucible of torture, chemical warfare and Islamic terrorism, swamped with insurgents pitched against the mighty US Army and its allies . . . but there's another western army in Iraq that dwarfs the British contingent and is second only in size to the US Army itself.

It's a disparate and anarchic multi-national force of men gathered from twenty or more countries numbering some 30,000. It's a mercenary army of men and a few women with guns for hire earning an average of $1,000 dollars a day. They are in Iraq to provide security for the businessmen, surveyors, building contractors, oil experts, aid workers and, of course, the TV crews who have flocked to the country to pick over the carcass of Saddam's regime and help the country re-build.

John Geddes, ex-SAS warrant officer and veteran of a fistful of hard wars, became a member of the mercenary army in Iraq for the eighteen months immediately following George W. Bush's declaration of the end of hostilities on April 16, 2003. Now, in this breathtaking book, John Geddes reveals the inside story of this extraordinary private army and the private war they are still fighting with the insurgents in Iraq.

'An eye opening book' *Daily Mail*

'A remarkable look at Iraq's invisible army' Frederick Forsyth

arrow books

Back from the Brink

Paul McGrath

Paul McGrath is Ireland's best loved sportsman and also its least understood. An iconic football presence during a professional career stretching over 14 years, he played for his country in the European Championship finals of 1988 and the World Cup finals of 1990 and 1994. But, behind the implied glamour of life in the employ of great English clubs like Manchester United and Aston Villa, McGrath wrestled with a range of destructive emotions that made his success in the game little short of miraculous.

That story has until now never been told. It is a story that runs from a hard, hidden childhood spent in Dublin's orphanages all the way to the pain of two marriage break-ups, his all-too public struggle with alcoholism, and the surreal highs and calamitous lows of a life lived habitually on the edge of chaos.

It is not just a football story. It is an extraordinary human story.

'Laceratingly honest . . . remarkably unflinching' *Mail on Sunday*

'Gripping [and] unflinching . . . His story is as complex as it is moving, as vulnerable as it is brutal' *Guardian*

arrow books

What If I Had Never Tried It

Valentino Rossi

First GP win aged 17. First world title at 18. First 500 class win at 21. First MotoGP win at 22. Current MotoGP World Champion. Living Legend.

Valentino Rossi is the greatest motorcyclist on earth. Wherever he goes, legions of fans follow him, in awe of his professionalism and skill on the track, and his style and charisma off it.

On the bike: Five World Championship wins. Top three ranking in the World Championship for nine years in a row. Wins on a Honda and wins on a Yamaha.

Off the bike: Super-cool, scorchingly engaging, unnvervingly rebellious, with pop-star fame and charm.

Valentino Rossi: Brilliant, talented, always relaxed, and very, very fast.

'While the autobiography details everything you could want to know about him and his career, you don't need to be a bike fan to enjoy it. It is truly inspiring stuff'
The Sun

a r r o w   b o o k s

Flood

Richard Doyle

Flood is a devastating and compulsive thriller that reads like fact. The country has suffered floods on an unprecedented scale in recent years, but have we seen the worst, an inundation that threatens millions of lives? Flood is the disaster novel of today.

A storm rages over the north of Britain, a troop carrier founders in the Irish Sea, flood indicators go off the scale, the seas are mountainous and a spring tide is about to strike the East Coast. Air sea rescue and military personnel struggle to save lives all down the coast. The worst is yet to come. When the storm reaches the south the two forces of wind and tide will combine and send a huge tidal surge up the Thames.

But surely London is safe: the Thames Barrier will save the capital from disaster as it was intended to do? The river is a titanic presence by now, higher than anyone has known it, and the surge thunders towards the Barrier. Scientists begin to talk of the possibility of overtopping. Can fifty feet high gates be overwhelmed by a wave? Then there is an explosion the size of a small Hiroshima: a supertanker is ablaze in the estuary and most of the Essex petrochemical works are going up with it. The Thames catches fire and the wall of fire and water thunders towards Britain's capital. This is the story of what happens next, and the desperate attempts to save the capital from destruction.

arrow books